BROKEN BONDS

THE BLOOD & FLAME SAGA
BOOK 2

E.A. WINTERS

DRAGONLEAFPRESS

Paperback ISBN: 978-1-958702-02-4

DragonLeaf Press, imprint of Snowfall Publications, LLC

To my incredible family, for putting up with me constantly talking about dragons, assassins, and word counts, and to Haley Boone, for being such an encouraging and enthusiastic cheerleader!

Mount Hara
Haizlin
Kalma
Carfus
Qalea
Ryden
Camar
Pillerae
N
W
E
S

Boan
Pilall
Ellix
Kinlock
Surion
Strip
Seddon
Horen

1

In practiced hands, knifework was elegant. Beautiful even. It was only possible for someone with remarkable skill, something most of the Framatar's children possessed. They were trained as elite assassins beginning at the age of four, eventually graduating from the program at sixteen. Semra, however, had graduated at fifteen, at a time when she believed their work made the world a better place and purged evil from its surface.

She never dreamed she would have gone from being one of the most promising graduates to where she stood today, facing off with a young brunette. The girl was a bit green for the children of the mountain, but mission-ready nonetheless.

"There's still time," Semra said. They were all killers, but they were orphans first. She hated hurting them, but if it came to it, she'd put a knife in their heart. "Last chance. The king's offer is a good one. Come with us, get trade training, start a new life. If you keep getting in my way, I'm afraid I'll have to kill you."

The girl blocked the hallway of the villa, cutting off Semra and two royal guards from the pursuit of another mountain child. In reality they were hardly children, hardened by a vicious lifestyle full of death and power. The girl swung a staff and pushed Semra backward, but her eyes held a flicker of fear, vanishing as she knocked Semra back. She kept Semra at long range and letting loose a furious scream as she whirled, bringing the staff down toward Semra's head. The turn was superfluous. The brunette was good but showy. Semra rotated her wrist and let the knife float across her fingers, tossing it into the air before catching it with the other hand. She fumbled it, then twirled the knife again before retreating two steps, doing her best to look sheepish.

Impress, challenge, ego-boost.

The girl smirked and struck Semra on the jaw. Stumbling backward, she was caught by the guards and set upright again. Her jaw smarted, but it was a worthwhile sacrifice. Semra flew forward and engaged the girl again before her brutish companions could take action. Her opponent swept at Semra's legs, brandishing the staff in a series of turns and twirls over her head. She grinned at Semra.

Ahh, yes. Hook, line, and sinker.

Semra spun the blade in her hands, dancing forward on the balls of her feet, feinting a high blow, and burst forward with a thrust to the lower abdomen as the girl left her torso vulnerable. Semra's knife buried deep into her intestines, slicing across to the hip out of the body, stabbing upward under the armpit, and slashing from the armpit across the throat. She grabbed a fistful of the girl's hair in her left hand and yanked her head down, reaching around with her right to drag the knife across the back of the neck through the carotid artery. The entire sequence had taken less than two seconds.

The girl crumpled, spilling blood and intestines onto the floor; Semra jogged forward, pausing when the guards' footsteps did not follow. She glanced back. The first guard, Findor, stared at the young girl's body with wide eyes. The other, Gaulen, looked at her with distaste.

Semra cocked her head. They were royal guards, trained to protect and kill when necessary. What was so shocking? The brunette had refused to accept clemency and was bent on slaughtering Semra and the guards, not to mention the civilians she and the other rogue assassins had already killed. Semra's work was clean, a precise and beautiful display of knifework. It would have stood to reason they should admire her form, rather than condemn her approach.

"She's a child," Gaulen said.

"She's an assassin," Semra corrected.

"Surely she could have died with more honor."

Gaulen never had a more punchable face. She pressed her lips together. "Why? Do certain methods make a killing better or worse? Dead is dead, and I couldn't have her following us. This group has already killed a number of people since Mount Hara was emptied, and she wouldn't have accepted trade training in a thousand years. If we're fast, we might still get to the others. Let's go."

She turned back down the hall and ran through a door leading out to a large sitting room. The brunette wasn't alone. Semra's leather-bound feet slapped against the stone floor, throwing herself into a roll as a young female archer appeared from the other side of a couch and drew back the string. Two boys, perhaps twelve and thirteen, ducked behind chairs as the arrow released with a *twang.* Luckily for Findor and Gaulen, the archer was a terrible shot, and the arrow hit the stone wall behind them and fell harmlessly to the ground.

The boys made a break for it, and Findor and Gaulen dove after them. Semra vaulted the couch toward the archer, in the same moment a lean-muscled blur flew down the stairs tackling the archer and pinning her to the ground. He dropped a knee into the girl's back, running a hand through his permanently disheveled brown hair and grinned up at Semra.

"Beat you."

Semra rolled her eyes. "I got one on the way in. And you can't properly take credit for this one – I distracted her."

Siler had been a child of the mountain too, the two of them growing up two class years apart. Individual birthdays weren't known or celebrated in the program, but they had both aged up at the recent new year – Siler to age twenty, and Semra to age eighteen. Siler helped her escape the mountain and joined her quest to expose the dragonlord. His gray eyes twinkled back, and he gave the girl a patronizing pat on the head. "Don't feel bad. She distracts me too...but I still manage to get the job done."

Semra's stomach tightened at his words. He'd been dropping more hints in the past week. Semra loved spending time with Siler. Their shared history led to an understanding no one else could offer, a welcome contrast from the side-eyed, suspicious glances she got from just about everyone else. Siler made her feel at home. Still, they had different goals. When emotions became obstacles, Semra was grateful her decisions tended to be ruled by reason. And their union didn't make sense.

"Get *off!* I'll rip your eyes out!"

Semra had nearly forgotten about the girl under Siler's knee. She examined her again and recognized her as fifteen-year-old Conet, who'd been deemed unsuitable for fieldwork and assigned to assist the indoctrination of the youngest children in the mountain. With archery skills like that, no wonder she was repurposed.

Siler pursed his lips. "Well, now, that's something. Do you expect me to *want* to get my eyes ripped out, or to not believe you are capable of it?"

"Get off!"

"Yes, you've established that desire already. I commend you for dropping the useless threat, but I admit some motivational factor is still lacking. Semra, do you have any suggestions for our friend?"

Semra smiled despite herself. "Perhaps a bribe? He likes money, but he also likes pastries. Do you have any pastries?"

A shout came from up the stairs.

"Ahh," Siler said to Conet. "My fault. I tied someone up and left them upstairs. I wanted to catch more of you than Semra, so I had to cut corners."

"If you have to cheat, you don't get the points," Semra said.

"I think I should get the points as long as they don't get away. Speaking of which, could a couple of you check on him? It's Treq. He's a wily fellow."

Semra motioned to the guards to check on Treq, and Gaulen passed off his young charge to Findor, dashing up the stairs at her side. Treq was a graduate of the year 4998 class. The soulless black of his eyes turned Semra's stomach sour. He was one year older than Semra, turning nineteen in the new year along with the rest of the mission-readies in his class. Semra had been bumped up to graduate with him, Isra, and Radix, becoming the first student to accelerate past their own year. Treq had despised her ever since. He lay on the landing, his wrists and ankles twisted bound together behind him. Treq had rolled from his front to his side to breathe easier, still effectively restrained. Gaulen knelt on his spine, taking hold of his arms.

"Cut his legs free so he can walk, and we'll get him downstairs."

"Don't get lazy. Treq is crazy. He once skewered two people together with a spear, and the frame job was nearly impossible."

"Thanks for the compliment," Treq said, wincing as Gaulen applied pressure.

"You're saying *his* murders are uncivilized?" Gaulen asked, shooting Semra an incredulous look.

Semra clenched her jaw, pulling a knife from one of the sheaths built into the thighs of her trousers. It would have been so much easier to chase down the rogue assassins without the guards, and only with Siler and Isra, whose skill level rivaled their opponents. They understood how she worked. She couldn't blame the king for wanting his own men, considering he was employing assassins to chase down other assassins. But she hated it all the same.

Prince Zephan worked well with her as well. He still technically led the task force, but the war with Belvidore had only gotten worse and split his focus. A pained twinge tugged at her heart. She missed having him on missions.

Semra cleared her throat. "I'm saying his *assassinations* are brutal and impulsive rather than elegant. And I'll remind you *telling* a murderer they are a murderer isn't considered the wisest of choices."

Gaulen smirked. "So you *do* consider yourself a murderer?"

Red hot anger gripped her chest. Semra sliced through the final threats of rope binding Treq's feet and let Gaulen haul him up. "I think if you think of me that way, you should watch your tongue. And I think you're a liability to work alongside if I have to coddle your feelings or worry about your trust issues at every step."

Gaulen's eyes narrowed, but he said nothing.

Treq coughed. "This sounds like a fun conversation. What now?"

"You're coming back to Qalea with us to await trial," Gaulen said. "The edict was issued. Assassins of Mount Hara would be offered leniency in coming forward, job training if necessary, and assistance in a fresh start. But that leniency applied to jobs completed as a result of indoctrination and manipulation by Azi Shamaran – or as you know him, the Framatar, or your dragonlord, or whatever – and considering the several missing people in your wake since we've been tracking you, I doubt the investigation will do you any favors."

"I see," Treq said. "And what form of execution awaits the guilty?"

Gaulen shrugged. "Above my pay grade. The King is generous – *too* generous," he added, with a side eye at Semra, "but even he knows that in an organized society justice must prevail."

Gaulen and Semra escorted Treq back down the stairs into the sitting area where Findor still held the young boys as Siler held Conet.

"They're going to kill us?!" Conet squeaked, tears welling in her eyes.

Semra remembered the girl's rough treatment of four-year-old Lesala, and her lip curled. The Framatar's great black dragon, Rotokas, recently snatched Lesala from the village of Kalma and deposited her into life on the mountain. She had fought tooth and nail to escape, and Conet caught her and dragged her back into the caves, slapping her across the face.

"Get it through your head; your family left you to die!"

"We are your family now, idiot! And you're doing a terrible job being part of it so far."

Semra ground her teeth. Still, in a way, Conet *was* Lesala. A bitter version of a person who believed lies. Young children often did if the same ones are told often enough, with only the smallest morsels of relational warmth tossed in to sweeten the deception. This prescription often worked on adults too, to a lesser extent, but if the lie was seeded in childhood and watered in adolescence, the passions of youth would defend it with pride. And that was the unfortunate position Conet found herself in. Better to believe the familiar story than face the implications of the truth.

Semra sighed. "You're young and impressionable. And a miserable shot. It's likely you'll receive clemency based on your age and failure to meet mission ready standards. I doubt you've personally been connected to any of the harsher crimes."

Gaulen glared at her. "Are you offering her hope? A magical escape from a traumatic and evil past? Or are you condemning her for not being as good as you are at evil things?"

"Who are you to say what's evil?" Siler snapped. "Watch your mouth."

"Maybe both," Semra said. Who was he to judge? And yet, he wasn't entirely wrong. Indoctrinated or not, Semra had taken part in horrific things before she learned the truth about her mentor and what they were doing. But she had been good at the only thing she was allowed to work hard at, and that was something. "I took pride in my work. It's the only thing I had. Something to appreciate about myself. If you don't work hard and apply yourself, what kind of person are you?"

"The assassin kind. They're all the same," Gaulen said.

"If we were all the same," Siler cut in. "Your condescending, highbrow comments would have been silenced ages ago. We would have traveled lighter, too."

Gaulen stiffened, and Treq guffawed. Semra stifled a smile, and the tension in her chest eased. Siler had never judged her. He understood her.

Siler passed Conet to Semra and walked next to Gaulen and Treq, Conet's quiver across his back and bow in his right hand left the other free to assist with Treq if necessary. Findor started to cross the room with the two young boys, back toward the hall in the direction they had come, but Semra stopped him. The first girl's body still lay where she had fallen – ripped open.

"Don't let them see. Perhaps their new life will not require they become as numb to violence as the rest of us."

The group exited the side door, Findor and the boys out front, Semra and Conet next, and Gaulen, Treq, and Siler at the back. They traipsed through a grand entrance and out onto an expansive garden behind the villa, lined with forest on the far end. Isra could just now be seen in the distance, dragging a teenage boy back with him. Semra closed her eyes and felt the tingling, mild burning sensation in the opal-like mark on her chest as she sent the call to **Zezura**, a rare Rangchanj dragon. The mark was mostly hidden by her loose-fitting tunic, smooth as stone just under her collarbone ever since she had saved Zezura's life – the action bound them together with the mark of the dragon's kiss in a way Semra still didn't fully understand.

The wind lifted Semra's dark hair from her shoulders and begged for a ride in its currents. *Soon enough,* she told herself, opening her eyes and soaking up the purples, yellows, and pinks of the curated garden flowers. Conet stumbled and as Semra reached down to catch her, an arrow whistled past her ear.

2

———

The arrow plunged into the soil, the air from its fletching sending a whisp of Semra's hair across her face. She jerked upright with Conet, catching a glimpse of a female figure dashing from a garden hedge . Siler attempted to return an arrow, but the girl ducked into the safety of the forest, the arrow piercing a pine instead.

"Lightning-quick," Siler said, shaking his head. "And the wind blew at just the right time. I shouldn't miss at this distance!"

Semra tilted her head at Siler and frowned. *No, you shouldn't.* He'd missed on purpose, and they both knew it.

Isra ran up from the other direction, out of breath. "That's two in the wind," he said.

Siler lowered his bow. "Let them go. We don't have the resources to track them after securing four hostages."

"She's one of them!" Gaulen protested, gesturing toward the trees. "We need to round them up!"

"Never leave a snake unattended to catch a hamster." Siler jerked his head at Treq. "Snake." He jerked his head after the runaway. "Hamster."

"I've honestly never received a better compliment in my life," Treq drawled.

Semra ignored him. "Once they hit the main city streets, they're as good as gone. We can always come back to continue the search, but it's too odd for them to be traveling in one group of this size and…composition. We were not fully prepared for it." She wanted to comment on the strange ages. It seemed there had been three mission-readies hiding out at the villa – the brunette Semra killed in the hall, Treq, and one more – but to take three children on the run together was risky. And that risk caught them today. The boys would have been Arrow class, focusing on hunting, making meals with the catch, learning tactical practice, and providing medical care to mission-readies.

Findor cleared his throat. "Who's going to, er, clean up inside the villa?" *The dead girl.*

"It's fine. I'll do it." Any excuse to get away from Gaulen. She needed to be alone. Semra turned to Treq. "Did you kill the villa owners, or are they away somewhere?"

Treq shrugged. Semra sighed and rolled her eyes. In the next instant, Treq headbutted Gaulen and wrenched free of his grasp, the rope holding his wrists together drifting uselessly to the ground. Treq spun behind Findor, yanked the guard's sword from its sheath, and held the blade to his neck. Findor's body was positioned between Treq and the others. Findor let go of one of the boys in the scuffle. Gaulen dove after the boy, pinning him to the ground while Semra and Siler stood poised opposite Treq. Semra had a firm grip on Conet in one hand and a knife in the other.

"Follow me, and I kill him," Treq said. "With great precision I have perfected for agonizing pain. Watch him die or let me go and I will release him at the forest's edge."

A powerful roar split the skies and Semra's mark throbbed

ever so gently as Zezura plummeted down through puffy white clouds and landed behind Treq, unleashing a stream of fire at his back. The Rangchanj dragon was fifty feet long from nose to tail, and her scales shifted color like a chameleon, flashing from her typical blue to red, purple, and back again. Treq shrieked and dropped to the ground in a roll, beating out the flames in his clothes and reaching out for the fallen sword. With a flick of her wrist, Semra sent her knife plunging into the back of Treq's outstretched hand.

Conet screamed and covered her head with her hands, and Semra let her go. She wasn't going anywhere anytime fast. Findor lay on the ground coughing, and Isra snatched the second boy as he tried to flee, and tossed him into the soil at his feet. Treq left the knife lodged in his hand and twisted to grab Findor's sword with the other.

Siler drew his sword and swung at Treq, and Treq blocked with one hand, holding the other close to his body, Semra's knife still embedded in it. Semra strode toward Treq, drawing a second knife, and motioned to the dragon with the tip of the blade. Zezura was all too happy to oblige, and Siler jumped back with inches to spare as the dragon knocked Treq on his back and laid a massive, clawed foot on his chest, drooling down at him with enormous slitted, serpentine eyes.

Semra stalked over, put her foot on Treq's wrist to hold it down, and ripped her knife free from his hand. Treq screamed. Conet covered her eyes.

What would Gaulen and Findor think of that? Part of her felt satisfaction that she might offend them. The idea of being prissy about assassins like Treq was asinine. He would only respect her in the language he spoke – threats and violence. But the other part of her almost wished she were acceptable to regular people.

The royal guard, and other people in the castle, for

instance.

"We'll get you back to camp and fix you up with supplies we brought," Semra said to Treq. "But there will be no more running, no more threats, not a single breath out of line from here to Qalea. Not unless you fancy death by dragon. We are supposed to deliver you safely to trial, but they're wild animals after all – totally unpredictable. Do you understand?"

Treq nodded, clutching his wounded hand.

Her eyes narrowed. "I need verbal confirmation, Treq."

"Yes."

Semra wiped Treq's blood from her blade on the grass. "Excellent. Play nice and you might even get dinner."

SEMRA ARRANGED logs for a fire in the woods, looking up to check on their four hostages every few seconds. Findor had bound the wrists of the two boys and sat them together against a large tree, Conet was sitting on the other side of him, and Gaulen was wrapping Treq's injured hand in clean cloth. Treq's wrists and ankles were tied once more, and he sat with his legs stretched in front of him and his arms lifted for Gaulen to work. Zezura eyed him, and Treq sent furtive glances her way.

Isra had been sent to clean up the mess in the villa, in favor of Semra and Zezura staying to deter any escape attempts, and Isra would collect their horses on his way back. The Framatar, the man who had started the program in the mountain to train assassins for his own ends, had also been a dragonlord. His dragon, Rotokas, had been responsible for snatching young children for the program and was an instrument of fear, punishment, or death to any who displeased him. Semra wasn't surprised Treq held the same fear for Zez.

Siler opened their pack of provisions and started handing out dried meats and bread. Gaulen finished Treq's bandage and ambled over toward Semra. Irritation immediately overcame her at his presence. He gestured toward the fire.

"Need a hand?"

Semra arched an eyebrow. "Do I look like I need a hand?"

Gaulen held his hands up defensively and passed her logs from the stack beside her instead. Utterly unnecessary, but gave him something to do with his hands, she supposed.

"I'm not your enemy," he said. "But when we get back to Qalea, I'll be asked what I saw from you. And so far, it's concerning."

"I thought you were here to aid us in offering assistance to any of the mountain children that wanted it, and stopping any outstanding threats from those that refuse." Semra had known the royal guard was also meant to spy on how she worked. Prince Zephan had been on most of the missions with her early on, but as the war with Belvidore became more and more involved, he was pulled away from the task force and replaced with Gaulen and Findor. The king still needed eyes on her.

"We are. It's just...you might be friendly with the prince, but the king's court is nervous."

Semra plucked a log from Gaulen's hands and added it to the tented kindling. "I was appointed to this task force to take care of a problem. So I did. If you're wanting me to be prissy, or asking me to kill people differently, well, that's not on the menu."

"Your approach doesn't look good. There are certain deaths that could be more...civilized."

Semra groaned. Because killing people was such a civilized business? Semra set her sticks down and turned to him. "She was bent on killing me. And you. My way might have *looked* dirty, but it was a clean kill and one of the fastest possible deaths. She didn't feel pain for long. Which do you care about? Image, or effectiveness?"

"Both."

Semra gritted her teeth. Siler would have done the same. But probably without offering the girl an extra chance to change her mind. Semra wondered what Zephan would have done. Would he have gutted the girl? Perhaps not. But was it wrong, or simply a different training style? A pang hit her chest to think of Zephan. When was the last time she had even spoken to him? Semra rolled her eyes at herself. The girl ended up dead either way, so what was the difference?

"You can't have both."

A quick puff of fire to caught Semra's attention and she saw Treq sit back down hard from where he had been edging away from Zezura. Siler spun just in time to see it, and scanned Treq's wrists. He snatched the bread from Treq's one good hand, and smacked him hard on the back of the head.

"Have that rope tied properly again in the next sixty seconds or I'll let Semra stab your other hand," Siler threatened. Semra's eyes widened as she saw what Siler was talking about. The rope on Treq's wrists had been worked loose so that it was passable at a cursory glance, but easy enough to escape from when the time was right. Siler snapped his fingers at Gaulen. "Get over here and watch him. I think Semra's enjoyed your stellar company long enough."

Semra's mouth twitched and she stifled a smile as Gaulen glared daggers back at Siler and moved away. Siler passed Semra her dinner portion and waved Treq's piece of bread in her face.

"I seem to have come into possession of extra bread. Be nice and I might give you some."

"Oh? What do I have to do to get it?"

Siler plunked down beside her and leaned back against a tree trunk. "Tell me why you let Gaulen bother you."

Semra pulled back. "Is it that obvious?"

Siler rolled his eyes. "When you bit his head off just now? I couldn't hear your words, but your face was clear enough."

"Oh. Right." Semra sighed and tore off a piece of dried meat. "All our lives we fought evil. At least, that's what *I* believed. That we really were 'purging evil from the world' – a ridiculous naïveté in hindsight. After exposing the Framatar I had nowhere to go and nothing to do. I have no transferrable job skills other than surviving on my own. And now, with the task force, I have a chance to use my skills to protect others like us who might want a different life." She bit her lip. *A chance we never got.* "As mission-readies, we swore to eradicate evil from the world, and doing this makes me feel like I'm finally keeping that promise to myself. But this is our last mission with the force, and there's nothing else left for me. I'm back down to nothing."

Siler eyed her skeptically.

Semra furrowed her brow. "What?"

"You got all that from Gaulen?"

"Come on, I'm being serious. They look at us like pariahs."

"You're not entirely wrong." Siler sighed. "It's not everyone. But Captain Firfell, the royals...anybody responsible for safety and security. They don't trust us. They can't come to terms with what we are."

It wasn't *quite* true – Semra thought Aviama and Zephan trusted her, at the very least, and maybe even Turian – but it was close. "I want to do something good with my life, but I can't live looking over my shoulder for assassin colleagues coming to kill me and the king's court waiting to condemn me the moment I sound 'uncivilized.' Staying out of trouble might be the best I can manage."

Siler shrugged. "Who ever said 'civilized' was better? Who gets to define what that even means? And since when did you care about the king's court? You're not under Jannemar's thumb. You've never served a monarch. You were born into trouble whether you like it or not, and staying *in* trouble is as good as it gets, as long as you get to pick what kind. For me, living in some fake, boring world of platitudes and fabricated politeness is a more dangerous reality."

Semra whistled at the dragon and Zezura lit the kindling with a short, fiery puff. He was right, of course – she'd never served a king or deemed herself a citizen of any country, even though Mount Hara was technically within Jannemar. And underhanded dealings of state could be just as evil, just wrapped up in diplomatic wording.

"This is about Zephan, isn't it?"

Semra's head snapped up, yanked from her thoughts. "Zephan?" Her stomach twisted.

"You and him...I don't know, you two are close. And you refused my offer to come hang out with me and find a villa somewhere." He gestured toward the villa through the woods. "This one's not bad, for example. Once we remove anyone trying to kill us."

Semra laughed. "Your villa idea was funded by money you skimmed from the Framatar and supplemented by work for hire, as I recall. I don't want to kill for money."

"I'll make enough money for the both of us. You could hunt for meals or go flying. You could retire."

"At the ripe old age of eighteen? Besides, the dragon would make our comings and goings a bit more obvious."

Semra wondered what a life with Siler would be like. Siler was certainly handsome, and his storm gray eyes sometimes held her a moment longer than they should. She was comfortable with him, and he understood her. But what could she find to do in villa of his? Could she be happy there, knowing he paid for it in blood? Zephan had once commented that Semra's assassination of Governor Mallen was unsportsman-like. Semra had snapped back that it wasn't a sport, it was a job – but if the purpose was simply to get rich rather than to eliminate evil, it wasn't honorable.

Siler twirled a twig in his fingers and tossed it into the fire. "He isn't Dahyu, you know. He might have seemed nice enough when he was pretending to be a regular person, but he's not and never will be. Even if he really wanted to be with you and you wanted to be with him, it wouldn't matter, because all his life decisions are dictated by the crown. And pretending otherwise is just as deceitful as anything else."

Dahyu, the healer's apprentice who offered to help strangers in the woods. The man who joined them in their mission to save the prince and break into the castle, before revealing *he* was in fact the prince. Dahyu ate roots and roast squirrel and slept in the dirt; Zephan wore silks and furs and ate the fine cuisine of royal cooks. Dahyu was warm, free, and safe; Zephan had become distant and burdened by impossible responsibilities, his nonexistent free time spent with his nose in a book. Missing Dahyu when Zephan was so close was exhausting.

Semra swallowed. "I'm not staying for Zephan. I just need time to figure out my next steps." It was true, wasn't it? Yes, of course it was. Semra knew they could never be romantic. They were friends. *But why hasn't he spoken to me? He left the task force just like that.*

"Okay, maybe you're not. I still want you to come with me, but in any case, you don't belong in a stuffy castle. You belong to mountains and trees and open road. And now, with Zezura – you belong to the skies."

3

———

Semra was grateful when Isra returned. Horses meant they were ready to be on the road. Being on the road meant travel, and traveling was a much needed distraction. The next morning they set out for Qalea, the capital of Jannemar. It took five days for the group to return to Shamaran castle. Semra frequently flew ahead with Zezura, hunting for dinner before the rest caught up. But once they were back, Semra prickled against a foreign, mundane life full of rules and social order.

Two weeks had passed since their return, and the courtyard was no escape. The greenery of the gardens brought some small comfort, but it was a poor substitute for fields and forests. Semra sat on a bench under the fruit trees, looking over the curated ward and soaking in the last of the quiet before the hustle and bustle of a thousand daily tasks descended on the fortress.

It was altogether a different sort of business than she was used to. Day after day gardeners, chandlers, cooks, and servants went about their tasks. Window washers spent the day breaking through cobwebs and cleaning glass, their diligent work undone by the time the day was over. Semra might have been free of the dragonlord's oppression, but the castle walls closed left her feeling claustrophobic. The wide-open sky beckoned. She needed a dragon ride, and badly.

The sun crested the horizon, wrapping around in a "U" shape and hugging the cliff. A young servant fled across the grounds as Saeb, the head of household, chased him down. One of the staff's children skipped along the path with her mother, stopping to pick up a particularly shiny rock.

The girl looked about five, only a year older than Semra had been when the dragonlord sent his great black dragon to snatch her from her humble village home. The child's mother clapped and smiled, and Semra wondered what life would have been like with a mother like that. Instead, Semra was brought into Mount Hara and trained as an assassin.

The little girl laughed and scampered away toward the outer wards, her mother trailing her. For a moment Semra thought of Lesala, the little girl she had saved from the mountain. Semra hoped Lesala integrated well into normal life now that the dragonlord was safely locked away in the Jannemar dungeons. Semra fingered the emerald snake amulet dangling from her belt. The same man who used to wear it would never again create killers out of children.

Someone screamed, and in an instant, Semra was on her feet. Zezura did a nosedive down into the courtyard and pulled up to land without a second to spare. The child's mother quickly ushered her away from the huge aqua blue dragon, and Semra could feel the beast's nervous claustrophobia as she sidestepped a perfectly trimmed bush but knocked a fountain statue clean off its stand with her tail. It fell with a crash, and a harsh voice cried out in protest.

"You!" A door to the first floor opened to Semra's right, and a heavyset woman stepped out, waving an embroidered

napkin and squaring her shoulders. "Stay off my garden statues!"

Semra sighed. This was the confinement piece. Walls hemmed her in, leaving limited space and fearful looks whenever Zezura came to say good morning. Castles might be lavish, but mountains were free. Semra strode to Zezura and stroked her head, feeling the nervous energy quiet under her hand. "Sorry Saeb. She's fifty feet long–she didn't do it on purpose."

Saeb jumped as she noticed Semra, but quickly collected herself. "Well, perhaps dragons don't belong around breakable things."

Saeb disappeared, but the reality of her words remained. Semra glanced behind her and three stories up, where the throne room's tall glass windows twinkled in the morning light. It had been two months since Azi, the dragonlord, had taken over the castle and his dragon Rotokas had shattered any windows Zezura missed. The windows were replaced, the roof was repaired, and Azi was living out his days in the dungeon beneath Semra's feet, but the memories of what happened there lingered.

"We're going on a ride today, Zez," Semra assured the dragon. "And I never liked that statue anyway."

Semra entered the castle's ground floor, two doors down from where Saeb had been, hearing Captain Firfell's voice drifting from one of the meeting rooms.

"Your Majesty, Mount Hara is emptied of assassins and every young child has either been reunited with their family or placed with one. You remember how we found the mountain...Kalma ravaged for supplies, young children abandoned, teenagers outwitting our trackers and dropping off the grid. There may not have been enough evidence tying them to crimes for trial before, but ever since Azi was captured, we've had more and more trouble with his assassins gone rogue."

Semra froze.

"I thought this was a military strategy meeting, Captain," King Turian's voice answered. "It's too early in the morning to mince words. What are you getting at?"

"The task force did its job. The small children are back with their families, or new families have been found for them, and Semra is back in the castle with the dragon terrorizing our city once again."

The task force had worked hard to find the families from which the children were stolen, but some of them couldn't be found, and Zephan had led the effort to find suitable homes to take them in. Lesala had been placed with the older childless couple that Zephan had lived with when he was under cover as Dahyu, which had made Semra happy. Shafii and Tinat were good people.

"I've not heard of the dragon so much as stealing a sheep," Turian said.

Firfell continued, ignoring the king's comment.

"The task force is officially disbanded now, and with Belvidore sweeping through the towns at our borders we need to focus our energies there. I don't feel comfortable having sent so much of our military far from home with multiple assassins and a dragon within our walls."

Semra cringed. Gaulen had said the court didn't like her, but it wasn't just the court. Captain Firfell, the guards, the servants...

Siler's words haunted her, turning round and round like a spinning wheel: *You don't belong in a stuffy castle.* Semra strained to hear the king's answer.

"Semra saved my life and my son's life," Turian said, an edge to his voice.

"Respectfully, sire, the queen is dead and we are at war," Firfell replied. "The assassins have proven the long con is their specialty, and there is no way to be certain what her intentions are, or what trouble she may bring from her past. And the dragon...well, it doesn't just make the nobles anxious, it sets all of Qalea on edge."

Semra's heart sank into the pit of her stomach, and she slipped into the hall. They were afraid of her. After everything she had done to dismantle Azi's plot against the king, they still didn't trust her. How could they? Trouble followed her everywhere, and she was more comfortable executing a perfect kill than dancing a waltz. But she'd vowed never to be used as someone's killing machine again.

Semra whirled into the stairwell to her right and leapt up the steps two at a time. Two servants jumped out of her way with surprised squeals as she fled from Firfell's words.

"Tornado in trousers!" hissed one to the other as she passed.

"She makes me nervous," the other agreed.

Semra's pulse pounded in her ears, and she quickened her steps. She'd learned not to hold onto every word and glance – or had she? The independent assassin part of her didn't care two figs what they thought, but the homeless orphan part of her carried the weight of their judgments every day. She stood out like a sore thumb in the castle, wearing pants strapped with knives instead of the silk brocade dresses and expensive lace-lined items Princess Aviama constantly stocked in Semra's wardrobe. Semra reached the second floor's landing, continued toward the third, and launched up the last three stairs in a single bound. Aviama could keep her heavy skirts to herself.

The open stairwell behind her carried the sounds of a quiet bustle into the hall, as castle staff moved about on the second floor in the laundry, storeroom, and kitchen. These peripheral sounds softened just a few steps into the third floor, since the private sitting rooms and bedrooms of the crown prince and two princesses were left largely undisturbed at this time of day. Semra crossed to Zephan's door, raised her hand to knock, and then hesitated. Something in her gut twisted. What was she doing? It was early morning, and he might not even be awake. What had she dashed up two flights of stairs to say, exactly? *Why am I staying here? What do I do with my life now? Did you know my presence in the castle was causing problems with the king's court?*

Semra shook her head. Of course he knew. How could he not, working closely with the military leaders, nobles, and the rest? And if he didn't know...well, wasn't that worse? Was the crown prince being shielded from important information because he was too closely connected with an assassin? Semra lowered her hand. No, that wouldn't do. Besides, she hadn't even seen him lately – only a handful of times since she'd returned to the castle. He'd been focused on the war with Belvidore and had been needed in matters of state.

Semra turned away, and when she did, she saw into the sitting room across the hall through the half-open door. Two women sat huddled on a couch in an embrace, one several years older than Semra's eighteen years, the other younger. Silk embroidered night robes adorned them and matching golden hair spilled down their shoulders, confirming them as Princess Avaya and Princess Aviama. Soft sobs wracked Aviama's shoulders as she curled into her older sister. Tears slipped down Avaya's face as she rubbed Aviama's back and held her close. Semra couldn't think of a time when Avaya showed emotion like this.

"I need her. I just need her." Aviama straightened slightly and wiped the tears from her face with her arm. Semra felt a lump lodge in her own throat. Surely Aviama was speaking of her mother, Queen Sharsi, who had been murdered by one of the dragonlord's assassins – one of Semra's colleagues – just three months prior. "Her perfume bottle is empty. I've been spraying it on my pillow. What if I forget what she smelled like?!" Aviama threw her hands up, then melted into a puddle in Avaya's lap, shaking with fresh sobs.

"We'll order more," Avaya cooed, stroking her sister's hair. "Saeb will know what scent she used."

Tears welled up in Semra's eyes as she was transported back to that night. The joyous gala where Princess Avaya of Jannemar and Prince Axis of Belvidore were meant to be betrothed and heal years of strife between nations. The whiff of garlic Semra had thought was arsenic, leaving the dance floor to follow the suspicious juggler, being yanked off balance and punched in the stomach. Semra reacted with a fight... screams erupting, guards grabbing her arms...and the mass of bodies opening just enough to see the queen dead on the floor with a knife in her chest, and Tymetin as the juggler wearing that sickening smile, knowing he had framed her beautifully. King Turian himself had since cleared her of all blame related to the incident, but Semra would never shake that memory. She had failed.

Avaya looked up at that moment and locked eyes with Semra, her piercing green eyes hardening to flint as if reading her thoughts. "We can't bring her back, Aviama. But we will stop the bloodshed. We can't rely on anyone but ourselves to protect us."

Semra blanched and drew back from Avaya's accusing glare. She stepped away and slipped back into the staircase, descending to the second floor and rushing into the guest room she had lived in for the past six weeks. A vanity shared one wall with an exquisitely carved wardrobe, and the style matched a desk on the other side of the room. An extravagant bed drew focus opposite the door, and intricate murals of white Nezil Myansara flowers spilled down the walls from a mountain scene on the ceiling.

Semra stared at the silks and furs, let her eyes rove over the gilded details of royal hospitality. A glimpse of a foreign life she was never meant to live, a guestroom built to host people of greater honor – and certainly more noble birth – than she. Zezura's restlessness tugged on her own heart through the connection they shared in the mark of the dragon's kiss. The dragon knew what Semra had been denying. It was time to move on.

Semra stepped in front of the mirror on the vanity and ran her fingers along the strange opal-like mark on her chest that peeked out of her tunic and reached up toward her collarbone. Semra had become a dragonlord that day when she saved Zezura's life, and Zezura saved hers in return. They were forever bound as a result. And a castle was no place for a dragon.

Neither was it a place for murderers, and it was clear Semra would never be free of her past as an assassin. The voice of Ramas, her mentor in the mountain, filtered in through the fancy façade of her bedroom and needled deep inside her brain:

You're a murderer, Semra. It's who you are.

The only thing you were ever good at was killing.

And yet, it was the man who snatched her from her childhood home, the man who pushed her to be the best tool for destruction she could be, the man in the dungeons of the castle that came to her in dreams and told her what her heart knew: *My dear, my dear ... you know I am the only one who has never left you.*

Siler liked her, and was becoming more pointed with his

comments, but he was a loner like her. He might enjoy her company, but he would do whatever served him. Money, mainly.

Zephan was kind to her, but he was already pulling away. Turian's nobles pressured him to get rid of her, and he would sensibly agree. Avaya pointed out yet again Semra's failure to protect them. Semra felt a burning in the mark of the dragon's kiss as she sent a message to Zezura: *Yes, we are going on a ride today. A long one, taking us far away.*

Semra sniffled and wiped a tear from her face, then turned to the drawer of her wardrobe. She had to pack.

4

———————

Semra's hands were still on her pack as the queen lay in her blood. She stepped back and ran to open the door, only to find Ramas, her childhood mentor. He was there to kill her. She closed the door, the room forming into a cell as her surroundings faded away. She turned around, and Tymetin smiled wickedly at her, waving a clove of garlic, mocking her. *Idiot girl!* Semra shook her head as her room came back. The queen was gone, replaced with her normal bed. She was alone. Semra yanked her pack from the wardrobe drawer, slinging the belt for her dagger around her waist. The memories were unbidden, but she no longer bothered trying to stop them.

Someone was shouting. *What is your name?!* It was Azi's voice – the dragonlord. *You knew what you were signing up for, and you wanted it. Loved it. What. Is. Your. Name?* It was the moment she'd rejected the only surname, the only family, she'd ever known.

Traitor.

Fool.

Weak!

Suddenly Semra felt fingers grab onto her shoulder. Semra whirled into her attacker, dagger drawn and pressing into their carotid artery, cursing herself for letting her awareness slip.

"Whoa, wait, it's me! It's me!"

Semra's attacker raised his hands, which made her flinch, and caught her eye. His amber eyes held surprise for a moment before melting into concern, and Semra let the dagger clatter the ground. She stepped away and ran a shaking hand through her dark curly hair. She assaulted the crown prince.

Zephan's familiar muscular frame was draped in a simple tunic sporting the Jannemar crest on his chest, leather gauntlets still bound to his forearms from what must have been an early morning sparring session. His dirty-blonde hair was mildly disheveled, and his boots were still tracking in dust. Her heart beat twice as fast at the sight of him, and an unbidden warmth flooded her head to toe.

"Are you okay? The guards saw you running, and I came to check on you. I said your name, and you didn't answer. I tapped you on the shoulder, hoping to get your attention. I can see that was mistake."

"I'm sorry, I'm sorry," Semra heard herself say. "I don't know what came over me."

Zephan stepped toward her, but Semra backed away. He didn't need to check on her before. Why should now be any different? No, this was not Dahyu. This was Zephan. She lifted her chin. "What would your guards say?"

"What?"

Semra clenched her jaw. "What would your guards say, with you this close to an assassin?"

"What are you talking about? They know who you are. They know you're with us. Where is this coming from?"

Zephan eyed the open wardrobe drawer and the pack on the floor behind her and crossed his arms. "What are you doing?"

"That's a good question," Semra answered, turning back to her pack. "More specifically, what am I doing *here?*" She pulled out a couple fresh tunics and stuffed them into her pack. The rest of her supplies were always ready at a moment's notice.

"You're not making sense. Something happened. What was it?"

Semra blinked back tears and took a breath to steady herself. Why did he have to care?

She ignored his question and pressed forward with her own. "Where have you been? I've been back two weeks and only seen you a handful of times. You eat and sleep here. You're around, but not around. You must have time somewhere. And now you show up, out of the blue?"

Zephan looked like he'd been slapped. "I really haven't had time. I've wanted to come, Semra. My schedule is full, and someone adds to it as soon as I think I've loosened it for a moment of escape."

"Firfell?"

"Sometimes. Why?"

Semra wiped her nose with her sleeve. Siler's voice came back to her. *You don't belong in a stuffy castle. You belong to mountains and trees and open road.*

"Firfell wants me gone. So does the entire court. I walk the grounds and people back away or watch me from the corners of their eyes, as if *I* were the dragon, not Zezura. And Zezura feels as claustrophobic here as I do. It isn't *free,* and I need to be free! I need not look over my shoulder every moment or wonder what toes I'll step on by being here. Rats and rot, Firfell is right. The task force did its job, and nothing is left for me here. What am I doing?"

Zephan frowned. "Providing security and consultation."

"You don't want me here. It wouldn't look good."

"Says who?"

Semra threw her hands up. "Says everybody! Are you telling me you haven't heard it?"

Zephan opened his mouth in retort, then closed it.

"See?" Semra said. "Like I thought. You know better."

"That doesn't mean they're right."

"What are the chances that they are *all* wrong? Hmm? And even if they *were* wrong, and I *could* fit in like some graceful lady of state, if the nobles decided I was a bad influence, it would be smart to create distance between you and me. They've already done it. And why shouldn't they? I have no rights to spending time with you, and the court can do what it wants – without their military aid and political power, the king can hardly be king. I might not know much, but distrust in the king makes him vulnerable. And if the crown prince looks bad, the king looks bad. Me leaving is the easy solution."

Zephan sighed. "They still aren't all powerful. My father is still king. And you're trying to make my decisions for me again. You've done it before, and I'm sick of it. If you think I'm making a stupid decision by letting you stay here, you may say so, but don't treat me like some mindless puppet. If that's why you're leaving, that's a ridiculous reason. Stay."

Semra took a quick step forward and tilted her head to look at him, her eyes burning into his from just inches away. "Are you commanding me?"

Zephan glared back at her, his hands balled into fists at his sides. He opened them and closed them again, his arms and hands clenched tight. But as he looked at her, his muscles slowly relaxed, and his voice was gruff as he spoke. "You know I never will."

Something in his tone stopped her in her tracks. Semra stepped back.

"I think you're making a stupid decision."

Zephan moved closer. "You're allowed to think that. But I'm allowed to make it. And I think if we give trade training to everyone else from the mountain, it serves you by finding something you can do is the smallest offering we could make. You saved us from certain death."

"Officially, I'm not doing anything anymore. The task force is over, and Firfell thinks I'm more of a threat to security than an asset. You don't want me here."

Zephan took in a long, deep breath and studied her. He swallowed. "I don't want you to go."

Something inside her chest tore apart at his words. There was no good reason for him to keep her there. Not unless... well, even if he did have feelings for her, it wouldn't matter anyway. Siler was right. The crown dictated Zephan's life. And besides, he might simply find her an entertaining distraction, a friend – if that's what she was – that waits around in the shadows until called for. No, that wouldn't do. Why did she care?

Semra examined his face for any sign of falsehood but found only earnest caring. Deep caring. She broke eye contact, picked up the dagger from the floor, and sheathed it. It wasn't fair for him to want her to stay, not when he had been impossible to find for over a month. Semra wanted to scream, *you haven't even been here! You've hardly even spoken to me!* What was she waiting for? Anger bubbled up over her sadness and poured out her mouth before she could stop it.

"What would your guards have done if they had seen me just now? They would have accosted me at the least and gutted me if they were smart. Because if I was trying to kill you, grabbing my arms wouldn't be enough."

Zephan shook his head. "Are you trying to scare me? Because the moment you found out Avi was lying to you and the others in the mountain, you dedicated yourself to stopping him at all costs. And you did. You are *good*. And you're welcome here; my father ensured it."

Semra shook her head. "Avaya blames me for your mother. She's not wrong. I didn't stop everything."

Zephan's eyes misted at the mention of his mother, and Semra wished she could take it back. He stepped toward her. "You did everything you could. Even the best of us can only do what we can do."

"My intentions don't matter. The reality is that I am an assassin, given free reign to waltz through a royal residence, and any guard or court or noble who *wasn't* nervous would be a fool."

Zephan reached out and pulled her into arms, and this time Semra didn't stop him. She hugged him back and rested her head on his chest. In that moment he was Dahyu, the healer's apprentice from a small village, when their friendship was simpler. In that moment she was home, comforted, protected in his arms.

Semra wondered what life would be like if she were the type of woman the castle approved of. Zephan was quiet for a moment, and when he spoke, his voice was solemn. "You've already convinced yourself you must go, and I have no right to keep you here. I know you can't live here in the guest rooms forever, but if it were up to me, we'd find something you might enjoy doing, help you achieve it, and give you a place to work. I'll miss you when you aren't here."

He lifted a hand, and his fingers grazed her arm. Safe and warm, he was the man from the woods, the commoner breaking into the castle and joining her on expeditions.

No. No, he didn't get to just sweep in and sound caring

after *not* caring to see her for weeks. He wasn't Dahyu, and he hadn't broken in at all. It had been his own house. He was Zephan, crown prince of Jannemar.

Her voice was thick when she spoke again. "I've hardly seen you as it is. It won't feel that different."

"We're at war, and I have responsibilities. As the philosopher says, *the weight of the sword is a weight on the mind.* It won't always be this way."

"Yes, it will. You might not always be at war, but you'll always have that weight, that responsibility."

Zephan pulled away and glanced up at the ceiling, where the mountain range murals stretched across the room and the painted flowers bloomed and trailed down the walls. "We have three gates: the Dragon Gate, the Spearhead Gate, and the Nezzi Gate. Three of our guest rooms are themed to match, and I chose this one for you. You're far from home, and though I can't picture mountain caves as a home, I hoped it would be some small comfort to see mountains."

Semra swallowed, but the lump in her throat didn't go away. She bit her tongue and glanced away.

Feet pounded down the hall and slid to a stop at the door. Semra and Zephan turned to see a guard pause as he glanced between them, taking in their proximity.

"Yes, Ashend?" Zephan said, authority in his tone and the picture of a prince once more.

"Your Royal Highness, your presence is required in the east meeting rooms."

"That's where Firfell is meeting with the king," Semra said to Zephan.

"I'll be there in a moment, Ashend."

"Sir, I was instructed to escort you."

Semra scoffed. Of course, he would need escorted across the castle. Who knew what unsavory people the precious prince might encounter on the way without careful supervision.

"Wait for me at the end of the hall, then." Zephan turned away from the guard, but he turned back again when he heard no receding footsteps. "Was I unclear?"

The guard snapped his mouth shut and dipped his head before whirling back toward the staircase. With Ashend out of sight, Zephan's shoulders sagged and turned back to Semra.

"I know the task force is ending, but let me find something, some position for you. I can talk to Firfell."

"More convincingly than the king?"

"Ultimately, Firfell can only advise. He can't banish you."

"True, but it isn't just Firfell, is it? And it's not wise for the king to continually ruffle the feathers of his closest supporters."

"You're going?"

"Nothing is holding me here, is there?" Somewhere inside, Semra hoped there was. She wanted to beg him, plead with him. *Want me.* But what would it matter if he did? Heartbreak and unnecessary pain.

Zephan stared at her for a long moment. His arms tensed, and a shadow passed over his face. His amber eyes searched hers, as if the answers to his questions could be found there. Zephan started to reach for her, but caught himself, and dropped his hand. He sighed, and his shoulders drooped. "Just promise me you won't disappear forever. Don't exile yourself because of guilt that you aren't...more than human."

Something wilted in her chest. Semra slung her pack across her back, nodding. "I'll always do everything in my power to protect the Shamaran family. I may not be particularly experienced as far as family goes, but I think yours is a pretty good one. I have observed a lot of leaders, and you and your father are just what Jannemar needs."

Zephan searched her face for a moment, then nodded once. "Okay. I'll see you soon."

"See you soon."

With that, Zephan disappeared down the hall, and Semra left the Nezzi Room for what she expected would be the last time.

5

———————

ARNEVON

King Arnevon of Belvidore popped a grape into his mouth, drumming his bejeweled fingers on the table. "The Surion Strip is the key to Jannemar. We need those reinforcements *now*. A victory at Seddon is our best route to the Strip."

And the Strip gives us the river, and the river, power. And the victory my forefathers failed to attain for Belvidore so long ago.

"Sire. If I may. Sending reinforcements to Seddon may secure you the city, but–"

"But nothing. I want Seddon." Arnevon glared at the young man before him: stubborn, brash, arrogant. Much like in years past, his son wore the Belvidorian crest, the same dark brown hair and beard as the king, but had much to learn before taking the throne.

"It's insanity to pour all our remaining troops into one location! We don't have the resources to give you the numbers you want." Prince Axis stood across from Arnevon's chair, fists planted firmly on the tabletop as he leaned into them, tension rolling off him in waves.

"You think me quite the dolt, is that it?" Arnevon

demanded. "Have you run as many campaigns as I have? How many battle scars have you earned, boy? I want reinforcements to Seddon, and I want them *yesterday*. We already outnumber them, but the topography gives Jannemar the upper hand. Turian won't stand a chance, not if we do it right. I want a battalion added to Seddon and a battalion added to Belera."

"It will take time to mobilize that many."

"You've been slack with the battalion commanders. They could do it on the discussed timeline if pushed to drill effectively. Fix your mistakes and get it done." Arnevon shredded a piece of chicken with his fingers and tossed a piece into his mouth, chasing it down with choice wine.

"Father – "

"How *dare* you!" Arnevon slammed his fists on the table, the silverware jumping with the impact. "In this room, I am your *king,* first and foremost, and don't you forget it!"

"My mistake, *Your Majesty*, but we have no provisions for these additional numbers." His son tapped furiously on the map spread between them on the table. "Do you think we can roll out two battalions in three days with all they need for the coming months? And it *could* be months. We need to think of our men's health, not to mention their loyalty."

Arnevon waved his hand dismissively. "Let them gather what they need from the people as they go. We'll raise the tax to support the war effort, and the charge will be relaxed once we secure the Strip."

Axis slammed his fists down on the table. "That's not good enough."

Arnevon picked up his goblet and tossed the wine in his son's face, smashing the goblet back down on the stone table with a great *clang*. "*You're* not good enough! Who was responsible for the readiness of those battalions? Who was lax on their training? And you think yourself worthy to sit on *my* throne and rule *my* people? *I* will restore our fortunes, and *I* will take my revenge on Jannemar!"

Axis's lip curled into a snarl as he glared at his father. He plucked a napkin from the table, wiped his face, then crumpled and tossed it down. "Like it or not, I am your son, your heir, and your people are my people. They will pay for the disgrace they have brought upon Belvidore. And I will wed their princess if it's the last thing I do, as promised, just to spite them."

6

———

Semra turned down the hall past Belon bustling by with a cart of laundry and listened to the chatter of the kitchen down the hall. She poked her head into the chandlery where she hoped to find Garbane, the candle-maker she had befriended, but the room was empty. He wasn't the emotional type; he would understand why she left.

She proceeded past the storeroom and kitchen, listening to the faint squeak of the dumbwaiter pulleys as breakfast made its way upstairs, then backtracked to fold a biscuit and sausages into a napkin. She glanced around, but nobody paid her any mind, and Semra scarfed down the food on her way to Ancestry Hall. Its double doors opened to a circular room leading into the Great Hall to her left, and two spiral stair-cases to her right, one leading up and the other down. Paint-ings of King Turian, Queen Sharsi, Prince Zephan, and the princesses smiled mockingly at her among all their royal lineage, Shamaran family history depicted from floor to ceil-ing. The castle was no place for the likes of an orphan assassin.

"I'm just saying, it's only a matter of time before that thing gets hungry and picks us off one by one," said a voice, from the staircase to the third floor.

Semra fled down to the main level, striding across a long hall to avoid the meeting rooms where she had overheard Firfell and Turian earlier. Servants eyed her as she passed, but she paid them no mind. She would never see them again anyway. What did she care about their opinions? Semra slipped out to the balcony to get some air. Striding forward and leaning heavily on the railing, she took a deep breath and let herself savor the sight of the sparkling Shalladin river curving into the base of the cliff.

"I'm surprised it took you this long."

Semra grinned and turned to see Siler. "And I'm surprised to see you. It's been two weeks, and I haven't seen you – I thought you were off to find a villa with all the spoils you skimmed from the Framatar."

Siler laughed and crossed the space between them, resting his elbows alongside her. "I like having friends in high places. It makes me feel important, and it comes with perks!" Siler waved a croissant under Semra's nose and took a bite.

"Pastries! How could I forget."

Semra relaxed next to him lounging there, his tussled brown hair and storm gray eyes reminding her of a simpler time. A time when they thought they were purging the world of evil, and her only preoccupations were of the mission at hand. Semra's world had flipped upside down since she learned of Azi's deception. She only hoped getting away could restore some of that simplicity.

"So," Siler said, gesturing to her pack, "where are you headed?"

"Wherever the wind takes us, I guess," Semra answered with a shrug. "I want to feel at home, and this isn't it. I want to go someplace where Zez and I aren't ogled or judged."

"Long flight then."

Semra rolled her eyes, and Siler threw his hands up defensively. "Hey, you're a knife-strapped, trouser-wearing woman with a dragon. What do you expect from people? I still think you should rent a room in my villa."

"The villa you don't have yet."

"Precisely." He grinned. "If you help me pick one out, I'll give you a discount on rent."

Semra laughed. "How charitable."

Siler angled his body toward her and his laughing eyes sobered. "Get a fresh start somewhere, Semra. Far away from all the assassin rumors–"

"*True* rumors," Semra put in. Was he going to ask her again to go with him? Maybe it wouldn't be so bad, going with Siler. She studied his face, his languid, unconcerned nature giving way to something deeper. He had a casual demeanor, but he was a deep thinker. If she went with him, she would have no financial needs, no obligation to be a part of society, and no requirements for what she must or must not do if she did venture out. She wouldn't be alone.

Siler waved her off. "The assassin part is true, but not all the stories circulating. But I digress. You either need to find a mountain of yours somewhere to live alone with Zezura, or a good identity that lets you rove about. You get to create a whole new life and then step into it. Could be fun."

Semra nodded. "Could be." *Then why did her heart feel so heavy?*

"Go somewhere new. Get that fresh start. Don't wait."

Semra nodded again. She closed her eyes and swallowed, but the lump in her throat had returned and refused to be ignored. As crazy as he was, Siler kept Semra grounded and understood her like no one else would. She would be free to move about as she pleased, without judgment. It would be easy. Maybe just for now...

Semra's eyes snapped open. Siler was gone.

"Siler?" Semra's chest constricted and she ran around the corner of the keep, but he wasn't there. "Siler!" Disappointment hit her hard in the gut, the emerging vision of having someone keep her company squashed like a bug. Her original plan of finding a cave suddenly seemed cold and desolate in comparison. Semra smacked herself on the side of the face. "He left fast for a reason," she said to herself. "You've run him off enough times by now. Get a grip."

Despite her pep talk, she ran back through the keep and out into the courtyard looking for him before slowly returning to the railing at the outer ward. The sun climbed the sky and warmed her face, and the clouds beckoned her. Semra felt for Zezura as she flew somewhere far off, and called to her through the mark. Her original plan was just fine. Siler was right, she didn't belong in a castle. And Zephan had proved it. It was time to go.

Behind her the door flew open and Semra turned to see Aviama run out and scan the outer ward. Her eyes landed on Semra and she ran forward, wringing her hands. "Semra! Have you seen Avaya?"

Semra furrowed her brow. "The last time I saw her was this morning. She was with you."

"No, no, no! She said she would meet me in the library, but she isn't there. But the thing is, she isn't anywhere. She's gone."

"What do you mean, gone? I'm sure she's around here somewhere."

Aviama seized Semra's arm and shook her head. "We've looked everywhere. She's *gone!* What if...what if something happened to her?"

Semra scanned the young girl's terrified face and sighed.

She glanced up, and could just make out Zezura's outline appearing on the horizon as her wings beat the air. Semra's heart dropped like a stone into her gut, and sent an apology to Zezura. *Sorry, Zez. We'll still go flying today. Just a small delay.*

Semra hoped it was true, and turned back toward the castle keep. "Where have you looked?"

Aviama threw her hands in the air. "Everywhere!"

Semra cocked her head. "That's not overly helpful. Could she be on a ride, or–"

"No. Her horse is in the stable. She's nowhere in the keep or on the grounds. Her breakfast is untouched. *Untouched!* And she never skips breakfast."

A shout went up from the courtyard and Semra flew through the door, through the keep, and out to the courtyard with Aviama hot on her heels; on the far end in the shaded garden, Avaya's lady-in-waiting was bent over something on the ground. Semra and Aviama ran up to her and she looked up, tears in her eyes, as she lifted a delicate gem-studded earring.

"Princess Avaya," the girl choked out.

Semra scanned the garden and broken plants by the wall. "Signs of struggle."

Two mounted guards cantered up, and the first slid from the saddle to investigate the scene. "Looks like there was an altercation here," he said grimly. "We should lock down the castle."

Semra rolled her eyes.

The second guard spoke up. "But what about Garfor? He just left with the carriage to repair, and the king needs it for tomorrow."

Semra snapped her gaze up to the second guard. "A carriage just left the grounds?"

The guard hesitated. "Yes..."

"Why isn't it being repaired here?" Semra demanded.

"It...I don't know. I think it needed some specialty work done."

Semra cursed under her breath. "Which gate?"

"Wait, what's going on?" Aviama asked, looking between Semra and the guards.

"Dragon Gate," answered the guard, "But I don't think–"

Semra didn't wait for him to finish. She crossed to the first guard's mare, swung herself up, and wheeled her around before the first guard could react.

"Hey! Halt! *Stop!*"

"Idiots!" she yelled back, kicking the mare into a canter down the courtyard, through the inner and outer wards, and toward the Dragon Gate. But something didn't feel right. It was too obvious, too easy.

The guard's horse was a good steed, and surged forward with little encouragement from Semra. Her black coat glistened in the morning sun and her muscles rippled as she found her rhythm pounding through the tunnel and out toward the main carriage road to Qalea. Semra heard the clatter of hooves, the murmur of voices as people scattered before her, and the sound of the Jannemar flag as it whipped in the wind overhead.

Semra glanced behind her and saw the second guard shouting as he rode, but as she turned back around she caught a glimpse of the carriage on the other side of the Dragon Gate rumbling down the road. Guards in the tower above her ran to the chain winch system to lower the portcullis. She wasn't going to make it. But there was no time to turn the horse.

7

———

Semra adjusted her feet firmly in the stirrups, let the reins fly free, and threw herself over the side of the horse so that her right foot hooked a stirrup and caught her, her knee draped over the saddle. Her torso stuck out at a precarious ninety-degree angle hanging off the side of the horse hands-free. Her heart pounded in her chest as she stared at the spikes of the portcullis gate and heard the chains release it right over her head, but the mare flew through with not a moment to spare. Semra gasped as she struggled to regain her seat, leaning forward and hugging the mare's neck as she returned her focus to the carriage at the edges of the city of Qalea. But the carriage was closer than it should have been. Had it made a stop, or was she remembering wrong?

No, it must have made a stop. Semra swept her gaze over the area and pulled herself sharply outside an open window two houses down from where the carriage now rumbled down the road. She could have sworn she had seen a blur through the window. Semra slid straight off the horse into the house window, her feet landing with a light *thud*.

It was a simple bedroom she found herself in, with a bed, a wooden bench, and a trunk. Semra crept to the doorway and saw a blonde woman sweeping the floor with a straw broom. Needlework lay abandoned on the table, a kettle sat next to an empty fireplace, and several baskets and pitchers lined one wall.

Semra crossed to the doorway, blocking the exit. "You should have picked the needlework."

The woman jumped and turned to Semra, eyes wild. She wore a wool cloak obscuring most of a silk dress. "Who are you? Why are you in my house?"

"The needlework would have covered the finery of your skirt, whereas the sweeping gives you away. The cloak would still be strange to wear inside your own house, though."

Semra stepped forward and her arm shot out to grip the woman's arm, twisting it behind her so that she cried out. Semra cocked her head in surprise. "You have no idea how to defend yourself. You aren't professional at all. How much were you paid to impersonate the princess?"

"I don't know what you're on about!"

Semra groaned and increased the pressure on her arm. "I'm afraid I'm in a hurry, so please don't make me break any bones."

The woman's jaw dropped. Her words came in a rush, her eyes still round as saucers. "I don't know a thing about the princesses, except they're lovely! Truly lovely, to be sure. I didn't know I'd be doing something bad, but it wasn't hurting nobody. I was paid five *jemari*."

"And the dress?"

"Was here this morning, and I get to keep it! I didn't break no laws."

Semra released her and stepped back. The woman sank onto the bench by the table and nervously poured herself a cup of water from the pitcher. "This is your actual house," Semra observed with surprise.

"'Course it's my house, and people used to knock, as I recall," the woman muttered, eying Semra warily. "Name's Polena. Not that you asked."

The door to the house flew open and four armed guards filed in, then paused uncertainly in the doorway.

"Dragons and daylilies!" Polena exclaimed, her hand fluttering over her heart. "I didn't do a thing wrong, not a thing! Surely, this woman is the one you want; she's an intruder!"

"Take them both," said a guard captain at the rear, and the guards seized both women immediately.

Semra looked at the guards' nonplussed faces and a wave of irritation swept over her. "She was paid to be a decoy. I'm a friend of the king, and his daughter is in danger. We need a full inventory of who was in the castle this morning, any newcomers, all comings and goings, and another full search of the castle grounds. I'll return to give my statement before leaving."

"Everyone is a friend of the king when they get arrested," the captain drawled. "You'll return because you're in our custody, and you'll leave when the king sees fit."

Semra and Polena were marched out of the house to the carriage that Semra had been chasing, which waited for them just outside, along with the black mare. The guards confiscated Semra's pack, dagger, and the multiple knives strapped to each thigh of her trousers. One of the guards, a young man with a round face, arched an eyebrow.

"What could you possibly need all this for?"

"Dolt!" said his friend, a guard with a long nose, escorting Polena. "She's the dragon girl."

Polena's eyes widened into saucers again, and the young guard drew back. "You're the one with the dragon?" His eyes traveled down to the mark beneath her collarbone, peeking out from under her tunic.

Semra pursed her lips and bit her tongue. She didn't like this kind of attention. And she would need some sort of makeup or new clothing option to cover the dragon's kiss if she entered the city again.

Long-nose spoke again, handing Round-face a coil of rope. "Better tie her hands. Rumor has it those petite things have killed a lot of people."

"Is it true you saved the king?" Round-face asked eagerly as he tied her hands. Semra decided she liked him. He didn't focus on the killing part, but on the saving. And he seemed genuine and earnest, if a little naïve.

"Or failed a coup, and played the winning side," Long-nose offered.

Long-nose was less likable.

"The blue dragon is yours?" Polena asked. "Was the black one yours too? How did you get a dragon?"

Semra swallowed but kept her mouth clamped shut. No need to add fuel to whatever rumors were flying about.

"That's enough," barked the captain. "We are transporting suspicious persons before the king, as commanded. Both charges will be treated as such until delivered."

Long-nose and Round-face escorted Semra and Polena inside the coach and sat. Semra leaned her head against the coach and closed her eyes, absent-mindedly loosening the rope on her hands bit by bit to slow her heart rate. All evidence led to Princess Avaya being victim to a planned kidnapping, with a decoy to draw attention and cover the real escape. When would Avaya have been taken? If Semra was planning it, she would have used several decoys. Semra wondered if more were in play around the castle that she wasn't aware of.

The coach pulled into the courtyard and four guards escorted Semra and Polena through the ground floor of the west side of the keep and into a receiving room. Polena was brought into a side room where Semra could not hear to give her story to the guard captain, and returned some minutes later. The two guards from the courtyard that morning with Aviama and Avaya's lady-in-waiting arrived and gestured at Semra to the guard captain. They withdrew for private discussion, and Semra settled in to wait. Yes, this might be less pleasant than the massive gilded guest room, but it certainly made more sense. This was a scenario that felt more familiar to her.

After speaking to someone standing at the double doors at the end of the room, the guards ushered Semra and Polena into a long room with a throne on the end flanked by more guards. One of them was Gaulen, the guard who accompanied Semra and Siler on their latest mission. Surprise flickered across his face. Captain Firfell, General Soldan, and Count Darbune stood around a table to one side where maps and other papers were spread, and King Turian sat with his head in his hands in a chair at the head of the table. Zephan sat beside him with his hand on his father's shoulder, speaking in low tones.

The guard captain cleared his throat. "Your Majesty, we found these two at the base of the carriage road in a house in Qalea. Permission to speak?"

The king slowly raised his head, confusion settling over his tired features as his eyes rested on Semra. Semra bit her lip as she glanced uncertainly at Zephan beside him, but his expression was unreadable. Neither moved. "Speak," Turian said, straightening slightly in his chair.

The guard obliged. "This one states her name is Polena and that she lives in the house where we found them. She reports she was paid to wear the fancy dress, enter the castle by a pre-planned route, and exit by the carriage at an appointed time this morning; this one I believe you are familiar with, Semra, who stole one of your guards' horses in the courtyard and fled pursuit in favor of a rogue mission, either to chase down the carriage or to create further distraction."

Turian ran a hand over his face and Semra felt a squirming in her stomach. Was he disappointed in her? Had she done something wrong? She had been trying to stop the kidnapping...

"Untie her hands."

"Your Majesty, we found a pack with her effects and provisions for a journey, and she was armed with multiple weapons. This fact, combined with her, ah, reputation and unstable demeanor, gives us pause in releasing her." The guard captain nudged Long-nose, and he quickly produced Semra's pack, dagger, and knives. Turian arched an eyebrow and when he looked at Semra, she saw only sadness.

"What exactly do you mean by unstable demeanor?" Captain Firfell asked.

"She has no reasonable fear of death, sir, and I consider this a dangerous trait," the guard said. "To regain control of the situation, sir, the Dragon Gate portcullis was dropped nearly on top of her, and she exhibited psychological instability when instead of turning aside she slid from the saddle and clung to the side of the horse and as it galloped through the gate, narrowly escaping death by impalement."

Zephan jumped to his feet. "You *what?*"

Semra's chest tightened, and she lifted her head to meet his gaze. Was he worried, or angry? Perhaps both. Or perhaps he was ashamed he had ever suggested she stay in the castle when she was so wild.

"Did she exhibit any additional instability upon your taking custody of her?" Turian demanded. "I note, for example, that she had a multitude of weaponry and certainly no lack in skill, yet still you have all your limbs."

Semra coughed to hide a laugh. She could have hugged him! But when she looked at his face, no humor was in it, and her amusement faded.

"She...was cooperative upon capture, Your Majesty."

"And this determination of her psychological well-being, based only on her risky behavior in an attempt to stop a kidnapping that you failed to stop, does this fall under the purview of your guard training?"

"Sire–"

"That will be all. I believe I told you to untie her."

The captain clenched his jaw and bowed curtly, then turned toward Semra to loosen her bonds. She tugged on the rope's end and let the slip knot she had made work itself free. She'd untied herself in the entry room, but now was certainly the better time to reveal it. Semra handed the rope to the captain, and his cheeks flushed a brilliant red.

"You there," General Soldan spoke up, nodding toward Polena. "How did you receive your instructions?"

"Some kid dropped off the notes," she answered. "I never met whoever gave them to me."

"Was there another decoy?" Semra asked, speaking for the first time.

Count Darbune shook his head. "I'm not sure that's information you need–"

"Yes," Zephan replied evenly, his manner all business. "One through the servant's quarters beneath the castle at the same time as the carriage, and a third on the east exit out to the cliffs and forest."

Semra nodded. "It's smart. I would still lock down the

castle. She's probably gone, but it's possible they're waiting for the search parties to assume they've escaped, and then making their exit under less surveillance."

"It's already done," Turian said. He turned to the guards standing with Semra and Polena. "You're dismissed. Take down a full statement from Polena with details, locations, everything."

"Yes, Your Majesty," Captain Firfell said. "And what about Semra?"

Count Darbune and Zephan spoke at once:

"She goes."

"She stays."

Semra glanced between them and winced. "I do love a welcoming atmosphere. Why don't I just see myself out? But I'm afraid I will be needing my effects back."

The count glared at Semra, but the king held up his hand. "Semra will wait outside the meeting room. She will have what belongs to her." The king looked directly into Semra's eyes. "You will not leave the castle before speaking to me again, as the most basic courtesies after this incident and after being a guest in my house. Agreed?"

Did he want to accuse her? Or express his disappointment that she would leave on a journey without so much as a word? Semra pressed her lips together in a hard line and paused, then dipped her head. The guards returned Semra's belongings to her and filed out with Polena, and Semra followed and seated herself on the bench in the adjoining room. Two guards stood at the double doors, but otherwise the room was empty. There was silence in the room beyond; for a moment, Semra wondered if she could excuse herself without being noticed.

Shouting erupted then, loud and angry in a cacophony of muffled voices she couldn't make out. Semra thumbed the green snake amulet on her belt, an anxious habit she'd developed, and played with a strand of her hair. She examined the stone floor and traced a crack parallel to the bench with her toe.

Silence fell again. Semra wished she could oil her knives – it always calmed her down, but taking out weapons near the king in front of his guards seemed ill-advised. She'd caused enough trouble. Just then the doors swung open and Zephan stepped out.

"Would you join us?"

8

___

I *think I'd rather not join you.*

But Semra said nothing and allowed Zephan to escort her back into the conference room, pulling out a chair at the end across from the king. General Soldan, Count Darbune, and Captain Firfell watched her intently from their seats, and King Turian stroked his beard, observing her. Semra took her seat, and Zephan placed himself in the chair next to her.

"My daughter has been kidnapped," Turian said evenly. His eyes were red, but his voice was steady. "The only suspects caught were the decoys the culprit planted for us to catch. Their scheme, whoever they are, has gone precisely as planned. All signs lead to Belvidore."

"We cannot afford to make false accusations against Belvidore, but we also cannot afford to allow her to fall into their hands and be used as a bargaining chip," General Soldan added. "King Arnevon is not known for his charity. The king must know Princess Avaya is safe."

Semra's stomach dropped. Avaya's proposed marriage to Prince Axis last year had been the first time Belvidore and

Jannemar neared a sense of peace in generations. When Azi had one of his assassins murder Queen Sharsi at the gala hosting Belvidore, the marriage agreement was off. Jannemar blamed Belvidore for the hit, and Belvidore did not take the accusation well. They retaliated with military force and plunged both kingdoms into war.

If Avaya symbolized the failed union between the nations, a broken promise and a mountain of fresh ill will, what else would a revenge-bent enemy do to her?

"I may be the king, but I am also a widower and a father," Turian said. "I admit my head is spinning, and military strategy does not come to me easily with Avaya missing."

Semra's chest tightened, and she swallowed. She never knew her father, and the man who raised her was harsh and unfeeling. She wondered what it would have been like to have had a father like this, tender and concerned.

Semra cleared her throat. "Why are you telling me this?"

"My son tells me Captain Firfell and I were less discreet than we thought during our early morning meeting today." Semra flashed a glare at Zephan, and he shrugged.

"They needed to know why you were leaving," he explained. "It was important."

Semra set her jaw. Of course, it made sense, but that information had come from a private conversation. What had Captain Firfell and Count Darbune thought about Zephan and Semra having a heart-to-heart that morning? Their expressions were sour, and Semra guessed it was precisely the type of interaction they hoped to prevent. Did they know it had taken place in her chambers?

Turian ran a hand through his beard and sighed. "I cannot lie...there is some disagreement over what to do with you, Semra. Some find the timing of your planned departure too convenient."

"That's ridiculous. I would never be so sloppy." Semra heard Zephan's sharp intake of breath beside her, and she grimaced. "I have no reason to kidnap Avaya, and all evidence points to the contrary."

There was a silence, and Semra wiped sweaty palms on her trousers underneath the table. Count Darbune spoke.

"For someone as skilled as you believe yourself to be, manipulating the evidence would hardly be a problem. Secondly, you would do well to refer to her Highness with appropriate respect moving forward."

Semra opened her mouth, then closed it.

General Soldan held up a hand. "Why don't you tell us why you were leaving, in your own words."

Semra scanned the faces in front of her, ranging from neutral, to sad, to angry. She glanced at Zephan, his gentle amber eyes trained intently on her. Semra clenched her fingers into fists beneath the table, and saw Zephan catch the movement out of the corner of his eye.

"I...have done what I came to do, or at least I did my best," she said. "I do not have a purpose here, and I believe my presence, and Zezura's, is causing trouble." *And Zephan doesn't have time for me.*

A brief expression of hurt flickered across both Turian and Zephan's faces at once, and Semra was struck by how similar their features were. The two of them were alike in many ways.

"Weeks have passed since Mount Hara was cleared," Darbune said. "Why hadn't you left before today?"

Semra shifted uncomfortably. "I don't know." She liked being close to Zephan. And his family, the only real family she'd ever seen.

"What is your occupation, Semra?" Darbune asked.

"This is unnecessary," Zephan objected. "We all know her situation."

Darbune waved his hand dismissively, and Turian shot him a warning look, but gestured at Semra to humor him. "I have agreed to allow the count to question you."

Semra nodded, and answered carefully. "I have no occupation, and few transferrable skills. That is part of why I was leaving."

"Fine." Darbune's lips turned down into an unsightly glower. "Would you admit to a lifetime of training and employment as an assassin?"

Semra shifted her weight. "Yes."

"And would you also admit kidnapping a princess is within your skillset?"

Semra leaned forward on the edge of her chair and leaned her forearms on the table. "I should hope there are many responsible for the king's security that have the skills to kidnap a royal. How else might they consider preventing such catastrophes?"

Darbune slammed his hand down on the table. "You are addicted to danger and revel in your deviant talents! You are out of control, and stealing a horse to flee the castle grounds on a rogue mission is deeply frightening. A person who does not acknowledge risks is not a person who deserves responsibility, and continuing through the gate shows extreme recklessness."

"Perhaps I am deviant," Semra said. Her nostrils flared, and her chest burned hot. "I don't care for fancy titles, or lip-service respect to nobility. I don't care who your father was, *my lord,* and quite honestly, I don't expect someone who spends their time collecting taxes and having their shoes shined to understand why a galloping horse cannot possibly be turned aside at the last moment. Had I been confident in the guard's ability to stop the kidnapping, I would have happily gone my way; as it was, they showed little concern for a suspicious carriage leaving the grounds and were more focused on *me* than on the recovery of the king's daughter."

"Why did you bother with the carriage at all?" General Soldan asked, his tone more curious than accusing. "And what are we to make of your death-defying feats beneath the Dragon Gate?"

"I chased the carriage to keep a promise to the Shamaran family. I slid out of the saddle at the gate and kept myself lower than the horse's body so that if we didn't make it through, the body of the horse might bear the weight of the portcullis enough to save my life."

Soldan grinned despite himself. "Incredible."

"Your Majesty," Captain Firfell said, turning to the king, "The fact of the matter is no matter how smoothly she speaks or how talented she may or may not be in her...ah, blood-stained line of work, she is a liability. Her lack of respect for authority is problematic."

"Respect should be earned, not assumed," Semra cut in.

"Even so. Your Majesty, I must express once more my deepest misgivings in having Semra involved in the recovery of the princess. If not the dungeons awaiting investigation, she could at least serve as a consultant here instead of in the field."

Semra's head snapped to the king. "What? Involved how?"

"The closest people she has to family are the ones who took the queen from us and threatened your own life, sire," Count Darbune added.

"They are *not* my family," Semra said. "*Involved how?*"

Turian spread his hands. "We cannot officially make any statement about the princess' disappearance, nor our suspicions of Belvidore, and Avaya *must* be regained. Belvidore is bearing down on Seddon, and if they take Seddon, the Surion Strip and a monopoly on trade routes will be next. We need another task force, and though your...skills would be critical, my advisors do not want you to help."

"Let Semra serve as a consultant, and I will go myself," Firfell offered.

Turian shook his head. "Asked and answered, friend. Your skills are better suited to leading soldiers than running small-scale operations in the shadows. But I must have someone I trust."

"Trust!" Darbune exclaimed. "It is absurd that she should sit with us to hear privileged information, much less galivant about freely. She is not nobility, she has no military rank, and hours ago she was ready to leave for good."

"It has to be me." All eyes turned to the prince, who thoughtfully stared into the grains of the wooden table before them. Zephan looked at his father. "Nothing else makes sense. You need someone you can trust, with a vested interest in keeping our family together, and in the political and military implications of each action taken. You need someone comfort-able with a sword, but more than that, if the situation devolves and requires negotiation, you need someone with authority on the ground at a moment's notice. I can take your signet ring and act on your behalf as necessary, freeing you up to redouble your focus on the war. Semra can't offer you any of that."

Semra looked at him quizzically, but he ignored her. He continued.

"The captain is needed by his soldiers, and the count, among other responsibilities, has a number of persons under him as well. The general obviously cannot be missed. On the other hand, I frequently dabble in a myriad of state concerns, and no one would be overly surprised by my absence."

The king leaned back in his chair, considering the idea.

Darbune furrowed his brow, then nodded. "It's the only

solution that makes sense. You can't go alone, but you're the right choice to take the lead."

Turian looked around the room. "Firfell? Soldan? Are you in agreement?"

"I don't like sending the crown prince far from home," Soldan admitted. "No one is a greater bargaining chip than the prince. However, if he were not on his mission, I know he would be headed to fight at Seddon, so I see no difference in risk."

Firfell pursed his lips. "I have no objections to the prince. He is young, but accompanied by an accomplished team, he may be our only option."

Was charisma awarded to all royals, or was Zephan particularly blessed? A moment ago there was a table of angry men, but now they were appeased and ready to follow him.

Turian sighed, then turned to Zephan. "All right. It's settled then. Zephan will–"

Zephan held up a hand. "I have demands."

Semra's eyes widened. He'd *just* gained peace and trust in the room. What was he doing?

Count Darbune folded his arms and scowled. "I thought you said you were the best choice."

"Oh, I am. And now that we all agree on someone *you* can trust – me – it's time for me to choose the people *I* can trust, to form my team. I can't take more than a couple people, or we won't be able to move stealthily, so they have to be just the right selections."

Firfell glared at him, and Zephan grinned. An awkward pause haunted the space between them, and Semra began to wonder what she was still doing there. If she wasn't being arrested, she should be free to go. She cleared her throat.

"If it's all the same, I think now is as good a time as any to excuse myself. I wouldn't want to hear any more *privileged* information, and don't want to cause any more arguments." She stood.

"I want Semra and Monac." Zephan drilled the four men with a cool stare. "And I'm not going without them."

She sat.

Shouts erupted.

THE KING RECLAIMED control over the room, and Semra tried to absorb Zephan demanding she be part of the mission to get Avaya back. He couldn't do that. She'd made her decision, and he'd said himself that he couldn't make her stay. The burning in her chest grew. Did he just want to stall her from leaving the castle, or did he want to keep her under observation? Captain Firfell had suggested she be locked in the dungeons during an investigation...what if Turian felt mounting pressure to keep the nobility happy, and changed his mind on her keeping her free?

Semra let the conversation fall to a dull noise and her senses honed in on the anger in Captain Firfell's face, Count Darbune's fists, and Soldan's gesturing hands. Zephan and King Turian responded with firm, understanding authority, but Zephan worked to defend his position and Turian passed a hand over weary eyes.

Semra wondered if the king would collapse from emotional exhaustion alone in his room after this. Turian now carried the weight of his kidnapped daughter, his son's negotiating terms to rescue her while putting himself in danger, his supporters at odds with each other over what to do, and the security of an entire kingdom at stake. If some small piece of that weight could be lifted by Semra's leaving, shouldn't she do it?

Semra's chest was heavy and hot, and she felt the burning desire to get out. Out of the cold, stuffy castle, out of view of judgmental looks, out from under expectations she could never meet. As much as she respected Turian and wished she could help him, it wasn't enough. The nobles would never accept Semra, and if Zephan continued to tie himself to her, he would damage his relationships with powerful supporters before ever taking the throne.

Besides, Zephan would never choose her. Even if he wanted to, his station wouldn't let him. And he didn't seem to want to. He was drifting farther and farther away, first with the task force, and then avoiding her in the castle. The thought of constantly seeing him, but never being close...

Her throat tightened. No, that wouldn't do.

Semra moved as if in a daze, unaware of the words still flying around her. She let her feet carry her out of the chair, into the entry room, and outside to the outer ward. Behind her someone was shouting, but she didn't care. She needed air.

Two minutes later, Zephan appeared at her side. Semra didn't move, and it was a moment before she spoke. "They couldn't let me be alone, could they?"

"I told them to let you go. They want you...in sight, so I figured I was the least threatening option."

Semra groaned and leaned both elbows on the railing. "I should have left weeks ago. Nobody would be fighting over me."

"That might be true, but my sister would still be missing."

Semra jerked her head sideways to look at him, and cursed under her breath. She had been so focused on herself that she had forgotten Avaya was his sister. After the loss of his mother, having Avaya gone and his father distraught had to be deeply devastating.

"How are you doing?" she asked tentatively.

A beat of silence.

"Not great. But I can hold it together for the nobles and such. When mother died, it was like this – at the beginning, while I was actively doing something, the reality didn't quite sink in. It wasn't until I was alone, trying to sleep, or even after Azi was defeated that I crumbled and felt the whole weight of it."

Semra nodded grimly. There was nothing to add to that. She didn't remember much of her real parents, but she cried herself to sleep at night for weeks when she first came to live in the mountain. A lump rose in her throat, and she swallowed hard. Semra paused, then angled her body toward him. As bad as the situation was, she had to speak her mind.

"Putting me on your team is dangerous for your relationship with the nobility. Did you see how they looked at you when you said my name? The way they looked at *me?* They will never accept me, and I'll drag you down as long as you associate with me. I should take Zezura and go, and you should choose someone else."

"Is that why you were leaving? Because you felt like you were dragging me down?"

Semra clenched her jaw shut and looked away. *Yes,* she thought to herself. *And because I'm claustrophobic and pointless here, and I hardly see you anymore.*

Zephan peered at her intently, but let it go. He began again.

"I need your skillset. The nobles can get over themselves. It's about time their prejudices were pointed out."

"Take Siler. Or Isra."

Zephan shook his head. "I need someone with your skillset that I can trust. Since your old acquaintances might be involved, you are essential to the mission. You don't think like a guard or a soldier, and having different perspectives is important. And if I brought *two* assassins with me, Darbune and Firfell might kill me themselves."

Semra could feel Zezura's nearness, looping in the air, anxiously killing time. She knew the dragon would have camouflaged herself with the color-changing ability of her species, so she would be practically invisible at this distance. It gave Semra comfort, knowing Zezura was close.

"This morning you promised me you would always protect the Shamaran family," Zephan said. "Did you mean it, or not?"

Semra struck the railing. "That's not fair!"

He shrugged. "'*The fox was a friend until the bear came.*'"

Semra rolled her eyes. "What, another proverb? What's that supposed to mean?"

Zephan's voice hardened. "You don't know the integrity of a promise until it's time to fulfill it. '*The fox was a friend until the bear came, and then it was shown to be only a claim.*'"

Semra's nostrils flared. "How dare you. How *dare* you! I've been called a lot of things. I've *done* a lot of things." She jabbed her finger at Zephan's chest. "But I've never broken a promise to you, and I've only *ever* protected your family. And the one time I decide for myself, the *one* time I choose me, you call me a liar."

Zephan's eyes burned amber fire and he rolled his shoulders back. His knuckles rapped the rail and he pressed his lips together. "Semra, I didn't mean –"

The door behind them opened and a servant stepped out. "Your Highness, my apologies. You are both needed in the lower throne room immediately. King Arnevon has sent correspondence."

Arnevon! Had Belvidore made a statement? A threat? Was it about Avaya, or were conflicts at the Strip getting more volatile? The surprise of the announcement jolted her from her fury, but her heart still hammered, and her anger still simmered. Zephan's breath caught, and his stony expression morphed to something vulnerable, penetrating, pleading.

A niggling curiosity begged her to go. *You know you want to know.* Semra looked away and tried to focus on the light playing in the ripples of the Shalladin's running waters. She didn't need to see the earnestness of his face, the intensity of those amber eyes. "The promise I made," she whispered. "I meant it, but that doesn't mean I'll do whatever you want."

The servant took a hesitant step toward them. "Your Majesty?"

In her peripheral vision Semra saw Zephan held up a finger to the servant, and turn toward her again. He plucked at the hem of his sleeve and stared at his toes. "You're right. I'm sorry. I just...I don't want to do this alone. There's not a single soul that can do a mission like this the way you do. I need you with me."

Semra's throat hitched. *I need you with me.* The river flowed on beneath her, but she hardly noticed.

Zephan cleared his throat. "Would you just...would you come hear what Arnevon said, and leave after? You can do whatever you want after that. But you can't leave now anyway. You promised my father you'd speak to him before you leave, and I know you'll honor that."

Semra turned from the river and glared at him. *Dirty move.* But he wasn't wrong. And she could always leave after she talked to Turian. What difference would another hour or two make if she was leaving for good? She groaned, and the corner of Zephan's mouth turned up. He knew he'd won.

"Thank you," he said.

"I do whatever I want after," she reminded him. "You said so yourself."

"Of course."

But there was a bounce in both of their steps as they

turned toward the servant. The servant let out a long breath and beckoned them back inside. Semra and Zephan hurried back through the keep to the room they had been meeting in before, and stopped cold in the doorway. King Turian was standing, knuckles on the table, face red and hard as flint. Zephan stiffened beside her. When Turian looked up at them, a shadow seemed to have passed over his face and his eyes were dark.

"Arnevon has officially taken credit for Avaya's capture and is using her as leverage. He demands we withdraw our troops and hand over the Surian Strip as compensation for the so-called 'accusations and embarrassment' to Belvidore at the gala. He says we have six days."

9

Semra needed time to think. Too many eyes followed her every move, but here in her guest room, she would find solitude.

"You're going to find her, right?"

Semra spun around to find Aviama standing in doorway of the Nezzi Room. Aviama's resemblance to Avaya was striking, the same long slender body and gentle curls. But her eyes were different – earnest, innocent, pleading.

Like Zephan's.

Semra flopped onto the bed and fell backward onto the mattress, staring at the mural on ceiling. The mountain scene with Nezil Myansara flowers greeted her, and Semra remembered Zephan telling her about them. The stunningly white flowers grew in harsh conditions at high altitudes, and their resilience made them a symbol of strength and beauty in Jannemar. Semra wished she could be like that – growing tall, wild, and free despite her roots, rather than chained down and judged by them.

Was she going to go after Princess Avaya? The question of

the hour. One the court, Zephan, the king, and now Aviama were waiting on. Semra squeezed her eyes shut, but the darkness didn't stop her racing thoughts. Opening them up again, she studied the painting. There was only one honest answer. "I don't know."

Aviama climbed up on the bed and lay beside her. "You have to go. You promised Zephan you would."

Not Aviama too. Semra sighed. "I promised Zephan I would protect Jannemar, but I frequently draw the wrong kind of attention. I doubt Avaya would be pleased to see me."

Aviama propped herself up on her elbow. "Avs is...she's difficult. She finds a reason to be mad at most people. But that's not all she is. I think losing mother..." Aviama's voice caught, and she took a breath. "Avaya wishes she could have made things better for mother, who was never fully accepted since she wasn't of noble birth. I mean, the people loved her, but it took years for the court to trust father's decisions after he married her. And Jannemar has old traditions, where only the men can inherit the throne. Avaya thought maybe mother wasn't as respected as she should have been for that reason as well. Avaya vowed if she had to marry someone she hated, she would use it to make things better for both countries."

Semra stared up at the carved wooden bed canopy and tried to imagine Avaya as the sacrificial type but couldn't quite picture it. "She seems so..."

"Prickly?" Aviama smiled sadly. "She's bossy and independent, but she's not all bad. Once when I was little, I broke an expensive family heirloom while she and I were playing together, and Father came running when he heard the crash. I thought he would just lose it." Aviama came alive, telling the story with various hand gestures. "He was so mad! Avaya took the blame. Then she scolded Father for letting valuables around children and demanded he be more careful in the future."

Semra laughed. "How old was she?"

"Oh, I was about five. Maybe she was twelve?"

"She watched out for you." Sadness hit Semra like a wave. How nice it must have been to have family like that. Loyalty should be treasured.

"Avs always watches out for me. Even when I think she's annoying about it, or a know-it-all. I know she loves me." The pitch in her voice took a turn. "Semra...I'm scared. I'm really scared. I caught Zephan crying the other day when he thought he was alone. I see the weight on Father. What if Zephan goes on this mission, and it doesn't go well? What if his grief makes him impulsive? What if Avaya tries to negotiate with Arnevon on her own and makes an even bigger mess of things? She would do that, too. She would try to talk her way out of it somehow. I need to know he's going to be okay, and if he's not going to be okay, I need to know somebody is there for him."

Semra sat up, and Aviama followed suit. She couldn't deny that the idea of chasing down a kidnapper, leaving the castle behind, and striding forward into the jaws of peril was attractive.

I need you with me. What was it about the phrase that forced her to replay it over and over since the moment he said it? Maybe because she felt wanted. The urgency in his voice sold it all. In that moment, he wasn't Zephan, but Dahyu.

Semra furrowed her eyebrows.

"Aviama...I can't promise how anything would go. Missions are volatile by nature, and there are always variables you can't control even with months of planning."

"But see, look! You didn't promise something you couldn't deliver on. You are realistic and smart, and you care about

Zephan, I know you do. And you care about me, because you haven't burned the dresses in your wardrobe, even if you never put them on! He needs somebody he can count on, who doesn't care that he's a prince and try to sugarcoat things. And I need someone who cares to look out for my brother, and not just the crown."

"But the trouble I cause with the court..."

"Is *nothing* compared to someone else in my family dying. Since when do you care so much if fancy people like you? For Zephan? Ha! He doesn't care either. Weak excuse." She crossed her arms and arched an eyebrow. "Besides, if any of your mountain friends show up, you're the only one who can identify them. Did you know King Arnevon has executed more people in the last ten years than any Belvidore monarch in their entire reign?"

Semra worried her lip and narrowed her eyes, thinking. She'd have a purpose again, and maybe even the chance to spend time with Zephan once more, in the woods, the way they'd met. Back when she didn't know he was a prince.

Perhaps Dahyu was there still.

Semra scolded herself for the thought. Even if Zephan did want her, even if a part of him felt like Dahyu, it wouldn't matter. He was the crown prince. Still, saying yes to this one mission wasn't the same as staying in the castle with nothing to do. She could do it for Turian, one last mission. She could do it for Aviama, and for the promise she made to protect the Shamaran family.

Aviama squealed and clapped her hands, bouncing up and down on the bed. "You'll do it!"

"I didn't say that!" Semra exclaimed, but she couldn't help but laugh.

"Oh, I know, but you were about to. I saw it on your face."

Aviama threw her arms around Semra. "Thank you, thank you! We need you."

Semra squeezed the princess back and sighed. In the face of Aviama's pleading eyes, she'd run out of reasons not to go. And the call of adrenaline beckoned her.

10

ARNEVON

Arnevon slammed his bedchamber door and leaned against it. Finally, some peace and quiet. *Quality time with the sensible one in the family,* he thought bemusedly. His daughter Blaise's chronic illness kept her bedridden more days than not, and she said little of interest on her good days. His only other child, his firstborn, his supposed heir, spoke of loyalty as an excuse for lazy military discipline and of weddings as if the princess twit from Jannemar would be trophy enough for Axis's astounding ego.

Arnevon walked toward his chair and desk, then paused. Two glasses had been set out on a tray on the side table. One filled with wine, the other empty. A sealed letter sat propped against them. No correspondence was ever left for him like this. Not since his wife's death. Arnevon's heartbeat throbbed in his ears as he yanked back the drapes framing his windows and threw open the wardrobe doors, looking for the culprit. Everything in the room was precisely as he had left it except for the addition of the glasses and the letter.

He snatched the paper off the table and examined the seal. A simple raven symbol he'd never seen before. Arnevon ripped the envelope from the top, careful to avoid breaking the seal. The elegant writ of a scribe greeted him:

His Most Glorious Majesty, King Arnevon of Belvidore:
I am a great admirer of yours and was disturbed to hear of the slander your name has endured as of late. I am sending you a gift to restore your fortunes and power. May the name King Arnevon never dare be mocked again.
Consider this my field interview. If you accept, you'll get glory, leverage, and legitimize the growth of an empire. Deny, and you miss the opportunity of a lifetime. My only hope is to serve you.
Your friend,
Raven
P.S. – I trust you know a good deal when you see one. I took the liberty of pouring us a toast, but unfortunately, I had to drink mine before you arrived. I do hope you understand. Stay in touch.

Arnevon re-read the letter twice. Three times. Then he crossed toward the fireplace and tossed it into the flames. *Most Glorious Majesty?* Was it more mockery or truly admiration? How did this Raven get into his bedchamber, and what gift could have been sent? Emperor...Arnevon's mouth twitched. Yes, he liked the sound of that, though he'd never been quite so ambitious as to seek it outright. He eyed the full wine glass and inspected the empty one. The base of the glass held residue, as if this Raven had indeed filled his own glass and drank it here in king's own royal bedchamber.

"*Kombel!*"

An older man in his seventies answered the call, appearing at the door. The man bowed.

"Your Majesty."

Arnevon plucked the glass from the table and shoved it into Kombel's hands. "Fancy a drink?"

"Your Majesty?"

"Come now, Kombel. You work hard. You deserve a drink now and then."

Kombel drew back, aghast. "But...but I'm working, Your Majesty!"

Arnevon clenched his jaw, then wagged his finger at Kombel. "It wasn't a suggestion. Drink. Half."

Kombel glanced at the cup, rapidly blinking back and forth between it and his king. Slowly, he lifted the glass to his lips.

11

———————

Semra pulled her cloak tighter as cool air wafted through her dark hair. She'd felt awkward when she'd first met up with Zephan and Monac to go over the exit plan with the lingering tension of her argument hanging over them. But out here, in the thrill of a mission, their roles were clear, and the distance seemed to ease.

Zephan signaled her, and she crossed the moonlit ward, joining him in the deep shadow of the outer wall. Monac was next, a broad-shouldered knight with shoulder-length brown hair and a trimmed beard. His movements were more lumbering than Semra's, but his strides were long. Semra rolled her eyes as Monac positioned himself between her and Zephan before the group crept along the shadows toward the guard's door in the wall. Semra had only just met Monac an hour ago, and he'd already taken every opportunity to create space between Semra and Zephan. *Bodes well for trust,* Semra thought sardonically.

As they neared the door facing the cliff on the northwest side, Monac passed Zephan, approaching the guard on his own. After exchanging a few soft-spoken words with the guard, Monac took hold of the man and cinched his arm around his windpipe. When he sagged, Monac carefully lowered him to the ground and placed his body against the wall. He slipped his hand in the guard's pocket and took the key to unlock the door.

Semra had to admit Monac was fast and smooth. He held the door open, Semra and Zephan slipping through and outside the castle walls. Monac shut the door behind them, locked it, and chucked the keys high over the wall to land near the unconscious guard.

"He'll be all right," Monac assured them. "He's a good man, and he won't be liable for anything this way. Besides, he once beat me at a choke-out competition to see how long we could hold on before blacking out, so now we're even." Monac grinned.

The trio walked along the edge of the cliff until they were covered by the tree line. Zephan nodded to Semra. "This should be far enough. Your turn."

Semra stepped to the brink and sent the message to Zezura. *Come to me.*

Dark as night, the Rangchanj dragon flew up the cliff and blasted into view only a few feet away from where Semra stood. The wind from her wings blew Semra's hair and cloak behind her in a gust, the thrill of freedom thick in the air. She was home.

Monac stepped back from the massive beast as it landed next to them among the trees. "It's too late to think this is a bad idea, right?"

Semra smiled and ran to Zezura, who allowed her scales to shift into her natural aquamarine color, accented by royal-blue patterning. Zezura nuzzled Semra, and she stroked the dragon's nose. The thrill of a mission, the adrenaline of free-dom, set into her bones like sunshine on a meadow of starving flowers. "Far too late. Besides, nothing beats a dragon for speed."

Semra fetched a simple, fitted leather harness from her pack and tied it around the dragon's neck and underbelly. Semra could ride without it by locking her feet between spikes on Zezura's sides and communicating with her directly to anticipate her movements, but with passengers, a harness of some sort was the best option. She planted a foot on one of the spikes running down Zezura's sides and launched herself up onto her back.

"A few things beat it for stealth, though," Monac grumbled.

"Zezura shifts her color to camouflage the best she can," Zephan said. "We're only flying a few hours tonight. Still, we'll have to travel by foot to get the lay of the land closer to the border. We can't risk being spotted, camouflage or not."

"You sure we won't fall off that thing?" Monac asked.

"*We* won't fall off," Semra said. "But we could have her carry you in her claws if it makes you feel better."

Zezura huffed and Monac jumped. Zephan laughed, climbing up behind Semra and slipping his arms around her waist to hold on. Warmth spread through her. Zephan glanced down at Monac. "Shall we sandwich you between us?"

"Oh, fine," Monac said, taking in their position together. "My options are holding onto the assassin or being dangled by her dragon! I'll take my chances at the back with you, thanks!"

Semra felt a pang in her chest when he called her "the assassin," but shook her head to clear it as Monac clambered up behind Zephan and wrapped his arms around the prince. "The truth of the matter, sir knight," said Semra, "Is that if you did not know how to kill, you would not have been invited."

With that, Semra patted Zezura on the neck and took no small pleasure in the girlish squeal that escaped Monac's large frame as they lurched into the air. Zezura's scales faded into the pigments of night and Zephan's arms tightened around her as they flew low along the Shalladin, sending a shot of warmth through her body. The soft rush of the river filled their ears and the moon and stars twinkled up at them from the water's glassy surface, and Semra reveled in the expanse of the world beyond the castle walls. To their right, the Dezapi Falls spilled down the cliff next to the Shamaran castle, and as they left the castle behind them, Zezura climbed high into the sky and angled southeast.

At last, she was free. The wide world beckoned, exchanging stuffy stone walls with the open wind and sky, and judgmental glares for the arms of the healer's apprentice – not some prince beyond her reach, but the alias he'd had when they'd met, man she could dream about, the man who'd once taught her to dance in the woods.

12

———

Semra, Zephan, and Monac rode well into the night but descended into Sibor Forest before sunrise. They "made camp" near the river, a generous term for dropping bags at the base of a tree and lying down. Semra heard Zephan and Monac talking as she started to drift off, her head on her arm and Zezura's tail draped over her legs.

"The first night in the field is always a bit rough, but by the second or third, I'm used to it," Monac said.

"It certainly isn't as comfortable as being at home, but it's nice to get away from the formality," Zephan answered. Then after a pause, he said, "It's cold tonight. Do you think she needs an extra blanket?"

"You have an extra blanket?" Monac asked.

"Well, no, but I could give her mine."

"She has a dragon. I think she'll be okay."

A beat of silence passed before Zephan spoke again. "She's already asleep, isn't she?"

Semra shifted against the leaves and dirt, only half-listening to the men's voices. She had adjusted somewhat to the extravagance of the Nezzi Room, but the woods still felt like home. As the wind whistled eerily through the trees overhead and gently rustled the leaves around them, Semra felt herself dropping quickly off to sleep.

"Are you sure she's safe?"

She heard no reply.

Semra woke to the sound of screams. Screams reminding her of the families of her victims before she knew the truth about the Framatar. Before she knew they were not purging evil, but had become evil itself. The forest was gone, and her mind's eye built the castle around her again. The screams were a blood-curdling echo in her ears as she made her escape. Semra fled, but the sound only grew louder as she burst into the Great Hall where a female body fell to the tiled floor, blood pooling on the ground with a knife protruding from her chest. One exactly like Semra's. Blood, red blood. Guards, everywhere. The smell of garlic. Tymetin's sinister laugh.

Arms grabbed her. Darkness engulfed her, and as the dungeon walls closed in, her childhood mentor's face shifted from a welcoming smile to a disgusted grimace. *"I always hated you."* Ramas reached toward her throat, and the Framatar's voice echoed, *"My dear, my dear ... you know I am the only one who has never left you."* Snakes began dropping from the ceiling, hundreds of poisonous asps, their scales wriggling around her toes, and curling around her knees rising like a tide as she drowned in a sea of serpents. The screaming was her own.

Semra lurched up, her heart hammering in her chest. She looked about her wildly, then squealed and jumped to her feet at the sensation of smooth scales rubbing against her legs. Semra swore under her breath. It was just Zezura's tail, keeping her warm all night. The great dragon lay curled in a ball, dead to the world, and Zephan and Monac still lay motionless ten feet away.

Just a dream. Just a dream. *Won't they ever go away?* Semra pounded her temple with her fist, as if sheer force could knock the nightmare memories from her mind.

Do you deserve for them to go away?

The thought pulled Semra's focus with a start. No, surely someone who killed people routinely in the past should have to suffer consequences. *I should be grateful I haven't been executed,* she reminded herself grimly. *I deserve to be executed.*

It was still early, and Semra pulled out her knives and sharpened and oiled them to perfection for the next half hour until sunrise. When the men started stirring, Semra pulled bread, dried fruit, and dried meat from her pack and divvied portions between herself, Zephan, and Monac. Zephan ripped off a huge chunk of his bread with his teeth and gulped it down.

"Some prince you are," Semra said, mockingly ripping off a chunk of her own and making a face at him.

He wagged a finger. "No prince! I get to drop the 'prince' part whenever I ride on dragons and sleep on roots and rocks."

The corner of Semra's mouth twitched. "Is that so?"

"Oh, yes. It's in the contract you sign to become a prince, right next to the consent to learn to be pretentious."

"Sounds nice," Semra said. "An old friend of mine used to ride dragons and sleep on roots and rocks. He looked like you, too, but his name was Dahyu."

"Great name! With a name like that, he must have been pretty wonderful. Handsome, too." Zephan tore off another piece of bread.

Semra laughed, and Zephan's eyes twinkled at her. Could he really have been pent up in the castle just yesterday, with the fear of war, pain of loss, and stress of the crown bearing down on him? Yesterday, the two of them had stood on either side of a great chasm, him with nobility, royal obligation, and military duty on his side, and her as a criminal commoner with no responsibilities and no future on the other. Here in the woods, he seemed so like the Dahyu he was when she first met him – witty, carefree, happy. She popped a piece of dried fruit in her mouth and when she glanced back up, Zephan was still looking at her, half a smile on his lips.

Monac was looking at her too, but he did not smile.

13

ARNEVON

Arnevon tapped his fingers on the arms of his throne, anxiously marking every millisecond which passed. The great bronze double-doors opened, and the silhouettes of a man and a woman were visible in the doorway. All conversation ceased as they garnered the attention of every servant and courtier in attendance.

The man wore a dark hooded cloak, woolen and ordinary, but his stride was long. His arms were strong as he led the lady forward, and she stumbled to keep pace with him. She wore an exquisite silk brocade gown and gem-studded necklace and arm band. Her attire boasted wealth, but her mud-caked hem told a different tale. Belvidorian guards on flanked them on either side, and Arnevon's eyes narrowed as the man gave a deep bow. The man hissed something under his breath at the woman, and she curtsied with practiced grace.

Arnevon's heart raced, but his voice was unwavering. "You deign to bow but not show your face before the king?"

"For you I certainly would, Your Majesty, but until we meet in private, I will remain as I feel comfortable."

"And why should I meet a stranger in private?"

"Stranger? I have only done as you asked. I have escorted your esteemed guest safely to your hospitality, as discussed. I regret I could not join you in our most recent toast. Was the wine not to your liking, Your Majesty? Perhaps we can toast again with a wine variety more to your liking."

Arnevon's breath caught and he felt his jaw slacken. *The Raven*. Arnevon glanced between the man's hooded figure and the woman's stony expression. Her chin lifted slightly at his perusal, but she showed no sign of weakness aside from mussed hair from apparent travel.

"And you are?" he asked the woman.

"Forgive me, sire," answered the man again. "Let me introduce Jannemar's brightest star, the king's eldest daughter, Princess Avaya Shamaran!"

Murmurs flew around the room before settling into a stunned silence. Arnevon drew back and stared at the woman before him, whose piercing green eyes bored into him with defiance and strength. What had this man done?

Arnevon clapped his hands and smiled with a warmth he did not feel. "No more visitations today! Tonight we welcome our esteemed guest, and whatever news she brings in these troubled times." He looked Avaya up and down again, from her muddied skirts to her mildly mussed hair. "Your Highness, I'll see that you are shown to a fine room to rest you're your travels, and we will meet again soon. Raven, adjourn with me to the sitting room."

The king descended from his throne and snapped his fingers, and guards materialized behind him as he swept out of the grand throne room and into a private sitting room. The room was hardly small, with couches and chairs arranged down its fifty-foot length, with low tables set among them in the middle, and three chandeliers hanging overhead. Guards stationed themselves at the doors and at intervals along the back wall.

Arnevon poured himself and his guest a drink from one of the tables and sat on a cushioned chair facing one of the couches. The chair had higher legs than the rest of the furniture, and as the Raven followed him into the sitting room and placed himself on the couch opposite him, Arnevon's position subtly looked down upon him. Hardly noticing the elevation difference, the Raven lounged back against the couch as if he had never been more at home. He plucked the crystal wine glass off the table, tossed back his hood, and spread his hands.

"Toast, yes?"

Arnevon studied the man. To Arnevon's great surprise, the man was young – younger even than Axis. His face was serene, controlled yet somehow mischievous.

"Your arrogance is both unmatched and unwarranted," Arnevon said. "You promise glory and instead bring liability. What exactly is she here for?"

The Raven took a swig of wine. "Whatever you want. Threaten Turian and expand your territory, or have Axis marry her and save face, or both. The prince didn't mention this to you?"

Axis did this without my knowledge? Arnevon curled his fingers into fists, tensed them, and relaxed. "How did you get her here?"

"Oh, she volunteered." He grinned.

Arnevon arched an eyebrow, and the Raven shrugged. "I'm not an unfeeling man. I gave her options, and she was free to choose. Turns out, she wanted to live."

Arnevon eyed the Raven. This young man had infiltrated Shamaran castle, kidnapped a princess in a time of war, and delivered her into his hands with the same ease that other people got out of bed in the morning. And Axis had provoked it. If Belvidore and Jannemar hadn't already been at war, Arnevon would have had his head! Still, now that she was here...

"In your letter, you said something about a field interview? What do you want?"

The Raven leaned forward and set his glass on the table. "You've seen what I can do. I am a man of many talents, and only the best purse strings deserve access to skills of my caliber. I want the honor of honest employment in the castle, Your Majesty. I'm persuasive, effective, and lethal. Whatever you need, say the word, and I'll do it."

"And how am I to trust you?"

"I saw what Jannemar did to you, Your Majesty. Years of strife between kingdoms, and finally when there was hope for a union bringing long-term peace, hope for hurts to be healed, you were ready and willing to extend an olive branch. Instead they embarrassed you, ran you out of the country, and accused you of espionage and murder. I don't think they deserve to rule, but more importantly, I like to place my bets where I think I can win. I'm a simple, selfish man, sire. Trust me to be serve myself. You have ambition that Turian never had, and your coffers will only deepen when you expand your kingdom into an empire. You will make history, and I will be a part of it."

The king tapped a finger on the arm of his chair and a small smile crept over his face. "You are persuasive, aren't you?"

The corner of the Raven's mouth twitched. "On occasion."

"You're hired. You are hereby assigned to Princess Avaya's bodyguard detail. I want to know everything she does, everyone she sees, and she is not to leave the castle. You'll stay on until the wedding, or until she becomes trouble enough to kill, at which point I'll reassign you. Do something stupid, and I'll forget I ever knew you. Do something worse, and I'll have your head."

14

───────

Semra padded the riverbank, breathing in the solitude. They had slept and walked on foot during the day. and flown Zezura again for the first half of the following night. Now, Zephan and Monac were still at camp. and Semra had scooped everyone's canteens up and headed off.

A twig snapped behind her. Semra jumped and whipped her head around.

"Whoa, settle down there, crazy," Monac said, holding his hands up.

Semra glared. *Failing to react to threats will leave me dead. I'd rather be crazy than dead.* She scanned his body posture, his muscles tensing despite his defensive gesture.

"Hands down please. Everybody thinks hands up is surrender, but it's not. It can be strategic." Semra turned back around and headed down the bank to the water. "And I'm not crazy. I'm cautious. There's a difference."

"Not paranoid?"

"Hard to be paranoid when trained killers want you dead," Semra said. "Doesn't paranoia require unrealistic fears?"

Monac studied her. "So they still want you dead, even with the puppet master in the dungeon?"

She shrugged, taking a few extra steps away from Monac before bending down to the river to fill her first canteen. Zephan trusted him, and he seemed competent, but being competent for a mission like this one also made him dangerous. Why had he sought her out alone? "In my line of work, you never really know. Many still think of me as a traitor."

Monac gestured at the distance between them. "Do you distrust Prince Zephan as much as you distrust me?"

Semra's chest tightened, and something in her gut twisted. She straightened and looked him in the eye. "I trust Zephan more than I trust just about anyone. My precautions are for you, whom I just met forty-eight hours ago, and though I'm sure you're perfectly lovely and only grilling me out of protective instinct for Zephan, it's just a force of habit for me." Semra capped off the first canteen. "What about you? You don't trust me either."

Monac mulled over her answer, letting the moment linger before he responded. "Zephan trusts you more than I would. From what I can tell, you're some kind of elite killer and you just upended your life by turning the tables on the man who kidnapped you. But living like that for most of your life has to leave marks. I'm concerned about what those marks might do to other people, even if you mean well. And if you don't mean well, and this is all an elaborate long-con, well, I'm intend to be close enough to you to find out."

Semra watched him, his bold brown eyes keen and somber, his stance relaxed but ready. Her gaze softened as she took in the prince's protector. He had reasonable concerns, and he wanted to figure her out for the same reason she was figuring *him* out. She laughed. "I can see why he chose you."

A chink in Monac's hard exterior melted away as he pulled back in surprise, then grinned an uneasy grin. "Why?"

A chuckle sounded behind them, and they turned to see Zephan walking down toward the river to join them. "Because he interrogates the people who save my life!"

Semra's heart leaped at the sound of his voice, and she cursed herself for such a juvenile reaction. She capped off another canteen and tossed it to Zephan. "He protects you. He sees potential threats. Those are good qualities, and as long as he can trust me on missions, we'll be fine." She threw Monac the last canteen. "But if you don't, you could get us killed, prince and all."

The three of them walked back to camp and ate the same dried food for dinner as they had eaten for breakfast, plus some leftover bread. Semra washed it down with water and leaned back against Zezura.

"So Qalea and the surrounding areas are being searched, but they won't find anything. We assume Avaya will be taken straight to Madensig Fortress, and we need to plan on going inside to retrieve her. What do we know about the man with the blueprints?"

They had been briefed on the loose plan before leaving the castle – head straight for the Belvidorian castle, Madensig Fortress, while others searched Jannemar for signs of the princess. Zephan, Monac, and Semra would look for the blueprints to the castle and do whatever was necessary to reclaim Avaya to remove Arnevon's leverage and save her from probable execution. Details on the *how* were a bit sparse.

"His name is Florin Thistlehorn. He's an architect," Zephan answered. "His family has been architects for decades, and he collects blueprints of everything his family has built. Supposedly it was his great-great-grandfather that designed Madensig."

"Why would he help us?" Monac asked.

"We are going to commission him to build something for us to get a look at his portfolio. He likes to drink, and he likes to talk...we'll provide opportunities for both, and we are going to pay him handsomely for his trouble."

Semra pursed her lips. "Not much of a plan."

Zephan sighed. "Agreed. But we didn't have much time."

Monac grimaced. "Is he sympathetic to Arnevon?"

"Sources say no, he isn't happy with Arnevon's rule. What are you thinking?"

"I'm thinking we start with your plan, and if it isn't effective in a timely manner, we explain our situation just enough to pique his interest and let him be a part of something big... plus the chance of padding his pockets. If all else fails, we resort to good old-fashioned threats."

Semra and Zephan agreed, though Semra worried about this part of the plan taking too long. Belvidore was only a two week journey on horseback, since Madensig was near the border of Belvidore and Shamaran Castle was relatively near Jannemar's border as well. Semra wondered why two nations would set up their heads of government so near one another rather than in a more central location, but shrugged off the thought.

What if this Florin didn't have older blueprints anymore? What if he couldn't be persuaded quickly? What if they were wasting their time? With a mix of dragon-riding and travel by foot, the detour to Florin's residence should still get them to the Madensig Fortress at about the two week mark. Still, if the man wasn't cooperative, perhaps she and Monac could motivate the man.

Semra tossed and turned that night. Though sleeping in wilderness was not unusual for her, this time every crunch of a leaf as she shifted on the ground rustled her awake. When sleep finally took her, it betrayed her.

Ramas fingered his serpentine amulet, smirking at her through the bars of her cell. Suddenly the snake on the amulet leaped from the bracelet and lunged at Semra, sinking its fangs beneath her collarbone above the mark of the dragon's kiss. Semra's head spun as she gasped for air, the venom spreading through her body and paralyzing her inside it. Ramas jeered at her, his words echoing through her mind.

"And you ... you are less than nothing. You are the nameless, faceless fly on the wall..."

"I always hated you."

As he spoke those final words, Ramas lunged forward right through the cell bars as if they were air. His right hand gripped a fistful of her hair at the nape of her neck and yanked backward, and his left pinned her dominant hand to her side. Panic and rage rose together through Semra's stomach and shot out her throat in a furious cry. In that moment Semra found her limbs again and flew at him, sending her left fist into Ramas' gut and clawing like a madwoman with all she had.

He drew back, and Semra jumped on him, wrapping her legs around his torso and pounding at his head. Ramas was shouting, protecting his head with his hands, but his voice was all wrong. The two of them fell to the cold stone floor, but it crunched when they landed.

"Semra! *SEMRA!* It's me, you're okay, it's me!"

Semra's eyes snapped open, and she froze. Ramas' harsh expression gave way to Zephan's soft golden eyes staring down at her. He had one of her arms pinned down, and Monac had the other; Semra lay on her back with her legs twisted around Zephan's midsection. He was bleeding from a cut on his throat.

Semra jerked her head right and left to shake the dungeon and get her bearings. Leaves and twigs crinkled under her head, and a soft wind blew against her face. Semra squeezed her eyes shut. *There is no wind in the dungeon. It was a dream.* Her chest constricted, her hands curled into fists, and something inside felt ready to burst. Hot tears welled in her eyes and fled down her cheeks, running into her hair.

Zephan moved to sit up, and Semra opened her eyes for a moment, then gasped as she realized her legs were still attached to his torso. Semra unwrapped herself from him and rolled away with her back to both men, sitting up hugging her knees. She felt for her belt loop and clutched at Ramas' amulet, running her thumb over its engraving. *Ramas is dead. You killed him. The dragon's kiss saved you from the snake poison.*

How could a man who had trained her for years hate her so deeply? Perhaps there was simply nothing about her worth loving. The Framatar's voice came softly then, whispering to her as it had when she was a child:

My dear, my dear ... you know I am the only one who has never left you.

"Semra?" Zephan's voice. "Don't kill me, okay? I'm just going to put my hand here."

Semra sniffled as she felt Zephan's warm hand on her shoulder, and when she didn't move, his arms wrapped around her and gently pulled her close. Her breath hitched on a sob and she lay her head on his chest, wetting his shirt with her tears. The blackness of the night enveloped them in the shadow of the trees as he held her. Time passed like a tide, emotion rolling in and through her, and eventually subsiding again. Semra's tears ebbed, and the fear of her nightmare faded. She stirred and sat up.

Zephan cleared his throat. "Um. Who was I? When you... you know..."

Semra glanced at him and stared down at the dirt. "Ramas."

"Is that the one who..."

"Tried to kill me. I was in the dungeon just now." Her voice was hoarse.

"Oh." The word came as a whisper.

Semra hung her head. "I'm sorry."

"How long have you been having these dreams?"

"Weeks. Since the throne room, I guess. They're not all of Ramas...some are of the Framatar – Azi. Or...past...missions." Semra's mouth went dry.

"Have you ever attacked someone in your sleep before?" Monac asked, piping in from several paces away.

"Monac!" Zephan hissed.

"We have to know. Wasn't sure how else to phrase it."

"No, it's okay. I haven't, but I've been in a room alone, and I usually come to myself pretty quickly once I wake up." A painful twisting feeling clenched in her gut. Semra unsheathed her dagger and knives and handed them to Monac. "I think maybe you ought to keep these. Just while I'm sleeping."

"Do you really think that's necessary?" Zephan asked.

Semra clenched her jaw. "I was in the dungeon just now. I'd been stripped of weapons. I'd hate to think what could happen if I were somewhere else."

Monac nodded. "I'll keep them safe. You'll get them back first thing."

A fresh tear escaped down her cheek, and Semra swiped at it angrily.

"It must be weird not to have your knives," Zephan said, watching her longing look at the blades in Monac's hands. Semra dipped her head. Zephan rubbed her arm. "I'm sorry. Thank you."

Semra took a deep breath. "What we're doing is important. It's worth it."

Monac furrowed his brow. "Why are you doing this?"

"Giving up my knives for the night? And it *is* just for the night."

He shook his head. "No. *This.*" He gestured to the woods around them. "Any of it. How does a girl raised to kill decide that the assassin life isn't for her? Why not just leave the mountain, instead of chasing down the royal family, putting yourself in harm's way, and continuing on crazy death trap missions like this one?"

"Harm's way is my normal. It's strange to imagine what it would be like not to have to constantly look over my shoulder. Do you have a family, Monac?"

"My father was less than ideal, but I had one."

Semra nodded. She bit her lip. "I hardly remember my parents, but they were good. They came up the mountain to save me when Rotokas – the Framatar's great black dragon – stole me from Kalma as a child. The Framatar killed them on our doorstep, and I never knew.

"I'll never be accepted at the castle. I have no title or formal position, Zezura drives Saeb up the wall and terrifies half the staff, and my background is...unsavory. It's not good for trust, and I'm not sure I'm built for four walls. But I always thought our missions were purging the world of evil, that they had meaning, and I'd like to think maybe I can do a little of what I thought I was doing before. Something good. I don't have a family, but Zephan, the king, Avaya, Aviama...they're a pretty decent one. And protecting that decency is worth doing."

Zephan looked stricken, and Semra couldn't decide if it was hurt or surprise that dominated his features. She hadn't meant to hurt him...but he couldn't really have expected her to stay in the castle forever. Could he? She had no good reason to. Monac took her in solemnly, then looked down at the forest floor.

"That sounds...like a good reason."

Zephan's eyes bored into her, and there was an edge to his tone. "You can't know you'll never be accepted."

Semra shrugged. "You can't know that I will. Decades of tradition don't change overnight, and regardless of my status, my past will never change."

Zephan's face softened into sorrow, then curiosity. "How do you know we are decent?"

"There is good in the world, and even the darkest of souls can see it," Semra said. "It's so rare, it must be permitted to shine."

"*I* accept you."

The statement caught Semra off guard, and her eyes welled with unbidden emotion. It was all she had wanted, all she had been craving, for Zephan to find her acceptable. But it wasn't true. She blinked back tears and swallowed hard. Her voice came out hoarse. "Maybe you want to. But you care what the court says, whether you admit it or not, and you're ashamed of me. In the rare moments when you have sought me out the past two months, it was always away from prying eyes."

A shadow passed over Zephan's face, and he looked away. His eyes glistened ever so slightly, and Semra thought she saw a tear. Why would he be sad about what she said? It was a compliment. His family was decent and good, and had a better chance of leading the kingdom into a peaceful era than anyone else she knew of. Though, admittedly, her pool of decent people she knew of was small.

"Well...we're all awake now," Monac said awkwardly as the silence stretched on. "Should we just get an early start?"

Zephan stood. "I'm going on a walk. We can get started when I get back."

With that he turned and disappeared into the trees, the gray of early morning following his silhouette. Monac and Semra exchanged glances, and Monac shrugged. "He does this sometimes, when he has to think. He'll be back in twenty minutes."

"I'll never fall back asleep now. Pass me back my knives and dagger. We should reach the war zone today."

15

ARNEVON

King Arnevon gritted his teeth. Did the princeling imagine himself more intelligent than his predecessor? Arnevon crossed the floor until he stood nose to nose with his son's smug face.

"I *know* bringing her here was your idea," Arnevon hissed. "You dare undermine my authority and threaten our reputation! If word gets out...the princess was *kidnapped* by Belvidore..."

Axis straightened to his full height, and Arnevon's face reddened, nostrils flaring, as he was forced to look up at his son. Axis leveled a glare. "I've already told you. I had *nothing* to do with this."

Arnevon crossed his arms. "What was it you told me? You will wed the Jannemar princess if it's the last thing you do?"

Axis threw his hands up. "What do you want me to say? That I'm upset she's here? I'm not. I intend to take full advantage of that fact. I don't know why this Raven character brought her here, but I'm not about to look a gift horse in the mouth. We'll tell the people she came of her own free will to make good on Jannemar's promise of marriage and unity."

Arnevon stepped to the table, poured himself a glass of wine, and then sat on an overstuffed chair. How long had his son planned this kidnapping under his nose? How weak had he made the armies for lack of focus on military matters? But Arnevon would spin it to his favor. Yes. And his son would be put in his place. It was the way of monarchs. He swirled his wine before taking a sip.

"You *will* marry her," he said slowly. "The House of Madensig will be strengthened, and the unity we swore to bring to the region will be restored. But mark my words, it will be done the way the *king* of the land commands it. Belvidore will not be mocked. Do I make myself clear? You will follow orders."

Axis scowled. "The king of the land makes wild accusations without evidence."

"I'm giving you a warning. I'll not give another." Arnevon took one more sip. "And should you fail me...there will be no princess to marry. Get out."

16

———

Zephan returned twenty minutes later as Monac had predicted, and they rode Zezura to the edge of the forest. Semra sent the dragon off with instructions to stay within a few miles, but out of sight. They moved forward on foot through Dulnor toward Kinlock where Thistlehorn was said to live. Monac gave Zephan a hat, and Semra wore her custom wrap skirt with hidden slits which concealed her weapons while providing easy access. Now was not the time to draw attention, and a knife strapped woman in trousers would be hard to miss.

Dawn broke in swaths of orange and red, lighting the city as they entered from the northeast. Qalea would he awakening by now. Vendors and castle staff would head up to the Dragon Gate, horse and wagon teams starting their days. Chatter and laughing would sound in the streets. But in Kinlock, the morning was eerily devoid of talk. Two wagons rumbled past them on the road, and to their left, a woman pulled laundry off her clothesline. No one spoke.

Semra cast a furtive look in Zephan's direction, but he was scanning Kinlock with just as much concern.

"We're close to the battlefront," Monac said softly. "This city borders on the Surion Strip, so if the fighting has advanced by now, then south of Kinlock may already be evacuated. Its effects will have spread north."

They continued through the city by foot until noon. As the day wore on, they passed more people, mostly holding quiet conversations in doorways or going about their business in silence. Even the market vendors were sparse, selling wares halfheartedly in the square. The common clamor of the market was missing, and half of it was blocked off with a crude fence and a large tent.

A scream came from the tent, and Zephan picked up his pace in long strides toward it, but Monac ran forward and put his arm out. "Let me look. Keep your cloak pulled up high and your hat on."

Zephan clenched his jaw but dipped his head in acquiescence. What would it be like to be so cut off from her instincts, so valuable that she was forbidden from acting freely? Dahyu would have run into the tent. But Zephan was kept outside.

Monac looked at Semra. "Nobody touches him. You are his bodyguard while I'm gone."

Semra nodded. "He's safe with me."

Monac gave a short answering nod and took off at a light jog toward the tent. Semra walked slowly with Zephan to the other side of the square, just around the corner of a shop where its shadow sheltered them from sight. Positioned here, Semra kept eyesight on the tent, the market, and the street.

"I'm adept with a blade, you know," Zephan said.

"I know. I've seen you fight." Semra kept her eyes on Monac as he reached the tent and was stopped at the door.

"If there *were* trouble, I'm not sure how I would feel about you protecting me."

Semra drew back and glared at him. "Why? Because I'm a woman?"

"No. Because if you're protecting me, then who is protecting you?"

"Nobody. Myself. Monac would do the same."

Zephan sighed. "Monac is different. He would die protecting me. He signed on to do just that when he became a knight of the Shamaran family."

Semra examined Zephan's face, but there was neither arrogance nor bitterness in his tone. Only matter-of-factness. Semra turned back to the tent, where Monac had spoken to someone and was now disappearing inside.

"I can't promise to be as sacrificial as that, but I would do everything in my power to protect you."

Semra peered back at the tent, but she could feel Zephan's gaze on her face. His voice was low and steady. "What if I don't want you to?"

"That's ridiculous," Semra said. "You're a highly targeted important person. Your eyes can't be everywhere at once; no matter how good you are, extra hands and eyes keep you safe. Unimportant people are best suited to do that, and Monac and I fit the bill."

"I think you're prone to being rather ridiculous yourself. You're addicted to extreme danger."

Possible. Probable. Semra pursed her lips. Or was it simply all she knew? Could a person be addicted to air?

Zephan cocked his head. "What if we just agree to save each other, as partners? Like we did at the throne room at the end. Not at the beginning when you shoved me out the window onto your dragon without warning, leaving yourself to fight alone."

Semra's mouth twisted into a grin. "Fine."

"If I fight with you, you agree to let me fight, and not try to hide me in a barrel somewhere?"

Semra laughed and turned to look at him. "Okay. No barrels. Besides, there are only three of us, and you're too good of a swordsman to sit out if any real trouble comes."

Zephan searched her face for a moment, then smiled, satisfied. "Good."

"Addicted to danger, huh?"

"Oh yes. *Extreme* danger. Isn't it obvious?"

The corner of Semra's mouth quirked up. "I frequently find myself in dangerous situations."

"You frequently *place* yourself in dangerous situations," Zephan corrected. "You nearly got yourself impaled on our portcullis for absolutely no good reason."

"Saving your sister isn't a good reason?" Semra demanded.

"It is, but going about it in a way that is likely to end in your death – and choosing that option without a second thought – isn't exactly what I'd consider normal."

Semra's gut twisted, but she put on an indignant expression. "Maybe I'm remarkably brave."

"Maybe you care less about your life than you should."

Semra's stomach soured, and she turned back toward the tent as her face fell. Nobody would really mind if she wasn't around. Her friend Brens used to mind. But the Framatar had had her throat slit in front of Semra. A chill ran up her spine at the memory. Zephan seemed to mind too, though his concern seemed a little out of place to Semra. Considering her history, perhaps she was reckless simply because being inside a body without adrenaline coursing through it was strange. *That's what addicted to danger looks like, Semra. He's right.*

Semra shook her head. So what if she was addicted to danger? Was it really that bad?

Monac emerged from the tent and crossed the square.

Semra stepped out of the shadows long enough for Monac to catch a glimpse, then waited for him to make his way over. His jaw was set and his eyes hard.

"Belvidore has control of Seddon and we are taking heavy losses at the Surion Strip. They set up an overflow medical tent here for more stable cases."

Semra glanced at Zephan, his face drawn. He stared out at the tent.

"We need more news," he said.

"I'm told there's a pub three blocks down," Monac replied. "That's our best chance to get the talk of the town, as it were."

The pub was a small establishment called The Fiery Chalice. There were tables scattered about the room and a long bar on the end, with perhaps fifteen people seated inside. Large whiskey barrels sat along the wall next to the bar and stood on end as small tables in the back. Semra gestured at them to Zephan.

"You sure you don't want to be stuffed in a barrel? Now could be your chance."

Zephan rolled his eyes but smiled in spite of himself, and Semra grinned in return. Zephan pulled his hat further over his eyes, and Monac gestured for Zephan and Semra to sit while he went up to the bar to order. Two middle-aged men and a teenage boy sat one table over, talking together over drinks.

"We won't last the month the way things are going," one man said, shaking his head and running a hand through his tangled beard. "They haven't gained the river yet, but we can't hold them off taking losses like this."

"The *month!*" The other man slapped the table. "My brother's been working in the tent. We'll be lucky to make it the week."

"They need more men," the boy piped up. He looked not a day older than fourteen.

"*Men*, maybe, Loudin," Tangle-Beard answered, wagging his finger. "Not you, so you can get off it. And they would need another entire company at this rate. Turian's lost his mind, that's for certain."

Zephan stiffened next to Semra, and she reached out under the table and touched his arm. *They don't know him.* He took a breath, but seemed to calm under her touch, and said nothing. The other man continued.

"We had peace for years. Why prod the beast now? If the king hadn't invited Belvidore the other month, this never would have happened. Sure, they're a nasty lot down south, but no need to rock the boat. We've survived their hatred this long. They're welcome to hate us from their side of the border, and we can hate them from ours!"

"What about the dragon riders?" Loudin asked, his eyes bright with excitement. "Maybe they'll come back, and fight off King Arnevon!"

"HA! Pray you'll never see a dragon in the flesh, Loudin. They're bigger than big, I've heard the dragons up at the castle were eighty feet long, and they'll sooner swallow you whole than serve any man. They're overgrown animals, like anything else, and they attack without sense."

Semra glared hotly at the wall over the men's heads. She used to think dragons were evil, too – but it still hurt to hear. Semra reached through the slit in her skirt to fiddle with the serpent amulet on her belt.

The other man continued. "No, the boy's right on this one. There were riders. One of them protects Shamaran Castle even now...Qalea sees it coming and going all the time."

Tangle-Beard down the last of his whiskey. "Well, if there *were* a dragon, and someone could control it, why isn't is helping? Our men are dying on the Strip, and the war is costing us all, in more taxes than we've paid in five years."

"What would you rather he do, give up and let Arnevon take us over? Turian's the best king we've had in three lifetimes, and Arnevon's the worst one we could hope for. He murdered our beloved Queen Sharsi. Imagine, a commoner speaking up for us with the royalty, became royalty herself, when Turian married her! Never has such a thing happened!"

"Maybe that's what happened," Tangle-Beard said. "Grief did a number on him, and he can't think straight anymore. It's a pity, a real shame, you know."

Tangle-Beard's friend shook his head. "I think he's desperate. He's doing the best he can to hold the Surion Strip. Once that's lost, our economy tanks, and Arnevon could push right on through Kinlock."

"Whatever his intentions are, he's up there making decisions in a gilded hall and down here, our families pay the price..."

The two men stood from their table and left with the young boy, and Monac slid into a chair with their drinks.

"Ungrateful lot," he grumbled, passing them out.

"Has news of Zezura spread everywhere?" Semra asked.

Monac lifted an eyebrow. "Two dragons wrestled on top of the castle's throne room, bashed in all its twenty-foot windows, and one still regularly flies overhead. Did you really expect all of Qalea to keep quiet about it?"

"Their trust in the kingdom is shaken." Zephan took a sip of ale and examined the tankard.

"They love your father, and they loved your mother," Semra said. "They don't know the context of what's going on, and they're confused."

"They're hurting, dying," Zephan snapped, "and we've failed to protect them!"

Semra drew back, but just as quickly as he'd said it, Zephan caught himself and lowered his voice. "I'm sorry. I just feel helpless."

Semra waved him off – *don't mention it. No problem.* But it was her failure to expose Azi soon enough, to protect the royal family effectively enough, that had led to the queen's assassination and the escalating war in the first place.

"You're doing exactly what you should be doing to help right now," Monac said to Zephan. "Besides, Semra's right, they don't have all the information. And those were just two men and a kid. Hardly a representative sample, and even *they* disagreed. They might not envy royalty so much if they knew the weight it carried.

"Now, let me tell you where Thistlehorn lives. The owner says Florin Thistlehorn lives in south Kinlock, but it's close to the Strip, and he isn't sure if Thistlehorn has evacuated or not. He gave me directions, and he knows a gentleman driving his wagon down to the border with supplies for the war effort. For the right price, he can get us a ride."

Beef stew was delivered to their table shortly thereafter, and Semra relished the taste of something that hadn't been dried and stuffed in her pack. They ate quickly, purchased more food for their travels, and caught a ride down south on the wagon. Evening fell as they followed the pub owner's directions to the house of the architect.

The storefronts in south Kinlock were connected in long rows with cobblestone beneath their feet, wooden signs swinging in a slight breeze to alert passersby to the services inside. But there was no beckoning smell from the bakery, no clang of metal from the smithy, and no gossiping women at the tailor. The streets were empty, and as the three travelers stood in the street, they heard only the sound of the wind against the swinging signage and the rustle of their own cloaks as they shifted their weight and took in the abandoned city.

"There." Monac pointed across the street to a shop on the end of the row next to the carpenter, with a sign out front depicting a pen and a hammer crisscrossed over each other. There were shop windows on either side of the large wooden door, and one small window on the second floor overlooking the street.

Semra crossed the street and lifted her hand to the door, with Zephan and Monac close behind her. Something inside her hesitated, and she looked at Monac. He nodded. Semra knocked.

There was no sound, and the shop windows were covered with curtains. Semra reached through the slit in her skirt and drew a knife, passed it to her nondominant hand, and stepped into the street scanning for a rock. Zephan beat her to it, plucking one off the side of the street and throwing it threw the window. Monac drew his sword and used the butt of the sword to push the remaining glass inward, scraping along the window ledge. Semra stepped up to the ledge, placed the edge of her cloak over it to protect her hands from remnant glass, and swung herself through the window.

Semra landed on her feet and scanned the room. Stacks of designs of buildings, archways, and bridges were spread on a table, maps and sketches of successful commissions hung on the walls, and a cold fireplace and kettle sat to her left. A short hall led to a staircase at the back of the room, with more paintings lining the wall.

And on the floor at the base of the stairs, the body of a man lay facedown, motionless.

17

AVAYA

Avaya twirled a perfect blonde curl between her fingers before tossing it over her shoulder. Axis was tall, taller than anyone in her family or court back home, with broad shoulders and well-muscled arms and chest to match. Being dragged across the border at breakneck speeds left Avaya feeling haggard. She looked like a peasant. Long days on the road left little chance for hygiene. But even in captivity, a luxurious scented bath and fresh silk had done her a world of good. She could make the most of any situation, so long as she was bathed and given access to an appropriate amount of velvet gowns.

Since her arrival in the fortress, Prince Axis had invited her to join him twice – once on a promenade in the courtyard, and once to join him in his sitting room which was where they found themselves today. He wore the swagger of a man confident in the affection of women, and Avaya intended to bolster that confidence. Her position in the castle was tenuous at best, and to stay alive was to present no threat and boost his ego. It was what she did best.

At long last, she could use familiar skills. Avaya sidled up to Axis and put a hand on his arm. "I was afraid, at first, of being married off to some stranger. I suppose most young princesses are, when faced with a political union. But when I saw you..."

Avaya pulled away shyly, letting her eyelashes brush her cheek, then turned into him suddenly and looked up at his face. "Tall and strong. Handsome, capable." His eyes widened before composure settled over his features again. *Yes...be surprised. Be complimented. But most of all, be on my side. I'll need you on my side.* "Even at the gala, I knew we could really be partners and bring our kingdoms together. That's why I was so heartbroken when...when my mother died, and everything else happened."

A lump rose in her throat at the thought of the gala and the night her mother was murdered. Her mother was dead, because of the assassin girl who brought dragons and death everywhere she went. The girl her father gave a job and a guest room to, and her brother couldn't keep his eyes off of. Even Avaya's little sister was taken with Semra. Avaya gritted her teeth against the emotion rising in her chest. She let the raw emotion linger just long enough for a single tear to escape down her face.

She had to finish the performance for Axis, and sobbing was decidedly *not* on the agenda. Avaya searched the prince's face, and his brow furrowed. Was it genuine concern she saw in his face, or was he playing her like she was playing him? She cleared her throat.

"No matter the circumstances under which I was brought here...I cried myself to sleep the first three nights. I have been placed under guard by my captor, following me everywhere I go, standing outside my door at all hours, reminding me of the ordeal I went through. But perhaps it is all for a greater purpose. If only we can do what we had planned to do, before this misunderstanding over Mother's murder, perhaps we can be partners."

Avaya took a steadying breath. This was it, the point upon which her freedom hung, her only chance to make things right between the kingdoms. She lifted her chin. "That is to say, there is no need for threats. I will marry you, Your Royal Highness, and I'll marry you willingly."

Genuine shock washed over Axis's face, and he stepped away from her. "You would marry me willingly, even now?"

A thousand times, yes. I can correct my father's mistakes. I can keep my head attached to my shoulders, I can make myself valuable, I can unite our lands. It was an immeasurably better option than living out her days in a Belvidorian dungeon...or failing to live at all.

"But of course. It was a good plan, and it's still the best thing for our nations. You and I can bring peace to the region again, and when you are king, we will make a greater Belvidore than there has ever been. You are stronger than your father, and we can negotiate to expand Belvidore past the Surion Strip while ending the war. The people will be pacified to know that their princess still has a role in watching over them, even a symbolic one."

Axis's eyes narrowed, considering her words. "I didn't order your kidnapping. I don't know who did."

Avaya frowned. "I thought your father ordered it."

The prince's features darkened. "He accused *me* of ordering it. That doesn't make sense."

Avaya shrugged. *Plant the seed, and pull back.* "I could be wrong. I could have sworn I overheard the Raven...but, I'm sure you're right. He wouldn't pin something so nefarious on his own son."

Axis's expression hardened, then melted away into diplomacy. A smile played at the corner of his mouth. "You really think I am stronger than His Majesty the king? Dangerous words in these halls, Princess. The king is terribly paranoid of disloyalty."

Avaya let her eyes grow wide in feigned fear. "Please, no disrespect to His Majesty, I wouldn't think of it!" *Make him feel safe. Make him feel powerful, in control.* "Oh, you won't tell, will you, Axis?"

Avaya caught a satisfied look in his eyes, and Axis slipped his hand to the small of her back. It was a daring move, but just where Avaya needed him. *Yes, I'll let you be my protector.*

"I don't see why anyone has to know...not if you behave yourself."

Avaya pressed herself into him, and his arms tightened around her. "I'm so sorry, and I will, of course I will. It's just... King Arnevon seems to have no ambition, but *you* are a man who knows what he wants."

She looked up at him and walked her fingers up his chest, a thrill of power running through her as desire lit his eyes. "Your father has wanted the Surion Strip for years and years, but has done nothing about it until circumstances forced his hand. But you...when you see something you want, do you take it?"

A smile spread slowly across Axis's face. He inclined his head toward her, and hesitated. Avaya lifted her chin just a hair. His lips were on hers, his arms crushing her against him. Avaya melted into him, kissing him back and running her right hand up his chest to his neck, his shoulders. Reaching behind her with her other hand, she felt for the tray of wine glasses and shoved it over.

The glasses landed with a crash, and Axis yanked her backward. "What was that?"

Avaya gasped. "Oh, I must have run into it! I didn't realize how close we were..."

A knock came at the door, and it swung open. The Raven appeared in the doorway, bowing slightly. "Highness? Is everything all right?"

"It's fine," Axis growled. "Disappear."

The Raven bowed again. "Unfortunately, Your Highness, His Majesty King Arnevon is requesting an immediate audience with you."

"Tell him I'll be there in a minute."

The Raven leaned against the doorframe and crossed his arms. "Ah, my poor choice of words. *Requesting* was polite, but inaccurate. His Majesty demands a private audience with Your Highness. Now."

Axis glared at him, then turned to Avaya. "It's been a pleasure. You've given me...much to think about."

With that, Axis strode from the room, and the Raven ushered Avaya out the door in the opposite direction.

18

____

Questions burgeoned in Semra's mind, twisting and turning like branches on a tree from one to the next. Each question lead to two more. *Dead or alive? Alone or with enemies? If there are enemies on the second floor, are they already taking aim at Zephan and Monac?*

Semra lifted the bolt on the front door and swung it open, ushering Zephan and Monac inside. She shut and bolted the door, and motioned for the men to stay put while she crossed to the body and turned it over on its back. The skin was cold to the touch, and she knew before she reached for his pulse that there was no heartbeat. Semra looked up at her companions and shook her head. Monac stepped past the corpse and went up the stairs, then returned a few moments later.

"It's clear."

"I should hope so," Zephan said. "Being quiet seems odd after breaking the window with a rock. I was just humoring you two."

"Better to be cautious than give away your exact position. Habit, I suppose," Semra answered. She walked to the window, glancing down the empty street, and returned to kneel next to the body. It didn't *look* like a murder. But that meant little, with so many Mount Hara assassins at large. Semra indicated marks on the neck of the body. "It looks like he took a tumble down the stairs. No signs of forced entry, and the door was locked from the inside. But the timing seems awfully convenient. He could have been poisoned."

"He fits the description of Florin," Monac said. "Short, brown hair, scar on the nose. It's him."

"The fingertips of one hand are clean but the others are dirty. Does that mean anything?" Zephan asked.

Semra glanced down at the body, then back at Zephan. He was right. Thistlehorn's fingertips were scuffed and dirty, not with pen ink or pencil marks as might be expected for an artist, but with dust and grime. How had she missed that? She arched an eyebrow. "Nice catch."

He grinned. "Impressed?"

"Actually, yes. Why is there dirt caked under his fingernails on this hand?" She lifted his hand and turned it over to inspect more closely. A splinter was caught in the pad of one finger.

Monac tilted his head and knelt. "Semra, move over. You're sitting where his hand was...look, here, on the floorboard."

"He scratched something into the wood! It's a zig-zag pattern...and a crisscross?" Semra ran a hand through her hair, studying it.

"Maybe he started to write a word, but died before he could finish it," Zephan suggested.

Monac gasped. "It's for us. Or, whoever would find him. If someone wanted to keep us from getting the blueprints, they would have come to beat us to it and silenced him. If he fell down the stairs, he wouldn't have left a cryptic message behind."

Zephan snapped his fingers. "Stairs. It's a drawing. Where is the crisscross?"

Semra looked down at the crude scratches. "Third stair. From the top, or the bottom?"

"I'll take this one, you take that one," Zephan said, crossing to the base of the stairs. Semra ran to the top of the staircase and counted three steps down, then squatted to examine the step, pressing on the boards.

"I'm going to look through the designs on the table and see what might be useful to us," Monac called, as he walked toward the main room.

Semra squinted as she ran her fingers along the edges of the boards, the lip of the step, and the riser. "I don't see anything."

Monac reappeared at the base of the steps, holding the rock they'd used to break the window. "We've got company. A team at least, maybe two."

Semra snapped her head up. "How are Belvidorian military this far north?"

"That's a great question to ask after we've escaped," Monac said. "They've surrounded the house."

"I've got something," Zephan said. "Semra, I need a knife to pry with."

Semra drew a knife and sent it flying toward Zephan with a flick of her wrist. It embedded itself a foot to his left, in the step above where he was sitting. He yelped, and his mouth dropped open.

"Thanks." He plucked it from the step.

Monac glared darkly at her. "Your life flashed before my eyes just now. Let's go."

Semra hopped up the last three stairs into a small room with a bed, nightstand, trunk, easel, and desk. Slowly she approached the second-floor window she'd seen from the street, and peered down. She softly called back down to Monac and Zephan.

"Two men in the street, one on the corner, one on the other side. Three men stacked at the door, well away from the windows. Zephan, how's it coming?"

"There's a compartment here. It's stuck, but I'm almost there."

"Don't lose my knife." Semra unclasped her skirt and stepped out of it to reveal her trousers, stuffed the skirt into her pack, and drew another of the knives strapped to her thighs. "Get it done and get up here."

"I'd rather stay on the ground level and fight our way out."

Five knives left. I can hit one or two now, and Monac can take them one at a time at the door. She glanced out the window again, and this time another man ran toward the architect's door with an axe from the smithy.

"They're breaking down the door! Axe!" Semra moved to unlatch the window, then leaped back with a yelp as an arrow flew through the window past her face, its feather fletching brushing her nose on its way to bury itself in the wall behind her.

Bang.

The axe made its first hit.

"Archer across the street!" Semra felt a tingling in the mark in her chest as Zezura picked up her distress. She spun her knife in one hand and sheathed it, drawing her dagger instead. This fight would be short-range.

Bang. Bang. Crack! Semra's heart skipped a beat at the splintering of the wood.

"ZEPHAN!"

"Got it!"

Steel met steel as Monac engaged the first of the men through the door of Thistlehorn's shop downstairs. Semra abandoned the window and flew back down the stairs, where Zephan and Monac fought three men at the door. A fourth leaped through the window and rolled to his feet; Semra ducked under Zephan's arm as he swung his sword at his opponent, then drove forward to meet the newcomer.

Semra's adversary parried her blow and struck quick as lightning; she weaved just in time and marveled at her opponent's incredible footwork. He was better than the average soldier. Semra fell into a rhythm of familiar movements as they fought like a dance: *clash, clash, step, turn, clash, step, dodge.* She kept herself between the soldier and Zephan, and as she feigned high and thrust toward her enemy's torso, a blur caught her attention through the open door.

Her opponent grimaced as Semra's blade nicked his abdomen, and a trickle of blood fell to the floor. He lunged after her at the same time three more men pushed into the small room from the street. Monac's man fell, only to be replaced by another; the three of them now fought six men. Zephan let out a guttural cry as he drove home is sword, and Semra drew a knife and sent it flying just in time to lodge in the throat of a soldier rearing back to strike the prince down from behind.

Semra jumped as she heard metal ring out inches from behind her head, and turned to see Monac had stopped another blade from hitting her as she had stopped one from reaching Zephan. Her eyes widened, and she dipped her head at Monac in acknowledgement before twisting to reengage her original attacker with a downward thrust. Two more men ran inside, pushing against the mass of warriors in the small shop so that Semra felt the walls were closing in on her.

She ducked to the floor and yanked her knife from the dead soldier's throat, stumbling backward from the force of her pull, then blocked an attack with the forearm of her dagger arm and slashed inward with the knife of her other hand. The man slumped, and Semra kicked him backward into his comrade.

They had been pushed back to the base of the stairs, Thistlehorn's corpse serving as a lumpy terrain feature; Semra planted a foot on the dead man's back and launched herself up to the second stair and plunged her knife downward into the nape of a soldier's neck as he swung toward Monac. Semra pulled the blade free, then slashed the blades of her dagger and knife across the man's neck again in an "X" motion. She straightened and her breath caught as archers appeared in the doorway.

19

ARNEVON

"The tournament is a nightmare." Arnevon crossed the room and poured himself another goblet of wine before taking his seat. Axis sat on the couch the Raven had occupied some time before, and the thought of the two of them colluding together against him rose in his mind once again. Axis waved a hand as if to expel the thought from his father's mind.

"It's three days of proving to the people that normalcy prevails, and the unpleasantries of the war will soon be over. If we are unconcerned, they are unconcerned. The tournament is precisely what we need right now."

Arnevon took a swig of wine and watched the remaining droplets slip slowly from the rim back down into the body of the drink. "It's too long to be away from the war effort. We will conduct business from the observation box. I want twice the messenger runners working throughout the tournament, and a supply of homing pigeons on site throughout the event. And –" Arnevon paused, considering his next words. His son would not like them.

"Double the prize for the final contest."

Axis pressed his lips in a tight line and drew in a deep breath. "Your Majesty. If I may, your obsession –"

"Careful."

"Your...prolonged interest in finding remnants of natural born *tabeun* magic melders has done little to profit the kingdom. The tournament is tradition, fine, let it be tradition, but it has now been six hundred years since The Crumbling. Aurin defied his king, dishonored his country, and brought curses on us all when he threw the spear that ended magic. Everyone knows the story, and in six hundred years no one has come forward with more than a party trick."

"Adding incentive will not do any harm."

Axis leaned forward. "The prize is already more money than any commoner would know what to do with. And if someone accepts the challenge and presents an illusion, and they're shown to be a fraud, are they still to be beheaded after you make the winnings even harder to ignore?"

Anger stirred in Arnevon's chest. "The consequences of deceit in the final contest have not changed in six hundred years. It was Mauve Madensig himself who set it up that way, and I see no reason to change it now."

"But you're willing to change the award."

"Yes, that's different. And I need your support to be enthusiastic. Speaking of which, I have something else in mind that might interest you."

Axis huffed a frustrated sigh and leaned back, crossing his arms. Ahh, the picture of humble anticipation. Arnevon regarded his son with disdain before deciding to let it go.

"Your fiancé will sit in the box with us, at your side."

Axis arched an eyebrow. "You're making a public pronouncement at the tournament?"

"Yes. It will give everyone hope of peace, belief that we are negotiating, and something to talk about besides the war. The timing of her arrival could not have gone better." Arnevon eyed Axis, scanning for any tells that he had orchestrated the timing of her arrival himself, perhaps just for this purpose. Axis's mouth tugged up into a sly smile.

"I'll spread the word. Thank you, father."

"Make sure the Raven is paired with one of our guards and both are assigned to Princess Avaya's protection every moment of the tournament. She does not accept a flower from the commoners, she does not straighten the hem of her gown, she hardly breathes without their say-so. They will be responsible for her life...and her death, if it comes to that. The only way Princess Avaya will die is if I order it. She shall remain protected for as long as she remains cooperative. While she is here, she is a diplomat, and she shall perform the political duties expected of her within the limits that we set."

Axis nodded. "Of course. I'll set it up."

"And double the prize for the final contest. If ever we needed magic, it is now."

20

———

Semra thrust her dagger into the gut of the soldier fighting Zephan, and yanking the prince down beside her behind the man's body as two arrows lodged themselves in the wall behind them, where their heads should have been. The burning in her chest grew stronger, and Semra all but threw Zephan up the stairs. Monac took up the rear, fighting two men at once at the base of the stairs. The rest bottlenecked around the opening. Semra itched for a throwing knife, but watching Monac's huge frame fill the narrow stairwell, she knew he had it well in hand. And she couldn't afford to lose any more knives.

Zephan reached his sword up and knocked an arrow from the air as it headed for Semra, and the two of them rolled onto the landing and out of range. A sapphire blur blew past the window, and Zephan kicked the window out in one swift motion as Zezura circled back to find them. Zephan cleared the rest of the glass, offering Semra a hand as the dragon hovered outside.

Semra shook her head. *Princes before assassins.* "You first."

Zephan tilted his head and leveled a glare. "Not a chance. Out."

Grunts and a great *thud* came from the stairwell, and Semra glanced over to see Monac backing up to the landing, heaving from exertion. Getting out of the window would take twice as long if she stopped to squabble with Zephan about who went first. Semra took Zephan's hand and climbed onto Zezura's back, sheathing her dagger to get a grip on the dragon and yelling back inside to Monac. "Our ride is here! Let's go!"

Monac stumbled and dropped his sword. Zephan leaped in front of him, blocking a downward kill stroke from a Belvidorian soldier. Semra gasped and half-stood on the spikes of Zezura's sides. Zephan ran the man through and engaged two more as they charged up the final steps.

Zephan whirled toward Monac. "Get out!"

Semra ground her teeth, staring at the scene before her with helpless turmoil. Going back through the window now would only slow their progress, but without her, they were even more outnumbered. She leaned forward for a better view, steadying herself on the smooth blue of Zezura's neck. Monac stood wearily and threw himself forward again with bare fists, decking one adversary on the side of the head and disarming him for his sword.

Zephan swore and took a flying leap out the window, landing behind Semra with a jolt and screaming something unintelligible at Monac as five more men swarmed him. Monac wavered on his feet. He wasn't going to make it. Panic swelled in Semra's gut and she felt rather than said the word to Zezura: *fire*. Semra gripped Zephan's leg to quiet him before shrieking, "*Down!*" at Monac.

He dropped to the floor with half a second to spare before Zezura reared her head to the window and released a torrent of flame on the Belvidorian squad inside. The Belvidorians fell back with cries of terror, and Semra lost sight of Monac in the chaos. Her mouth went dry, and Zephan's arm cinched so tight it hurt to breathe. *Get up Monac! Where are you?*

A flash of motion caught her eye to the side of the room. Monac rolled and coughed as the fire caught old papers and licked at the easel and wooden bedframe. He ran to the window, launched off the sill, and dropped down on Zezura's scaly hide behind Zephan. No sooner was he out of the window than the Zezura launched upward, the shop of Florin Thistlehorn nurturing tendrils of dragon flame down below.

Zezura pulled away, and a rush of air tickled the back of Semra's neck as Zephan let out a breath of relief against her skin. Goosebumps ran up her arms, and she was grateful for the breeze.

Below them, the surviving five men fled the building into the empty cobblestone street. *Well, there goes laying low.* Semra sighed. Zezura shook her head, and her scales shimmered from aquamarine blue to soft reds and purples as she melted away into the gentle sunset sky. Night fell quickly, and by the time they flew over the Surion River and the trade route it was famous for, little could be seen but the lights of army encampments. Somewhere down below, Jannemar licked its wounds and geared up for another battle, taking heavy losses but holding Belvidore south of the river. The lights of Madensig Fortress, the Belvidorian castle, came into view as the night stretched on, and finally Zezura descended into a patch of forest west of the castle.

Semra let Monac and Zephan slip down first, then patted Zezura's neck and slid to the ground herself. She stretched her aching limbs from the long ride, and checked the sheaths on her trousers. Semra looked up at Zephan.

"You owe me a knife! You never gave it back."

Semra could barely see Zephan's face light up in the dim

starlight. The amber of his eyes lit up, and the fact that she had caused it wrapped her in a blanket of cozy warmth.

"Aha! You of little faith!" He took his sword out of its scabbard and turned the scabbard upside-down. A knife tumbled out. Zephan plucked it from the ground and handed it over, grinning. "I rode the whole way with my arm securing the hilt to me, since it didn't fit securely in the sheath with the knife at the bottom."

Semra smiled at his excitement and something inside her fluttered. *He brought it back for me.* A small thing, perhaps, but not one she was used to. "A true gentleman," she teased, taking the knife.

Zephan's grin widened, and Monac groaned.

"Did you get the mystery item in Thistlehorn's secret stair box, or what?"

"Ah. Yes, and I think it's precisely what we came for."

Zephan pulled crumpled parchment from a pocket inside his cloak and spread it out, but in the darkness, under a canopy of trees, little was visible. The three huddled around it, and Semra bumped into Zephan's side in her haste to see it. She grimaced in the dark. Would he think she did it on purpose? Did she seem forward? Was she annoying?

He nudged her back in return. Semra's stomach dropped, but she said nothing.

Monac leaned over the map, squinting. "It's the right shape. I can't make out the labels, but this is it. We can't afford to draw any more attention to ourselves, so we'll forego a fire and plan in morning light."

"Let's get a few hours' rest," Zephan said. "After that, we'll have to keep moving and plan as we go. As Monac pointed out at the beginning of all this, dragons are not particularly excellent for stealth. Now Belvidore knows we're here, and any hope for the element of surprise is gone."

Despite his suggestion of rest, Zephan lingered over the map for a long moment. He leaned into Semra's side so that his arm touched hers from shoulder to elbow. Semra shifted her weight, and her fingers brushed the back of his hand.

She hadn't meant to do it; her eyes widened in the dark and she made a short, barely audible gasp. Monac didn't seem to notice, but she could have sworn she saw the hint of a smile on Zephan's face in the low moonlight. He took his time folding the map, his arm still pressed against Semra's, before handing the map to Monac and turning to walk into the shadow of the trees.

THE MORNING BROUGHT a crisp chill to the air, and Semra wished they could risk a fire. They were seated in a tight circle on the ground with the blueprints to Madensig. Zezura slept soundly off to the side. Semra pulled out the oil from her pack and laid out her knives.

"We can't hide in shipments or in a trunk like last time without a friend on the inside or considerably more planning," Semra said.

Monac rummaged through his bag, producing a chunk of dried meat, and tore off a piece with his teeth. "What about the moat?"

Zephan shook his head. "They have sharpened spears hidden in it. They roll them in feces. Anyone who tries to cross will get severely infected by the cuts from the stake."

Semra wrinkled her nose. She could almost smell the putrid process, and picture the green of infection setting in. "Gross. But also smart."

Zephan nodded. "That which seems beneath you, will end you.'"

Monac raised an eyebrow. "Philosopher?"

Zephan grinned. "Norin Bruit, *The Pursuit of the Lonely Road.* Whatever you think is too gross, too dangerous, too anything, is exactly what will be successfully used against you."

Semra understood the sentiment. Ethics on warfare only handed the enemy more weapons. Azi called ethics a weaknesses.

Zephan stretched his legs out in front of him and leaned back against a tree. "When Aurin and the Elemental Melders stopped magic once and for all at the Origin Wellspring, Mauve Madensig was furious. He had built his fortress with its moat fed by the Surion River specifically to bring with it rich magical power as the water flowed from the Origin, only to have the Melders destroy that power before he could harness it. When he realized the water had no power at all, but was now ordinary, Madensig poisoned it with the infection spears, and people have died from their attempts to cross. Rumor has it the tradition carried down through the generations and continues today with Arnevon."

A nasty tradition, but effective. The stories alone would be enough to keep most at bay, but with Arnevon as paranoid as he was, leaving the fortress protection to the archers and castle guards was not enough. A disgusting ploy to infect and kill invaders of the moat was right up his alley.

"Speaking of which, once word reaches Arnevon of our little skirmish in Kinlock, he'll have the guard doubled throughout the castle." Monac bit off another piece of dried meat and swallowed it. "He probably already knows. The tournament might force him to thin his resources a bit in the fortress, but that doesn't mean it won't be well guarded. Especially if he expects we might come for Princess Avaya."

"Arnevon will expect us to strike during the tournament,"

Zephan said. "His defenses will be elevated now, but it's not going to get any easier. I think making our move *before* the tournament is our best shot."

Semra poured oil onto a cloth and ran it over the blade of the first knife. "We need to know the procedure for getting in and out, and we need it fast. Crowds are our friend, and if we can find some chink in the process to get inside, the main gate with castle staff is still my vote."

Monac nodded. "The tournament is in four days. We'll travel today, get to Horen tomorrow, hear the talk of the town and get some information, and reconvene in the evening. By day three, we'll need to make our move."

21

AXIS

Axis cocked his head to one side as he took in the mysterious figure who caused so much trouble. "You have some nerve, pitting me against my father." The Raven was handsome, confident, and not a day older than Axis himself. Maybe even younger.

"On the contrary, I have put Belvidore in the most strategic position possible. Let the strongest, most able king take the seeds I've planted and water them to their full potential."

"And you think that someone is me?"

The Raven shrugged. "You're certainly best suited for it. But I've been wrong before."

"So...you kidnapped a princess as a resume builder, delivered her to her enemies, and hoped for the best. No one hired you."

The Raven spread his hands. "And now I'm employed at the castle in an official capacity. I hope you understand I do expect compensation for my work. But if I'm hired for a large enough project, I'll waive the kidnapping fee."

"A kidnapping no one hired you for." Axis raised an eyebrow.

"Naturally."

Axis grunted in response. If his father had half of the Raven's boldness, Jannemar would have been defeated long ago. His gaze narrowed to slits. "Why is my father convinced someone hired you, and why is he convinced that someone is me?"

The Raven clucked his tongue. "Family drama, I see. Perhaps I can help you with that as well."

Axis gripped the arms of his chair. The Raven waved a hand. "Certainly not without money, of course. No need to fear me going off the rails. You can keep your miserable father, and your petty arguments too. But the real question is how you are going to capitalize on the free gift I've given *you*. Like I said, I'm not interested in Arnevon at all. I'm on his payroll as the princess' bodyguard for walking around money, and I have access to the castle and to you, so he's served his purpose. Let him think I work for him. But I'm after bigger fish, and *you* are the king of the new era."

Axis relaxed his grip on the armrests and picked up his wine glass, cradling it in his hand. "When I do become king, marrying Avaya will strengthen my claim to Jannemar territory and my position in negotiations with Turian. The people will acknowledge *me* as their ruler, but she will be the face of familiarity and comfort bridging the gap. I need to make her play the game. Is she toying with me?"

The Raven scoffed. "Is the diplomatic, spoiled princess toying with you to regain control after being kidnapped and dragged into another kingdom? Your Highness, you should expect nothing less. It is the only survival mechanism that serves her in this setting. But a woman who enjoys games is a woman you can manipulate. Give her a game she can't afford to lose, and let *her* convince *you*. Let her think she has to earn the privilege of being your queen. The alternative for her is death, after all, and yet she is running over you. And as she fights for your hand, let her façade become her reality, and she will be putty in your hands by the end."

Axis smirked. "And you know just how to do this."

"I'm an excellent coach, Your Highness. Let me teach you how to play."

"For a price."

A frantic knock came at the door, and Axis opened it. The guard bowed

"Your Royal Highness." His gaze flitted to the Raven. "I have urgent news."

"Go on."

"We received word that the Jannemari dragon rider had an encounter with one of our squads in Kinlock, leaving half of them dead, and was last seen flying toward Belvidore. She was accompanied by two men."

Axis froze. *The dragon rider.* She killed half a squad? Impressive. And worrisome. Perhaps this dragon rider girl was more dangerous than he'd given her credit for, having only seen her at Shamaran Castle when she was dragged away for allegedly murdering the Jannemari queen. Avaya was in danger. He thanked the guard and dismissed him, then turned back to his guest.

"Raven, your company has been most stimulating. We will speak again. For now, you are dismissed to guard my fiancé. I want to know everything she does, everywhere she goes – rest assured I'll make it worth your while. And I want to know every correspondence you have with my father."

22

———

On the morning of the third day, Semra sat in a wagon next to a gruff, bearded man driving on the drawbridge into Madensig Fortress. Semra adjusted her cap, her hair tightly wound beneath it, and glanced at the driver. He shifted uneasily in his seat, but nothing else appeared out of the ordinary. The castle loomed ahead in dark gray stone, a stark contrast from the bright sandstone of the Shamaran Castle. Although function was certainly prioritized over beauty, Madensig was impressive, with its four floors, six high towers, and enormous front gate. The entire thing was surrounded by an outer wall and an expansive moat.

Four more supply wagons of various sorts preceded them and six trailed behind, waiting their turn to be inspected at the gate. Since the gala fiasco in Jannemar, each vendor was required to present a certificate to enter, and subject to individual search. Monac had spent time in the pubs near the castle hoping to hear off-duty guards and knights gloat and gripe, and learned of an increase in security at the castle over the past two days. Arnevon had received word of the dragon in

Kinlock.

The wagon at the gate moved through. The driver shifted again next to Semra, and the chestnut mare tossed her head.

"You're doing fine," Semra muttered under her breath. "You've done this a thousand times, and today is no different. The second half of the fee will be at your house by dawn, and these wartime taxes will be paid three times over."

The man nodded and wiped his brow with the back of his hand. If he didn't keep it together, they'd both lose their necks. Another wagon went through the gate. Their turn came, and the guard glanced up and smiled at the driver.

"Morning, Bevel. Got me anything good today?"

"Always. Want a sample?" Bevel reached into a sack behind him and tossed the guard an apple. The guard caught it and laughed.

"You know I do. Alright, hand me your certificates, you know the drill."

Bevel passed the guard his certificate along with his apprentice's certificate, whom Semra was filling in for. The guard gave it a cursory glance, then squinted at Semra.

"That your usual boy?"

"Benna is sick, but my nephew here has filled in before. The certificate is his."

The guard looked at Semra, and she tilted her head so the shadow of the cap fell further onto her face. The smell of dried sweat from the borrowed hat nearly made her gag, and a bead of her own perspiration slipped down her neck. The guard straightened, satisfied, passed the certificates back, and waved them through. Semra wondered how Monac was faring with the stable hand. Monac would be waiting for shift change and then coming through with the stable hand in an hour. Semra would have preferred outfitting the wagon with a hidden compartment in the bench for

Monac to hide in, but there wasn't time and Monac was too broad.

The wagon rumbled through the gate, past the outer bailey, and turned left across a spacious yard between the inner and outer walls. The stables were around back, where Monac would be headed, but Bevel stopped their wagon in a row of several other supply wagons and hopped down to unload. The storehouses were located near the kitchens and accessed through a door in the inner wall, where suppliers were coming and going as they unloaded their product.

Semra grabbed a basket of apples as three castle servants appeared to help unload, turned to carry it into the storehouse, and stopped cold. Through the door, Semra saw sacks of flour, sugar, produce, and meat, bustling activity that would have made Saeb proud, and gray eyes like the sea staring intently at her from a familiar frame leaning against a barrel. Siler.

Semra's heart flipped three times and landed somewhere between her soured stomach and her toes as she shoved the basket into an unsuspecting servant's arms and whirled back to the wagon. The game was up. If Siler reported her presence, she'd be dead by morning. He wouldn't do that though, would he?

Why is he here?

Bevel stood in the wagon handing down sacks. Semra climbed up with him and chucked another sack into waiting arms. Her throat constricted. Siler was supposed to be off on adventures making his contract killing fortune. But if he was here...

"We're leaving," Semra hissed, with a furtive glance back through the door. Siler was gone.

"You're coming back with me?" Bevel handed off another sack. "We aren't unloaded yet. Just a few more."

"If you don't want to be found out, we are leaving *right now.*"

"Okay, okay, just a minute. We'll have you out of here in no time."

We might not have a minute, moron. Semra got down from the wagon, turned away from the servants, doubled over at the waist, and shoved her index finger down her throat. A wave of nausea rocked her and she lurched forward, emptying the meager contents of her stomach onto the grass.

He's going to kill Avaya. The thought struck her like a gong, a thousand alarm bells going off in her brain. She stabilized herself with a hand on the wagon wheel, hacking up stomach acid from her throat.

"Watch it!" someone yelled.

"Hey, sonny, are you all right?" another voice asked.

"Grab these last things," Bevel called to someone. "He's sick. I've got to get him home!"

Semra climbed up onto the bench and Bevel snapped the reins, the chestnut mare picking up a brisk pace as the wagon circled the yard and headed back out the way they had come.

"A little warning would have been nice," Bevel grumbled. "No need to go and–"

"Bevel, *go!*" Semra looked back over her shoulder as two guards run out on foot from the kitchens, stopping briefly at the servants, who pointed in their direction. "Get *gone!*"

Bevel cursed, and the mare surged toward the front gate. Semra tugged her cap down and coughed and gagged as they slowed briefly by the guard Bevel knew. Bevel waved his arms frantically at the guard. "He's sick, he's sick, his mother will kill me! We need to get him to a doctor!"

The guard waved him through. The wagon rushed down the drawbridge, and as they reached the main road, two mounted guards flew through the gate after them. Semra looked back once more, and Siler stood at the gate, motioning to the gate tower. *He did this. He turned me in.* Breath left her body as the realization hit like a wave crashing against a bluff. Was there no one in life who would not betray her in the end?

The drawbridge was drawn up at Siler's word, as the two horsemen left it behind hot on their heels. *Please let Zephan be ready. Let him be ready.* A burning in her chest warned her that Zezura was alerted to her stress, but Semra stayed her. *No, Zez. We can't have a dragon at the castle today. I'll find another way.*

The chestnut mare thundered into the heart of Horen, the wagon bouncing along behind her, and Semra gathered her feet under her on the driver's bench.

"Drive hard until you're halfway home," Semra called to Bevel against the wind.

Bevel jerked his head her direction and his eyes bulged. "What are you doing?! You're going to get yourself killed!"

"Don't worry about me. Take the alleyway and get me close to those buildings."

The wagon swung through a harsh turn and down the alleyway out of sight of the pursuing guardsmen, flying a foot from the walls of shops.

"Closer!" Semra yelled.

"How close do I need to be?!" Bevel screamed back at her.

"Kiss it!"

The mare glistened with sweat as she cantered closer and closer to the buildings, and Semra gathered herself and leaped for a shop signpost hanging overhead. As her feet left the bench, a single thought invaded: *the last person to truly understand you has sentenced you to die.*

23

Semra caught the signpost of a tailor shop with a grunt as the wagon careened down the street without her. Semra dropped to the ground. Three fine ladies dropped their jaws at the sight of her, but she paid them no mind and ran one shop down, ducking into a cobblery. The cobbler and two customers looked up, and Semra put a hand on her hat and whistled.

"Did you see that? Crazy man nearly run me right over!"

Semra jumped and turned as the guardsmen cantered by, and the cobbler shook his head.

"Any man dumb enough to run from the king is a man I don't want a thing to do with."

"The street's large enough for the both of us, no matter who he's runnin' from!" Semra shook her fist in the direction of Bevel's disappearing wagon and turned back to the cobbler. "Thanks for lettin' me catch my breath."

Semra stepped out of the door, hurried down a block, and into the flow of people on the main thoroughfare of Horen. Quickly she picked her way through the crowd. One woman sold meats on the corner, a florist offered roses to young men for their sweethearts, and a mass of humanity went about their daily drivel. One young man fiddled with his cap behind his back, blushing under the gaze of a stunning young lady a few feet away. Semra turned her back to the woman as she passed and stumbled backward into her so the lady fell toward the lad with a cry.

The gallant gentleman dropped his cap to catch her, and quick as lightning, Semra spun behind him, snatching his gray cap from the ground and dropping her brown one in its place. She melted back into the sea of people and adjusted the gray cap over her pinned up hair. She needed a bigger change to her appearance, but the hat would do for now. And the young man would rather have the beautiful lady in his arms than his old gray cap, anyway. Semra smirked.

"Nice hat."

Semra jumped and swung around to see Zephan observing her from the shadowed corner of an alley. His mouth tipped up into a lopsided smile. Semra relaxed and laughed sheepishly.

"Saw that, did you?"

"Oh yes. Quite entertaining. And helpful to the poor bloke. If only I had a you, to help me with *you*."

Semra gaped at him. Did he say what she thought he said? "That seems...weirdly forward," she said at last.

Zephan frowned. "Ah, what every man wants to hear from a woman. 'How oddly forward.'"

Semra grimaced, and pressed her lips together. It didn't make sense for him to flirt with her. And even if it did, her flirting back made even less sense. It would all be for nothing anyway...no matter what warmth flooded her whenever he looked her way.

He cocked his head and examined her with those melted amber eyes. She looked away. Across the street, sun glinted off the metal of a guardsman's helmet, and Semra gasped and stepped into the shadows, pressing Zephan out of the way and into the wall.

His lips parted in surprise, and Semra found herself staring at them, lingering a moment too long. Her hands rested on his chest, his heart beating fast against her palm. His hand grazed her arm, reaching for her almost reflexively. He dropped his hand, but a tingling sensation ran through her at his touch.

"And *you* were accusing *me* of being forward," he mocked. His voice dropped back into seriousness, and he looked over her head to scan the street. "What do you see? And why are you back so early?"

Semra reached into the pack over Zephan's shoulder and pulled out her skirt. Her cheeks flushed at their closeness. She quickly wrapped the skirt around herself and secured the waist, grateful for the distraction.

"Siler is here. Inside Madensig. I didn't even make it past the inner wall." She took off her cap and pulled the pins from her hair so that her curls fell freely about her shoulders, then dropped the pins back into the bag. "He saw me, two mounted guards made chase, and they pulled up the drawbridge. The guard never changed in that time, so Monac must still be outside. We need to find another way in. If Siler is here, someone is going to die."

24

Semra paced the forest floor. "Siler was supposed to be off somewhere buying a villa with the money he skimmed from Azi."

They found Monac, who went off to gather more intel, and Zephan and Semra returned to hide out in the woods and regroup. Semra held in her burning anxieties for the long walk out of Horen, but in the quiet of the trees, she could contain them no longer. She spun on her heel and stormed the other direction, the same back and forth she'd been repeating for several minutes.

"He's not hiding; he's got position. The guards know him and listen to him. I spoke to him just that morning in Jannemar. The same morning Avaya disappeared..." Semra's mouth went dry.

Zephan sat at the base of a tree trunk, fiddling with twigs while he watched her. He froze. "It was him."

"He said to me, '*Go somewhere new. Get that fresh start. Don't wait.*'" Semra swallowed against a lump in her throat. "*Don't wait.* Rats and rot. He was trying to get me out of the way." Tears welled in her eyes. Semra swiped them away angrily.

"Siler is making all of Captain Firfell and the rest of your father's court's concerns real. If he took her...if he kills someone...then they're right about us."

"No. If he did this, then they are right about *him.*" Zephan snapped a twig in his fingers and stood to his feet. "You aren't Siler."

How could he not understand? Ramas's voice came to her then, whispering a painful truth: *You're a murderer, Semra. It's who you are.* Semra shook it off and pressed on. "If he kidnapped Avaya, who hired him? And if he was hired to kidnap her, why is he still there? He was watching, waiting for me. He knew I would come."

"He knew you were coming once word got out of Zezura in Kinlock, at the very least."

"By now Siler will know the map of the castle by heart and every weakness we would attempt to exploit. He knows me, he knows how we think, he knows what I would try. Was he going to kill me today?" Semra's breathing came fast and heavy, and her lungs constricted as she drew ragged breaths. "I don't know if I can beat him."

Siler would know what to do, in that unconcerned way of his. The irony that he was the one she wanted to talk to about this struck her in the face. *He should be here, helping me. At the very least, he should be in a villa, keeping his word. But he left you, like everyone always has, after all you've been through together — and he's willing to see you get killed.* A chill ran up Semra's spine. Would he do it himself?

Azi's voice echoed through her mind again. *My dear, my dear ... you know I'm the only one who has never left you.* Semra let out a guttural cry and slammed her fists into her temple.

"Get out, get OUT!" she screamed. The voice came again. Though inaudible, it was taunting and soft as silk. *Siler has already left you. Zephan is next. Who else is left? Your parents are dead. You have no family. Your family is with me, in the mountain, but you destroyed your family...*

"Semra!"

Zephan pulled her fists down away from her head and pinned them to her sides. Semra reacted, thrashing and pulling away, but Zephan held her fast, pulling her arms behind her back and wrapping his around her. Semra pulled against his iron grip, but he was too strong, and as the immediate reaction passed she felt herself releasing the tension and leaning into him as she gave up the fight.

The two of them stood there, Zephan's arms still encircling her, his hands gripping her slowly relaxing fists. Semra melted into his chest, the warmth of him around her soothing her tired mind. Tears streamed down her face and her shoulders shook in silent sobs. Zephan held her until the sobs ebbed, then slowly he began to rock her back and forth, back and forth. Two minutes passed, and he began to step forward and backward, moving her with him. Zephan took her hand and tenderly brought it up to his shoulder, then left it there and placed his arm at her waist. He took her other hand in his.

Semra followed his lead, moving with him, her stomach turning tiny somersaults with every step. He was warm and inviting, a calm presence in the middle of a storm. She was drawn to him like a vessel at sea to a lighthouse. She looked up at him. "Why aren't you freaking out about everything? You seem strangely...together."

"I *have* been freaking out. When you and Monac left and I was alone, I lost it a bit. Had a big long cry, to tell you the truth. The war with Belvidore, Avaya gone, rogue assassins... when I'm alone with my thoughts, they get to me. But right now, keeping you calm has been keeping me calm. It might not make sense, but it helps."

Semra frowned, taking in the information. "Why are we dancing?"

"Because teaching you to dance – in the forest, before the gala – is one of my favorite memories, and I've been dreaming about doing it again ever since. And because dancing has rhythm when life doesn't, and it's calming and nice."

Was it really one of his favorite memories? She had to fight a smile every time she thought of it. And try as she might to avoid it, the dance in the woods came to her mind often. Semra scanned her muscles to test his other rationale. The tension in her shoulders and the weight on her chest and lungs had lessened. "Huh."

Zephan spun her around and pulled her back to him. Semra stumbled as she turned, and Zephan caught her in his arms. He grinned. "And I didn't even lose my hat."

Semra laughed, and in that moment she wasn't an assassin and he wasn't a prince. They were like the young people in the square, just a man and a woman with the whole wide world blotted out around them. She gazed at him and absorbed every feature: the twinkle in his eyes, the cut of his jaw, the way his mouth moved when he spoke. A tingle in her belly made her squirm as she took in the soft way he looked at her, a way that made her feel out of control and simultaneously want to run and want to stay forever.

"Want to try something fun?" Zephan asked, a mischievous look in his eye.

She raised an eyebrow. "I admit the dancing is sort of... nice, but *fun* seems extreme when I learned my last friend from the mountain betrayed us."

"You need the distraction. If it makes you feel any better, he'll still be a traitor after we do something fun."

Semra eyed him, but made no complaint. He wasn't wrong, exactly. Zephan lifted his arm, brought her around in a slow turn, and drew her close again. Semra tripped over her feet and steadied herself, and then they were a man and a woman dancing, to no music but the crunch of leaves and the waft of the wind. His hands were gentle and guiding at once, moving her through a simple sequence she had never learned, directing her to the proper steps. Following along captured her concentration. Her mind was tired. It was comforting, having one simple thing to focus on.

"Can we do a lift...over my head?"

Semra drew back. "Um...what?"

Zephan, so confident a moment ago, suddenly looked sheepish. "It's this thing Aviama saw entertainers do in a dance. She thought it was romantic and wanted a man to do it with her one day, and I told her it was ridiculous and unrealistic, so she made me try it with her and – well anyway, I can do it."

"I don't know about that."

"Oh, come on. I want to be able to tell Aviama I got you to do something girly. She'll absolutely *die* if I get you to do a dance lift before she gets you to wear dresses around the castle."

Semra grinned. "I am *not* going to wear dresses around the castle. She got lucky *one* day, but whatever she kept stuffing in my wardrobe is still sitting there."

"I know! So give me something funny to tell her when we get home. You're athletic, so I think it'll go better than it did with her. You need to run and jump."

Semra swallowed. "I need to...are you kidding?"

"Well, no. Run and jump, and I'll catch you." Zephan released her and ran backward about twenty paces.

Fear crept up through her, and she shook her head. "That's too far off the ground. You'll miss."

"The woman with the dragon is afraid of heights? I don't buy it. And I won't miss."

Semra bounced on the balls of her feet, and Zephan widened his stance. She shook her head.

"This is stupid!"

"It's also fun! I'll catch you. Trust me."

Semra shook her head again, but nerves and adrenaline wove together in her chest, and she loved the call of a thrill. She took one deep breath, then sprinted toward him. Her feet pounded into the earth, her heart beating like a drum. In the last moment as she reached him, halfway into her jump, panic gripped her, and she bailed. Zephan half-caught her as she half-jumped, and Semra felt a moment of sheer terror in the air completely out of control, gravity pulling them down hard like a stone. They fell to the ground with a *thud,* and Semra rolled away and sprang to her feet. Zephan stood and brushed himself off.

"Are you okay? You didn't jump!"

"And you chose the wrong person to flirt with!" Semra blurted it out, anger suddenly flaring hot.

Zephan stepped backward. "What?"

Why had she said it? Semra broke away and ran trembling fingers through her hair. Her outburst had been nearly as surprising to her as it was to Zephan. But how did he expect her to react? He abandoned the task force, hardly saw her, then demanded she join a mission with him! And now he had the gall to be charming and sweet, tender and free like Dahyu.

Semra threw her hands up. "Why are you doing this? Why would you tell me you want me to stay at the castle when I have no sustainable job there, tell me in Horen that you wished you had someone to help you with me like I helped the man hold his sweetheart? Why would you dance with me, and look at me like that?"

"Look at you like what?"

"Like you *care!* Like you care too much, the kind of look the nobles–"

"Why do you care so much about the nobles?!"

Semra waved him off and forged ahead: "That the nobles in your father's court would have a conniption over, the look that pretends you are simply Dahyu, the healer's apprentice in Ryden with no responsibilities or title. Because when we danced in the woods the first time, that's who I danced with. In fact, tonight was the first time I've danced with *you*...the *prince* you, that is, the first time since I've known who you really were."

Zephan closed the distance between them and her breath caught. She looked away, but she could feel the heat of his glare boring into her. "I'm allowed to care. I *do* care. And Dahyu feels more real to me than the prince does, some days. Maybe I want that part of me to be free every so often. Is that so wrong?"

Semra whipped her head back toward him, a renewed fire in her eyes. "Yes. Yes it is. Because the heir to the throne can't be with a murderer. King Turian got into trouble for marrying someone without royal blood. Can you imagine the backlash of your people, and everyone you depend on supporting your future reign, if you entertained a relationship with someone like me? It's wrong because it's playing games that were never meant for us. Because it's stupid."

Ramas' voice rang in her ears.

You're a murderer, Semra. It's who you are.

The only thing you were ever good at was killing.

I always hated you.

Semra winced.

Zephan's voice rose. "My life is *dark* right now and if you're a bright spot in it, I think we deserve to have a little light, don't you? I didn't mean anything by it, I didn't mean to make you angry, but here we are anyway, and you know what? You're making a big deal out of a dance. And I'm sick of how you degrade yourself all the time and use it as an excuse to keep everybody out."

"I'm not like you! You grew up with servants and money and a family. How could you understand? I'm not making excuses to keep people out. I'm taking care of myself because no one else will. Flirting might seem fun now, but it's mean later when nothing can ever come of it. You'll move on to legitimate prospects, but why was I strung along in the meantime? You don't have to think about other people as often when you're elite."

"*Elite!*" Zephan yanked down the sleeves of his tunic, and Semra couldn't help but notice the irony of his nervous habit being something a person would do in fine clothes. "I can't help how I was born and raised, like you can't help how *you* were born and raised. It's not my fault. You can't blame me for being a prince, like you can't blame yourself for being indoctrinated as a child! You think I don't understand you? Well, maybe I don't. Who would you be with then, Siler? He *kidnapped* my sister, and you honestly aren't sure whether or not he was going to kill you today!"

Semra's voice rose two octaves. "Who says I have to be with anybody? Who thinks that's even a good idea? I nearly killed you for tapping me on the shoulder the other day! Does that sound like a stable person who should be romantically involved with another human being? I'm getting Avaya back, and then I'm headed to some deep, dark, solitary cave where nobody expects anything of me, where I can be who I am, where mothers and their children don't move away when I walk by, and no one speaks about the inconvenience of my existence behind my back. Siler shouldn't have sold out, but at least he isn't under any pretense that he's better than he is. I may not have worn any of Aviama's dresses, but I've been playing pretend at Shamaran Castle. I'm not one of you."

"Can't you see I'm trying to tell you something good? You're more than what they see. I want to show you what *I* see. But you shut me out at every turn." Zephan's face hardened to flint. "Hiding is easy. You think being a prince is easy? You think I'm some *elite* priss who eats pastries and languishes on extravagance all day? You think I haven't wished for another life? But I only have this one life, and I can't abandon my father or my people. I wish you'd let me have one thing, a way to keep from abandoning myself while I'm at it."

Semra's breath hitched in her throat. She didn't think of him as elitist, not really. He had things she wanted – a loving family, food that was already dead and dressed and cooked whenever hunger struck, and a purpose that he could feel good about—an identity.

Who was she but an assassin? If she gave that up, what was left of her? But if she held onto it, she wasn't someone to be proud of.

She hadn't thought about his sacrifices in the way he described them, abandoning himself, his own desires, for the sake of the crown. Dahyu was his escape. But if she was part of his escape, who was she when reality came crashing back down?

Her breathing quickened. What if she leaned into it? What if she escaped with him, just for the moments when he was Dahyu, and not the prince? But she knew the answer already. If she let herself lean into Dahyu, she would be lost in a fiction she could never have. Attachments were weakness, weren't they? No, that was a lie from the dragonlord of her childhood. But the stronger she attached to a figment of her imagination, the greater the pain of being torn apart as the mirage crumbled.

Semra swallowed. "I don't want you to abandon yourself. I want good things for you. But I think it's selfish of you to use me as some inane distraction. I've been used all my life. I won't be used by you."

"That's what you think of me? Selfish, using you – like Azi? You think we're the same?" Zephan's eyes burned amber fire as he leaned in toward her, his voice low. "Maybe it was foolish for me to flirt. Maybe you'll find all that you need by dying alone in a hole somewhere no one can find you. But maybe you refuse to broaden your view to anything other than your self-deprecating pity party, and maybe entrenching yourself in an assassin identity you *say* you rejected is as harmful to yourself and to the kingdom as me taking a break from the smothering identity thrust upon me at birth. Wake up, Semra. The world is bigger than you, and you have a bigger role in it than rotting in some forsaken corner of the earth."

Zephan spat out his final words and wheeled around, disappearing into the trees, leaving Semra's head spinning.

25

Indignation burned in Semra's chest. She tilted the knife in her hands, hoping to catch a glimpse of Zephan in its reflection. He clenched his jaw and shredded another leaf. He'd disappeared for half an hour, and the two of them had been sitting on opposite sides of the wooded space ever since. How could he walk off like that? How dare he accuse her of self-pity and selfishness when *he* was the selfish one?

Or was he? Whose perspective had she considered? Hers, and only hers. She focused on whether Zephan was paying attention to *her,* whether *she* was alone on the task force, whether the court liked her, and what it would mean to her if she dared to like a prince and was inevitably rejected.

But weren't those reasonable thoughts? Wasn't she right about him? It was irresponsible of him to act that way, both to the crown and her own conflicting emotions. Semra twirled the knife in her fingers. What would it be like to turn her brain off and quiet all the racing thoughts?

Monac had come back to find Zephan sitting with his back against a tree, plucking leaves off a bush and glaring off into the distance. Semra leaned against Zezura, who had found them a couple hours after they made it back to the forest. Semra looked up at Monac as he walked over, and he gestured toward Zephan and arched an eyebrow. *What's up with him?* Semra rolled her eyes and shook her head, returning to oil her perfectly clean blades once again.

It's not worth explaining. And she didn't *want* to explain it.

Semra sheathed one of her knives on her trousers and picked up another. He was the one flirting without thought to its consequences and complaining about living as royalty. *Elitist priss.* But he wasn't, was he? Semra poured a dab of oil onto her cloth, capped off the oil jar, and tossed it to one side.

"Well, this is pleasant," Monac commented drily as he took a seat on the ground and leaned back against another tree. Semra and Zephan both glared at him, and Monac shrugged. "I don't care. You two are being weird, but whatever happened, you need to get over it, because I have news."

"What news?" Zephan asked in a clipped voice.

"Madensig is on high alert. Which is saying something considering it already was *before* the Siler debacle." Monac crossed his arms. "It's going to be nearly impenetrable now, and the drawbridge is only let down for limited times and purposes...neither of which we are privy to. Rumor has it Arnevon and Axis have been fighting over Avaya, but them fighting is nothing new. My guess is one wants to use Avaya's political position to continue with a wedding and the other wants to kill her, but I'm not sure which one of them wants which thing. Maybe they're working something out though, because Avaya is going to be at the tournament."

Having Avaya at the annual tournament meant declaring her presence to all of Belvidore. Once the cat was out of the bag, there would be no going back.

Zephan dropped the leaf in his hands. "Impossible! How does he justify it to the people?"

Monac frowned. "The king's crier announced that Her Royal Highness Princess Avaya of Jannemar would be joining the royal Madensig family in observation of the tournament as an esteemed guest. The people are commanded to act with decorum and respect as our two kingdoms seek peace."

Zephan's eyes narrowed. "There are no peace talks. The war is ongoing, and his army is made up of citizens. How could they think peace was being negotiated?"

"It doesn't matter what the people think." Semra ran the cloth along the blade of her knife one last time and sheathed the blade. If there was anything she'd learned as a mission ready killing and setting up a cover story, it was that the masses were easily manipulated. "They'll believe what they've been spoon-fed, or they'll be quiet to avoid punishment. What matters is getting Avaya."

Monac plucked forest debris from his tunic and dusted it off his hands onto the ground. "Either way, we have to move fast. And our options for getting in are even more restricted than before."

Zephan grimaced. "Even if we got in, we might never get out. We'll need a diversion big enough to draw away a lot of guardsmen."

"There has to be a way across the moat without getting an infection. Maybe the sticks are just rumors."

Semra sniffed. She could bypass all the ground security. "I'm going in on Zezura."

"That's not a great idea." Zephan glanced at the dragon, and Zezura let out a puff of smoke in his direction.

Semra ran her hand along her hide. "It might be our only option. Have a distraction, get somewhere I can lie low until security eases a little again. I don't know where I can go to hide out."

"Maybe you could hide in the cisterns. You know, a deep dark hole alone." Zephan's jaw clinched. "You'd like that."

Semra shot him a dirty look, and he met her gaze evenly.

Monac sighed. "This is asinine. Your Highness, you look like a petulant child, sitting there in a pile of broken leaves. I think you've soundly defeated the forest shrubbery, so you can stop now. Semra, we all know your blades are already clean, and when I walked up you were using them to spy on the prince without him seeing. Now that that's out of the way, can we quit being petty and focus on saving the princess and stopping the war?"

Zephan snapped his head her direction. Semra grimaced and dropped her knife. If Monac noticed her spying, she was slipping.

She lifted her chin. "The cisterns aren't actually a bad idea"

Zephan's mouth dropped open. "You're not serious. It's the worst place to be trapped, and it isn't sustainable for as long as you might need to be in there."

"I've been through worse."

"And exactly how long *would* you be in there?"

Semra shrugged. "A day, maybe two."

"Ridiculous. We're not doing it. Period, the end. We'll get Avaya at the tournament. If we can snatch her before she gets to the royal family's box, maybe we can avoid even deeper international issues than we already have. It's a major concern that they are presenting her publicly to the people. I'm afraid of what their agenda might be, and I'd like to cut it off before getting to that point."

Monac ran a hand through his beard. "Although, confirming the rumors that she *is* in Belvidore might suggest they don't plan on killing her yet."

"*Yet.*" Semra pursed her lips. "They would need it to look

awfully believable if they killed her now. It would be a night-mare of a job, but with Siler employed, it's certainly possible."

Zephan twirled a leaf stem in his fingers. "Subtlety isn't Arnevon's style. I'm not sure he would care if people guessed what had happened, as long as no one could prove it."

Silence hung in the air between them, and Semra took in a deep breath. She let it out slowly, then glanced between Zephan and Monac, both staring into space as they absorbed the problem.

Semra straightened. "We're out of time. Monac and I will have to get her when she comes in for the tournament. It's the only option left."

Zephan glared at her. "I'm going with you."

"No, you're not. I'll need another set of hands, so I'll bring Monac. He's the only one Siler doesn't know."

"And I'm the best bet of my sister trusting you, so I think I should be there."

"It's a terrible idea to have two important people in danger on one mission, for no good reason."

Monac crossed his arms and arched an eyebrow. "You need a lot more sets of hands than two. It's risky, but so is this whole mission. Zephan can handle himself."

"*Thank* you." Zephan's shoulders relaxed and he exhaled. "It's about time somebody acknowledged I'm not that breakable."

"Not *that* breakable, but still *valuable*," Monac said. "The reality is, no matter how good – or how cocky – Semra is, the two of us aren't going to be nearly enough. Not to pluck a royal hostage from the army of protection smothering the king and his family."

Semra rolled her eyes. He was right, of course. With no time to plan, even three would be too few. The mission was insane.

"It's settled then," Zephan said. "I'm going. It's my task force, my mission, my sister. I'm pulling rank, and I'd appreciate you both remembering who leads this mission the next time you try to sideline me."

Semra lifted her chin and ground her teeth. "Fine."

"Fine."

"If you die, I'm running away. I won't tell your father his son died by volunteering to be stupid." She wasn't sure she meant it, exactly, but it was true she wouldn't want to face Turian if Zephan was killed.

"Ah, running away. Sounds about right." Zephan snapped the stem.

Semra's jaw dropped, then she closed it. His words stung. *Wake up, Semra. The world is bigger than you.* But she'd tried that, hadn't she? Being part of something bigger? She'd joined the task force. The one Zephan left.

Monac glanced between them, then slapped his thighs. "Well, that was a high-quality discussion. I'm going to bed. I think we'll all think better with a little sleep. Semra, give me your knives for the night. There's a chill in the air that isn't from the weather, if you know what I mean, and if the prince stars in any of your nightmares tonight, I don't want you deciding to kill him for real. Because then I would have to kill you. Which would be a shame because I kind of like you now."

Semra pursed her lips, then unsheathed her knives and threw them into the tree over his head – *thwap, thwap, thwap* – one after the other. He yelped, then scowled as he pulled them from the trunk. Semra smirked.

She unclasped her dagger and belt and tossed them to him before laying down on the ground to sleep, but sleep wouldn't come. Semra tossed and turned for over an hour before drifting off into a fitful sleep, where Ramas came to kill her, and Avi stood laughing as the paralytic venom set in. King Turian's court crowded about the bars of her cell, smiling and laughing as the blight among them was killed. Turian himself looked on, sad but unmoving, as the memory of no-name Semra was removed forever.

Ramas' voice came to her again, leering at her through the bars. He crossed into the cell and whispered in her ear as the snake wrapped itself around her neck.

"And you ... you are less than nothing. You are the nameless, faceless fly on the wall in a moment of time..."

Who was Semra, anyway? She didn't know her real surname. She had taken on the name of all the dragonlord's children at the naming ceremony, Bandaka, but renounced it when she learned that the Framatar was really Turian's manipulative twin brother, building an assassin army to support his coup for the throne rather than purging the world of evil as he had told them they were doing all their lives. She came from a little nothing town and her parents were dead, murdered by Azi on the mountain for trying to rescue her. She truly was less than nothing.

Zephan stood next to his father, watching her take in ragged breaths and shaking his head. "Addicted to danger. Shame."

Semra tried to run, to turn away, but she was trapped inside an immovable body as she watched everyone wait for her to die.

"Semra, save me!"

Semra jerked her head toward the voice, and her friend Brens looked back at her with wide eyes. "I messed up, but you'll cover for me, won't you? You always look out for me... you'll protect me..."

A faceless assassin stepped forward and slit Brens' throat, and she crumpled to the ground. Semra tried to scream, but no sound came. Her chest burned with pain, and the lump in her throat threatened to choke her completely. Her gaze darted about, frantic to find someone, anyone left to help her.

And then there he was, the only person left who might care she exists, who truly understood her. Siler leaned against the wall of the dungeon, observing her in that casual manner of his. Semra begged him with her eyes. *Help me. Before it's too late...*

Siler shoved off from the wall and reached down to Brens' body. He grabbed Brens' ghostly hand and dragged her to Semra's feet. He disappeared and returned dragging Queen Sharsi's corpse next, depositing her on top of Brens, the knife still in the queen's chest. He said not a word. Next he brought Governor Mallen, Semra's knife in his neck, and one by one the pile of murdered remains grew. Siler leveled her with a cold stare.

"It's just business. It's what we do." Slowly he raised his sword until the tip of the blade touched her chest. "Killers get killed eventually. It's the circle of life, and your head brings a hefty sum." He gave a shrug and reared back to deliver the stroke of death. Semra's lungs unleashed at last, and she screamed.

Semra lurched upright. Her arms were pinned to her sides and Zezura's tail draped over her legs, rooting them to the ground. Semra gasped long pulls of the morning mist into her burning chest. Gray haze diffused the early light into a pensive softness, and as the dungeon melted away to the forest, Semra noticed for the first time that it was Zephan whose arms wrapped around her and pinning her arms down.

Of course. She'd nearly forgotten she was a danger to her companions when she slept. Her stomach soured. Monac knelt three paces away, anxiously watching his prince, and

Semra wondered why he had let Zephan be the one to hold her down in the first place.

Zezura nudged Semra in the face, and she let her body relax as the tension of the nightmare eased. With a gasp she realized she was now resting against Zephan's chest, fully encircled by him, and she squirmed to get her arms free. Zephan dropped his arms and scooted away.

Monac eyed her. "You good?"

Semra nodded, and he grunted but returned to his place on the ground ten feet away, and rolled over.

"Sorry," Semra mumbled, her eyes on the forest floor. She snuck a glance at Zephan. His face was etched with concern, but he was silent. "How did you get over to me before I woke up?"

"I think Zez tried to wake you and couldn't. She ended up waking me up and you looked like you were having a fit or something in your sleep. The two of you share feelings or something, right?"

"Something like that." Semra hadn't considered that the emotions in her dreams might translate to Zezura. Sadness washed over her, and Zezura sent sadness and worry back to her. Somehow the solidarity was comforting, though she felt guilty for sharing the terror of her dreams. Semra wiped tears from her face and swallowed. "Thanks."

"It's nothing. Don't mention it."

Semra paused. "I'm still mad at you," she said softly.

"I know. I'm still mad at you too."

Semra inhaled and nodded. It was a simple exchange, but some piece of her felt a little more whole. "Okay."

Monac moaned from his place and rolled over. "It's great that you're okay and such, and I recognize you're in the middle of some kind of weird moment – I've never heard people be angry so sweetly before – but I'll be mad at you both if you keep me up all night. We have a big day tomorrow."

Semra bit her lip and eased back against Zezura. The dragon nosed her gently and wrapped her tail around her. Tomorrow. In a few short hours, they would sneak into the Tabeun Tournament hosted by Jannemar's greatest enemy – in an arena filled to the brim with witnesses.

26

———

"Why did it have to have *ruffles?* I'll wear the ridiculous hat, but I draw the line at ruffles." Semra tugged the chemise higher, concealing the bandage covering the mark of the dragon's kiss. They had blended the bandage with her skin as best as they could with powders and paste and followed up with as high of a neckline dress as Monac could find.

Monac had returned with a simple off-the-shoulder white chemise dress and blue overgarment that fit over the shoulders, a form-fitting bodice lacing in the front, and wide flowing sleeves. At the top of the chemise across the neckline there was indeed a small ruffle, to Semra's dismay.

"For a person who prides herself on not caring about clothes, you are being pretty high maintenance about a simple ruffle." Monac twirled his hat in his hands before placing it back on his head and tugged at the ends of his somewhat billowing sleeves. A long leather vest fit over his shirt, and he wore high boots over dark trousers.

Monac, Zephan, and Semra were walking toward the tournament grounds to arrive early and scout the route Arnevon,

Axis, Blaise, and Avaya would be taking on the way in. Monac had been able to confirm the route posing as an off-duty guard the night prior, an easy role for a man who was in fact a castle guard.

"I never said I didn't care about clothes. I said I don't care for *dresses*. And anyway, you could have found a different one."

Zephan gave a playful tug to the ruffle on her dress. "You've been through worse."

Semra turned to glare at Zephan as he walked behind Semra and Monac. He grinned, showing off what looked like a missing tooth, and Semra laughed in spite of herself. The tension of the evening before had dissipated with the light of the morning, and Semra was grateful to have clearer air between them.

Both Semra and Monac were outfitted as middle to upper class commoners of Horen, but Zephan had been scaled down to a more invisible station. One of his teeth had been blacked out by using some poor woman's missing eye paints, and he wore a long, threadbare woolen tunic belted at the waist, low scuffed boots, and a stained hooded mantle to top it off. The smell of walnut and garagor root still lingered from the temporary hair dye they had boiled and applied just that morning, turning his natural dirty-blonde hair so brown it was nearly black. His torso was also a bit thicker than usual owing to the thick extra shirt that Monac had insisted he wear under his primary apparel as a security measure – in case he should have to change his appearance quickly.

"Many fashionable necklines do not come up as high as we need to cover the mark," Monac added. "I was lucky to find it, and you'll be happy to wear it."

Semra huffed. "I just don't see why I *had* to come as a woman."

"I hate to be the bearer of bad news, but you are, in fact, a woman." Zephan nudged her and chuckled, then caught himself and drifted away to give her space. A part of her saddened at the distance, but it had been her idea. He was trying to respect her, so why did a pang still hit her chest?

Semra shook off the question and rolled her eyes at Zephan. "Yes, but who came up with the infernal idea that women should wear dresses all the time, no matter the occasion? I mean, surely at the beginning of time when there were hardly any people, they didn't invent clothes and think, 'Oh, we should definitely make half of the population wear more restrictive clothing.' So somewhere along the line, some woman took a tablecloth and wrapped it around herself and thought, 'you know what, this should become a critical aspect of being a woman. In fact, we should make everybody look down on any woman that doesn't wear tablecloths to slow her down and make everyday activities cumbersome.'"

Zephan's eyes twinkled, but he took out the canteen from his bag and concentrated on taking a drink, concealing the rest of his face.

Monac pressed his lips, stifling a smile. "If only you had been there to stop her."

"I probably would have killed her. Actually, it was probably a man. To make it harder for women to run away from them when the men are being stupid."

Zephan snorted water out his nose and spewed the rest of the mouthful on the back of Monac's neck as they walked. Monac pulled back in disgust and wiped it off with his hand, then rolled his eyes and smirked as Zephan was seized by a coughing fit. Semra twisted around, glancing between the men. She frowned. A normal girl wouldn't have made a joke about killing people. A normal girl wouldn't be so opinionated against dresses, either.

Semra's cheeks flushed, and she walked on in silence. They passed a gaggle of giggling young girls in frilly dresses, skipping and twirling in what looked like brand-new frocks for the occasion. Semra's head swiveled as she watched them go, looking on with involuntary distaste. She could never.

Semra caught Zephan watching her out of the corner of her eye, and turned to glare at him. "Why are you smiling? You're being weird."

Zephan smoothed his face into a mocking neutral expression and shook his head. "Nope. This is my face."

Semra raised her eyebrows skeptically. "Monac, why is he being weird?"

"Oh, I'm not getting anywhere near this. You two are on your own."

A buzz of excitement lit the air as the people of Horen and the surrounding area converged for the tournament. The closer they got to the arena, the more people fell into the sea of humanity, until Zephan, Monac, and Semra were caught up in a proper throng of people. The dark gray stone of Madensig Fortress stood out on the hill in the distance, and the city of Horen poured out of doors and down streets to claim the best seats they could wrangle.

Two young boys ran by with toy spears in their hands, raising them over their heads like a battle cry. As the crowd thickened, they were forced to slow down, and the boys paused near Semra.

"You've *never* seen the annual tournament?" said one to the other, absentmindedly tapping the spear on top of his own head. "You've at least heard about The Crumbling, right?"

The other kid rolled his eyes. "*Obviously.* But we've never been rich enough to travel this far before. This time, my father got work nearby."

"Wow." The first boy hopped from one foot to the other. "But don't worry! I'll tell you everything you need to know! It opens with a play of *The Crumbling,* when Aurin betrayed Belvidore by destroying magic instead of using it to become powerful enough to defeat Dorugo. It was cool at first, but now it's boring. We all know what happened. But after that, we get to see the Spear Throw and the Burning Stake events! The other events – the Artifacts of Power, the Undoing, the Human Target, *and* the Final Challenge – all happen tomorrow, and mother says we have to go home after the Undoing. But I say we slip away this year and see the rest!"

Semra grimaced. A *burning stake* event didn't sound like fun. Neither did the others, to be honest. *Human target?*

The arena rose before them with pillars running around its outside, and as they passed under the shade of this outer portion, a portion of the arena was visible through an arched tunnel. The arena was lined with rows of long benches on the sides set higher and higher, angled upwards from the middle so that competitors would stand at ground level, and the sides rose all around to give the audience a better view. There was only one entrance into the arena, and the road Monac had learned the royal family would be taking was wide open and poor for any type of ambush. Considering the landscape of the road and the size of the entourage planned to accompany them, snatching Avaya on their way into the tournament would be impossible. With some preparations during the tournament, getting her on exit was their best bet.

The boys squeezed through imperceptible gaps in the crowd and scampered away, and the arced double doors into the open-air arena greeted them as they were carried along by the current of people. The moment they passed the double doors, the anticipation was palpable. A dirt floor opened up before them, and rows of elevated seats lined the sides with steps in several places leading up through the rows to the walkway at the top level. A stone wall separated the arena from the seats, and an open gate in front of them provided the view into the arena floor. Twisting around, Semra the observation boxes for the royal family and nobles sitting over the arched entrance they had come through, with two sets of semi-circular stairs leading up to it on either side.

Monac leaned in and spoke in a low voice. "We need a position close to the box. And we need eyes on the coachmen after the royals and nobles are in the box and the carriages are brought back outside the arena to wait."

Trumpets sounded, and Semra jerked her head toward the sound. Trumpeters strode forward through the entryway with blue, red, and gold Belvidorian banners dangling from their instruments, and the crowd hastily scattered to either side to make way. Monac was pulled across to the opposite end, and Semra and Zephan were pressed backward toward the stairs. Semra glanced at Zephan. They were early. By an hour.

The clip-clop of horse hooves and the rumble of coaches met Semra's ears as she craned her neck for a better view. Four elaborate carriages rolled into the arena flanked by a mounted guard escort. The fourth and final carriage was dripping in gold and gemstone accents, flaunting an opulence like Semra had never seen. An announcer called out the names of several nobles as they exited their carriages.

"Duke Foran of Yulineset."

The duke exited his coach and made a dramatic bow to the audience, sweeping a feathered hat low to the ground as he did so before straightening and angling confidently toward the stairs into the box amid cheers.

"Lady Generiva Swathel."

Zephan chortled from behind Semra, and she twisted to give him an odd look. He grinned and leaned forward to whisper in her ear.

"You don't remember Lady Swathel? I believe she fell ill before our gala, but sent her trusted representative Axelia Berinon in her stead. Ah, if only we had known how to best represent her ladyship."

Recognition dawned on Semra and her lips tipped into a smile as she took in the large woman with immensely flouncing silken skirts and layers of ruffles draped about her from head to toe. Axelia Berinon had been the alias Zephan and Aviama created for Semra to attend the gala in Jannemar. Semra turned her head into Zephan to whisper back.

"I'm sure you did the best you could. Clearly, the quota for ruffles in the country had been met with that dress. No seamstress in Belvidore could be called upon to make another with half its glory."

Zephan let out a burst of laughter, and it sounded like home. Her heart twisted.

"Her Royal Highness and the esteemed guest of the king, Princess Avaya of Jannemar!"

The final carriage door opened, and Princess Avaya stepped out into the arena. The woman was every bit the princess, composed and dressed in a gorgeous emerald green gown that accentuated her figure and perfectly matched the shade of her eyes. Semra marveled for a moment at her beauty and the grace with which she walked. Semra walked quickly, efficiently, and – when the occasion called for it – imperceptibly. Avaya walked to gather the attention of everyone around her, and she succeeded. A murmur rolled through the crowd, and a smattering of claps mixed with boos.

"Her Royal Highness, Princess Blaise!"

The contrast between Avaya and Blaise could not possibly have been overstated. Surely this pale, skin and bones creature was not related to the two broad-shouldered Belvidorian royals Semra had seen at the gala in Jannemar! Blaise emerged from the carriage with her arms glued to her sides, her white-blond hair plastered into a tight hairstyle, and the rich blue of her gown the most impressive thing about her. She looked as though she might be carried away by a light gust of wind. The two princesses made their way toward the stairs to the observation box, in the direction the nobles had gone before them, with several members of the guard following closely.

"His Royal Highness, our Crown Prince Axis!"

Axis drew himself up to a towering height and turned to offer winning smiles to every angle of the audience. Two young girls to Semra's left let out longing sighs and a giggle. Semra snorted, and they glared at her. Semra rolled her eyes and returned her gaze to the arena. *Everybody hates assassins, but what about empty-headed flirts?* They deserved at least as much derision.

"His Glorious Majesty, Ruler of Belvidore, King Arnevon!"

Thunderous applause rang out as the king stepped out, dressed in fur-lined cape, exaggerated gilded attire, a gem-studded chain around his neck, and a crown upon his head. The gems on his chain made Semra think of the Framatar's gem-encrusted collar, but the Framatar's collar was far more extravagant than even the jewels of King Arnevon. The king raised his hand to the crowd and smiled.

The first piece of rotten fruit hit Avaya as she reached the base of the stairs. *Whizz, splat. Whizz. Whizz.* A smattering of tomato juice splashed onto Axis's shoe from the place where it hit the ground near Avaya's feet. Semra reeled back in time as an apple flew by her ear toward the princess. One of the Belvidorian guard reached out and snatched it from the air inches from Avaya's face, then spun in Semra's direction to face the thrower. Semra gasped and ducked down, tugging the edge of her hat further over her face. It was Siler.

The apple whipped through the air and pegged the young man behind Semra with a *thwack* that would certainly leave a bruise. The culprit cried out and melted into the crowd, and Semra peered around the woman in front of her in time to see Siler's furious face before turning back to check in with Avaya. Semra's head spun. There was no reason for Siler to become so angry. It wasn't his role to take revenge. His job was to deliver her to Arnevon, and potentially keep her alive, and it was going to take more than a little fruit juice to kill Avaya. Did he really care about her?

Her mouth went dry. Here he was again, the last assassin colleague who was supposed to care about her, standing in precisely the place he should not be. Who had hired him? Why had he taken a job that betrayed Semra?

Azi's dark voice slipped into her consciousness. *My dear, my dear...I am the only one who has never left you.* But he had betrayed her, and far before she'd been aware of it. He'd slaughtered her parents on the mountain. He'd threatened Brens so that even her closest friend turned against her, and he had her killed when she dared restore their friendship.

But Siler was stronger than Brens. He knew exactly what he was doing. Bile rose in Semra's throat.

Indignation gripped her. Even keeping to his mission, Siler should have minded his business, stayed invisible as one of the guardsmen, and let the fruit tarnish that perfect gown, on that perfect body of the perfect royal. She would look as sickeningly beautiful with a little extra color on her silk than without.

Axis caught up to Avaya and used a handkerchief to gingerly wipe juice off her face and arm. Siler paused and withdrew again to the sidelines. The crowd sat in a stunned hush. In full view of everyone, the Prince of Belvidore ran his thumb over the Princess of Jannemar's chin, then took her hand in his and quickly led her up the stairs to the box, his jaw set and his eyes dark.

Zephan took an involuntary step forward, bumping into Semra, and she reached back and gripped his wrist. With a start, Semra realized in that moment she had nearly forgotten Zephan was there. Now it was impossible to miss, red hot anger curling his lip into a sneer as his glare bored into an oblivious Axis from the mass of commoners.

At her touch, he stiffened, and then relaxed. His eyes held a battle of torn emotion as he turned to Semra, seeming as though he wanted to skewer the prince of Belvidore for touching his sister, yet unwilling to blow his cover. In a moment of realization, Zephan glanced down at his wrist where Semra still gripped it, and Semra swore under her breath and released him. She stepped away, cursing her stupidity. *Right.* It would be odd for a well-to-do lady to associate so boldly with a ragtag peasant boy. Better to be socially predictable, normative, and invisible.

Semra refocused her attention on Avaya and shook her head. Even as a hostage, stained by rotten fruit, Avaya was confident and poised, as elegant as she was hateful. She lifted her chin and practically floated up the stairs with an air of indifference and the endorsement of the crown prince. Despite her arrogance, Avaya truly was excellent at playing the cool, collected diplomat.

The king's smile had vanished, and he marched up the stairs with purpose. The people watched with rapt attention, and Semra thought she would have been able to hear a pin drop. King Arnevon stood before his throne positioned in the front of the box overlooking the arena, with his daughter set on his left and his heir on his right. Avaya sat, gown stained, on the other side of Axis. Arnevon stepped forward and put his hands on the wall to address the crowd.

Semra glanced across the arena to the audience across the way and spotted Monac. He made eye contact with her briefly, then sent an anxious glance to the arena entrance. With everyone listening to the speech and attention fixed directly above the archway in, slipping out to track the coachmen would be impossible. They would have to wait. Zephan shifted uncomfortably behind her.

"Welcome one and all to Belvidore's annual Tabeun Tournament!" The king spread his hands and the crowd roared, eager to move on from the tension of the rotten fruit debacle. He waited for the sound to die down, then gestured for them to sit, and began again. "On this day we remember a distant era hundreds of years past, an era of strength, innovation, and magic. We remember when Belvidore was respected across the nations as bringing forth the most formidable mages, the bravest men and women demonstrating grit, determination, and a spirit that refuses to accept defeat. That same spirit lives in us today!"

The sea of people stamped their feet and *whooped* their approval. Zephan clapped, though his face remained stony, and Semra followed suit. Arnevon soaked in their praise, in no hurry to stop the outpour. The crowd quieted, and he spoke again.

"The original tournaments brought nations together, celebrating strengths, learning from one another, and admiring talent the world over. It is fitting, then, that despite the dark times in which we find ourselves, we should welcome a foreign guest – once again bringing kingdoms together." The people were silent, with a smattering of awkward applause. Arnevon looked sternly upon his subjects. "I will not have my guest scorned. My hospitality and reputation as host dishonored is to dishonor me and our great nation. I trust that there will be no further outbursts. They would surely be met with dire consequences.

"Our history with Jannemar has been long and bitter. Our northern neighbors' desire for magical monopoly, and desperation to control both Rivers of the Wellspring and the power they contained before The Crumbling, brought about much of the friction that remains today. Still, the individuals in power today are not the same as those whom my forefather His Majesty Mauve Madensig fought so valiantly all those years ago when he built our great fortress and moved our country's capital to Horen."

Avaya lifted her chin at the condescending mention of her home and family, drawing her shoulders back ever so slightly. Semra squinted to make out the figures standing along the sides by the nobles, and was rewarded with finding Siler's silhouette, standing in the shadows. Unreadable. Semra wondered if he had double-tapped his wrist before today, that thing he did before missions. She wondered if he suspected Semra was in attendance, and what he might be planning to do were he to find her. Was she reduced from friend to target? A mission? *Why did you betray me?* Anger burned in her chest, and she jumped when she heard Zephan's low voice in her ear.

"It's laughable, his portrayal of Jannemar. The Surion and Dezapi rivers were Jannemar's territory long before The Crumbling, and Belvidore was so frantic to control magic that they started a needless war for the Surion Strip. Ultimately they failed to take the Strip, but gained ground and expanded their borders to where they are today and built Madensig with a moat fed by the Surion River. They drowned themselves in water from the Wellspring, hoping beyond for shreds of leftover magic."

Arnevon spoke again. "King Turian has made a multitude of mistakes, but today his own flesh and blood has been sent to us, a representative of Jannemar, to negotiate peace, to remedy wild accusations against Belvidore, and to make good on a promise. Today we are again neighbors, and hope of unity shines bright." The king turned to Avaya and inclined his head in a slight nod. "Welcome, Princess Avaya of Jannemar. We extend our gratitude at your traveling to be with us today, and we look forward to establishing good memories together at this year's Tabeun Tournament: the birth of a new era!"

The people erupted in applause, leaping to their feet, clapping, and hollering. The far left corner of the arena started chanting, *Belvidore forever! Belvidore forever!* An older woman clapped her hands near Semra and leaned over to a friend, saying, "Oh, what wonderful news! Peace talks – our boys will be home soon!"

A twinge of guilt knotted in Semra's stomach. Not because she was exactly guilty, but because Semra knew it was a lie. There were no peace talks. Avaya had not been sent willingly by Turian for negotiation or apology, as he had made it sound. And the body count continued to rise in the name of the war effort. Semra hadn't known the history before, but now she saw that Belvidore and Jannemar's conflict over the Surion Strip spanned more than a generation or two of animosity. It was hundreds of years in the making, and as always, there were two vastly different sides to the story.

Avaya leaned over to whisper in Axis's ear, and after a moment Axis nodded and spoke privately with his father. Arnevon's face clouded for a moment, and there was a pause as everyone waited for what might happen next. They spoke for another moment before at last Arnevon gave a short, hesitant nod, and turned to the people once more.

"Our esteemed guest, Princess Avaya, will now address you herself!"

27

———

Arnevon wagged his finger toward the audience as though they were naughty children. "Mend the first impression you gave of yourselves and give the Jannemari princess a warm welcome."

Semra felt Zephan stiffen beside her, and anxiety burgeoned Semra's insides as Avaya stood, curtsied low before Arnevon and turned to the people with a smile. The audience applauded politely for fear of angering their king again, and all eyes rested on her obnoxiously perfect face.

"Thank you for your generous hospitality," Avaya said with an incongruous earnestness that made the people squirm. She moved on without batting an eye. "It is long overdue we form our opinions of one another not by rumor but through experience. I am proud to fulfill the hope for unity that you have carried in your hearts so long. Our enemies shall indeed be struck down, but let our swords hesitate. I have come not as your opposition but as your friend."

Semra and Zephan exchanged glances. She sounded good. Every hair was in place, every muscle poised, every feature of Avaya's face devoted to delivering the appropriate expression at the precise moment. Semra noted the "us" and "we" language as Avaya placed herself firmly on the audience's side as a partner rather than a threat. Maybe it was a good strategy, but hearing the words still felt like a slap in the face. Surely, she could have made herself sympathetic to her listeners without being quite so bold. And who did she mean when she said, *"our enemies"*?

"Six hundred years. Six hundred years we have been living in a magicless society, and though the economy has recovered and our problem-solving has shifted, the core of us all remains the same – to control our destiny, to live for freedom, to find some corner of happiness.

"We are living in historic times. It is time that the only thing rotten be fruit left out too long, and not our divisive spirits. My father and I are so encouraged by the welcome of King Arnevon and his willingness to negotiate the peace that both of our kingdoms so deeply crave. Though the misunderstandings between our nations have been many, it is time we heal old wounds."

Semra's hands balled into fists. As if a kidnapping could help international relations. What had she been threatened with? And worse, what large-scale damage might Avaya create in the effort to maintain her safety?

"Heal old wounds how? By faking negotiations that will fail?" Semra hissed to Zephan.

He snorted. "Or by sucking up to Belvidore and ignoring the fact that they started a needless war and feud six hundred years ago, have been obsessed with the lost magic ever since, and in the last two months literally started another war and *kidnapped* her to coerce Jannemar into surrendering control of the Strip."

Avaya continued.

"So today I say to you thank you, for your attention, for the resilient spirit I will continue to see today in your people in the tournament, and for the chance of ushering in a new era of peace – one of unity and love."

The corner of Arnevon's mouth tipped up, and Axis smiled widely at Avaya. Avaya gripped hand and Axis swung it high in the air; the throng leaped to their feet in response and thundered their applause.

"She's really something isn't she?" said the woman to Semra's right, speaking up again. "Perhaps the Shamarans have someone sensible in the family after all!"

Doors on the opposite end of the arena opened, and a rolling stage was pushed into the center. The bustle of movement and hum of conversation picked up again as a man ran out to the center of the arena to introduce the play of *The Crumbling*. It was more of an elaborate illusion show than anything, and Semra imagined a series of mirrors, trap doors, and other tricks hidden beneath the stage to pull off the deceptions.

"Welcome to the Tabeun Tournament, where elemental melders gather from across the world in harmony, to celebrate the finest Tabeun talents and sportsmanship ever seen!"

Semra glanced across the arena to Monac. He was already moving. It was time. Semra waited until Monac was through the exit and out of sight before edging her way to the end of the stairs, leaving Zephan behind. He had reluctantly agreed to play lookout from inside the arena, only coming out to alert them for emergencies. She glanced up at the observation box at Siler's shadow, but he still stood facing the show. Semra reached the edge of her row and paused, waiting for a distraction to cover her exit.

She focused on her breathing until it was slow and steady. Adrenaline laced her body with the thrill of the mission, but her mind dropped into that focused space that she relied upon to keep her on task and alive.

The announcer continued narrating the show. "But Aurin allowed the curse of the *ogon* to grow in him, his fireblood corrupting the pure Belvidorian blood in his veins..."

The man playing Aurin threw his hands in a dramatic arc over his head, and from his hands – *or sleeves,* Semra thought – fire shot high up into the air. The crowd gasped and applauded, and Semra slipped beneath the archway under the box. To her right a door in the wall of the tunnel was cracked open to reveal a small sitting room, the raucous laughter of the coachmen carrying out through the door. Someone inside barked at them to keep it down, and Semra crossed the entryway tunnel to the outside covered portion where pillars lined the structure all the way around it. The carriages would be lined here in the shade somewhere, waiting for the event to end.

Semra turned to the left and around the curved side of the arena to find the four ornate carriages waiting with their horses. Relationships with princes and schmoozing of nobles did not come easy to her, but this – the scent of horse mixing with dust and danger in the air, the promise of chaos – *this* she could do. She quickened her pace and reached the first carriage when a hand grabbed her wrist and yanked her behind one of the pillars. Semra threw a punch, but her abductor caught her fist in his hand and clamped his other palm over her mouth.

Her eyes widened. It was Monac. Monac mouthed, *Siler,* and jerked his head in the direction she had come from. Semra's blood ran cold, and a chill ran up her spine. Every plan they could hastily concoct would be at risk with Siler around. He'd had longer to plan, and he threw everything out of balance. She strained her ears for cues of Siler's approach, but heard nothing aside from the applause of the crowd inside as they reacted to some spectacle or other.

A footstep sounded on the other side of the pillar, and Semra jumped. He was far closer than Semra had imagined. She stiffened and Monac held eye contact with her as he dropped his hand from her mouth and motioned for her to stay where she was. Monac gave her a nod and then leaped around the corner.

"Ahhh!" Monac screamed into Siler's face on the other side of the pillar, then laughed maniacally and stumbled forward and to the side, out of Semra's view. Siler grunted and Semra heard the shuffle-drag of feet as Monac collided with Siler and one half-dragged the other. Semra could only assume Monac had thrown his weight onto Siler and Siler was the one pulling Monac along.

"What are you doing out here?" Siler demanded.

"Whaaaat're yew *not* doin' here?" Monac drawled. "Yews are in the out, whens yew guards should be in the guarrrds' houses! Guarrrds houses...guards *hooses*!"

Semra marveled at Monac's complete dedication as he transformed from solemn, disciplined bodyguard to utterly sloshed buffoon. If he were putting on the act for anyone other than Siler, she would have laughed. Semra held her breath as the scuffing, shuffling sounds continued.

"You can't be out here." Siler's voice. "Go in and don't cause any trouble, or go home and sleep it off."

"I'm not de waaan causin' troubles! I had nooo troubles befores yew come to be hollerin' yer hollers ah meee."

"Mouth off at me again and you'll catch my fist. *Aughh!!* Get off me!"

A *thud* signaled a body hitting the floor, and Semra winced. Monac grunted. Siler must have thrown him to the ground. She pressed herself tight against the pillar. If he walked four paces forward, she'd be caught.

"Get up or be dragged," Siler said to Monac from the other side of the pillar. "If you can't walk, you're not going back in there."

"No, no, not right. My ferrrmly in der." Semra's brows furrowed as she tried to make out the unintelligible sounds that came from Monac after that, but it was no use deciphering the babble. The sounds receded toward the entrance, and Semra slowly let out a breath.

Semra stood there against the pillar for a long time, not moving. Finally she pulled up her heaping skirts to withdraw a knife, and slid to stand at back of the first carriage. She examined the leather straps suspending the carriage body from the chassis, and carefully sawed the underside of one of the straps, enough to weaken but not quite break. She drew the knife along the strap once more, when running footsteps echoed down the path toward her.

Semra lurched upright, knife in hand, then huffed a sigh of exasperation and relief. "You two have *got* to stop surprising me."

"Better me than Siler," Zephan said. "You need to hurry up. Give me a knife and I'll help."

Semra hiked her skirts up to her thigh and pulled another knife free, then tossed it to Zephan. He caught it without breaking eye contact, then patted one of the horses on his way down to the next carriage. Semra weakened the strap of the opposite corner on the coach she had been working on, then moved to follow Zephan.

The royal carriage was the last one of the line. Zephan had just started on it when two sets of footsteps hurried out the entrance once again. Zephan spun and wrapped an arm around Semra's waist, tugging her behind the royal carriage as the pair of guards approached.

Semra's breath caught as they stood nose to nose, each of them still holding a knife. A thousand butterflies burst in her stomach at his proximity. She could hear his breathing quicken, and his arm tightened. The footsteps drew nearer, and Semra slipped an arm around Zephan's neck and spoke in a hushed tone with her lips at his ear.

"I need my knife back."

"Slaughter doesn't seem like the best idea," he murmured back against her hair.

Goosebumps ran up her arms. What would have been like to let Zephan flirt with her, to be his brightness in the dark, the way he had described? To let him care for her however deeply he wanted.

The guards' paces slowed as they approached, patrolling the area. Semra's lips brushed Zephan's ear as she spoke, and his arm pulled her in. "No, I mean we shouldn't be seen with knives next to the king's coach."

Zephan pulled away and rested his forehead on hers. "We still have one more strap to cut."

Semra's heart stopped. Zephan's thundered under her palm. Somewhere the mission ready part of her was screaming about attachment and weakness and focus, but it all felt a little hazy.

"You! You there!" one of the guards yelled.

Adrenaline shot through her body. It was bad enough to be caught near the royal carriage, but if the guards learned they'd tampered with it, they'd be dead. Mere seconds stood between them and capture, and in the space of those seconds they would provide a convincing reason for commoners to be at the king's carriage, or pay the price. It was her heart that produced the solution, but the mission ready part of her could not deny its usefulness.

Semra tilted her face up to Zephan and said the only words that came to mind, the only excuse for two people being precisely where they should not be. "Kiss me."

"W-what?" Zephan stammered, but she didn't leave room for any further argument. Semra brought her lips to his and kissed him, breathing in his scent, flooded with warmth from her head to her toes. Zephan hesitated, but only a moment, kissing her back earnestly yet somehow soft all at once.

Semra lifted her leg and pulled at her skirt, breaking their kiss long enough to breathe, *"knife,"* as the guards ran up before Zephan claimed her mouth again. Zephan pressed her up against the coach and ran his knife-holding hand under her skirt and up her thigh, searching until he found the sheaths strapped there. He slipped the blade inside, and her mind went fuzzy at his touch. Their connection, this kiss, was everything she'd refused to admit she so desperately wanted. At last, under the guise of distracting the guards, she released every ounce of restrained emotion, giving in to every craving of closeness.

But they had one last thing to do, and the guards were nearly upon them. Semra reached behind her, stabilizing herself as they kissed, on the last leather strap they needed. Her knife hid in her palm on the underside of the strap.

"Hey! Get away from there!"

Semra slashed at the strap, but slipped, making a shallow cut. Zephan's hand lingered on her thigh, and Semra brought her knife around her back to drop it into another sheath on the same leg before they straightened.

What if the kiss was not enough? What if the guards examined the coaches? Was there another reason to be there that wouldn't lead to death? Her swirling skirts concealed her knives once again, and she ripped a handful of decorative gemstone baubles off the extravagant coach as she stood. Zephan eyed her and quickly grabbed her hand, the gems trapped between their palms.

It was risky. Theft of that caliber had a solid possibility of death. But murder or attempted murder of the monarch left no question at all.

One of the guards looked positively flustered, refusing to make eye contact with Semra. The other was angry.

"How dare you approach the king's coach? If you want to mess around, do it somewhere else."

"Of course, we're so sorry," Semra gushed. "Please, please forgive us. Our parents don't approve, and our moments together are short."

"It's really none of my business to care. I'm escorting you back into the arena, and if you cause any more trouble, you'll be lucky if you're kicked out instead of something more severe. Move."

Semra and Zephan mumbled their apologies and hurried back toward the entryway. Semra's heart still pounded from the fire of their kiss, an electric current running through her body from the touch of their linked hands. She dared not look at him as they reached the tunnel, desperately trying to think about anything else. *Was the strap weakened enough? Did Monac get away? Did Zephan get the same butterflies I did when our lips touched?* Semra played the kiss through her mind again, his hand on her leg, their bodies close...she shook her head. *It needed to happen to cover us. It doesn't matter. It can't matter.*

Semra picked up her pace to compensate for her racing thoughts, Zephan keeping up with long strides, until she bumped into something solid. She looked up, startled, and found herself staring directly into piercing gray eyes. Siler stood inches from her face, arms folded, a furious disdain playing across this face.

Siler glanced between them, and Semra and Zephan instinctively dropped their hands. Zephan rolled the gemstones into his palm as they parted and clasped his hands behind his back. Semra looked at him in alarm, then relaxed her expression. She wanted to have the gems. It was their backup excuse to being at the carriage, and whoever held them carried the highest risk.

Semra smoothed back stray hairs from her face and her cheeks flushed as she realized how the two of them must look. Of course, a moment ago for the guards, that's precisely how they needed to look. Heat washed over her at the lingering sensation of Zephan's lips on hers. Did he feel it too? She chanced another glimpse his direction, to find him already looking at her. They both looked away.

The irritable guard drew himself up tall and cleared his throat. "You were right, sir, there were people outside the arena. Just these lovebirds, though. Nothing serious."

"I don't recall asking for your opinion," Siler snapped. Semra drew back. The guard was years older than Siler, yet Siler's position as a royal bodyguard elevated his status. Siler drilled the guard with a cool stare. "Search them."

Semra's stomach lurched into her throat. Siler knew exactly where she always kept her knives. Semra wondered what penalty there would be for carrying weapons into an event with the king and his children, and stealing jewels off their coach. If Arnevon was as paranoid as rumor would have them believe, Semra doubted the policy was lenient. Would Siler really sell her out if he knew she might be killed?

The guards reached for them and Semra bolted, reaching for Zephan's hand with the gemstones in it and yanking him with her. His hand opened to receive hers and fear gripped her –it was empty. She ripped her hand from his and spun behind him to grab his other hand as they ran, but he pulled his fist in toward himself. He was going to take the fall. No, no, no! It was all wrong. Zephan would be killed. If this mission went any more south, Turian would have sent his son with Semra to save Avaya, and wound up with two of his three children dead along with his wife.

The guards chased them through the tunnel as the announcer rang out, "Please welcome our competitors for the Spear Throw!"

Semra dove for Zephan's hand and he slapped her hand away with his free hand as the bashful guard lifted Semra off the ground. A low guttural growl escaped her throat as her fingers grazed Zephan's shoulder and she was dragged backward. Zephan spun and landed a punch on the guard's jaw before the irritable guard barreled into him from the side, and Zephan and the guard careened into a line of competitors standing with their spears outside the gate about to run into the arena.

The competitors took off into the arena at the same time Zephan and the irritable guard bowled over the last contestant, who threw his arm out to break his fall, only to have the full weight of two grown men snap it like a twig as the three of them tumbled to the ground. The stolen gemstones from Zephan's fist scattered in the dust as gasps from the crowd went up at the commotion.

The deep voice of King Arnevon bellowed from the box above them, silencing the arena. Every ear strained to hear his words, each body in the mass of people inclined toward the scuffle at the arena gate. "What is the meaning of this?"

Semra's eyes flew wide as saucers as she saw Zephan's life delicately held in Siler's clenched fists. Zephan looked at her only once as he was hauled to his feet, his eyes filled with resolve. He would take the blame and distance himself from her if he could.

The desperation she'd felt for Zephan against the carriage surged through her, a powerful wave that refused to be ignored. *The kiss wasn't an excuse for the mission. You meant every moment of it. The mission was the excuse for the kiss.* Fear worked its way through her like icy fingers. She couldn't lose him.

Semra tore her eyes away from Zephan and met Siler's stony gaze. Questioning. Angry. She mouthed the only thing she could think of. *Please.* He had to know they were there for Avaya.

Siler glanced up at the box, hesitated, and then bowed. "It seems this piece of riff-raff didn't want to compete for prize money. He thought he'd steal it from the royal carriage instead."

Arnevon's eyes narrowed and flicked to Semra. "And the girl?"

Semra bowed her head quickly as the king looked between Zephan in his rags and her in her ruffles. Would Arnevon know her from the gala in Jannemar?

Siler shrugged. "Gemstones were not the only prize he was after, Your Majesty. But she is clearly above his station."

Something inside her twisted at his words. She looked up from the guard's arms, but Siler refused to meet her eye again. Semra chanced a glimpse of Zephan across from her, and he too was looking down at the ground. The fallen competitor lay on the ground, moaning as he cradled his broken limb. A healer ran forward to tend to him, examining the unnatural angle of his arm. The five other spearmen shifted their weight awkwardly inside the gate to the arena.

Arnevon leaned over the observation box to peer down at Zephan. Zephan grimaced in silent apology, exposing his blacked-out tooth. Semra marveled that the paint remained, and Arnevon let out a harsh laugh. Murmurs rippled through the crowd.

"So you want a chance at fortune, young man? To win the heart of the lady, hmm?"

Zephan said nothing, but dipped his head into as close a bow as he could manage in the irritable guard's grasp.

"You are in luck. It seems my need today is not for rolling heads, but entertainment. You've removed a contestant from the tournament, and therefore you shall take his place. If you win, you get the prize money, the girl, and your freedom. If you lose, you will be arrested on the spot and thrown into the dungeon until such a time as I am in the mood to properly punish you for daring rob the royal family. What do you say to my gracious offer?"

Zephan swallowed and tilted his head up toward the king. "I accept."

28

Semra's chest caved in. There had to be another way. Every second Zephan spent under the scrutiny of Belvidore was another opportunity for them to see past his disguise. But if he were arrested now, what chance would she have of breaking him free?

Siler ripped Semra from the guard's arms and marched her outside the arena gate. She craned her neck to see Zephan released into the arena and handed a spear. Six small hay bale targets were rolled out and set in a line on the far end as each man took his place. A large backstop was pulled in behind the targets to protect the audience from bad throws, and a line they would not be permitted to pass when throwing was drawn in front of the contestants.

Zephan adjusted his grip on the spear. He was a skilled swordsman. She knew that for certain. But how was his spear throw? His life may well depend on the answer.

"You're an idiot for coming here," Siler hissed in her ear. "You should have taken Zezura and gone."

Red-hot fire flared in Semra's chest. Siler had gone into

business with slimy Belvidore and betrayed her twice, and still *he* was giving advice? "I'm going to kill you."

"Considering that publicly revealing any advanced level of skill would blow your cover, and that you are in my custody, and I have in fact beaten you before, I can only assume you are being facetious. Focus on not getting yourself killed. Behave."

Semra clenched her jaw but bit her tongue, instead turning to watch as Zephan pulled his arm back. His stance and grip were decent, but she hadn't seen him test the spear to find its balance point. Had she missed it, or had he forgotten? How confident was he that the Belvidorian spears were made with the same weights as Jannemar?

The first round of spears flew at the targets. Two contestants hit the inner bullseye, the third and fourth hit the outer ring, and fifth fell short. Zephan hit the outer edge, and Semra winced. Siler let out a low whistle.

"Not looking good for princey."

Semra's face flushed. "If you don't stop threatening his life, I won't care whose cover I blow when I take you down. Don't use that word. How many throws do they get?"

"Six. Best throw counts, and whoever is in last place is eliminated."

The second throw had three on the outer ring of the target, one in the dirt beyond the target, and two on the second ring. Zephan landed his in the second ring – an improvement from his first throw, but he would have to do better to move forward. Semra sucked in her breath as they threw a third, fourth, and fifth time. The announcer called out the final throw.

A piece of fruit sailed through the air toward Zephan, hitting him in the shoulder as he reared back to throw. Zephan released the spear, but his face was contorted with the knowledge that the damage was done. His form suffered from the blow to his shoulder. The first spearman hit bullseye. The second and third hit outer ring. The fourth hit inner ring, the fifth his bullseye, and Zephan's throw sailed past the target into the backstop, quivering there in the wood.

Semra gasped. They were going to take him. The two guards started jogging out into the arena, when the assessor on the field held up a hand. "Contestant number four is disqualified," he called out. "His foot passed the line on throw. Contestant six remains in play."

Semra leaned against the gate for support as the air in her burning lungs came out in a rush. How long had she been holding her breath? Zephan was safe! For now.

Siler tugged on her arm. "I'm going to send you back to the guard room. Get away once I'm gone, but if you try to escape while I'm with you, I'll catch you. I have a reputation to uphold."

"I'm not leaving him." Semra planted her feet, but Siler dragged her backward with little difficulty. Her fingers dug into Siler's skin, but he didn't flinch. He didn't react at all. She was no more trouble than a sack of potatoes.

Semra twisted around to look back into the arena, and Zephan's eyes locked onto hers. *Fear.* It struck them both, straight to the bone. Where was Monac? Did he feel as helpless as she did?

The announcer's booming voice called out across the stadium. "Next, the Burning Stake event!" Murmurs rumbled through the crowd. The announcer continued. "An important person from each contestant's life has been selected to participate in this event, serving as a reminder of what we fight for. We fight for what is good, for those we love. Magic protected us and our loved ones."

Siler picked up his pace and Semra stumbled, breaking

eye contact with Zephan and turning to watch her feet as she hurried after Siler. His grip on her arm tightened and she winced. Something in his expression grew strained.

The announcer spoke again. "Your Majesty, I'm afraid the loved one retained for the sixth contestant was released to care for him when he was injured. We are short."

King Arnevon's loud voice barked from the box overhead. "Bring out the girl."

Semra's heart skipped a beat. They wanted her as leverage in the arena. How realistic was a burning stake event? Siler kept walking. Footsteps ran up behind them and a guard called to Siler.

"Raven, the king commands the girl be brought to the arena. Surely you heard him. I can escort her."

Siler stopped and slowly turned, his grip nearly cutting off the circulation in Semra's arm. "I am fully capable of escorting the woman," he said, with a bite to his tone. Siler set his jaw and whirled Semra around, angling them again toward the arena.

"What exactly is the Burning Stake event?" Semra's chest tightening and her eyes darting across the open space. The tall gate on the opposite end opened and six platforms were wheeled out, wooden stakes standing six feet high fixed on top, with kindling arrayed at its base.

"The fire is controlled in a ring around the platforms, not on the platforms themselves. They lit the actual platforms on fire the first year under Madensig – the flames grew too quickly and the smoke killed two loved ones in minutes. They rescued the others, barely, but they had burn scars the rest of their lives, and a third died later from complications."

A series of wooden structures were brought out and erected next. Six climbing ropes dangled from thirty feet in the air with a knife fixed at the top of each rope, followed by an eight-foot wall, a sandbag pulley hoist.

A gruff, bearded man working the arena met them as Siler marched Semra across the grounds toward the last platform and stake. "I'll take her," he rasped.

Siler pursed his lips, then gave a curt nod and handed her over. Semra glanced back at him over her shoulder as she was led away. Did he have any remorse for his betrayal? Didn't he understand they never would have come to the arena if he hadn't stopped them at Madensig?

Siler looked at her hard before turning on his heel and striding back to the observation box. Zephan's gaze was fixed on her from across the arena as the raspy-voiced man tugged her to the final platform, helped her up, and brought her wrists behind her.

Semra shifted her feet on the dry sticks and grasses arranged at the base of the stake. Kindling. Were tournaments usually so dangerous? Wasn't it a shadow of the Tabeun Tournaments? But then, plenty of people had died in those too. Semra glanced to her left at the five other platforms and saw an older man, perhaps someone's father, a young man, perhaps a brother, and three women, all tied in the same way she was. The young man's eyes were wide, but he lifted his chin when he saw Semra looking at him. The woman next to Semra looked cool as a cucumber, standing there with her shoulders back, flashing smiles at the contestants.

Semra swallowed hard and followed her gaze to Zephan, then looked away again. *Don't let them see a strong attachment.* Where was Monac? She scanned the crowd, trying to ignore the bite of the rope as the knots were cinched tight around her strained, flexed wrists. Curious stares greeted her, some doubtful, some excited. All filled with anticipation of the event. The announcer spoke, and the pressure of their attention was diverted.

"As always for this event, each contestant must climb the rope, retrieve the knife, scale the wall, hoist the sandbags, and free their loved one. Once they have done so, each pair shall race to ring the bell at the gate. The pair to finish last shall be disqualified – or in the thief's case, arrested."

The six men took their places behind their starting lines, and Semra relaxed her fists. Tensing her muscles while being tied gained her only the smallest of advantages when relaxed. The knots were strong. The bearded man had done a good job.

The horn blew, and the men ran for the ropes. The man next to Zephan leaped up and caught the rope in his hands while his legs hung free, flying up the rope hand over hand with nothing but the strength of his arms. Zephan looped his foot around the rope and pulled himself upward one bit at a time, landing him squarely in the middle of the pack.

Semra slowly began rubbing her wrists against each other, using the stake between her wrists to pull at the tension. Flames jumped up in circles around each of the contestants, the fire clinging to some substance drawn on the ground. Her heart jumped, and she glanced to her left, where flirty smiles girl stood unconcerned. A harmless visual display for drama.

Semra took a breath and returned her focus to her wrists, casting her gaze back to the rope climb to check on Zephan. He plucked the knife from the top of the structure and scurried down the rope, passing two more contestants as his feet hit the ground. The man next to Zephan was already at the top of the wall obstacle, holding a significant lead on the other contestants, and grinned back at his cocky beau next to Semra. He balanced on the top of the wall and bowed to the crowd with a flourish before leaping to the arena floor and rolling to his feet.

Great. I see what they see in each other. Semra grimaced as the rope rubbed against her skin. It was still far too tight to slip free.

A *click* sounded beneath her feet and Semra's stomach dropped as a trap door opened in front of her and snakes began to slither out onto the platform. Ramas' serpent amulet burned into the trousers under her dress, a faint lump reminding her of how epically it had failed to protect *him* from a venomous death. At her hand.

The weight of a thousand bricks seemed to drop onto her chest, her lungs burning at the extra effort, her breathing quickened. The snakes kept coming, five, ten, twenty serpents swirling up from the trap door, slithering in silent menace as the crowd roared their approval. She pressed herself against the stake, the rough wood cutting into her back. She bent her knees to drop the bottom of her skirts on the wooden slats as a shield to keep the snakes away from her shifting, trembling feet.

One of the other girls screamed, and the audience laughed, then jumped to their feet and pumped their fists as Flourish Man completed his sandbag hoist and leaped through the flames to his save his girl. Zephan reached the top of the wall and swung his leg over to the other side, holding second place in the obstacle race. Flourish glanced back and gritted his teeth. Back on Semra's platform, a snake found an opening and slipped beneath her skirts.

Visions of the venomous snakes from the dungeon of her memory and nightmares flew to center focus. Her heart beat wildly, and a tremor rocked her body. Silky scales slithered against the skin of her ankle. Her blood ran cold. Furiously she scoured her wrists against the rope and each other, welcoming the painful bite of the rope – if only it saved her from the serpents. The snake moved off her ankle, and Semra shuffled her feet behind the stake as far as she could, images of Ramas and his asps filling her mind.

Where was it? Where was it? Two more snakes slithered on top of her dress and began scaling up her skirts, the rest of the serpents' mingling bodies in a roiling, interwoven pool at her feet. She couldn't breathe.

No one will even miss you when you're gone.

The sound of her own scream consumed her senses from her memories, transporting her back to that dark dungeon of death where no one came for her. *Help, someone! Please!*

Pathetic. Ramas snarled in her mind, riffing off her own self-condemnations.

The Framatar clucked his tongue in mock concern. *My dear, my dear...*

A *thud* on her left rocked her from her rumination. Flourish had reached his loved one and cut her free, and in her haste she stumbled and fell off the platform, scattering the kindling where she had been standing. The girl looked up to see Zephan already at the sandbags, still holding a strong second place, his muscles straining at the effort as the bags rose toward the bell. The girl's face twisted from flirty smiles to disgusted snarl, and as Flourish lifted her from the ground, she scooped a handful of flaming kindling and flung it toward the dry wood where Semra stood.

Flourish took off with his girl to go back over the wall and into a sand pit toward the finish line as the twigs under Semra's feet caught fire. The swarm at her feet writhed in livid indignation, hissing and coiling away from the dancing flames. Slippery, scaly bodies wrapped themselves around her legs underneath her skirts and her chest tightened, her lungs burning, her head beginning to swim.

This is a death too good for you, Ramas quipped at her, his face contorted in hatred as she imagined him standing before her. *Murderer. Traitor. Failure.* It was then that she felt the fangs sink in.

Utterly silent until this moment, Semra let out a blood-curdling scream that shook the air. Her eyes squeezed shut against Ramas' disdainful face, against the sting of the smoke, against the snakes as they desperately tried to flee back through the trap door, and the fire turning the Tabeun Tournament imitation into a very real execution pyre.

29

———

Sweat pricked at Semra's skin, burning. Her hands yanked against the rope in a frenzy as terror overwhelmed the measured strategy her brain had employed before. Something seized her hands, and she shrank back before hearing a voice in her ear:

"It's me! It's me."

Semra's knees weakened in relief as Zephan cut the rope back enough to wrench her hands free from the loosened bonds. "I've got you. Hold on."

Zephan snatched handfuls of snakes off her dress and flung them into the ring of fire around the platform. Taking her hand firmly in his, they jumped as one through the flames. Semra released Zephan and threw herself into a roll. Yellow and orange wisps danced before her, heat burning against her legs. Zephan stripped off his shirt and beat out the flames consuming her skirt. On reflex, Semra pulled at her skirt to get to her knives, but Zephan gripped her fingers to still them and shook his head. *Don't blow your cover or this is where we die.* He twined his fingers through hers instead and drew her after him, taking off together toward the wall.

Three other contestants were past them now, putting them in fifth place with only one contestant behind. Zephan ran forward and knelt at the wall; Semra picked up her hem and ran at him, planting a foot on his knee, another on his shoulder, and flying upward. She gripped the wall and reached a hand down to Zephan. He leaped up to take a hold of it and she pulled him up after her, the two of them passing another contestant as they hit the ground in no time flat.

The sand pit stretched before them, and Semra and Zephan dropped to their bellies to crawl under a low hung net, jumped up to scale a hurdle, and leaned forward as they picked up speed in a sprint toward the finish. Semra coughed and wheezed, her lungs still burning from smoke, but she welcomed the pumping of her legs and the adrenaline in her veins as comforting old friends. Ramas' accusatory voice dimmed as her focus narrowed in on the line in the sand, the guards at the end...and Monac outside the gate.

He shook his head. *Zezura,* he mouthed. *Now.*

"We can't," Semra wheezed to Zephan beside her. "Avaya."

Zephan slowed his run and faked a stumble, dragging her down with him. "Something's happened. I don't think we have a choice."

Semra's heart lurched into her throat and the call flew out to Zezura. One of the contestants they had passed on the wall blew past them again as they lurched to their feet and ran toward their fate. They crossed the finish line second-to-last, the last man half-carrying his older father the last few steps.

"And the last contestant has crossed the finish line!" the announcer cried. "Those moving on to the Artifacts of Power event will be–"

Zephan and Semra shifted uneasily, catching their breath with the other five pairs and eying the announcer and guards warily. The smell of singed hair wafted through the air and

Semra ran a hand over her matted, sand-filled hair. She couldn't remember the moment her hat had disappeared. The announcer paused as he was handed a piece of paper, opened it, and glanced at the king's observation box. King Arnevon nodded back at him, and the announcer turned back to the crowd.

"The five original contestants will be moving on to the Artifacts of Power. Our new addition, the thief, was disqualified at the sandbag hoist for letting the bags drop rather than lowering them to the ground before moving on."

Semra's breath caught and she looked at Zephan. His mouth parted. "I let them fall to get to you when you screamed. You were on fire."

This was her fault. If she had kept her mouth shut, if she'd been strong enough to keep Ramas' voice out of her head, Zephan would have had the extra seconds he needed to properly complete the obstacle. Her mouth went dry. Semra sent out another desperate pulse to Zezura. *Where are you?*

Coming. Flying. Coming.

The announcer cleared his throat and spoke again. "The thief will be arrested and punished for–"

Whap. Half of a mushy apple sailed through the air and connected with the announcer's temple, and all eyes turned to see Monac as he spat out his bite of apple and decked the guard nearest Semra and Zephan, dropping him to the ground. He made eye contact with Zephan for only a moment to jerk his head toward the exit before knocking the other guard onto his seat.

Zephan and Semra took off through the gate. She could feel the prickling burn of the mark of the dragon's kiss under the bandage as adrenaline rocketed through her once more. A thrill of hope washed over her as a great dark shadow swept over the arena.

Frightened screams rang out from the audience and a clatter of uncertain movement rippled through the people. Three guards hesitated their pursuit to cower under the shadow's looming presence, and a rush of wind from the wingtips of the great blue dragon cut across them as the beast dipped into a low fly by.

"Cowards!" Arnevon bellowed from his covered box. "Guards, kill them, *now!* Raven, prove your worth!"

Furious cries followed them as they fled through the tunnel.

"It's the dragon girl!"

"Cut off its head! *The girl is the head!*"

Semra dodged a guard's swing and came up with an uppercut to the jaw that cast him stumbling backward into the wall; Zephan barreled through two more, and a spear cut through the air in the tunnel and plunged itself into the chest of a guard as he laid his hand on Semra.

Monac ran up behind them. "I have a plan. Go!"

Semra needed no prompting. Zezura followed their course overhead, looping in the air once to double back, and dropping altitude over the square on the other side of the tunnel beyond the arena. Monac veered left to the coaches and leapt onto the back of one of the carriage horses, still harnessed and patiently waiting. The guards split to chase both Monac, and Semra and Zephan. But as they drew into the city, only one pursuer concerned Semra.

Out of the corner of her eye, as they turned into the square, she saw Siler, racing after them, gaining ground. Ten paces. Five.

Zezura dropped to the dirt and Semra planted a foot on one prominent spike along her side to propel herself up onto the dragon's back. Zephan followed suit and started reaching his arms around her to hold on when a blur knocked him off, the two men tumbling down Zezura's other side. Twenty guards descended on them, spears and swords in hand, and Zezura let out a spew of flame to keep them at bay. She beat her great wings and lifted into the air.

"No, no, no!" Semra's voice was hoarse from screaming. She looked down. Siler bowled Zephan to the ground and straddled him. "Zephan isn't on yet! We need Zephan!"

Zephan flipped Siler and hit him in the jaw, but found himself pinned down again. Zezura growled in protest and let out a puff of smoke. *Not safe,* she seemed to say.

Semra punched the hard scales of the dragon's neck, then wrung her injured hand. "I don't care. He comes, or I slide off right now!"

Zezura angled into a steep dive straight into the pack of men below, reaching down with massive claws, and plucked Siler and Zephan off the ground together as they pummeled each other.

"Auuughhh!" Both men exclaimed in angry surprise as they were snatched into the air. Semra flinched, remembering her own ride in a dragon's claws as a child. It was not pleasant. The guards stared up at them in disbelief as they pulled away. One threw a spear, but it fell short and landed harmlessly a short distance away.

Beyond them, Semra saw Monac riding one of the carriage horses, still hooked up to its coach, a two-horse team galloping into the streets of the city with more guards streaming out behind. The coach hit a rut in the road and the weakened leather straps snapped, dumping the chassis in the road behind the horses and leaving Monac to flee without the extra weight.

Zezura flew over Horen to the outskirts and descended over an empty meadow. Zezura dumped Zephan and Siler into the grass, and Semra slid off her back. Relief at their escape mixed with fury at their ruined plan and Monac being abandoned in the city as a result. She ran at Siler as her anger boiled over, and slapped him with an open hand across the face.

30

ARNEVON

Arnevon could have skewered the princess where she stood. He wanted to. She was useless as an informant, having never been privy to the crucial affairs of her father. Yet she was far too poised for the level of manipulation he had hoped for. "You're telling me you knew nothing about the dragon girl's presence at the tournament?"

"Like I said, Your Majesty, I learned of it at precisely the same moment you did – when the dragon appeared."

King Arnevon clenched his jaw, changing the topic. Perhaps he could catch this fly with honey.

"Have your accommodations been to your liking?"

"Yes, Your Majesty. Aside from the constant surveillance and removal of my free will, I've almost enjoyed my stay." She said the last of her words with more bite than he anticipated.

So much for honey. Arnevon clamped his lips in a tight line at the young princess's disrespect. When she had arrived at the castle, her fine clothes were bedraggled and worn from travel, but now she was every bit the pampered beauty he recalled meeting at the gala in Jannemar.

"I realize this must be a difficult time for you. But surely as a royal yourself, bodyguards are a normal part of life." The girl said nothing, and Arnevon drummed his fingers on the arm of his throne. He continued, "It was reasonable of you to follow through on your family's promise, despite your father's betrayal."

Avaya lifted her chin. "My father was a fool to attempt to forego the union between Prince Axis and myself. I want to rectify his mistake."

"And this willingness would have nothing to do with the threat of death looming over your pretty head?"

"Your Majesty, I am a woman of my word. And I was flattered that Axis wanted me so badly that he went to such lengths to bring me here – at least, I hope some of the reason was for me, and not the political advantages I bring. Truth be told, I'm grateful to be marrying a real man, from a fine nation, instead of a fat old relic from somewhere I would die in obscurity."

Arnevon's drumming fingers froze. Had he heard what he thought he heard? *He went to such lengths to bring me here.* "Axis..."

Avaya's eyes widened. Her hand flew to her mouth. "Oh, I've spoken out of turn! Forgive me! *Prince* Axis, of course, His Royal Highness! It's that he's made me feel so welcome here, despite everything. The Raven seemed so acquainted with him, I wasn't surprised to learn it was the prince who orchestrated my capture. But the Raven was under strict orders not to bring me to any harm."

If his son had conspired with the Raven to kidnap Avaya behind Arnevon's back, it didn't matter whether the idea had been a good one. It was an international level of subterfuge of which he had hardly deemed his son capable. It would mean that in all Belvidore's sordid history, Axis was the greatest traitor of them all. Arnevon's lip curled in an involuntary snarl. "How acquainted were they, the Raven and my son?"

"Your Majesty, forgive me, I know you are hard on the prince because you want him to be the best he can be. Axis told me you are a bit paranoid – no, no, that's not right, *cautious,* yes, cautious is all! Please, don't look at me like that, I only mean to tell you that I believe the prince to be more thoughtful than you give him credit for, and perhaps he is already becoming the great ruler you have pushed him to be."

Arnevon crossed his arms to keep them from shaking, and leaned back in his chair with an air of repose that he far from felt. *He thinks me paranoid, does he? Is a rabbit paranoid when the arrow is on the string?* Well, if that were the situation, Arnevon would show his son that he'd picked a fight not with a rabbit but with a lion.

He swallowed the bile that rose in his throat and smiled winsomely at the naïve idiot before him. She'd been useful after all – her tongue wagged when she was comfortable.

"Perhaps you're right, my dear. Perhaps I have been too hard on him, but my work has paid off, and he will be a fine ruler one day. Thank you for meeting with me today. I won't take up any more of your time."

The princess beamed and curtsied low. Arnevon nodded at the guards, and they opened the double doors and followed the princess outside. Arnevon beckoned his advisor, who stepped forward; Arnevon clutched the arms of his throne and wiped sweat from his clammy brow.

"Insolent boy! He's staging a coup. Get me the healer, *now.*"

31

———————

AVAYA

vaya spun around the moment the doors of the king's hall closed behind her. She was shaking. She'd meant to play both sides, to toy with Arnevon's paranoia and Axis's anger, but this – she had not wanted this. *What would he do with the healer?*

The Raven still hadn't returned from being dragged off by the dragon, and another bodyguard fell in step with her as she swept down the corridor.

Avaya quickened her steps. "Is he back yet?"

The bodyguard glanced at her. "Who?"

"The Raven."

"I haven't heard."

Avaya bit her nail. Her mind replayed her audience with King Arnevon. She had played him like a fiddle, performing her role exquisitely, and Arnevon had eaten it up. Large doe eyes here, a few curated slips of the tongue there. She made King Arnevon and Prince Axis more of a threat to one other than she could ever be to either of them. Still, adding tension to an already rocky father-son relationship was one thing, but poison and treason were another. Would Arnevon really go that far?

A dragon had just swooped over Arnevon's annual tournament, forcing it to be indefinitely postponed. It was meant to ease people's fears, convincing them peace talks were underway and family members would safely return from the warfront. Avaya wondered about her own family...and recalled the moment she realized it was Zephan beneath the black hair, blacked out teeth, and disguise getup. Her heart had stopped beating. For the first time since she arrived, she'd felt true fear. She replayed Zephan being dragged into the arena, remembering him dropping the sandbags to rescue the murderous dragon girl. And to top it all off, her brother and her protector were both snatched up to the sky by the great beast.

Enough was going terribly wrong as it was. She couldn't let Arnevon kill Axis.

Avaya jerked her head at her security guard. "You, what is your name?"

"Bonan. What do you want with it?"

"Bonan. Does the healer have any specialties?"

The man shrugged. "There are multiple healers."

"Yes, but the king favors one, does he not?" Avaya bit out the words impatiently, and she bit her lip, catching herself too late.

"I'm not sure it's any of your business."

Heat rose in her chest, and she curled her hands into fists at her sides. Fool! How could she get him to understand? Avaya forced herself into composure and lowered her voice to above a whisper. "What really happened to the queen?"

Bonan shot her a dark glare, and hurried them past a servant in the hall, and down two more corridors. "She was sick, for a long time. Took a turn for the worse after Princess

Blaise was born. And if you appreciate your head being attached to your body, you'll leave old rumors alone."

"Didn't you hear the king as we were leaving? If you care about your prince, you'll care that the king believes his son has betrayed him and intends to take action."

Bonan picked up his pace. "Shh! You can't know he would do something like that."

"I'm sure that will be a comfort to you at the funeral."

"This is ridiculous."

Avaya cocked an eyebrow. "Is it? Tell me, is the king's favored healer particularly adept with treatment for poison?"

"Aren't healers supposed to be good at treating things?"

A guttural groan escaped Avaya's throat. "You need to help me!"

Bonan whisked her through the tower and onto the last hall. Only one more turn, and they would arrive back at Avaya's room, where she would likely be forced to remain until called for. And Bonan still seemed unmoved by her pleas, committed to the singular purpose of returning her to her lavish prison.

They passed an open doorway into a sitting room and bedchamber, and Avaya spotted a frail stick of a woman sitting at a chair surrounded by books, her feet tucked under her. Avaya twisted out of Bonan's grasp and fled through the doorway, passing a guard standing outside it and knocking on the open door hurriedly as she passed. Bonan followed closely, but stopped short at the door, probably boring daggers into her back with his eyes. *Well, let him.*

The person in the chair, as surely she must be a person despite her haggard appearance, looked up as Avaya came in. Her hair was mussed, her silk brocade gown expensive but relatively simple, and she wore only the fabric of her dress rather than any waist trainer or corset. She seemed not to be allowing her servants to do anything to help her appearance, as her face hadn't even been powdered or painted. Deep shadows fell under her eyes and cheekbones, and she had her finger on the page of a book and the end of her braid in her mouth.

Avaya curtsied low. There could be no mistaking who this strange, sickly person must be. "Forgive me for the intrusion, Your Highness, but I simply had to introduce myself. I hadn't yet had the chance, and I do so hope to learn new friendly faces here in Belvidore. I am Princess Avaya of Jannemar."

The Belvidorian princess was only a little younger than Avaya, but unhealthily thin, and pale. It was no wonder she had been left at home for the gala in Jannemar – she wouldn't have fit into the regal display of power and prestige as a rival nation. On the contrary, Blaise looked like she could be blown over by a sneeze.

The girl glanced up but said nothing. Avaya smiled. "Princess Blaise, I am honored to make your acquaintance." *And keep Bonan from dragging me back to my room.*

Blaise stood and dipped her head. "And I yours," she said, in a high, reedy voice that perfectly echoed her sickly, sallow features.

"I had hoped to see you in Jannemar, but I heard your illness was debilitating." Avaya smoothed her skirts and fidgeted with the rings on her fingers. "It was good to see you feeling well enough to attend the tournament."

"My father frequently hides me from the public eye, but he insists I attend the annual tournaments. Of course, it's not generally so interesting as it was this year." Blaise's gaze darted to Bonan, still in the doorway, and back to Avaya. "My condition has afflicted me since childhood." She lowered her eyes to the floor.

"Does it keep you from doing many things?" Avaya asked.

"Yes."

"Oh." Avaya clamped her mouth shut and scanned the area. The princess' rooms were no more splendid than Avaya's guest room, but was significantly more cluttered. Plants overflowed the room, making it look half its actual size. Books, drawings, and journals littered the couch and small table next to Blaise, and a tray of untouched food sat to one side. "What do you do with your time, then?"

"When I'm feeling well enough?" Blaise spread her hands, indicating the table, open window, and books. "This, mostly."

"I see." A miserable existence, but then, she was an invalid. What else could she do with her life? Clearly, She'd resigned herself to stuffing her rooms full of plants and escaping her dismal reality through books.

Avaya sat uncomfortably in the awkward pause that followed, chewing on a nail. Arnevon was going to kill Axis. And though this conversation might delay the inevitable return to Avaya's room for a few minutes, the conversationalist, weakling Blaise would be no ally for her.

But perhaps she had some helpful information even so. She'd press her luck once more. "What about the healers? What sorts of specialties do they have to help?"

Avaya heard Bonan shift his weight and clear his throat behind her. *Subtle.* She ignored him, and crossed to the couch instead, perching on its arm.

Blaise shrugged. "I've seen them all."

This wasn't working. Blaise was absolutely worthless. Avaya tried a new angle.

"What is it really like here? I've heard King Arnevon is a reasonable, but hard man."

Blaise's brows furrowed, then relaxed. "Where did you hear that?"

"Hear that he's a hard man?"

"Hear that he's reasonable."

Avaya eyed Blaise. Her eyes were innocent, and too big for her gaunt face. It was the closest thing to a challenge she had heard from the stick in the overstuffed chair, but there was no malice in her eyes. "It's just – something I heard, I suppose. I'm not sure I remember."

Bonan cleared his throat again. "Your Highness, we really must be going."

"Yes, of course." The conversation wasn't going anywhere anyway. Avaya curtsied low and followed Bonan back out to the hall. Frustration built in her chest, chased by a surge of hopelessness as they followed the hall to its end and rounded the corner.

"Bonan, please. I need information to help stop the king from killing the prince."

"Not so loud," Bonan hissed.

"You have to help me. The threat is real."

They reached Avaya's quarters, and Bonan held the door open.

"All I *have* to do, Your Highness, is prevent you from entering or exiting this door without permission. Bearing in mind that I enjoy my life, even if you hate yours, I respectfully recommend you resign yourself to staying in your room and out of trouble."

The door swung closed, sealing her off from freedom once again. Avaya grabbed a pillow off the bed and screamed into it. She threw the pillow to the side and paced the room, chewing on her nail. He couldn't die, not yet...

32

Semra's chest heaved and her nostrils flared. Her mind spun with the question she'd been battling since she saw Siler in Madensig: *How could you betray me?* Siler stepped back from Semra's slap, stung, but made no move to counter.

"What is wrong with you?" Semra demanded. "You tried to kill me, *twice!*"

Siler balled his hands into fists but did not move. "I've never tried to kill you."

Zephan scoffed, and Siler bristled. He glared at Zephan and turned back to Semra. "Weren't you in that arena? Arnevon gave a kill order. Getting to you before the guards did was the only way to keep you alive, and I was going to have to do some heavy convincing to get Arnevon to keep you that way so I could save you later."

"*I* was doing just fine. *You* dragged me back into the arena."

"You were *not* fine. You've faced death many times, and I've only ever heard you scream once before. *And* you couldn't get out of your ties. You were off your game."

Semra opened her mouth, then shut it, throwing her

hands up. "What are you doing working for Belvidore? How could you be wrapped up in this?"

"*Me?*" Siler's shoulders tensed, and he jabbed a finger at her chest. "No. *You* were supposed to be starting a new life somewhere, getting away, getting safe. Not making out with some pretentious pansy who wants you at his beck and call like a puppy without any intention to offer you more. You escape a controlling liar who manipulated you into serving his own political aims only to end up doing the exact same thing. Manipulated to serve someone else's agenda."

Her throat tightened. "That's what you think of me? A mindless puppet serving another lord?"

Siler shrugged. "Maybe for all your big talk, the bribe of the crown was too much to turn down."

Zephan glanced between them. Semra reeled. Siler was the one who always wanted money. Siler was the one who hated political spheres and diplomats, yet here he was under an enemy king. How dare *he* accuse *her*? The sting of unshed tears pricked her eyes. She blinked them back hard.

Zephan took a step toward Siler. "You're one to talk. How much money were you paid to kidnap my sister? How big a role would you say your actions will have in the political sphere, with the upheaval of the entire region and clash of kingdoms? People are dying in the wars, in huge numbers, and still you aid Arnevon's vain ambitions that will bleed both peoples dry!"

How could Siler think what she was doing was the same? Semra's cheeks flushed crimson again as his accusation replayed in her head. She backed away from him, shaking her head. "I've never done anything just for money. And I've never wanted any crown. If you think I took a bribe, you don't know me at all."

Siler rolled his eyes. "I know you better than anyone, and

not all bribes are silver and gold. Empty promises come in all kinds."

"And you," Siler growled, turning to Zephan. "You think you're so high and mighty, with such lofty, self-righteous motivations. Where were you when Semra and I emptied the mountain of the last assassins, chased down the scattered threats, and saved the last of the little kids? Where were you when *your* task force did your work for you? Taking credit, I imagine, from the comfort of your gilded halls."

"I don't need to explain myself to you. I fought tooth and nail to spend more time on that mission. I was there every second I could be." Zephan paused, and his features darkened. "And you didn't empty it of all the assassins. Threats remain, for here you stand."

Heat flashed through Semra's body. Which assassins remained in play but her and Siler? Her lips flattened. "You didn't feel that way about us before, when you put us on the task force to begin with."

"There is no '*us*' with you and Siler," Zephan spat. "Don't lump yourself in with him. You stayed after Azi was defeated because you knew it was the right thing to do. *He* only stuck around for *you*, and when he finally accepted that you weren't interested, he turned mercenary."

"I've never pretended to be something I'm not." Siler crossed his arms. "And that's more than I can say for either of you!"

"Some of us want to improve our vices rather than brag about them," Zephan said.

Siler ignored Zephan and drilled Semra with a cool glare. "You were supposed to expose the dragonlord, end his child-snatching, and free us all, not fall for the means to the end. Zephan's only job was to stay alive and feed us information. We didn't know princey here was actually the prince at the time. But no, you had to go and fall in love with him, like a dummy."

The indictment sounded like something Azi would have said. *Sentiment will cost you the mission.* Semra's voice rose. "I *did* expose the dragonlord and end his child-snatching! What else do you want from me? Or are you angry I am less motivated by money than you are?"

"The star pupil, the early graduate, and you flunk the easiest rule in the book. Don't get attached. It's a good thing Ramas is dead. He'd keel over to see you as some naïve little puppy."

Semra screamed her frustration at Siler, an open-mouthed, wordless gush of anger. A torrent of racing thoughts and ire built up inside her, but the thoughts flew by so quickly she could hardly pin one down. "Well, then, it's a good thing I killed him, isn't it?" she blurted. "To save him the pain of seeing one of his victims try to be human. And Zephan isn't a mark. And anyway, I didn't fall in love with him!"

"Could have fooled me."

"That's the point, isn't it? To fool people?" Semra's lip quivered and she turned away, raking her shaking fingers through her tangled hair. She used her own act of murder as a jab at someone she cared about. What was wrong with her? *You're not normal,* a voice inside her seemed to say. *You're damaged, and you'll never get that back.* Semra shook her head to clear it, but the thoughts only became stronger. *Failure. Belvidore on alert. Avaya lost. Monac abandoned. Failure.*

A new thought struck her.

Maybe you're a liar too. Do you love him?

The touch of his lips, the warmth of his arms around her, haunted her like a counterfeit daydream.

Zephan took one look at Semra's expression and stepped into Siler's space, separating him from Semra. "Leave her alone!" His voice lowered to a rumble, and he spoke to Semra without removing his eyes from Siler. "Don't listen to him. Whose idea was it to stop the hit on my family at the gala? Siler's? Don't make me laugh. He's never served anyone but himself."

"Says the man who flirted with a girl with a dragon, who now has her sticking around to support his crown, even after avoiding her for weeks at the castle."

A pang of bitterness flooded Semra's body, and she gritted her teeth. Siler had a point.

Zephan shook his head. "I never avoided her!"

Siler clucked his tongue. "Not true," he said, examining a scratch on his forearm. "I heard you and Firfell talking. He said it's bad publicity for crown princey to be seen with a killer for hire. Nobles nervous, support shrinking. You promised to be a good boy and steer clear."

Semra's gut wrenched and her face fell. "You did what?"

Zephan shook his head. "No. No, that's not how it happened. You're twisting it."

Semra's jaw dropped. Siler pushed Zephan backward. "So Firfell didn't ask you to stay away from her?"

"No, he did. How...how did you..."

Siler arched an eyebrow. "And you promised him you would stay away, isn't that right?"

"Not...not exactly. He was doing his best to keep me away from her, strategizing with other military leaders and nobles to add to my already full schedule. I told him it wasn't his place. We argued. I said I would be more careful of my public image in the fragile time frame of the beginning of the war, for my father's sake."

Semra's heart rate doubled, and she tried to focus on the pounding feeling of it hammering in her rib cage as his words sunk in. "You obeyed him. The prince obeyed the captain, instead of the other way around, and you let him win. You didn't even tell me. You left me wondering."

Zephan glared daggers at Siler one last time before turning back to Semra, exchanging his anger for pleading. "I was trying to figure things out! The war effort is critical. The nobles' opinions don't matter long-term; we would have time later to convince them enough to avoid further problems, but in the short-term we needed to patch things up. I was afraid if I told you, you would leave for good. And I was right. Before Avaya disappeared, when you thought you were causing problems, you were packing."

Semra put out a hand to steady herself on Zezura. The dragon nudged her gently with her huge nose, from the place she had coiled herself on the ground. Perhaps by now she was accustomed to humans standing in one spot to talk indefinitely. Semra shut her eyes against the truth. Her fears were realized – she was a threat to the king's court in Jannemar, being with Zephan caused him problems, and even he had recognized it and avoided her. She should never have stayed at Shamaran Castle so long. What had she expected?

Zephan spread his hands helplessly. "I'm so sorry I didn't tell you. I've always wanted to protect you...I never meant to hurt you."

Semra winced. *But you did, didn't you?* All her fears about Zephan, his position, her place in his world, were true. And Siler had known it. He'd overheard Firfell, or learned it from Avaya or someone else, and hadn't told her. Semra's shoulders drooped and her eyes watered. She turned away.

Siler slow clapped behind Zephan. "Oh, bravo! Well done. How do you best protect a woman? Send her on a mission sandwiched between an obligation to protect *you* and an obligation to snatch *another* person requiring protecting from a vicious, paranoid, rival king. Oh wait –

that's not good enough. Let's get every eye in the city trained on her in an arena and watch her nearly burn to death at the stake!"

"Says the one who left her alone when you thought she was being manipulated, to go serve the rival kingdom bent on destroying the castle where she was living, and nearly got her killed *twice* in the last *week*!"

"You kissed her, but what would you ever really do with her? Make her central to a scandal before a lazy cover up so you can marry some diplomatic flooze? Because you can't break free of that crown, now can you?"

A tear slipped down Semra's cheek. What were they competing over? Who could hurt her more? Because they were both doing a phenomenal job.

Zephan glared at Siler. "What do you want from me? To say it's a problem, that the person I want to spend all my time with was raised by the man who murdered my mother? That my entire life has been about preparing me to lead our people, and it would be unbelievably selfish and ungrateful to everyone who has poured into me if I threw it all away for a girl? Yes, it's a problem! I think about it when I lie awake at night, I dream of a simpler life, but you know what, I don't have one. I have this one. And there is quite simply no one who could take my place without turning the kingdom over to ruin."

"Idiots!" Semra screamed. "Both of you! Shut up!" She couldn't think. She couldn't listen to them insult each other to justify themselves for another second. She whirled on Zephan.

"I thought you were so perfect. You grew up with a functional family. Avaya casts some doubt on that, but certainly a lot more functional than mine. You had a dad who loved you, a sister who would die for you, and the other sister, with all her faults, is still trying to protect you – she didn't say a word at the tournament, and I'm sure she knew it was you.

"You were different. You and Turian gave me hope that good rulers might exist. You said we would respect each other, that I could trust you. You promised you understood me, that there was good in me. That you weren't bitter or angry at me. Yet here you are. You lied. Raised by the man who murdered your mother? Is that all I am now, all you can see? An obstacle to the throne? When you look at me, do you think of the Framatar, and everything he's done? Do you wonder how many people I've killed at his command, and if you could really stand the sight of me if you knew?"

Semra's eyes bored into Zephan's, and the shock and pain in his face tore at her soul. But there was something else. He hesitated, when she asked him if he thought of the Framatar. That sliver in time was all she needed to know. Her heart splintered to pieces.

She spun to Siler.

"You were supposed to be on my side! You were supposed to be the one who understood me, you were supposed to be the one..." Semra paused, taking in a ragged breath to steady herself, and let out a long, bitter sigh. "You were supposed to be my support." Her voice broke. "You were the only one who could understand me. Everyone I've ever known has either tried to kill me, or been killed, and you are the only one left. My one last tie to my childhood, the only one who knows me for who I really am. And now I've lost you too."

Semra felt the chasm in her chest widen where her worthless, splintered heart had been held together with hope of connection with another human being. Vain hope. She was alone, and had been since Azi slaughtered her parents and brainwashed her when she was only four.

"Semra – " Zephan started, but Semra cut him off.

"Not a word," she hissed. "We are getting to the rendezvous point and finishing my obligations to you and your family. And that's that."

"The obligations are a sham," Siler said. "You're pinning yourself to him. I *do* understand you. Let me prove it to you. Come back with me."

Semra's lip curled as it trembled. "Don't touch me. By Aurin, don't breathe another word. I'm sick of you both. Take a hike back to your boss." Semra rapped Zezura's hide with her knuckles. "Let's go, Zez."

Zezura stretched her long muscles and stood as Semra launched herself up onto the beast's back. "Zephan, get on. If you say anything, I'll push you off and have Zezura carry you in her claws."

33

AVAYA

Avaya threw open the door to her chamber and leaned into the hall, tapping her foot anxiously. Bonan raised an eyebrow, and Avaya clenched her jaw. "Where is the Raven? Why isn't he back yet?"

"I haven't the slightest idea." Bonan's mouth quirked into a – what was it? A smile? A grimace? Was he mocking her? "But someone else will be here for you shortly."

"Someone else?" Avaya's heart stopped. Axis? Had he gotten her message? It had been a bit cryptic...had he figured it out?

"One of the healers is coming. You said you were sick."

Avaya blinked at him.

Bonan sighed. "You look terribly healthy for a sick person. Hard to believe that only an hour ago you were nauseous and aching all over."

He'd decided to be helpful after all. "The healer! Yes, now that you mention it, I'm a bit woozy as well. I better go and lie down."

"Lay on your hair or something. It looks too perfect for you to feel so ill."

A bold statement and a welcome suggestion. Avaya smiled and leaned toward him. "Thank you," she whispered, and then pulled back into her room and shut the door. Avaya ran to the water basin and sprinkled water in her hair and arms, mussed her hair with her hands, then slipped under the covers of the lavish bed and tossed about for good measure. Twenty minutes later, a soft knock came at the door and an older woman stepped inside.

"Your Highness? I'm told you're feeling ill. My name is Laurel."

A thrill ran through her. A chance for answers. Was Laurel the favored healer of the king, or one of a dozen castle healers? Avaya let out a soft moan, and the woman came closer.

"I've brought you some herb mixtures and broth. I am going to check you now."

Laurel's long, narrow fingers were surprisingly strong as they moved along Avaya's hands and arms and felt her forehead. "You seem a bit clammy, but not particularly warm. Perhaps you are nervous, having been here so short a time. It must have been quite strenuous, traveling here so quickly from Jannemar!"

Avaya looked at Laurel. She had gray hair, whisps too short to stay in her bun falling to frame her face, and her kind eyes surveyed the princess. "I feel achy and nauseous," Avaya said. "And dizzy, too."

The older woman nodded empathetically and offered Avaya tea. Avaya hesitated, but the woman smiled. "Wormwood, mint, balm, lavender. Nothing dangerous, I assure you."

Avaya managed a weak smile in return and sniffed at the cup. The sweet smells certainly seemed to support Laurel's claim, and Avaya took a sip. She wrinkled her nose and coughed. "It's bitter."

Laurel laughed. "That would be the wormwood. It will

help settle your stomach. Not a bad blend with the lavender and mint, though, hmm? Now tell me, what do you think of Madensig?"

"It's beautiful, but I'm afraid my first impression wasn't under the most favorable of conditions." Avaya grimaced at the memory. She'd crossed the border with a grumbling stomach, bound hands, and untold layers of dirt and grime.

Laurel clucked her tongue. "A shame. It really is beautiful. And there are some wonderful people here too."

"How long have you worked here?"

"Oh, fifty years or so."

"Fifty years! You've been here longer than the king!" Someone with so much experience in Madensig was an excellent person to know.

Laurel nodded.

Avaya shifted onto her elbow. "What do you wish was different in the kingdom?"

Laurel was silent for a moment, then squinted hard at Avaya. "Your Highness, that is a challenging question."

"Is it hard to answer?"

"I didn't say that. I said it was challenging." Laurel folded her hands and leaned in. "Why do you ask such questions?"

"Well...I may one day be queen, and maybe I could help improve things when I am. Bridge the gap between Jannemar and Belvidore as was intended before everything went horribly wrong."

Laurel examined her, then dropped her voice low. "And what leads the future queen to fake her illness?"

Avaya pulled back, but as she looked into Laurel's eyes, she saw neither judgment nor derision, only calm concern. Avaya paused, then took a breath.

"Everyone is afraid to speak around here, but the prince is in danger, and I need to get to him. I'm afraid I won't be a particularly effective queen if my intended dies and I never become one...and even less effective if *I* die. I think one of the healers may be involved."

Laurel sat upright. Avaya held her breath. She had either saved her future, or signed her own death certificate.

Laurel tilted her head. "Do you love him?"

Avaya opened her mouth, surprised. Something about Laurel was disarming. Perhaps it was her directness, or how she felt warm and familiar, without care for either the fabricated closeness or calculated distance most people had with royals.

"It is the duty of the royal family to serve their people above themselves, and therefore to marry whomever best promotes peace in the land and suits the political aims of the monarchy. But heaven help me, if the people demand that I marry an *attractive* man and make the world better by his side, I'll do it! I count myself lucky." Avaya looked intently at Laurel. "And I do care for him."

Laurel smiled. "Your Highness, you speak with wisdom beyond your years. Those that marry only for love are fools, but those that marry without compassion are worse. Forgive me, but if I'm wrong about you, my head ends up in a basket."

Avaya reached out and took Laurel's hand. "Take confidence in this – if your head ends up in a basket, mine will be its neighbor."

The older woman nodded slowly. "I can help you. What do you need?"

34

———

Zezura flew them a short distance away to the wooded foothills where they had set the rendezvous point. Monac had managed to meet up with them on foot several hours later, having released the carriage horses a short time before. After a meager meal Monac had managed to scrounge from the city, the three of them strategized once more on how to get into Madensig.

"These are all terrible ideas that will get everyone killed." Zephan let out an exasperated sigh.

"They are all terrible ideas because there are no good ways in." Monac stretched out on the ground and wove his fingers behind his head. "Not with Arnevon as paranoid as he seems to be. Wartime, a hostage, the tournament debacle, all things working against us."

Semra shook her head. "The cistern. It's the only thing left."

Zephan jerked his head up. "You can't be serious."

Semra shrugged. Zephan's eyes narrowed. "I don't think that's a good idea."

"I don't care."

Monac glanced between them, and the tension in the air grew thick. "If you're planning on sitting in a cistern for a couple of days while the search parties exhaust themselves in Madensig, you can't fall asleep in there. You might have more nightmares. And I don't mean to be rude, but the siren of your scream is not ideal."

Semra glared at him. "I never planned to fall asleep."

"Good."

"Good."

Zephan folded his arms. "You're actually doing the cistern idea?"

Semra drilled him with a stare. "Hand me the blueprints."

Monac dug the blueprints out of his bag and handed them over, and after several hours, they had formed a semblance of a plan. Monac declared he needed his beauty sleep after his hard work throwing apples at people and beating up guards, Zephan went on a walk, and Semra changed out of her tattered, fire-scorched dress and into a fresh tunic overtop her trousers. She pulled out her throwing knives and cleaning cloth and set to work, content to be left alone with her racing thoughts. Until Zephan returned.

"How long are you going to punish me?"

Semra looked up long enough to glare at him, then looked down again at her knives. "I'm not punishing you."

"Right. I must have misinterpreted your stomping and eye-daggers. Clearly you are in the sunshiniest of moods."

Semra didn't look up this time, but the strokes of the cloth against the blade quickened to short jerks. "You think I'm a threat. Raised by the person who murdered your mother."

"No, I think *Siler* is a threat. His motives are different than yours, and always have been. What I meant when I mentioned being raised by Azi was that it doesn't look good on paper to the court. They don't understand it. But I don't just know you on paper. I know *you*."

Semra bit her lip.

Zephan sat down beside her. "I think by and large, we do pretty well together. But I think today when you were angry, you used the dragon like a bully. You didn't feel like talking so you used Zezura as a power trip to get me to shut up when you wanted, to control me. I didn't appreciate that approach."

Semra picked up another knife to clean it a third time, though it was already sparkling. She considered his words. She *had* used Zezura like a bully. Guilt washed over her. Everything he said made sense. Of course it did. She was a fool. Semra replayed the conversation with Zephan and Siler in her mind, mulling it over again and again. This time something new snared her attention.

I didn't fall in love with him. She had said it to Siler. But if that were true, why did her breathing quicken whenever Zephan was close to her? Why did she find herself gazing at him at random, only to catch herself and try to look away before she was caught?

Zephan let out a heavy sigh. "I should have told you about Firfell. What he wanted me to do. I should have been open about everything, told you my dilemma, told you what I wanted. Maybe you could have helped. I guess I tried to control you, too. I didn't want you to leave. I hate it when you leave."

Semra felt a chink of the ice in her heart melt before his vulnerable offering. She lifted her chin, not ready to release her anger. "Yes. You should have."

"You have to understand. I don't mean this to be high and mighty, as Siler put it, but the reality is, in my position I am not allowed to tell everyone everything that I know." Zephan leaned forward. "I know sensitive information, and it's valid for the nobles to be worried about who I might share that with, even accidentally. And with Azi's recent attempt at a coup, and the shocking discovery of a whole slew of assassins floating around, having a strong, competent heir is even more important than before."

Zephan crossed his arms and leaned against a tree, and the intensity of his gaze was insufferable. Semra shifted uncomfortably. She snapped the cloth along the blade, and her finger slipped, the tip of the blade drawing blood from her thumb. She gasped involuntarily, then clenched her jaw. *Moron. You're not thinking straight.*

Zephan leaned over and reached for her hand. "Let me help."

Semra slapped his hand away. "Stop it!"

He drew back. "Stop what?"

"Stop being so nice! It's annoying!" Semra winced at the sound of her own words, spilling out before she could stop them. She clenched her jaw. *Why can't he just stay mad like a normal person, and leave me alone like everyone else?* Everything he said made sense. She'd put the cart before the horse and made assumptions about him – again – and he was still gentle with her, as if she were made of glass.

Zephan furrowed his brow. "What are you talking about?"

"I'm mad at you. So stop being so perfect, because it's obnoxious. Stop being nice when I'm being mean. Stop treating me like some delicate flower when I'm a weed in a gutter. Stop acting like I deserve good things."

Her words hung in the air and her lip curled into a grimace of disdain. But not for Zephan. Never for Zephan. *For what then?* Semra's chest blazed with a furious flame, every nerve on edge. He was too good. Too kind. It wasn't right.

I hate myself. Nobody else was doing it properly. They had all lost their minds, letting her live after what she did, giving her a feather bed with rich tapestries and expensive foods to eat and missions to go on.

How could justice reign in the world if no one would hate her the way she deserved to be hated? Even the Framatar's hate didn't count. He was evil in his own right, and making him angry at her was one of the few things she had done right. But Semra saw the blood in her ledger every night in her dreams. The wicked despised her, but despised her as a dog fighting another dog. That was natural – dogs fought other dogs. It was the good people that had it wrong. Good people should hate her.

Zephan slammed his fist into the leaf-laden earth beside him. "Stop trying to make everybody else hate you the way you think we should!"

Semra's blood ran cold, and the heat of her anger fled before it. She blinked. Was that what she was doing? How long had he known? Her throat tightened as emotion threatened to take her, but she pushed it down. *Down, down.*

"I'm sick of hearing you act like I'm some fragile, pristine thing." Zephan snatched a leaf off the ground and stripped it from the stem. "I'm sick of hearing you berate yourself. And I'm sick of you pushing me away."

"Good. Go, then." Semra shifted her body away and plucked at invisible dirt particles on her knife blade. It wasn't right, the way he kept pushing, as if insistent on finding the depths of her soul. But her soul was drenched in blood. The amber of his eyes when he looked at her would never again be warm, but cold, if he discovered her true self. The emotion she'd tried to stuff down flew right back up again.

"You – *uuuugh!*" Zephan threw his hands up and ran them through his hair. He sprang to his feet, stomped four paces, and stopped. He was going to stalk off. Satisfaction mingled with panic at the thought. It would mean she won, that she ran him off, that she got what she told herself she wanted when she told him to go. But then the one person who had hope left for her would have given up, and any hope she had for herself would be strangled.

Zephan pivoted and crossed the space in three long strides and knelt before her in the dirt. *Finally.* He would give her what she deserved. Say the things he had been holding in all this time. His real opinion of her, his secret bitterness and blame. Semra steeled herself for the onslaught and drew her shoulders back. His jaw clenched and his eyes were fire, his hands curled into fists, and Semra met fire with fire in her eyes. But as she watched, something unexpected happened. As he searched her face, the muscles in his face slowly loosened, his jaw relaxed, his fingers uncurled.

Slowly, softly, Zephan took her hand in his and removed the knife, carefully setting it aside on top of the cleaning cloth. He reached for her other hand and held them both, the warmth in his hands chipping away at ice in her heart she had hardly been aware of until the moment it started to melt.

"Whatever you think of me," he said, his voice low and earnest, "Whatever stupid thing I do or say, whatever stupid thing *you* do or say, there is one thing you cannot do. Promise me you won't send me away unless you mean it. I can't play those kinds of games with you. I won't. Respect me enough to do the same."

Semra's heart stopped in shock, then turned in on itself as remorse poured out, mixing with shame, and an odd sense of safety. Tears pricked at her eyes, and she nodded, a lump in her throat rendering her unable to speak. She attempted to swallow, unsuccessfully, then tried again.

"I'm sorry," she squeaked.

He took a long breath, and let it out. "It's okay. Just know –

maybe you don't accept yourself yet, but I do. Borrow my view of you, until yours catches up. There is *good* in you."

The floodgates opened then, and tears poured like rivers down her face. The pain of a hundred nightmare memories, the guilt of a pile of corpses, and the cry of a four-year-old child ripped from her chance at a normal life all merged into one raging wave. Her body racked with sobs, and she clutched at Zephan's shirt. He pulled her in and let her weep into his chest.

He accepts me. There is good in me. It couldn't be true. It didn't make sense. And yet...and yet there was no one in the world Semra had come to believe more fully than Zephan Shamaran.

Semra didn't know how long they sat there together. Time suspended as her body wearied and her tears ran dry. Exhaustion crept over her, and a with the ebb of her weeping there came a strange release, dimly reminiscent of peace. She lay curled against him for a long time before she sniffled, somewhat bashfully, and sat up.

Zephan reached a hand up and brushed a stray wisp of hair out of Semra's face. He leaned in and her breath caught, those abominable butterflies that had not ceased to plague her in Zephan's presence bursting in her stomach. She started to pull away, but his hand slipped up to the nape of her neck and gently held her there. Zephan brought his lips to her ear and spoke in a whisper.

"I think you are remarkable...brilliant...and stunningly beautiful. You *do* have a good heart. And I won't be going anywhere anytime soon."

35

AVAYA

Avaya tugged the quilt over the servant girl's shoulders as she lay in Avaya's enormous guest bed, surrounded by pillows. Laurel arranged the common woolen mantle over Avaya and put an arm around her shoulders. "Keep your head down," she whispered. "I'll sort things out."

Laurel opened the bedroom door and stepped out in the hall; Bonan gave her a nod and Avaya marveled at the ease in which Laurel slipped him four gold coins. If she blinked, she would have missed the transfer entirely. Avaya fiddled with the cloth over the basket on her arm, fixing her attention downward as Laurel ushered her through the halls to Prince Axis's chambers. They arrived without incident, and Laurel knocked on the door of the sitting room with purpose.

"Your Royal Highness, the healer you called for."

A gruff voice called through the door. "I did not call for the healer."

"Your Highness, I was told it was urgent that I assess you. I'm afraid I can't be sent away without at least confirming your wellbeing in person."

The older woman's confidence under stress was commendable. Laurel was well connected and respected in the castle. It was good Avaya had made her acquaintance so early on in her stay.

There was a loud sigh and a grunt, then the door swung open. Axis stood in the doorway and spread his hands. "Now you see me. I'm quite the picture of health, thank you, and was about to sit down to dinner. Who sent you?"

"My deepest apologies, Your Highness." Laurel curtsied low. "Perhaps my new assistant can remain with you to ensure you are feeling well?"

Axis swiveled toward Avaya for the first time, and she lifted her eyes to his. She smiled, and his lips parted.

"Of course," he said, sweeping his hand into the room. "Please."

Laurel curtsied again and disappeared down the hall, and Avaya stepped inside a lavish room with a chandelier hanging over an exquisitely set table in the middle, surrounded by a ceiling and walls completely covered in murals. In the center of the ceiling overhead, a spring was drawn, with the chandelier spouting from it like a fountain and mountains surrounding it; on the wall across from her, a powerful man was depicted with his arm pulled back, aiming a flaming spear at the spring on the ceiling. Three other figures surrounded the spring on the other walls, one holding back a rushing river with her bare hands, one with the palms of his hands on the earth beneath them, and one swirling in the air, her long hair whipping about her face as she conducted a tornado around them all.

"The Elemental Melders," Avaya said in surprise, her gaze drifting from one figure to another on the four walls.

Axis nodded and shut the door behind them. "Tell me,

what do you think? Was Aurin using *Tabeun* or *Sifal* when he ended magic in the known world?"

"Surely it was *Tabeun,* or natural magic. Their abilities were inborn, and their goals were pure, even if misguided."

Axis crossed his arms. "They nearly died in the attempt. *Should* have died. Magic was never more twisted beyond its limits than on that day; it is *Sifal,* or 'dirty magic,' that they tried to combine with *Tabeun* to get their way." Axis pulled a chair out at the table and gestured for her to sit, then moved to his own chair. Avaya eyed the stew, bread, and wine and eased into the chair.

"There's always more than I can eat. Join me." Axis clapped his hands and a servant appeared with another place setting. The young man placed it in front of Avaya, dished stew into both of their bowls, and stepped back. "Thank you, Perton."

"How very kind," Avaya said. Axis sat across from her and picked up his spoon. Her chest hitched, and for a moment she couldn't breathe. "Wait!"

Axis paused and looked at her.

Avaya swallowed. "Perton, would you indulge me...the first time a servant waits upon a royal in Jannemar, we thank them for their service by allowing them first taste of their first served meal. I thought since this was the first time you waited on me...?"

Anger flickered across Axis'sface, and Perton glanced between Axis and Avaya.

Axis picked up his napkin and smoothed it out. "It is not customary for servants to partake in royal mealtime here in Belvidore, and I daresay I have never heard of such a thing."

"Perhaps you would humor me just this once. To feel more at home. I assure you, it won't happen again." Avaya twisted the rings on her fingers underneath the table. Her stomach tightened.

Perton's eyes darted back to his master, and Axis rolled his eyes and waved his hand in permission. Perton nervously picked up the serving spoon and tasted the stew. He dipped his head and stepped back. "It is excellent, Your Highness."

"A taste of the whole meal, Perton." Avaya felt Axis'sglare fall harshly on her face, but she lifted her chin and drilled a stare into the young man before her. "Try the bread next. Please."

Perton hesitated, then took a roll and bit into it, and Avaya lifted her own wine glass and offered it to him. Slowly he raised the glass to his lips and took a sip.

"It is most excellent. Thank you, Your Highness."

Avaya's eyes narrowed. Perton's pupils remained normal size, his breathing was regular, he seemed the picture of health. Still, what if the poison took time to set in?

Perton stepped back and clasped his hands behind him, and Axis picked up his spoon once more. "Are there any other charming Jannemar traditions I need to know about? Something to interrupt my sleep in the middle of the night, perhaps?"

"Certainly not," Avaya answered. She couldn't let him taste the food. She needed to stall. "I wouldn't dream of–oh!" Avaya knocked her wine glass over onto Axis and jumped forward. "My apologies, Your Highness, let me help!"

Avaya bumped into the table roughly as she got up, sloshing the stew out of its bowl and into the prince's lap on top of the wine. Axis threw down his napkin and flew from his seat.

"That is quite enough! Does no one in Jannemar know how to have a proper meal or glass of wine without it ending up on the floor? Or is it a flaw you alone possess?"

Perton leapt into action, grabbing serving towels and getting down on the floor to clean up the mess, and Axis stepped away in a huff. Avaya followed and bowed her head with a deep curtsy.

"My sincerest apologies, Your Highness." She dropped her voice low. "I believe it may be poisoned. When I did not hear from you after writing you the note, I feared the worst."

Axis'shardened expression shifted to surprise, then back to caution again.

"I had forgotten about your note. I was drawn away..." He put his hand into his pocket and drew out her note, perused it, and looked at her.

"Well, the boy seems to have survived your experiment. Unlike my shirt."

"Yes, but some poisons take time. Perhaps we can keep him close for an hour or two and watch? If nothing happens, I will pay whatever penance you deem appropriate for my actions and keep my suspicions to myself henceforward."

Axis drew himself up to his full height and gave a curt nod. "Just this once, princess. If you're right, and the boy dies, you will have earned my trust; if not, you may have lost what little I had in you." Axis raised his voice. "Please excuse me to change, Princess Avaya. Perton, help me out of these clothes. You can clean up the rest later."

Avaya perched herself on the edge of one of the chairs and chewed on her nail. *What if he wasn't poisoned?* What if she was wrong? Or, worse, what if she was right that he would be poisoned but wrong about when? Axis would think she made the whole thing up to make him look foolish, or to create a rift between him and his father.

Of course, she *had* been trying to create a rift originally, but she hadn't known Arnevon was already so paranoid and at odds with his son that he would consider having him murdered. Avaya leaned over the bowl of stew. How wildly concerning that something so ordinary could be so deadly.

Axis re-emerged several minutes later, shooting ominous glances in Avaya's direction and back at Perton, who carried about his duties as if nothing out of the ordinary had transpired. Perton cleaned up the spilled wine and stew, and Axis told him his appetite was gone, and to clear the table entirely. Perton quickly obliged and disappeared back into the adjoining room.

Axis and Avaya sat across from each other in silence in the sitting room, Axis with crossed arms, taping his foot, and Avaya chewing her nail. Twenty minutes passed before Axis spoke.

"Jannemar doesn't have any custom of servants tasting their masters' food, does it?"

Avaya snorted. "Preposterous. But I wasn't sure he would be inclined to taste it had I said I thought it was poisoned and he was likely to die."

"If you're right, a very decent servant will be dead," Axis said.

"Better him than you, Your Highness," Avaya answered. "And might I suggest you invest in hiring a taster so as not to dispatch with any decent servants in the future."

"How sure are you?"

Avaya paused. She had to be confident to earn his trust, but not arrogant, or she would threaten his ego. She needed to give answers, but not so many that he wondered how she knew them. Better to lead him to make the appropriate conclusions on his own...

She took a breath. "Your Highness, King Arnevon interrogated me first about my father, and then about you and about your meetings with the Raven. He knows you are in communication with the Raven and is afraid. Like you said, he's paranoid. What is the truth about how your mother died?"

"Peacefully. In her sleep. But we have our suspicions." Axis drummed his fingers on the arm of his chair, and Avaya saw Arnevon in him in that moment. They shared the same broad build, nose, and jawline, though Axis was significantly taller.

"He asked about your meetings with the Raven, and then he wanted to speak to a healer right away and said you were staging a coup. Why would he think you were staging a coup?"

"A coup! I haven't the slightest idea. That's utterly absurd." Axis ground his teeth and curled his lip. "If you are found to be lying to me, about any of it, I'll make what life you have left a misery you will beg to end."

A chill ran up Avaya's spine, but she forced herself to hold the prince's gaze with a firm dignity. "Every word is true."

"If Perton is still alive, you'll be remaining in your room until I determine otherwise. You will make no more unauthorized visits anywhere in the castle, even to me, and I will send for you when it suits me. Is that clear?"

Avaya bit her tongue as tension sprang into every cell of her body at his dictatorial demand. Her expression remained smooth and unmoved, and she forced her body to relax before she spoke. "I mean only to please you, Your Highness. I seek only your health and the wellbeing of our two great nations."

Axis waved her off and clapped his hands. Perton appeared, and Axis examined him for a moment as the young man waited patiently in the doorway. Axis tossed up his hands. "Show Her Highness the door, Perton."

Avaya's eyes burned and balled her hands into fists, focusing on the feel of her nails digging into her palms to distract her from wanting to scream. She stood, dipped her head hardly a quarter of an inch in respect, then swept from the room with all the grace befitting her station. *He underestimates me now. But oh, let him. He will learn.*

One of Axis'sguards returned Avaya to her room, and Bonan was replaced outside her door with someone she'd never seen before. There was still no sign of the Raven. Avaya ate nothing the rest of that day and night, disturbing her plate on its tray and pouring her wine glass into an opaque flower vase on the vanity. After lying awake for much of the night, Avaya finally fell asleep – only to be rudely awoken early the next morning by an incessant banging on the door.

"I hear you!" Avaya called gruffly as she swung her legs out of bed. "Can't a girl get any rest these days?"

"You've been summoned," a voice answered. "Someone is dead."

36

———

Semra, Zephan, and Monac waited three nights for the moon to be shrouded in cloud before making their next attempt into Madensig. Monac purchased a horse, three quivers of arrows, and a bow he approved of, setting himself up on the north side facing the postern gate. Zephan was outfitted as a stable hand with a hooded cloak, holding three metal stakes each with a long rope fastened to one end and the other fastened to a tree across the moat. Semra wore a simple female servant dress with her signature trousers underneath and a small pouch tucked into her bodice with food provisions.

Zephan climbed up first, Semra agreeing to ride behind him since she would be disembarking first. Zezura lurched into the air and Semra's stomach dropped. She always loved the rush of taking off, but this time Zephan would be more exposed than ever, and they ran the risk of him getting trapped inside the enemy's fortress.

"Only an idiot would put his own life *and* the future king in such a vulnerable position," Semra had chastised him. "Politically, Avaya is a valuable pawn but a pawn nonetheless.

You are the lynchpin. If they kidnapped Avaya, they won't think twice about capturing or executing you."

"Is that concern I hear?" Zephan had teased. She'd shot him a look, and he'd sobered. "I'm also a son to my grieving father and a brother to a sister in harm's way. What kind of man am I if I don't protect my family? What kind of military leader would I be if I were unwilling to take on risk? I would rather earn the respect of my men than lead them from an elevated position unaware of the sacrifice they make."

Ultimately, the prince had his way, and the plan required three anyway. There was no way to insulate him from danger; every step of participation in the plan was dangerous for each of them. Monac had hemmed and hawed, but was outranked, and reluctantly agreed.

Semra wrapped one arm around Zephan's waist and stretched out the other on Zezura's smooth, near-black, indigo scales as they blended into the night. Her heart pounded as Zezura flew low, so low, beneath the walls of Madensig Fortress. Her wingtip grazed the water of the moat, and she turned sharply to hug the outer wall on the other side.

Zezura tilted sideways to get Zephan closer to the wall, and he drove one of the three metal stakes into the mortar between the stones. Zezura crushed her tail against it as they passed, sinking it securely, and the process was repeated twice more with the other two stakes. Semra shook her head and smiled. *Who needs a hammer when you have a dragon?* Semra's smile faded. *Would they find all three?* They were meant to find two, but the third was better concealed and would serve as Zephan's way across the moat and up the wall after the inevitable search party went after Monac.

Zez banked away from the castle and picked up speed low over the moat and land, then turned skyward and rocketed up, up, up. Semra hid her face behind Zephan's back against the wind of their ascent, and pulled away again to look over Madensig, Horen, and the deep blackness beyond that held all of Belvidore. The night was black as pitch, and Semra saw only a few dim flickering lights in protest against it in the castle below.

The dragon centered herself directly over the open court-yard in the center of the square of the fortress, and Semra took a steadying breath. *Slow, Zez...slow.* The dragon descended over the courtyard, then swooped sudden and low; Semra dropped to the courtyard and rolled to absorb the impact. In the center of the courtyard, flush to the ground, was a three-foot-wide circular opening lined with stones and the garden curated beautifully around it as the centerpiece. Semra darted toward it and dropped inside as the Zezura soared above her, angling for the north tower, and shouts rang out. Running feet pounded overhead as Semra gripped the hand and foot holds set into the sides of the cylindric stone chute around her.

Semra quickly descended until she met a platform, then turned and felt with her foot for a set of steps leading to one side. If the night above was pitch black, Semra had no vocabu-lary for the darkness in the cistern. The emptiness echoed her steps on the smooth stone floor, and as she went down the steps, she abruptly hit cold water. Semra sucked in a breath and pulled back at the sloshing sound. Had anybody heard?

She paused to listen for any sounds coming down through the cistern opening behind and above her. Screams rose in chorus, their remnants bouncing around the vacant cistern's lofty ceilings. The fear of the dragon would drown out any noise she could make down below. As for sight, all the guards would be able to see in the darkness was a hooded drag-onrider and an enormous dragon terrorizing them from above – just in time for Monac's flaming arrows to start from beyond the postern gate. Already the guards were consumed by the inescapable crisis over the castle on the north side.

Semra picked up her long skirts and pulled them to the front between her legs, tucking them into the waist of her trousers underneath, and waded into the water as she continued down the steps. The sound of the water emanated out, revealing a larger underground room, and Semra waved her hands in front of her until she ran into the cold stone of a pillar holding up the structure on the other side of the stairs. She imagined the pillars continuing at intervals the length of the room, and she felt along one far enough to note they were thicker than she was wide. The water deepened and Semra slid into it, envisioning herself in the familiar cold river running through the mountain where they used to bathe growing up. It had been dark and chilly there too, and the sensation felt strangely comforting. Of all the places to wait for long periods of time, this one was certainly passable.

Above her, Semra listened to the yells and screams of Madensig's protectors as Zezura terrified them with close passes, dips, and flames. She could feel the dragon's excitement, moving fast up into the wind and spiraling down again. Their archers would be sending volley after volley, but arrows were like chaff to Zezura's impenetrable hide. As long Zephan stayed safe, everything would be fine. A finger of anxious doubt filled Semra at the thought. *They'll be aiming at the dragonrider. They think he is you.*

It wasn't long before Semra felt a peaceful glide from Zezura, and Semra knew she had lifted off and was flying free somewhere. Semra breathed a sigh of relief and settled in for the long wait. The castle would be in a frenzy for the first twenty-four hours, searching everywhere. This would be the most volatile, dangerous time for Semra. After that, Semra would find a time to come out of the cistern and find her way to Avaya's quarters.

Semra bided her time, pacing herself in eating the rations she had brought with her, pinching herself to stay awake as the night drew on. Once, someone in heavy armor clattered down the steps of the cistern with a lantern, but they only took a brief survey of the still water and empty pillars before returning to the surface. The hubbub in the courtyard died down and Semra remained in position all night and all the following day, until the next night. She listened intently and, hearing nothing, slowly crept from behind the pillar to the steps and out of the water. Semra wrung out her skirts and remained on the steps for half the night, stretching her aching muscles and untucking her dress from her trousers, allowing her skirts to go from soaked to only lightly damp.

Semra ascended the steps and climbed up the opening of the cistern until only her eyes showed above the dark ground of the courtyard. When the changing of the guard came, Semra slipped out and made her way into the castle through empty kitchens and to the storeroom where Siler had prevented her entry the first time. Only, now she was on the inside. Semra found a plate and put a simple breakfast together of bread, breakfast meat, and fruit that she found. She set it beside her and spent the remainder of the night tucked behind sacks and barrels of foodstuffs, only shifting from her position as the castle began to stir.

At first light, Semra slipped out of her hiding place with the plate and into the adjoining tower, picturing the fortress blueprints as she ascended to the third floor. She passed two guards and another servant, none of whom acknowledged her, and proceeded out of the tower, down the hall, and around the corner. This hall was lined with what the blueprints notated as guest apartments where Semra, Zephan, and Monac assumed Avaya would be held. Semra took in the long hall at a glance and picked up her pace toward the only room with a guard outside the door.

The guard didn't give her a second look as Semra knocked on the door and slipped inside.

"Oh! Those aren't the things that I can eat."

Semra stopped dead in her tracks. A young woman lay on the couch of her sitting room, but it was not Avaya. She looked to be made of all skin and bones, and was slouched half-propped against the back of the couch. Flowers sat in the window and on the table, but were starting to wilt, and the ones on the table sat dangerously near the edge. Books stacked on the vanity against the wall and the table next to Blaise. An easel sat by the window, with a blank sheet of paper set up on it. Verses of poetry, drawings of horses, rivers, and plant life rustled lightly against each other from a slight breeze from the window and a hand-written poem with notes in the margins drifted to the floor.

Semra leaned down to grab it, and caught a glimpse of only two lines before the thin girl snatched it from her hands and leaned back against her pillows on the couch.

> *Ashes, ashes, hail her coming, magic in her leaves,*
> *Her solemn strength is weathered wild even as she grieves.*

More plants were drawn in the margins. Semra arched an eyebrow. Perhaps whatever condition or sickness she had was not restricted to her body. Or was she just odd, and loved plants an excessive amount?

Somewhere in her brain, Semra registered the woman was still talking.

"I have a rather restrictive diet. Wait – Why haven't I seen you before? Are you new?"

Semra took a moment to take stock of the situation. Avaya's room would most certainly be guarded, and no other room on the hall had a guard posted outside. Why would there be a guard for a guest? Semra's heart skipped a beat at her mistake. Of course! This must be Arnevon's daughter, Princess Blaise. But why was she down here, on the guest floor?

"You got lost." Blaise spoke in a thin, squeaky voice more befitting a mouse than a princess. She folded the poetry inside a book from the side table and set it in her lap. "Looking for Princess Avaya, no doubt."

"Well, this is the guest floor...and there is a guard outside..."

"An understandable mistake. The guard outside my door isn't there to keep me safe. He's there to save the king from hearing my undignified opinions."

Semra frowned. "Opinions, Your Highness?"

Blaise laughed, but the sound was hollow and melancholy. "I've been removed from his sight already. Not even on the same floor, as you noticed. He doesn't want the daughter he regrets having, to make him remember she exists by having opinions."

Semra hesitated. She needed to extricate herself from Princess Blaise and find Avaya as quickly as possible. Every moment spent in Madensig heightened the risk, which was more than considerable even if the plan were to go smoothly. But she also couldn't draw too much attention as she did so.

Blaise sighed. "You haven't come to hear my opinions either. Nobody ever does. Are you trying to find Avaya's room?"

"Erm...yes. A thousand pardons."

Blaise waved her hand and leaned back wearily on the couch. "She's down the hall, around the corner. She's the only other room on this floor with a guard posted outside. Have you met her yet?"

"No, I haven't," Semra lied. "What is she like?"

"You're just asking to be polite, aren't you? I should like to give you the answer you are looking for. Oh, she's lovely. Just as they say in Jannemar, anyway. Here in Belvidore, opinions of the Shamarans aren't so glowing."

Semra's mind pricked with curiosity. Blaise was not at all what Semra had expected, and her controversial opinions might be the only opportunity for honest insider information. And the sickly princess was desperate to give it.

Semra bit her lip and folded her hands. "Highness, I am new to my position, and everyone tells me I'm naïve. I would be grateful for any genuine information at all, and if you forgive my saying so, perhaps you wouldn't mind someone to hear your thoughts for once."

Blaise tilted her head and looked at Semra intently, then relaxed. "Well, she *is* lovely, I'm afraid. I wish she wasn't, but she is. The rumors have it that she's ugly, but she's drop dead gorgeous, poised, well-mannered. Slender but not skinny, color in her face – all the things a woman of birth should be. Except a couple of her nails are all raggedy, and she seems *too* comfortable. Like a diplomat here on business. She's more confident in my home than I have been all my life, but she seems arrogant about it, you know? I do hope you find her arrogant. If you do, come back and tell me, because it would be most comforting. I don't like her. I don't think she cares an ounce for me or my family."

Blaise's voice ticked up to an even higher pitch, and Semra winced. "And, if I'm right, I don't like that she's so good at pretending that she does care. If Jannemar allowed women in politics, I'm certain she would have a lot to say! But perhaps there, she's as silenced as I am here."

"She did something concerning?"

"No, no. Not a thing, that's it. She's the perfect hostage. Oh, rats, they told Horen she came voluntarily and it's all part of a big negotiations diplomacy deal. Listen, if I spoiled the illusion for you, forget it. And if you don't forget it, but remember it instead, and you decide to tell somebody that I said it, well, I'll deny it, and I'll have you hanged. Oh, and the same goes for telling anyone my opinions, okay?"

Semra blinked. "You..." She swallowed. "Opinions about what?"

Blaise gave a curt nod. "Precisely. Precisely. Well, then, go on, but I mean it that if you decide you don't like her, or she does something interesting, please do come back and tell me. I'll make it worth your while if you're quiet about it. I promise."

Semra curtsied and bowed her head, then made her escape. "Of course. So sorry for the mistake."

Semra turned away from Blaise's room and hurried down the hall with her plate of unacceptable breakfast items. She turned the corner at a clipped pace and nearly ran into the single guard outside a room on the next hall. Semra stepped back and dipped her head in apology. The guard straightened and looked her up and down, but said nothing. Semra turned away from him and knocked on the door. She listened, but there was no answer. Semra paused, then rapped on the door again, this time louder.

"She's been summoned," the guard said. "She's not here."

Semra turned to the guard. "You're guarding an empty room?"

"I guard whatever I'm told to guard."

Semra lifted the plate. "I was told to deliver this."

The guard shrugged. "She can't eat it if she isn't here. Leave it and go."

Semra hesitated, her mind spinning and heart racing. She nodded, and the guard opened the door. Semra walked into an elaborate guest room with a canopy bed, an army of pillows, a vanity, and sitting area with a small table before it. Every moment inside the castle was a risk, but she couldn't afford any more unexpected delays – not with Zephan waiting, Belvidore invading, and all Madensig on high alert.

A thought popped into her mind, as natural as breathing. *Kill the guard, hide him in the room, and wait for Avaya to return.* Semra shook her head. *No, you don't take life anymore. Not without reason – he's doing his job. He has nothing to do with this. Ugh, life was so much simpler when killing was the endgame.*

Another thought. *You're taking too long.*

Semra snapped her head up at the sound of approaching footsteps. The guard appeared in the doorway, his face hardening as he observed her standing frozen in the room with the breakfast plate, securing his fate as he sealed her off from freedom. She didn't want to kill him, but if she had no choice, she had no choice. Semra clenched her jaw and set the plate down on the vanity, then turned to face the guard.

37

———

AVAYA

Avaya swept down the hall, her mind reeling. The king interrogated her the night after her meeting with Axis. The following night there was screaming throughout the castle. Everyone refused to talk about it. She'd seen spurts of fire and the outline of the dragon against its flame through her north-facing window, but when she'd banged on her door demanding answers, she was told to stay put. The next morning Axis had sent for her.

"It seems I am in need of a new valet. Perton is dead, thanks to you." Avaya had nearly fainted with relief to find Axis alive. Perton's death had been an added perk. Perhaps she'd be back in Axis'sgood graces.

"Surely you mean thanks to your would-be murderer."

"We shall see. It would be elaborate for you to have arranged something like this to manipulate my trust, but I plan on launching a full investigation nonetheless."

"It will be short. I've been nowhere, save when summoned, and spoken to very few. But I don't understand — last night you said if he died, it would prove my faithfulness. And I did prove it. At great personal cost, I might add."

Axis had stepped toward her then, brushing her arm with his hand, then tucking a strand of her hair behind her ear. *"You have saved me from my own father. Whatever your motive, we'll spin the story of our love and your dedication to me,to Belvidore, and release it to the people. And if you really did save me"* – here he had leaned in to let his lips brush her ear – *"you will want for nothing, and I shall provide every desire of your heart every day of our marriage. But if you are found to be deceitful, our matrimony will be an inescapable snare to you, and your lavish rooms and frivolous sweetmeats will be the only comforts afforded you."*

A shiver ran up Avaya's spine at the memory. She had lifted her chin.

"Double your investigators. Resolve your doubts. My heart is for my people, and in that pursuit, I offer it to you. Do with it what you will."

"And the dragon?"

Avaya had shrugged, hoping the nonchalance masked the anxiety pounding in her chest. *"No match for my intended, I'm sure."*

His eyes had roved over her face, then lingered on her lips before his mouth met hers. Avaya could feel his guard slipping. She would let him run his investigations. When they found nothing, he would hers. But what would the king do if he learned of her involvement? Would Laurel break under pressure?

Avaya quickened her pace as she neared her room, stalking down the hall with her guard hot on her heels. *Where was the Raven?* She stopped in her tracks at the sight of a guard staring into the open door of her bedroom.

"What exactly do you think you're doing?" she demanded.

The guard jumped. "Your Highness. One of the servants brought your breakfast plate, but she isn't leaving."

Avaya's stomach growled at the suggestion of breakfast. She'd eaten no formal meals since before she made Perton eat the poisoned food in the prince's chambers. Avaya strode past the guard into the room, then stopped short. There, wearing servant's garb and a stupid dumbstruck expression, stood her brother's assassin guttersnipe.

The woman who'd destroyed her family. The woman who had duped her brother, sister, and even her father into believing she was some poor, victimized passion project that they could fix. Avaya's lip curled for only an instant before she smoothed her expression over into impassivity.

"Good, I'm starved. And I'm bored. She can clean my room and entertain me before returning to the rest of her duties."

Avaya swept into the room with an air of importance, but her chest constricted and her breathing quickened as the door closed behind her. Anger bubbled up from within her and she whirled on Semra. She checked her rage in the last moment, biting out a more subdued option instead.

"If you're here to kill me, you're doing a terrible job."

38

K ill Avaya? Semra pressed her lips together. Aurin's Spear, what had gotten into the girl's head? Semra looked at the princess for a moment. "In what deranged world would I be here to kill you?"

Avaya shrugged. "You're an assassin, aren't you? Assassins kill people."

"Ah. I must have forgotten. Should I adjust my plans to meet your expectations?" Semra crossed her arms. She wasn't sure exactly what she had been hoping their encounter would be like, but this wasn't it.

"Smart. Move straight to threats – *that* will convince me you're innocent and misunderstood."

Semra rolled her eyes.

Avaya glared back at her. "The servant thing suits you."

Semra nearly bit her tongue clean off at her words, but she stayed the course. She took a deep breath. "I'm getting you out of here."

Avaya strode to the plate Semra had brought, plucked the breakfast meat from the plate and dropped it on the floor. "As intrigued as I am at how you would do such a thing, I'm afraid you've come all this way for nothing. I'm not going."

"Yes, you are." Semra watched as Avaya ripped off a piece of bread roll, crumbled it to bits, and dusted the decimated morsels from her fingers. Zephan might eat the cuisine of royals at home, but he was happy to eat roots and scant dried provisions on the road. She would never understand how the two were related.

Avaya set her hands on her hips and drilled her with a cool stare. "No, I'm not."

"King Turian sent me to retrieve his daughter. I can't return emptyhanded."

"Send him my warmest regards."

Semra tossed her hands up and lowered her voice to a sharp hiss. "What reason could you possibly have for choosing to stay with your kidnappers?"

Avaya sniffed. "I have responsibility you couldn't dream of. The weight of the crown on my family is unshakable, and I am finally in a position to *do* something. I'm not sitting on the sidelines anymore."

"How do you feel about sitting in a coffin? Because that's a real possibility if you stay."

Avaya's eyes went dark and flat as she stepped into Semra's space and stared her down. "I don't need to prove myself to you. I've made my decision. You can tell my father I plan to ease the tensions with Belvidore from the inside out."

Fear gripped Semra by the throat like a vise. What if she couldn't get Avaya out? Turian would be furious, and his court would think she had orchestrated the kidnapping herself. If she was seen as guilty she'd be sent on the run, and for all Semra's claims that she was leaving her old life behind her, Avaya's blood would be on Semra's head if she was murdered in Belvidore. Semra swallowed hard, her eyes narrowing.

"You speak of the weight of the crown on your family, but your *father* is the king and *he* commanded you be brought back. He's terrified of losing you. And, speaking of the crown, the *crown* prince is here to save his sister. So if you're going to justify letting them mourn both your mother *and* you, you could at least have the decency to tell your brother yourself."

Avaya faltered, steadying herself on the side table, uncertainty in her eyes for the first time. "Zephan is here?"

Semra nodded. "He convinced everyone he was the best man for the job. Refused to take no for an answer."

"I'm not an idiot. I know my brother; I saw him in the arena. Is he in Madensig?"

It wasn't a question Semra wanted to answer. Truth be told, there wasn't a question in the world that Avaya could ask that would cause Semra to want to give her information of any sort, however innocuous. But she had to know, or she might not come. It was the reason they'd risked Zephan's life to bring him his close.

"He's here. You need to come with me."

Avaya chewed on a fingernail, staring off into a distant corner of the room. "Tell him to he has to go back. Tell him to give me time."

Semra grimaced. "You know he won't. Certainly not if *I* tell him. He needs to see you."

Avaya paced for a moment, then stopped. "It can't look like I left willingly."

Oh, that was a problem Semra knew how to fix. Solutions to Avaya's predicament filed through Semra's mind. Uppercut? Elbow to the face? The corner of Semra's mouth tipped up. "So you're coming? Are you saying I should I deck you in the face?"

Avaya pursed her lips. "I didn't say that. But I need to protect myself here – I'm on thin ice and trying to build trust."

She stopped, then eyed the breakfast plate Semra had brought. "Where'd you get that?"

"I threw it together in the kitchens as an excuse to come up here."

"You made it yourself? From the general castle store-houses, not anything set aside?"

"Yes..."

Avaya snatched up the plate and crammed the fruit and remainder of the roll into her mouth. It was the only less-than-elegant thing Semra had ever seen Avaya do.

She must have been starving. *She thinks she's going to be poisoned. She knows how precarious her situation is.*

Semra cocked an eyebrow. "Have your meals been that bad, or is that coffin I mentioned looking a little more likely these days?"

"Shut up. Now get me to my brother and back."

Semra concealed a smile and breathed a sigh of relief. *All that matters is getting to the stables. Once we're beyond the inner walls, she's coming with us whether she wants to or not.*

A knock came at the door, and the guard's voice barked at them.

"Your Highness? That's long enough for the servant to clean up in there."

Semra's heart quickened, and adrenaline laced each pump of blood. She kept her voice low, and her eyes on Avaya. "Tell him you need him to move the couch."

Avaya nodded and raised her voice. "Yes, yes! But she's insisting on rearranging all my sitting furniture before she goes." Avaya turned toward Semra and yelled for the guard's benefit, "I've told you twice now, it's fine where it is! What is wrong with you?!"

The door flew open, and the guard stormed in just in time for Semra to run to the couch and tug on it as if repositioning it. Avaya brought her hands up to her face in a show of dismay and flitted off to the side.

The guard crossed the room in four long strides and took hold of Semra's upper arm. "That's enough of that, now. Her Highness was more than clear."

In a single fluid motion, Semra brought her arm up, over, and down, breaking his grip. She slung her forearm into the top of his head and brought it down hard, knocking him on his back, twisted his head around with both hands so his body was forced to follow and he flopped on his stomach. Semra pressed a knee into his spine, wrapped her elbow around the guard's throat, and cinched it tight until his body went slack.

"What, no slit throats?" Avaya taunted. "I'm disappointed."

"It's your turn to shut up." Semra fished a knife from the trousers under her skirts and passed it to Avaya. "Hurry and cut off the cord at the base of the wall tapestry and bring it to me."

Avaya brought Semra the cord, and Semra tied the guard securely and dragged him behind the couch. He stirred, and she slugged him in the temple. He slumped.

Semra snatched the lit lantern from Avaya's vanity, wrapped it in bedlinen, and smashed it against one of the four posters of the bedframe. The glass shattered, and Semra dripped oil over the feather bed and wall hanging as the bed caught flame. Avaya's eyes widened, and she looked truly uncomfortable for the first time.

Good. About time.

"Time to go." Semra gripped Avaya's arm and pulled her out the door, down the empty hall in the direction she had come, into the tower, down one flight of stairs, and out into a hall of long tables and chairs. Semra pulled Avaya down with her between the chairs and the wall just in time for footsteps to cross through the room and continue out behind them. The sound faded away and Avaya moved to stand, but Semra tugged her arm downward again and shook her head. *Not yet.*

They waited only a few minutes before shouts claimed the air around them.

"Smoke! Fire!"

"Southwest side! Go, go, go!"

Hurried footfalls pounded through the hall and into the stairwell, and screams from servants echoed through the tower from the floor above. Semra pulled Avaya to her feet. Sometimes simple solutions were the most effective. The fire was the level of diversion they needed.

By the time they reached the stairwell, it was in chaos. Three servants ran screaming on their way down the stairs, and two more hauled buckets of water up the stairs, while a guard bellowed for more water from above.

Semra gripped Avaya's arm tight as they ran down the last flight of stairs, emptying out into the kitchen area where twenty servants flitted about anxiously with meal preparation interrupted by demands for buckets upon buckets of water.

"We need more!" someone screamed.

"We don't have more!" someone yelled back.

The voices mingled together.

"All of Horen must see the smoke! Get quilts, heavy things, beat it out!"

"Are you sure that's going to work?!"

Semra plucked a quilt out of the arms of a young girl staggering under the weight of a stack of them and shook it free of its neatly folded form. She wrapped it around Avaya's shoulders before motioning the princess to duck her head down, and ushered her out into the grassy yard between the inner and outer walls, through the very door Siler had been standing in just days prior. Semra ran under one of the archways into the stables with her arm around Avaya's shoulders.

The stables were long, with horse stalls lining both sides and ladders leading up to hay lofts and storage spaces at intervals down its length. Semra motioned for Avaya to get up the ladder.

"You can't be serious," Avaya whispered. "I'm in a dress."

If a dress was all it took to keep valued hostages from escaping, it was no wonder they'd been instituted for half the population. Semra groaned and hitched up her skirts. She and gestured at Avaya's gown. "So am I. Figure it out, princess, before both our heads roll."

Avaya huffed, but reluctantly acquiesced, lifting her embroidered hem and climbing up to the loft with Semra on her heels. The hay loft was large, perhaps forty feet long, filled with stacks upon stacks of hay bales, and barrels of barley. Semra tugged Avaya away from the edge of the loft and further into the stacks of hay bales. Avaya sneezed and Semra elbowed her in the ribs.

"Ow! You didn't need to–"

A hand clamped over Avaya's mouth and yanked her backward into the hay; she stumbled and let out a muffled scream. Semra's heart leaped into her throat, and she was halfway into her right hook before she saw who it was. She dropped her hand, and Zephan grinned. Monac materialized out of the hay behind him and nodded at her. She nodded back.

"Did I surprise you?" Zephan asked, his voice hushed.

Semra pressed her lips together to suppress a smile. "A little."

He beamed. "That's quite the accomplishment, I'd think! Glad you both made it." He turned to Avaya, who was glaring daggers at him. "If I let you go, will you behave? No squealing like a stuck pig when you get nudged."

Avaya rolled her eyes, and Zephan snatched his hand away. "Eww! You didn't need to lick me!"

Avaya smirked and crossed her arms. Semra's gut cinched tight as she watched them. It wasn't a perfect relationship, but in that moment, she saw a brother and sister who could have acted the same way when they were small. What would it have been like to have a brother? Did she have siblings somewhere?

Zephan caught her eye and turned sheepish. He cleared his throat. "Right. Avaya, I'm so relieved to see you safe. We'll wait for the right moment to leave and get you out of here as soon as possible." He glanced at Monac. "We have some bad news."

"So do we." Semra glared at Avaya. "She doesn't want to leave."

"You *what?*" Zephan hissed, glaring at his sister.

She clenched her jaw. "I'm not going. Now that I'm here, I have a chance to fix what happened at the gala...I can restore Belvidore's relationship with Jannemar and stop the fighting by marrying Axis and creating unity between our kingdoms. The union was a politically solid move then, and it's an even more strategic one now."

Monac shook his head. "Word on the street is King Arnevon is highly paranoid, and he could kill you for looking at him sideways. The fact that he was willing to kidnap you to get what he thinks he deserves is incredibly dangerous. What if he decides a dead trophy is better than a living one?"

Avaya took a breath as if to speak, then pursed her lips and said nothing. Semra arched an eyebrow. *She knows something.* The memory of her scarfing down the food Semra brought surged to mind. If she was in danger, why wouldn't she share it? Was she really so proud?

But of course, Zephan would never let her stay if he knew. What Avaya didn't know is that he'd never let her stay anyway. She was leaving with them whether she wanted to or not – but transporting her bound and gagged was less than ideal.

Semra shook off the thought and turned to Zephan. "What's your bad news?"

"We're taking heavy casualties at the Surion Strip. Jannemar is losing ground, and Belvidore has greater numbers than we thought. Our leaders are stretched thin, especially since General Gresvig was deposed along with some of the other rats in our court that Azi had influenced. We heard them bragging about severely injuring one of our generals too, so we must be down another one. I need to get to the Strip."

Monac leaned wearily against a hay bale. "Also, we were able to use the rope you secured to the wall to get across the moat last night, but the guards have since found all three and removed them."

"You can't go to the Strip." Avaya put a hand on Zephan's arm. "It'll be a bloodbath."

Zephan stood a little taller as he looked down at her. "'A king who wears his sword for show – a man unworthy as a foe.' I can't leave *our* men, whom *we* sent, to fight alone. I won't."

Semra's stomach flopped over at his words, at the thought of something happening to him. She watched his amber-brown eyes search his sister's green ones, a resolved firmness mixed with tenderness for his sister. Semra's gaze drifted down to his muscled arms as he put a hand on Avaya's shoulder, and back up to his face.

With a jolt she realized he was looking at her, and she straightened. "Hmm? What?"

Something in Zephan's eyes flickered and he cocked his head. Avaya's stare darkened.

Monac grunted. "We still need a way out of the castle. His Highness asked if you thought we could make it out in a wagon somehow."

Get it together. Semra took a breath and shook her head. "No, it's too long to wait, and with the, erm, distraction I made, they aren't going to be lax with any incoming or outgoing wagons."

Avaya's tone was flat. "She *burned* my *room.*"

"Yes, we saw the smoke," Monac said nonchalantly.

"Such a pity that your fancy prison room is ruined," Zephan added, dripping with sarcasm.

Semra cleared her throat. "We need to cross the moat."

Avaya looked at her. "As long as the guards are distracted, why can't you?"

"Punji sticks," Zephan answered. "They're planted in the moat. If you find one and cut yourself, you could die from the infection."

Avaya scoffed. "You believed that? It's a rumor Belvidore started. It isn't true. They do have archers at the walls, but the archers and the outer bailey are your main problems."

Zephan's jaw dropped. "How do you know it's a rumor?"

Avaya shrugged. "What, a girl can't do research?"

"Are you sure?" Monac asked.

She nodded. "I wouldn't send my brother into a death trap. I'm sure."

The group exchanged glances, and Zephan nodded. "Okay, so we just need to get over the wall and across the moat without getting shot."

Semra held up a hand. "It's too far to swim."

Monac grinned. "We've got the equipment we need. We can make it."

Avaya crossed her arms. "Why doesn't dragon girl bring beasty in to save the day?"

Why doesn't the princess keep her trap shut until she decides to be helpful?

"Because as great as she is, Zezura draws a lot of attention and she'll reveal our location before we have a chance to hop on." Semra answered. "It could take her a bit to get here depending on how far she's flown to hunt, and we are sitting ducks during that time. We may use her yet, but I don't want her exposed and vulnerable between the inner and outer baileys of the fortress for long. Arnevon was aware of her before, but especially after the other night, he may have sought out strategies to hinder her."

"For a dragonrider, you don't seem to take advantage of it as often as you should."

Semra's blood ran hot. "Zezura isn't for being taken advantage of. She and I are a team, and as much as she protects me, she deserves me to protect her in return."

Hurried footsteps from down below silenced the group in the hay loft, and they bent down to be fully concealed behind the hay and barley. Two sets of footfalls entered the stables, and Semra heard the latch of a stall door and the hooves of horses as the animals were led out. A voice came from the stable beneath them.

"Ride hard. You should arrive early on the fourth day. The next company should arrive another four days after you do. Deliver the correspondence and the pigeons directly to General Rewan."

"What do I say about the dragon and the fire?"

"Not a word. They're looking for the woman who set the fire now, and she was seen going down the southwest tower with the Jannemar princess. We'll have her by the midday meal. It's well in hand."

39

———————

The three-beat gait of a canter reached Semra's ears as the horse beneath the loft was kicked forward. She let out a breath as the sound of its hoofbeats faded away in the distance. Zephan, Monac, Avaya, and Semra waited up in the hay loft. One minute, two minutes, three. Avaya stirred, but Monac shook his head, and she stilled.

Five minutes passed, a light creaking sound came from below, and at last, the second man could be heard exiting the stable, his suspicions apparently satisfied. Semra's mind whirred with what they had heard, piecing together their full predicament. Zephan ran a hand through his hair, and his hand shook as he did.

"I need a minute. Get me if something changes or if you think of a solution." He walked across the loft and disappeared behind another stack of haybales twenty feet over.

Monac's eyes followed his prince, then fell back to Semra. "We don't have time for this. He knows it. If they don't search the stable soon, they'll know we are here and surround it instead."

Semra nodded. There was only one sensible response to their situation, and Zephan's stalling wouldn't change what they had to do. "We need to split up. Avaya and I will draw them away, and you and Zephan can get over the wall and across the moat. I'll have Zezura pick us up after you're across. Right now, the focus is on who is *inside* the walls. If Zezura comes before you get into the moat, guards on the wall will be focused outside the castle again and you might be caught before you hit the border. We'll keep them focused until you're safe."

"Did everyone forget that I'm not going?" Avaya demanded.

"Oh, you're going," Monac said. "The king's order trumps yours, and you can negotiate with King Turian for your political union after you're no longer a pawn for Belvidore's blackmail."

"Fine. But Belvidore needs to know I didn't want to go."

Monac shrugged. "You can tell them whatever you want next time they try to kidnap or kill you."

Avaya's jaw dropped.

Monac pursed his lips. "Your Highness," he added dryly. Avaya huffed. Monac turned back to Semra. "Zephan isn't going to want to split up."

"Like you said, we don't have time for this. I'll talk to him."

Semra crept the twenty feet from her place to where Zephan had disappeared and found him pacing in a narrow rectangular space hemmed in by hay bales and barrels. She patted the hay as she approached, and it rustled lightly under her touch. "I'd knock, but...you know..."

Zephan gave her a dark look but continued pacing.

"We don't have time for this."

"I know." More pacing.

Semra let out an exasperated sigh. This approach wouldn't

work with Zephan. The fastest way to get him moving was to slow down. She took a deep breath. "You losing it a little?"

"Yes."

"It takes a lot to make you lose it."

"A lot is going on."

"Want to talk about it?" Semra hoped to high heaven the answer was no. She had no idea what to say, and the clock was ticking.

"I thought we didn't have time for that."

"We don't."

"I need to pull myself together."

Semra pursed her lips. "Yes. You're a liability in this state."

Zephan stopped pacing and glared at her. Semra put her hands up defensively. "Sorry. Not accusing. Just observing." She grimaced. "I guess that doesn't sound better."

Zephan's shoulders sagged and he passed a hand over his eyes. The answer came to her then like a spark in a void. *His world makes no sense right now. It has no rhythm.*

Semra stepped close to him and he looked down at her questioningly but didn't move away. Slowly, Semra reached for Zephan's hand and drew it around her waist, then ran her hand up his arm and rested it on his shoulder. With her other hand, she took his, and swayed back and forth.

This is the dumbest thing you've ever done. Semra bit her lip and blushed beet red. This was a stupid idea. She never should have done it.

"Are we...are we dancing?" he asked. Semra couldn't tell if he was incredulous, or mocking her.

"Maybe. Because...because it's calming and nice. Or something." *Lame. Stupid. Rats and rot, Semra, the Belvidorian guard is going to show up any minute and you're going to die with those idiotic words as your last.*

Against all reason, Zephan chuckled. His arm tightened

around her and pulled her against him, and Semra's pulse began to race . He moved her lightly, adding expert footwork to the tiny space around them, and she let him maneuver her feet beyond where they had been rooted to the floor. Zephan pulled her into a hug and held her close, and Semra felt him take a steadying breath.

"Thank you," he whispered.

Semra swallowed, trying to ignore the warmth wrapping around her, the safety and softness of his presence. "You're welcome."

There was a pause, and he spoke again. "We've been here too long. We need to move."

"Yes. You and Monac first, Avaya and me next. I already spoke to Monac."

"I don't think we should split up."

"Avaya will be in no more danger than she was in this morning. She'll look like a pawn dragged here and there by opposing parties. You have to get out."

Zephan squeezed her tighter. "What about you?"

"Zezura will pick us up as soon as you're safe." *Would they last that long?* She doubted it. Semra's stomach soured.

"I don't like it," Zephan said.

"I don't like you going to the front lines."

"Ugh, gross." Zephan and Semra looked up in startled surprise to see Avaya, her face scrunched up in disgust. Semra dropped her arms and tried to pull away, but Zephan held her for a moment longer before releasing her. Avaya rolled her eyes. "We've got company."

"How many?" Zephan asked.

Monac appeared. "From what we can see through a few windows, I'm not sure. Maybe a dozen."

Semra dipped her head. "They're looking for Avaya and

me. They don't know about you two, so once we draw them out, they'll follow us and abandon the opposite side. Stay in the loft until we're gone, then climb out one of the back windows."

"We should help," Zephan said.

Semra shook her head. "That's a terrible idea. You'll get yourselves killed and I'll probably get blamed for it somehow. And I've already summoned Zezura." Semra hoped she looked convincing, and sent out the call through the mark of the dragon's kiss . *Come to me.* She felt for Zezura's answering call, but it was distant.

"Is she close?" Zephan pressed.

"Yes," Semra lied. She looked at Monac. "Promise me you won't let him follow us. Your duty is to your king and your prince. Protecting him even from himself, if he wants to do something stupid."

Zephan's eyes narrowed, but Monac nodded. Monac reached out and clasped her forearm in farewell, and Semra gave a curt nod. A lump lodged in her throat at the simple goodbye. Rats and rot, did she care about Monac? She was coming to care about far too many people these days.

Avaya glanced between the three of them. "What happens now?"

Semra stripped off her servant's dress and tossed it aside, revealing her signature trousers strapped with knives, and a long-sleeved undershirt. Monac handed her his sword without a word, and Semra took it in kind. "You stay close, we run, and we buy time until Zez picks us up."

"So it's up to the beasty after all."

Semra glared at her. "Stay close, or I'll cut you."

Avaya's eyes flashed and she opened her mouth, then closed it. Semra looked once more at Zephan, a torn expression plaguing those amber eyes. She knew he wanted to stay, to fight with her. Maybe he was even calculating how far he could get before Monac stopped him and hauled him back to concealment and safety. But he mustn't. For the weight of the crown.

Zephan stepped toward her, but a firm resolve hardened in Semra, and she stepped away. They were out of time, and any closeness to him now could compromise her courage. She adjusted her grip on Monac's sword.

"Out the window after we're gone," she repeated. "Stay safe."

Semra turned on her heel and pushed Avaya in front of her toward the ladder, then descended first and waited for Avaya. She didn't look back. Semra's breathing quickened as she scanned the stable. No one was visible, but she knew Monac's report would be sound – they were surrounded.

Semra spun the sword in her hand and bounced on the balls of her feet, then gripped Avaya firmly by the arm and ran forward to meet whatever opposition might await them. Five armed guards ran forward from the yard to meet her; Semra threw a knife into the neck of one before the first adversary reached her and drove into the second at full force with the sword. Shouts went up, and the guards circling the back of the stable abandoned their positions to assist in taking Semra down. *Now's your chance, Zephan,* Semra thought to herself. *Take it.*

She stepped over the body of the second man and swung at the third, dashing in and out of his space like a bird. The sound of blood rushed in her ears, adrenaline coursing through her veins, the movement of her body as she stab, slash, stabbed her way through each opponent, brought her home. Dancing might bring rhythm to Zephan's life, but the art of the fight was a dance to Semra. No matter how hard she tried, no matter how often she said she had left assassin life behind, *this* is what she excelled at. *This* is what she was made for.

The only thing you were ever good at was killing.

You're a murderer, Semra. It's who you are.

Semra parried a blow to her head but left Avaya vulnerable; she saw the guard hesitate and she threw a knife into his throat. *They have orders to keep her alive.* Semra absorbed the information as her mind continued to whir.

Perhaps her assassin identity wasn't a part of her that she could kill. *What if this really is who I am? What if I can't shake it, can't rise above it?* Zephan wouldn't understand. Society wouldn't understand. That hole in a mountain with Zezura would be all that was left for her, if she survived today.

My dear, my dear ... you know I am the only one who has never left you.

The Framatar's voice in Semra's head, clear and unbidden in her mind, filled her with newfound fury, and she flew with three times the strength she had borne before. Semra lunged, blocked, and reached for Avaya; she twisted Avaya's arm behind her back and pulled her against her own body as a human shield as she sliced into the torso of another man.

Four bodies littered the yard between the inner and outer walls of Madensig, but nine more rallied for a chance to draw blood. Semra knew her endurance and skill wouldn't last against large numbers of fresh fighters, especially with a non-skilled important person along. Avaya sagged, half-falling against Semra so that she had to bear up the weight of the princess while fighting. Semra's shoulders drooped and her breathing came heavy as she maneuvered Avaya's body like a sack of potatoes. A heavy sack of potatoes. One that was unco-operative. And made a person want to stab it.

She wasn't even fighting. She couldn't possibly be fatigued.

"They can't kill you, but I can," Semra hissed, and poked her in the back with a knife. Avaya yelped and straightened, and Semra flung the knife into the thigh of an oncoming attacker. He kept coming, and she ducked, weaved, slashed with her sword, and suddenly found herself disarmed by a guard to her right, appearing from nowhere and stripping the grip of the sword from her while she was distracted with Avaya.

Semra lunged forward, gripping the handle of the knife in the first attacker's thigh and ripping it free; he shrieked in pain and fell back and Semra released a blood-curdling yell as she broke through the block of the guard to her right. Semra buried her knife in his gut, then dragged the blade across to his hip and tore it free. He gaped at her as his eyes began to glaze, and dropped Monac's sword as he fell.

She parried a blow from above as Avaya was torn from her grasp, and Semra looked up in time to see Siler running toward her with five more guards on his tail. He was barking orders and the guards were responding, but Semra heard nothing beyond her own pounding heartbeat. Someone tackled her to the ground and her body crumbled under his weight. The force of the hit reverberated through her body in a way that would leave her blue by tomorrow, if tomorrow ever came.

Pain radiated from her chest where she'd struck the ground. Rage washed through her, at the one person who should have understood her, should have protected her, was supposed to be living a better life.

"Traitor!" Semra screamed. *"Traitor!"*

Siler's eyes met hers and with a cold and cutting stare. Somewhere next to her Semra was dimly aware of Avaya crying and squalling about being kidnapped and threatened.

Her voice grated even as Semra's brain shut it out. Semra's heart hurt as she Zezura's distant silhouette formed on the horizon, flying fast but not fast enough. *It's okay, Zez. It's too late.* Siler motioned to someone behind Semra, and her world turned to black.

40

———

Ramas smiled wickedly, cocking his head.

"*You are the nameless, faceless fly on the wall in a moment of time...*" He laughed as his hand shot out and sunk into the soft tissues of her throat. Semra wondered briefly if he would rip out her esophagus.

"*Five dead in minutes. So much death. You hardly thought about it, didn't you? The implications. The families torn apart. You think being an assassin is in your past, yet who do we have to blame for all the deaths, for the dragon business, for the queen's death, for the conflict in the king's court?*" Ramas clucked his tongue. "*That's right. You.*"

Semra gasped as ice cold water smacked her in the face and soaked her shirt and trousers. Her eyes flew open, and she winced, throbbing pain in her head where she'd been hit. Semra found herself lying on the stone floor of a great hall with ebony pillars running its length on both sides, rich tapestries lining the walls, and an engraved stone throne set on a dais on one end.

She struggled to her knees and discovered her hands were bound behind her, and her ankles were crossed, also bound.

Avaya stood on Semra's right, Siler beside her, and four guards flanked. There was a middle-aged man on the throne, stroking his beard with a hand dripping with gemstones. Semra recognized him from the gala back in Jannemar: King Arnevon.

He tapped his fingers on the arm of his throne as he considered her. "What is your name?"

"Semra."

"Semra what?"

Semra Nobody. Her vision swam, and she licked her lips. "I have no surname."

"You're one of the assassins from Mount Hara?"

Semra clenched her jaw. How much did he know? How much did Siler tell him? "Yes."

"And how much were you paid to break into my castle and attempt to kidnap our esteemed guest?"

Semra balked. Even for Arnevon, that was a stretch. "I didn't try to kidnap anyone."

Arnevon's fingers stopped moving. "Your purpose was to remove Princess Avaya from Madensig, is that correct?"

"Yes." Telling the truth in captivity was a strange experience for Semra. But these were basic questions that did no harm to answer. Her gaze flicked to Siler, but his features were stone.

"Kidnapping, then."

Semra shrugged. "If you say so." *And if rescue constitutes as kidnapping.*

Arnevon's face reddened. "Who hired you?"

"No one."

"You expect us to believe that you risked life and limb to break in, threaten the princess' life while she is under *my* protection, landed yourself in chains, and all for nothing? Not a cent?"

"My reasons are my own."

The guard to her right slugged her in the ribs. Semra cried out and fell forward, catching herself on her forearms. The double doors at the end of the hall opened, and someone swept in with a swift, strong gait, wearing the colors of his kingdom. Prince Axis walked up behind Semra and came to a stop next to Avaya, then turned to his father.

"I heard there was a meeting that might interest me. I've come to offer assistance."

Arnevon waved a hand dismissively. "We caught the arsonist and would-be kidnapper, but she seems to be quick with her mouth and empty in the head. Your fiancé is safe, so I thought not to trouble you."

"Nothing is more important to me than the security of Madensig and the safety of our family and royal guests. I've been so sick with worry since the dragon attack, I've hardly touched my meals."

A tense look passed between father and son, and Semra glanced first at one, and then the other. The tension could have been cut with a knife. Clearly some thinly veiled message was being transmitted, but what it was, she couldn't guess.

Axis tore his stern gaze away from Arnevon and trained it on Semra. "When did King Turian hire you to steal my bride?"

Semra watched as Axis slid his arm around Avaya's waist, and she stepped into him. Had Avaya really followed the illusion that far? "As I said before, I wasn't hired."

Axis nodded at the guard behind Semra, and she rolled on instinct as the guard took his swing. His fist *wooshed* harmlessly through the air, and she popped back up on her knees. The guard's face reddened. Semra rolled her eyes and stiffened, rooting herself to the spot, to let him slug her in the ribs again. It was no use. He would only get angrier the more foolish she made him look. She clenched her fists as the sting of the impact rocked her torso, but she would not cry out again.

Axis's brow furrowed, his face lined with anger. "Who hired you?"

Semra groaned. "Which name would stop the beating? Should I lie now, and get beaten later when the lie is found out, or tell the truth now, and get beaten immediately for an unsatisfactory answer?"

"Insufferable," Derision dripping from Arnevon's voice. "The girl can't possibly have been working alone. Princess, how many were there?"

Semra and Avaya's eyes met. "I think there was one other, but she never let me see him." A careful answer. No matter what plans she had for staying in the castle, Avaya meant to protect Zephan.

"And what was your experience?"

Avaya let out a pained sigh as though she had waited all her life for the chance to share this particular grievance. Her expression contorted into anxious hurt at the memory she screwed up in her mind to share, and she wrung her hands. "She overpowered my guard, burst into my chambers, and threatened me to cooperate. She tied the guard and left him to die of smoke fumes, smashed a lantern, and let the whole room go up in flames. She's a maniac!"

Semra scoffed. "The guard was away from the origin of the fire and wasn't even gagged. How long was he there before rescue? Two minutes? Three?"

"As long as you've decided to be useless, you are not permitted to speak," Arnevon said. He turned to Siler. "Raven, you've proven your utility in preventing her break-in attempt before and catching her now. What do you suggest we do?"

Semra looked at Siler. "Raven?"

Siler ignored her and faced the king. "Your Majesty, she's

decently rested, healthy, and feeling confident. Give it time, let me take care of it, and we can revisit the issue with her after making her more...cooperative."

Semra's jaw dropped. Her stomach churned and she bore a hole through his skull with a withering glare he didn't even turn to appreciate. *Expose him,* a voice in her mind said. *Tell them who he really is — unmask whatever this Raven persona is that he's built.* She shook her head to clear it. *What is he doing? He can't mean it. He can't...*

But the voice needled in the back of her brain and wouldn't let go. *Why not? Because you're so lovable, the cuddly killing machine? Because you're overly trusting, with no evidence that humans can be good? Because you're desperate for connection and you manufacture it in your mind when it doesn't really exist?*

Avaya was talking, and Semra willed herself to focus.

"...and I hereby pledge myself to the Belvidorian throne in an effort to unite our two kingdoms, choosing my future husband's people as my own people, and bridging the gap to Jannemar secondarily. Please accept my allegiance as penance for my father's misguided actions."

Semra reeled, unable to stop a disgusted look from creeping over her face. Semra squeezed her eyes shut and opened them again, but there she was, Princess Avaya of Jannemar, with the same stupid expression she'd had on her face a moment prior.

A thin smile played across Arnevon's thin lips. "I accept your allegiance, daughter." He studied her, and tapped the arm of his throne. "Only, prove your devotion with action. There is much to atone for, and it remains to be seen whether betrayal is a family trait."

Avaya whirled to Semra. "Let me start with this. Allow me to personally assist in persuading the intruder to spill what she knows. If she doesn't talk tonight, have her hanged in the morning."

Semra's heart stopped, but Siler remained expressionless and Arnevon tented his fingers in a nonchalant, thoughtful pose. He pursed his lips. "Raven? What do you think of this?"

"If I may, Your Majesty," Siler said, "One day may not be enough for the results you want. As for the princess' participation, I wonder if her skills would be better suited to politics than information extraction."

Avaya drilled Siler with a cutting glare, and he met it with a minute shrug. As Semra watched their exchange, understanding dawned on her. Siler had kidnapped Avaya...or had he?

"How long?" Semra's voice sounded far away as her mind raced a thousand miles per hour, as if totally detached from her body. She looked from Siler to Avaya and back. Siler's gaze jerked to Semra and fear flickered in his eyes for the first time. He knew exactly what she was asking. *How long have you been planning this? Was it for weeks, when we were in Jannemar together? When we passed the time on the Shamaran Castle wall, or when you spoke of villas and a new life?*

Siler swallowed, and he transitioned into his usual unconcerned demeanor once again. "Oh, we'll see. However long it takes."

"Raven, I'll remind you that we are at war," Arnevon said. "Perhaps you'd like to experiment on tactics with the girl, but we haven't the time. You have two days, or she hangs according to our guest's suggestion."

Siler gave a curt nod. "We must assume that she and any associates have knowledge of the layout of the whole of Madensig and its dungeons. The dungeons may be good enough for some, but she is a highly trained operative with the highest of connections in the Jannemar kingdom. I recommend keeping her off the schematics of the fortress."

"What do you know of the fortress schematics?" Axis asked skeptically.

"Enough to know what *she* knows," Siler answered, nodding at Semra, "Plus some." He grinned. Semra's heart ached. She used to love that smile.

"Raven, Axis...approach," Arnevon commanded. They complied, and after conferring privately together for several minutes, Siler and Axis descended from the dais as the huge bronze double doors behind Semra opened and a guard strode forward and bowed, a bundle of cloth under his arm.

"Speak," the king said.

"Your Majesty, we have searched the stable loft and found nothing aside from this, ah, erm, servant's dress. No sign of any associates in the surrounding area."

Semra breathed a sigh of relief.

"And the dragon?"

"It circled and dove at our men for an hour before taking to the skies, Your Majesty. We have two wounded, but they are in non-critical condition."

Warmth flooded Semra's chest and she sent that warmth to Zezura. *You did great. It's not your fault that I'm in here. Stay safe.*

Siler gestured for Semra's dress, and the guard handed it to him. Siler ripped off a long strip of the cloth and turned toward Semra for the first time. Kneeling in front of her, he held the strip up toward her face. "Good thing you hate skirts," he murmured.

Semra's lip curled into an involuntary snarl as red-hot anger erupted from her gut like a volcano. He had set himself against her, aided in her capture, kidnapped Avaya, joined the enemy, and he expected to be able to make comments about how well he knew her? While blindfolding her as a hostage?

Semra roared backward and slammed her head into a headbutt as Siler leaned forward to bring the blindfold around to the back of her head. Her head met with his shoulder instead and he let out a short yell, pushed her over onto her back as the blindfold slid down to her neck, and dropped a knee on her chest. He secured the cloth around her eyes and Semra felt herself hoisted over his shoulder a moment later – though she noticed with some satisfaction that she was placed on the opposite shoulder from the one she had hit. Semra hit him in the back as best she could as they went, but with her wrists tied, and using her elbows to stabilize herself against him as she swung upside-down over his shoulder, she was less than effective.

Siler grunted and carried her through a series of halls and stairs. At one point he paused, she heard a soft click, and the light she sensed through the blindfold went dark. Semra knew they were going down, but couldn't place where they were on the blueprint. The air grew colder, and they progressed down more stairs. Semra tugged at her blindfold, but it was tied tight. She fought with it for several minutes before gaining freedom, but seconds after she got it off, Siler deposited her on the ground. The small dirt room they found themselves in had a single lantern set on the floor by the entrance, and two sets of chains secured to the wall. Siler locked Semra's wrists into the chains and stepped out of range.

"I won't let them kill you," he whispered.

"Could have fooled me," Semra spat. "Isn't it your job to torture me now?"

Siler shook his head. "Arnevon wants my input, but he doesn't trust me enough to interrogate you for information. He knows we're acquainted."

"Ah. So who gets that distinguished honor?"

Footsteps padded down dirt steps and three figures appeared at the door. Semra squinted in the low light and identified Prince Axis and Princess Avaya, but it was a third that captured Semra's attention. Stalking into the room, head low as if on the prowl, came a large man built like a brick, carrying nothing but a pipe.

41

Semra's mouth went dry, and every muscle tensed.

"Nothing too visible," Axis instructed the man with the pipe. "She needs to look a little fresh for my father's interrogator."

Great. Arnevon and Axis aren't on good terms. Now I get beaten up twice. Semra looked Axis in the eyes. "You think I have secrets, but you have plenty of your own. What would your father do if he knew you were down here?"

"That's the advantage of being me," Axis answered coldly. "I get to keep mine. You get killed if you don't tell yours."

I'll learn your secrets yet. Semra lifted her chin. "I don't tell high level secrets to lackeys. I tell them to kings."

Axis's face reddened, and his jaw clenched. "You think the crown prince a lackey?"

Semra shrugged. "Some lackeys wear silks and furs. I think you're on a short leash, and you're puffing out your chest without the authority to back it up."

The corner of Siler's mouth twitched as he leaned against the dirt wall, but he said nothing. Axis scowled and stepped forward, his impressive height looming over her.

"My father is a small-minded fool. He would let Belvidore languish in disrespect and obscurity. By rights the land is ours, and the land beyond it. You will honor me not as a king but as your emperor."

Semra kept her composure, but a chill ran up her spine. *Emperor.* If Axis became king, he would be three times as aggressive as Arnevon – and far more unpredictable.

Avaya laid a hand on Axis's arm. "You don't need to defend yourself to someone like her." She turned to Semra. "You will tell us what we want to know, because Zephan is walking into a trap, and only I can save him."

Semra leveled a glare back at her. "What would you like to know? That the prince's intended has conspired with an assassin?"

Avaya waved a hand dismissively. "He knows Siler kidnapped me for his own purposes to gain position at Madensig, and that I was grateful for the opportunity to prove myself and keep my promise of marriage. We need to know what the king of Jannemar is planning."

Something in Semra's gut twisted at the distancing language. *The king of Jannemar.* Semra raised an eyebrow. "Your *father*. You need to know what *your father* is planning."

Avaya spread her hands. "Precisely."

"I don't know anything."

The man with the pipe stepped forward and swung at her torso, and Semra raised her chained hands to block the blow with her forearms. He struck her again and she fell to the ground, and again against her exposed back as her hands flew to collect herself.

Semra shook her head, spitting out her words between gasps for breath. "They don't trust me. Why should they?"

Avaya crossed her arms. "My brother seems to trust you – you've even hoodwinked him into being smitten with you, so there's no telling what sensitive information he's shared. My *father* seems obsessed with your cause. You lurk about Shamaran Castle, soaking up intel like a thirsty sponge. You know something."

Semra grunted and coughed. "You're the one that loves gossip. Don't you know the talk of any castle you enter? Surely you know secrets of Shamaran and Madensig alike by now."

Another blow. Semra brought her arms over her head to protect it as pain exploded in her ribs.

"What reinforcements does Turian have?" Axis demanded. "How many are coming down through Kinlock?"

A low moan escaped her lips. "I don't know." The pipe came down. *Whap!*

"I don't know!"

The pipe came down again and Semra grabbed it, pulling the man off balance and downward, and sent a swift kick to his temple. The man dropped the pipe, caught her leg, and slugged her in the stomach; Semra slung the chains of her wrists around his neck and yanked hard. The man thrashed, knocked her in the jaw, and Semra released him, gagging and sputtering.

Semra touched her bleeding lip, turned to Axis, and smiled. *Let him explain* that *to Arnevon.* "Someone will know the king was not the first to interrogate me."

Axis snatched the pipe from the ground and sent a punch to her stomach that sent her sprawling. His eyes blazed and he spat into her face. "If you aren't ready to give me something actionable by the time I return, the king will be the least of your worries."

42

AVAYA

Avaya swept up the stairs with Siler on her heels, racing down the hall toward her newly assigned prison cell. Zephan was headed straight for disaster, and she had to stop him before he got to the battleground. She ran inside, closing the door, but Siler stepped in the way.

"Are you going to let Axis kill Semra?"

Avaya groaned. "Siler, I don't have time for this right now." The pretense of *the Raven* felt unnecessary now.

Siler put his hand on the door and opened it further. "Make time."

Avaya threw her hands up. "What do you want me to say? That the monarchs of the kingdom should deal lightly with an intruder, kidnapper, and spy?"

Siler's lip curled. "Perhaps I should inform them of who really orchestrated your kidnapping."

Her heart skipped a beat as she fiddled with a lock of her hair before catching herself and releasing it.

"Don't be ridiculous. You're in a good position now, and if they knew you didn't need their money, they would trust you even less. If she shares something interesting, I'll push for leniency, but my goal right now is to build bridges – not strain them by making unreasonable requests."

Avaya shooed Siler out the door and shut it, then hesitated as she moved to bar the door. The bar was missing. *Arnevon doesn't trust you. You're not allowed to lock yourself inside your own bedchamber.* Avaya gritted her teeth and ran to her wardrobe. The bottom drawer had been left cracked open, and a soft warble sounded from inside. Avaya opened it to find two carrier pigeons sitting on bits of straw and loose clothing lining the bottom of the drawer. Avaya stroked the head of the carrier pigeon and shifted the cloth around to find the tiny cannister and empty parchment.

She chewed on her nail. What to say? *Make Zephan leave the front lines and go hide in a hole somewhere, because Belvidore is going to win, so he doesn't have to bother.* Well, that wouldn't do. *Jannemar needs to lose this battle, so kindly pass on the location of hidden explosives only to Zephan so he doesn't get blown to pieces...*

Avaya froze. He'd traveled with Semra and Monac for two weeks to get to her, and after what she saw in the stables, Zephan might leave the front lines if he were properly motivated. *But he's smart and principled. He's not going to abandon his men.* Avaya went to the desk in the room and retrieved an inkwell and feather pen. *Oh, we'll see about that.* She dipped the pen into the ink.

To His Royal Highness, the Crown Prince Zephan of Jannemar: Princess Avaya and companion captured. King Arnevon demanding an audience on the border of Belera to negotiate terms of release and control of the Surian Strip. Alternative is death to hostages.

AVAYA DATED the note and added that he had five days to meet. It would take him three and a half to get to the Strip, and he would have to leave right away to make it to Belera on time. Avaya rolled the small paper and stuffed it inside the cannister, removed a pigeon from the drawer, and attached the cannister to one of the bird's legs. Avaya carefully lifted the bird in her hands and crossed the room to the window, when she heard a pounding on her door.

"Your Highness, open the door! Open the door *now!*"

Fear gripped her at the demanding tone. What could have changed their attitude toward her so quickly? Avaya opened the window and threw the pigeon into the air as three guards burst into the room.

One guard ran to the window, one came to stand uncomfortably close beside Avaya, and the third surveyed the room. He spied the remaining pigeon in the wardrobe drawer, walked toward it, and rifled through the drawer. The guard pulled out the second cannister and small bits of parchment, then snapped his fingers and the other two guards ran over and threw open the wardrobe, pulling open drawers and doors and searching every corner.

"Feeling homesick?" the guard in charge asked.

Avaya tossed her blonde waves behind her shoulder. "Not at all."

"What was in the note, Your Highness?"

She shrugged, but a knot formed in her stomach. "I simply hate animal captivity and released it back where it belongs."

"And where precisely does it belong, Highness? Jannemar, perhaps?"

Avaya opened her mouth, then closed it. There was nothing to say. The two other guards continued to search her room, opening the vanity, yanking back bedsheets, and tossing pillows.

She crossed her arms. "This is all highly inappropriate! I demand to know what this is about!"

"Treason," said the guard, and Avaya's mouth went dry. "You've been charged with treason and have been summoned to stand before the king."

The guard snapped again at the other two guards and turned on his heel, and the other two men each gripped one of Avaya's arms and dragged her out into the hall.

"No, no, no, you're making a mistake!" Avaya cried, pulling back to no avail. She paused, and the guards moved forward unconcerned. She tripped and hurried to keep up with their long strides. "Where is my own guard? Where is the Raven?"

"Excellent question. How did you slip away?" the head guard called back over his shoulder, never turning his head as he walked before them.

"I didn't. He was there, moments before you arrived. You didn't see him? He was there!"

Avaya was met with silence, and she cursed under her breath. Where was Axis? Had anyone seen them take the secret passage down to see Semra? Was he accused too? What did they think she had done?

The guards dragged her down the hall, through the tower, and toward the throne room. A horrible screeching sound filled her ears, and Avaya jumped as a shadow passed over one of the many windows lining the hall. The head guard spoke quietly to one of the men posted at the entrance to the throne room, but Avaya couldn't hear a word. She stared out the window and was met with a great violet dragon opening its huge serpentine jaw to pour flames out on the soldiers in the courtyard armed with bows and arrows, swords, and terror. The dragon's scales flashed black, crimson, and violet in quick succession, and Avaya watched as two men with spears ran out into the courtyard, taunting the dragon and waving their weapons in the air.

A hideous *crunch* from the courtyard raised the hair on the back of Avaya's neck and she shuddered as the double doors to the throne room opened, and she was ushered from the dragon behind her to the snake before her. King Arnevon sat on his throne, nonchalant and positively lounging as he leaned back. He was as comfortable as Avaya had ever seen him. He examined his cuticles and looked up at her, his eyes glinting with a sadistic joy.

"Well?"

Avaya glanced at the guard, but the king's eyes were trained on her, not him. She faced Arnevon. "Your Majesty?"

He spread his hands. "You know why you're here. Have you nothing to say for yourself?"

"A thousand pardons, Your Majesty, but I do not in fact know why I am here. I was told I have been accused of treason, but since the guards failed to provide any evidence or explanation for such reckless allegations I assumed there was a misunderstanding.

Arnevon tented his fingertips and peered down at her. "You have enjoyed our hospitality less than a month, and in that time you have faked an illness, duped your personal guard on your whereabouts twice, had an unsanctioned visit with a prisoner, and now I learned you have somehow managed to keep messenger birds in your room and are sending information back to Jannemar."

All breath left Avaya's body. With a list that long, she would be dead by morning. "No, Your Majesty, I assure you it isn't true! I *did* feel sick, honestly I did, but it must have been a brief stomach bug. I've been under an enormous amount of stress, and I'm sure that had something to do with it. As for the guard, Your Majesty, I'm afraid I was summoned by the prince and the guard was not present for my return. Perhaps this is an issue with the quality of your guard…?"

Arnevon's lip curled and Avaya swallowed. That was *not* the right thing to say.

"Are you quite finished with your pathetic excuses?"

"I don't have an answer about the guard, Your Majesty, because their absence was not under my control. As for the birds…" Avaya racked her brain. Surely there was a good reason. She couldn't tell the truth without exposing the fact that Zephan was near Madensig, but she couldn't realistically be given permission to have them except by someone with authority. "They're your own birds. I was embarrassed to tell the guards when they came at me so aggressively in my own chambers, ransacking it as if I were some criminal, but I have always loved birds and found them a small comfort in a new place. Prince Axis was kind enough to provide them for me when he heard I was homesick." Avaya dearly hoped Axis's-confused beguilement by Avaya would protect her and make Axis curious rather than murderous that she had dragged him into her defense.

Arnevon's eyes narrowed to slits. "You have not struck me as homesick."

Avaya dipped her head demurely. "Naturally, I would put my best foot forward for the king of the land."

"So what is the parchment for, then?"

"Nothing. I wanted to learn how to send a message with them, so it's for practice."

"Mhmm. We will check all messages coming by pigeon then – surely it's back with us by now, since its flight was only brief. And we will release the remaining pigeon and ensure that it does indeed fly to the Madensig pigeon loft. Did you know that messenger birds can find their way home from well over a thousand miles away? But of course you did. Birds are a passion of yours, are they not? If the pigeon leaves Madensig's grounds, I'll see to it that you are beheaded. Meanwhile," he added, "the man who brought you here is missing, and seeing how espionage has been added to your list of offenses, it seems appropriate that all accomplices might meet the same fate as you do."

Arnevon raised his eyes to look directly into the face of the head guard next to Avaya. "I want the Raven brought before me, and I want him here *now*."

43

———————

The dark of the dirt hole Semra was chained in enveloped her, and the damp cold air sent a chill through her bones. Avaya, Axis, Siler, and the man with the pipe had all left together after Axis's threat, and Semra wondered what kind of death Axis might order. A standard beheading would be nice, but at least having her throat slit would bring death in thirty to sixty seconds – provided it was done properly. If not, it could take as long as ten minutes, which would be less than ideal.

No, Axis wasn't the throat-slitting type. Sword through the gut, axe to the head, or slow torture seemed more his speed. Would Avaya look on as he gave the order? How long would it take Zephan to learn of her death? *Would he even care?* Semra squeezed her eyes shut. *Of course he would care, idiot. He always cares. Too much for his own good.* It didn't make sense. It wasn't practical, and therefore was not helpful, for him to care about her as much as he did...especially considering the way her stomach flopped around when he gave her attention.

Perhaps it was better this way. He wouldn't have to feel any guilt over their inevitable parting, and he could turn his eye toward someone more worthy of his status. Perhaps a beautiful noblewoman with a shred of propriety and political knowledge. Someone with a history that would make his advisors smile and nod, rather than vomit. Someone appropriate.

Dull footsteps sounded from the narrow passage outside her room. Running. Semra straightened from her position, sitting against the dirt wall and peering into the blackness. Arnevon's interrogator wouldn't run.

The light of a lantern cast dim yellow tones against the ruddy brown of the walls and tossed strange shadows ahead of it, bobbing brighter and closer. A silhouette appeared in the doorway.

"Siler!" Semra's heart leaped – and then lodged in her throat. What was that name supposed to mean to her now? Was it the safe familiarity of a friend, or the bitter dregs of a traitor willing to capture, torture, and kill for money?

"Happy to see me?" A grin flickered across his face, but it died on his lips and a troubled expression replaced it.

"I used to always be happy to see you. But, well…" Semra lifted her wrists, and the chains rattled with them. "You are no longer a comfort to me."

Siler searched her face for a moment, then looked away. "Maybe this will help." He pulled out a set of keys and unlocked her wrists from their bonds. "We have to move fast. Zezura is divebombing the courtyard right now, and we can't ask for a better distraction than that."

Warm gratitude filled her chest. Zezura was a better friend than any human she'd ever known. "Where are we going?"

"I'm getting you out, but this place is wickedly effective as a fortress. How did you get inside in the first place? Did Zezura drop you off somehow when she terrorized everyone a few nights back?"

Semra shook her head. "Not a chance. Your loyalty could turn on a dime, and you're on the king's payroll."

Siler pulled her to her feet. "Fine, fine. But the king's money is only icing. Avaya's deep pockets are the ones I'll be buying my next villa with."

"Next villa? You already have one?"

"Maybe. If you ever left Shamaran without an agenda, maybe I'd show you."

"Maybe I'd like that, if you didn't kill for money."

"First of all, we *all* killed for rewards–"

"No," Semra hissed, "I killed to purge evil. It's embarrassing, looking back, that I believed Azi's lies hook, line, and sinker, but I really thought I was making the world better."

Siler groaned. "You're perfect, you're better than the rest of us, I *know* already! But if you'd let me finish, what I was saying was that we all killed for reward – monetary or otherwise. Your reward was feeling like you had a purpose, like you were in control of something for once. And *secondly,* I thought you'd be proud of me. I've killed hardly anyone since leaving Jannemar, and I didn't even kidnap Avaya."

Semra's eyes narrowed. "It was you. We already know it was you."

Siler clucked his tongue. "I took her from Shamaran Castle, but it's not kidnapping if they pay you to do it. She paid me to stage her kidnapping and bring her here. *You,* on the other hand, killed five people just this morning. So get off your high horse and let me help you."

Semra's lips parted, but only silence stretched between them. She hardly noticed Siler tugging her into the dirt passageway. Avaya orchestrated the whole thing. No wonder she was so poised at the tournament! No wonder she didn't want to leave! Even Princess Blaise had caught on – Avaya was too composed for a hostage, and she gathered information less like a prisoner trying to gain her bearings, and more like a... like a what?

A spy. She paid Siler to create a kidnapping, and sent her entire family, *royal* family, into a tailspin while they attempted to lead a kingdom. It was a risky game, and for what? An image of Avaya comforting Aviama rose into Semra's mind. Aviama was sobbing, and Avaya was petting her hair.

We can't bring mother back, Aviama. But we will stop the bloodshed. We can't rely on anyone but ourselves to protect us.

Did Avaya really believe that marrying Axis would stop the war? Was she so desperate for control in her own life that she would rather rely on herself to take care of business than any other more reasonable, qualified choice? Why be kidnapped instead of getting out of Jannemar and arriving in Belvidore with pomp? Siler's words about control intruded on her thoughts of Avaya.

Your reward was feeling like you had a purpose, like you were in control of something for once.

Semra's eyes widened in the dim lantern light as they dashed down the passage. He was right. Semra's motives were precisely the same as Avaya's – purpose and control. Semra was not nearly so noble as she had thought. Or had she?

You're perfect, you're better than the rest of us...

Semra's mind stumbled. Why would Siler say that? She was far from perfect. Semra knew she was a dirt person for all she'd done. She'd distanced herself from Zephan because of it. But she did expect herself to rise above, to repay in protecting life what she owed the world by taking it. She hadn't been successful so far. Her blood debt was too high to overcome.

So she had planned on running away with Zezura and "dying alone in a hole somewhere," as Zephan had said. How could she push that sort of thinking on anyone else? How far had it gotten her?

"I *am* proud of you," she whispered at long last. An uneasy burning feeling gripped her heart. "And I think you're wiser than you let on when it comes to deep thinking stuff about life. But then you go and do stupid, self-serving things like take Avaya's money."

"I'm not skimming from the dragonlord anymore, so I've got to make a living. And there aren't many good paying jobs for assassins unless you're assassinating people, you know. There's no reason I shouldn't put my skills to use to look out for myself – no one else will. I guess you got in my head, and when opportunity came to stay free, to stay *me*, and still not kill anybody, I took it. I'm still doing it, too, by the way. I have to get Avaya through this next thing before I can back out. It's a big payday."

Semra moaned. "You need to get out of here. Come with me."

"See, there you go again, telling me what to do with my life."

"Only when you're making stupid decisions."

Siler grinned and his stormy eyes twinkled at her. "See what happens to me when you're away?"

Semra's lips twitched into a crooked smile, and she shook her head. "I can't decide whether to laugh or hit you over the head. Aiding in my capture does make me lean toward hitting you. Hard. With something solid."

"Getting you out again has got to count for something!"

"We're not out yet. I'll defer my thanks until I'm outside the walls."

"Let's go then. I'll escort you as my prisoner to get past anyone we see. Hold your hands behind you so it looks like you're shackled – there, that's it."

Siler gripped Semra's upper arm and pressed lightly against a panel at the end of the passage. It swung outward at his touch, and they stepped through the opening. Glancing back, she saw the secret panel was a large, framed painting on the other side, among a gallery of other paintings lining an empty hall. A great clamor came from down the hall behind them, and Semra looked out one of the tall windows to see Zezura's scales flash purple, red, and blue as she unleashed a torrent of fire on a group of soldiers before her.

Semra's pulse ticked up a notch. "We have to get to her."

"Let me hide you somewhere for a day or so. I can protect you, take care of Avaya, and get you out safely. Zezura is a dragon. She can defend herself."

Semra glanced down at the mark of the dragon's kiss on her chest, peeking out from beneath her disheveled tunic. The closer she was to Zezura, the stronger the connection seemed to be, and the mark was screaming emotions straight to Semra's core. "I got this mark because I saved her life. You can't save a life unless it was at risk of being taken in the first place. I can feel her, Siler. She's angry, but mostly she's scared. If I can get to her, she'll take me away, and the problem is solved."

Siler sighed, but wheeled her around by the arm and strode confidently toward the end of the hall toward the court-yard doors. He paused by the door, and Semra stood on her toes to peer out with him through the small window at the top. Zezura had scattered the soldiers in the corner of the courtyard, snatching a bow from one of them and snapping it in half with her jaw. Two more men ran forward with long spears. The men danced in and out, waving their spears, taunting the dragon. Zezura turned on them, and as she swung her head toward them and opened her enormous jaws, the men saw their chance.

The two soldiers jabbed their spears into the lining of her mouth, and the dragon recoiled, sputtering and wheezing. Smoke curled up from the pots and Zezura reared back, tossing her head and opening and closing her mouth, but no fire escaped. Something was wrong. A swirl of smoke rose from her nostrils as she wheezed again and coughed, her scales flashing crimson, black, and green in swift sequence.

In one smooth motion, Semra wrested her arm from Siler's relaxed grip and slipped through the door and out into the courtyard. Zezura's panic seized Semra's chest through the mark, and Semra pushed an ounce of calm back toward Zezura as the dragon bucked against whatever they had done to her. An ounce was all she could muster. *Poison-dipped spears? Chemicals? What was in the pots?*

One of the soldiers holding the spears reared back his arm to jab at the dragon again, and Semra took a flying leap at him, leaping on his back and pummeling his head and neck. The man stumbled and fell, and Semra rolled and felt the glide of a shallow cut slice its way up her upper arm as she sprang to her feet. She glanced to one side and saw the second soldier had grazed her with his spear. A wave of nausea and heat washed over her, and Semra wavered on unsteady legs as weakness hit her like a wall.

Zezura stumbled into one of the courtyard's pillars and half-heartedly unfurled her wings, and Semra tripped over her own feet and pitched forward before a solid body tackled her to the ground. Semra's head spun and she shook it to clear it, but instead the world around her whirled even faster, coming in and out of focus. Someone was shouting – was it one person, or many? – and she was hauled to her feet. *What exactly are feet, anyway? They're what you stand on, but what are they? Is there a definition for feet?*

Semra was dimly aware that her thoughts were

nonsense, but somehow, they were the only thing she was able to focus on. She swayed and swung an arm out to stabilize against a pillar behind her, then snatched it away as her fingers touched an arrow embedded in the pillar. *Was that for me?*

More shouting. The person who tackled her plucked her from her feet and lifted her up across his shoulders, looping his right arm around her knee, her hips and torso laying behind his neck, and gripping her right wrist with the same hand. Siler. He had tackled her?

The arrow. Of course. He knocked her out of its path.

Semra's head pounded, and the bouncing movement of Siler's quick jog did nothing to assuage the throb. Soldiers fell in around them so that they were surrounded, and Semra lost sight of Zezura as they re-entered the fortress, ascended a spiral staircase up one floor, and crossed a hall. Large bronze double doors opened and Semra found herself in the throne room once again.

Siler put her on the ground and a wave of nausea hit her at the sudden movement. Siler jumped back just in time to save his shoes as Semra vomited onto the gleaming tile floor. She put her head down, and the coolness of the tile was comforting against her hot skin. She closed her eyes. It would only be for a moment...

Semra's eyes snapped open and she gasped, lurching up from the floor as someone waved a bottle of smelling salts under her nose. Ammonia filled her nostrils, and with it, some of her weakness left her. Semra glanced about the room and saw nobles lining either side, King Arnevon on his throne before her, and the king's advisor, standing to his right. Siler standing behind her with a gaggle of guards, and Princess Avaya standing six feet over, facing the king. Prince Axis was nowhere to be seen.

"Raven, how good of you to join us. I was saying you needed to be invited to our little discussion."

"I was unaware the princess was here, Your Majesty. I found your intruder wandering the grounds, and nearly escaping to the dragon in the courtyard. I'm afraid whatever security measures you had in place for her were woefully insufficient."

The king lifted his hand and turned to the captain of the guard. "Is this true?"

The captain swallowed. "I was not responsible for the prisoner, Your Majesty, but I did see the Raven tackle her to the ground in the courtyard before she could reach the dragon. He hauled her back into the castle and straight to you, with our escort."

"Interesting." Arnevon drummed his fingers against the arms of his throne. "We were assessing how our esteemed guest, who pledged her allegiance to Belvidore and her hand in marriage to my son, is a traitorous spy and even more troublesome than her father. I thought perhaps she and her accomplices could share a basket for their heads to roll into when we chop them off. What do you think?"

"I think it's wise to dispatch of all known traitors at once, Your Majesty. Provided that is the most advantageous option at your disposal."

Semra marveled at Siler's smooth, practiced nonchalance. His only tell was the light tap of his left wrist with the index and middle fingers of his right hand – a move so miniscule few would have noticed. It was Siler's small way to gear up before a mission.

"And what, pray, is my most advantageous option?"

"To keep Avaya alive as a potential bargaining chip until your hold on the Surion Strip is certain, and kill her once you have what you want." Avaya's head snapped toward Siler with a dark glare, but there was fear behind her eyes. Siler continued, unfazed. "Take it from a man of experience in these matters, sire – the killing part is easy. But the consequences are rather permanent, so it's critical to suck them dry of any use before ending them."

A murmur went up around the sides of the room, and the hairs on Semra's neck and arms stood on end.

Arnevon leaned forward. "Approach. Bring the prisoners to me."

Siler took hold of each woman by the arm, pulling Avaya forward and half-dragging Semra as she struggled to get up off the floor. Semra still felt some weakness, but the world had stopped spinning. She glanced out the window looking for Zezura, but saw nothing. The three of them stopped at the foot of the dais, and Arnevon trained his eye on Semra, speaking loud enough for Semra, Siler, Avaya, and the king's advisor to hear.

"And what purpose do you serve me?"

"None. Not unless you can offer me a better deal than Turian."

"You told us no one hired you," Arnevon growled.

Semra shrugged. "I didn't want to answer those questions before. The status quo has changed."

"You insult my intelligence to think I would trust you even an iota."

"You don't have to trust my character. Only my greed. It's a similar arrangement you have with the Raven, is it not?" Semra touched Avaya's shoulder beside her to steady herself as a dizzy spell rocked her on her heels. Avaya slapped her hand away.

"And are you greedy?" the king pressed, his eyes locked on hers.

Semra felt numbness in her arms and legs, and began to

sweat. She shifted her weight. Good – she might have mild numbness, but she was steady again. "Aren't we all?"

"Ha! You lie through your teeth! Is your life worth so little?"

"It's certainly not worth much," Semra answered. It was the truest thing she'd said.

Arnevon snapped his fingers, and the waiting soldiers surged forward and brought Semra and Avaya backward away from the dais. He waved a hand. "Kill them both."

44

———————

Semra had deserved to be executed for years, but this was the closest she'd gotten to it. In the blink of an eye, soldiers moved to strike. Siler wrestled a sword from the soldier near him and tossed it to Semra in time for her to block the blow from a man attacking her left. Adrenaline coursed through her veins as she met opponent after opponent. Siler drew his own sword, spinning across to defend Avaya.

Still so loyal to your master? Semra slashed at the soldier before her and flicked a glance toward Siler and Avaya. *Let her die. She brought it upon herself.*

But that was the assassin in her talking. Was she as different as she'd claimed, or was she another killing machine? For all she'd done, Avaya was still Turian's daughter and Zephan's sister. Semra ducked and retreated as a dizzy spell came and went. She attacked in an upward thrust and kicked the second man backward as he tried to come in range.

"Get me a sword!" Avaya yelled, covering her head and jumping behind Siler as he parried another swing.

Semra let muscle memory and instinct carry her as she

moved through her footwork, but her body was still weakened. The extra energy spent getting Avaya a blade was out of the question. Siler passed his sword back to her, bursting in close to his adversary with an elbow to the jaw, snapping his neck, and plucking the man's sword from limp fingers.

"Don't get yourself killed with it," he called back.

Semra sent out a pulsing need through the dragon's kiss and felt for Zezura. She was weak but responded with an answering pull. A roar went up from the courtyard. They were fending off ten soldiers, with more on the way, and Semra knew her endurance wouldn't last long against so many. She was already fading. She sprung up the dais and the guards threw themselves between her and the king; a wave of numbness and dizziness hit her, and a moment was all it took. Semra was knocked off the dais to the ground, her sword clattering to the floor four feet away.

Her head swam and her vision blurred.

The only thing you were ever good at was killing. And now you can't even do that.

The thought intruded into her consciousness without warning. Zephan would die on the front lines. Arnevon would take control of the Surion Strip to expand Belvidore and would exploit the people of Jannemar, and Axis would pursue an empire when he took his father's place. Avaya would die. Siler would die. Semra would die. Ramas' face sneered at her in her mind's eye.

Oh, but don't worry. No one will remember your failings. No one will think of you at all.

A guard ran forward and swung his sword downward at her neck; Semra rolled to the side and hooked his ankle with her leg so that he stumbled and fell. The bottle of smelling salts she'd been offered earlier tumbled to the ground and rolled toward her, spilling half its contents on the floor as the topper bounced off in another direction. Semra inhaled sharply at the harsh scent and felt her head settle. She scooped up the bottle and sprinted for the doors, dodging three guards on her way.

She spun to the left and ducked under a guard's swing, then jumped on his back and twisted his neck with one hand, her other still gripping the bottle of smelling salts. She landed with a *thud* that reverberated through her skull. Semra looked up to see Siler and Avaya hot on her heels, the soldiers giving chase, and King Arnevon standing and shouting from his throne behind them.

Two guards flew down the hall toward the throne room, and Siler screamed at her from behind as he drew his own knife, "Knife, high left!"

Semra jerked her head left in time to see it bury into the frame of the heavy doors. She grinned and yanked it out of the wood with both hands before sending it flying into the throat of one of the guards. He dropped like a stone. Oh, how beautiful it felt to have a knife in her hands again!

The second guard kept coming, and Semra ran to meet him, dropping low to the ground and sliding the bottle of salts on the floor past the guard to free her hands before ramming into her opponent feet-first. Semra knocked him backward and rolled to avoid his sword swing, ripped the knife from the dead guard's neck, and instead of engaging the guard, she fled down the hall, snatching the bottle up once again. Guilt ran through her at leaving Siler and Avaya, but she didn't have much strength left. Still...

Something in her stomach wrenched, and as she neared the stairwell, Semra turned back to see the guard nearly upon Siler, the two of them chased by an army of men. Semra hurled her knife into the back of the first guard at the base of his neck and flew down the stairs. The quicker she got to Zezura, the quicker they'd be free – if Zezura was fit to fly.

The bottom floor rushed to meet her, and Semra put her hands out against the wall to stabilize herself as she staggered off the steps. She lingered only a moment before pushing herself off the wall and through the door out into the open courtyard. The breeze nipped at her face and ruffled her hair, bringing with it energy and hope. Zezura plunged past three terrified men when she caught sight of Semra, knocking the long, useless chains from their hands as they tried to ensnare her. The spears lay crushed in pieces on the ground, and few men had remained to attempt to control the dragon in the confined space of the courtyard. Semra dumped the rest of the salts on the end of Zezura's nose and she reared back, her eyes widening, and tossed her head.

Energy. Less woozy. Better.

Semra climbed up on Zezura's bare back and nudged her toward one of the tall windows of the second floor, with Siler and Avaya enveloped in bodies inside it. "Break it, Zez. We have to get them out, and then you have to fly."

Zezura lowered her head and smashed it into the window, shattering the glass and scattering the fighting inside the hall. Zezura sidled up to the open window and Semra stood up against the stiff spines of the dragon's back to see inside. Avaya had lost her sword, and a superficial cut ran down her forearm, but she was free of the fighting and scrambling to her feet amid shards of window on the floor. Siler had obtained a quiver slung across his back and scooped up a bow and arrow, firing at the soldiers as he retreated toward the open window to cover Avaya's escape.

"Avaya, *now!*"

Avaya grimaced at the sight of the dragon and Semra's outstretched hand, but as the din behind her grew into a furious clamor, she leaped down onto the back of the dragon and slipped her arms around Semra's waist to stay on. Zezura beat her wings with effort, and slowly they lifted off the ground. Siler stood in the window, notching his final arrow to the string.

"Zez, get Siler! He'll die if we leave him!"

Zezura flushed her scales an angry crimson and as they pulled away from the fortress, she snatched him from the edge of the window in her front claws. An archer took his place and raised his bow toward Semra and Avaya, but as Siler hung sideways from the clutches of the dragon, he pulled back the string and released his final arrow, hitting home between the archer's eyes, and he fell facedown to the courtyard below.

Zezura weaved and dropped in the air for a moment, then let out a puff of weak smoke and beat her wings furiously until finally she rose above Madensig and caught an air current to glide on. Semra breathed in deep and let out a sigh of relief as the fortress dropped away and they angled toward the forest on the outskirts of Horen.

Make a quick stop here, and then we have to fly on. Zezura sent a reluctant weary feeling back to Semra, and Semra put a hand on the dragon's neck. *We have to fly further. We have to, or we'll be caught by nightfall. I'm sorry.* Semra wasn't sure how much of the words Zezura understood, but the urgency emotion and the intent to press on was clear.

The dragon dropped altitude fast, catching herself in halting jerks on the way down. Nausea washed over Semra, and Avaya's arms threatened to squeeze her to death. Siler yelped from where he hung beneath Zezura's belly in her clutches, and as she came to an abrupt stop inside the forest, Siler landed with a jolt and rolled away.

"What's the big idea?" he demanded.

Avaya loosened her arms around Semra's waist to get

down, but Semra sent Zezura another message: *Up.* It wasn't what Zezura wanted to hear, but she huffed and puffed and slowly gained altitude again, with Semra and Avaya on her back.

"I'm sorry, Siler." Semra's throat tightened, and she clenched her jaw. "I want you safe, but your priority is getting Avaya's money, and I have another objective. I can't have you meddling. Take care."

"Wait! *Wait!*"

Semra looked down only once, seeing Siler standing there with his bow and empty quiver, waving his arms at her as he grew smaller and smaller. A twinge of guilt crept into her heart, but it had to be done. He had betrayed her once in favor of his employer, and would do it again given the chance. Siler had saved her life today at great personal risk, but when the king ordered them both to be killed, Siler also fought to protect himself and his earnings. With Avaya dead, there would be no payout.

And if Semra didn't bring Avaya back, King Turian's court would trust Semra even less than they did already. Besides, if Zephan really was walking into a trap, Avaya might have critical information. Unless Avaya was bluffing about being the only one who could save him.

The air was cool on Semra's skin, but she still felt warm, and then a chill ran through her as the wind met the beads of sweat on her brow. *What was on those spears?* Whatever it was, its effects were somewhat lasting. Zezura dropped altitude suddenly, then caught herself, then careened sideways out of nowhere and sputtered another puff of green and black smoke.

Avaya yelped and tightened her grip on Semra, then screamed into her ear against the wind, "What does she think she's doing? Is she trying to kill me?!"

Semra turned her head back toward her. "Your in-laws poisoned her or something. She's ill!"

Zezura pitched forward into a nosedive and Avaya screamed. Semra's head swam and dark spots danced across her field of vision as her stomach dropped and roiled with the unexpected movement. The dragon leveled off somewhat as they reached the tree line, her legs and wingtip brushing the tops of the trees, but she still carried too much speed.

"Hang on for a bumpy landing," Semra called.

Avaya grunted as Zezura glanced off a treetop and jerked a few feet upwards again. "You think?!"

Zezura crashed through the branches of the forest and skidded to a stop, Semra and Avaya rocked off balance and tumbling to the ground beside her. Semra put her head between her knees and let a wave of nausea roll through her. She closed her eyes. Avaya rustled the leaves next to her as she sat up, and Semra's hand shot out to grip the princess' wrist.

Semra's eyes remained closed, and she took in a ragged breath before she spoke. "You have no transportation, and I have a feeling your survival skills are less than stellar. If you try to run, I will catch you. We are going to get to Zephan, and we are going to do it together."

Avaya scoffed. "You look terrible. I'm not sure how much chasing you are capable of."

Semra slowly straightened and opened her eyes, swallowing down bile and leveling a stare at Avaya. "You saw me fighting at Madensig, killing multiple men? I felt sicker then than I do now, and yet here I am alive while they lie dead. Please include that piece of information in your calculations."

Avaya looked at her skeptically, but didn't argue. Semra and Zezura took turns puking throughout the evening and night, long past the point when either of them had anything left in their stomachs. Avaya sat with her back against a tree for several hours, gathered wood for a fire when the evening air brought a chill, and demanded Zezura start the flame. Zezura spewed purple and green smoke out of her mouth, but no fire came. Avaya screamed at her and threw the sticks, and Zezura roared and swept her tail to knock Avaya off her feet. She fell hard on her bottom and Zezura put her head down again, apparently satisfied.

"Does screaming get the fire going?" Semra asked dryly from her position half-sitting, half-laying against a tree nearby.

"Does lounging in the woods all day while people are dying feel productive to you?"

Semra stared back at her, sickness dulling her facial expressions. That was one mercy to be grateful for, as defensiveness descended. Semra hated doing nothing.

"You could try making a fire like a normal person." She eyed Avaya's mess of haphazard twigs on the ground. "Have you ever done anything normal?"

Avaya lifted her chin. "Have *you*?"

"Fair point." Semra's stomach clenched and bile flew halfway up her esophagus, then went back down. She groaned.

"How did you get what Zezura has?"

Semra indicated the tattered sleeve on her upper arm. "They had spears dipped in something strong, and I got cut. I'm assuming it's poisonous."

"You thought you were going to *die*, and you *still* dragged me out into the middle of nowhere to be stranded with a dragon carcass and assassin corpse after you die? With no one to save me?"

That outcome didn't sound all bad. Semra pressed her lips together. "To be honest I hadn't thought about it much. I've been focused on other things. I hope I don't die, but if I do, Horen isn't far."

"You would kidnap me, destroy Belvidore's already shaky trust in me, and then send me back to be murdered?"

Semra shrugged. "Seddon then. You probably don't know what plants are safe, so you won't be eating much, but you'd get there on foot eventually."

Avaya rolled her eyes. "Good news is, you're not going to die."

Semra arched an eyebrow. "You kidnapped yourself. I wouldn't trust your judgment right now."

"The spears were dipped with *konnolan,* genius. It's a chemical that deadens magical essence." Avaya crossed her arms. "Dragons' mechanism for fire is biological rather than magical, but their systems are still built on magical essence, and without it their functioning declines. The magic is housed in the tissues, or bloodstream, or something – I forget, but it's something throughout the whole body."

Understanding dawned on Semra. "Of course. Zezura has some magical attributes, and that's how the dragon's kiss works. It's some sort of remnant to the dragon's magical roots?"

"Exactly. And konnolan neutralizes *tabeun* magic. But it wears off, so you should both be fine eventually. Actually, it shouldn't have impacted you at all. The healer who told me about it said it's inert to nonmagical species."

"Maybe they mixed it with something?"

"Maybe. They were concerned it wouldn't work fast enough, so they were considering adding something to it."

Semra considered this. "How did you get access to a healer who told you their plan for Zezura?"

Avaya tossed her golden hair behind her shoulder. "I have my ways."

Semra put a hand on her stomach and wavered as nausea washed over her. "So this should pass, and I'll be fine, and we'll keep going."

"Yes. I'm just not sure how long it will take, and I'm hoping Zephan isn't dead by then."

45

————

They wasted another day recovering before Zezura was well enough to fly again. Flashes of heat still came over Semra, but as her condition improved, she was better able to hide their effects from Avaya. At first, she tried to fight the heat, tensing up and worsening her nausea, but after the flash rolled through her, it was typically followed by a period of some respite. By the next day, Semra was ready to fly.

Semra laid a hand on the dragon's neck. "Zez, are you able to take off?"

Zezura grunted and huffed, but slowly unfolded herself from where she had been coiled on the ground. A leaf crunched behind her. Semra whipped her head around to see Siler, arm already wrapped around Avaya's neck from behind. Semra reached for a knife, but the sheaths on her trousers were empty.

She dropped into a combat stance. "What do you think you're doing?"

"Let's try again," he said, drilling her with a cool stare. "Maybe, 'oh, hello Siler. Nice to see you. I do hope it wasn't too inconvenient for you, tracking us down on foot after I dumped you in the middle of nowheresville.'"

"Let me go, Siler." Avaya's voice was surprisingly strong for the prissy sort of princess Semra imagined her to be.

Semra ignored her. "Maybe I wanted to make sure you were working hard for Avaya's money."

"The flight from the castle wasn't enough? I saved your life back there. In case you forgot."

Avaya waved her arms. "Hey, hello, you two! I'm here, and I'm the one with the money you're discussing. Siler, if you want to see a single cent, you'll let me go *now*."

Siler smirked. "Which do you prefer? Your money or your life? It's quite simple. You'll agree to my contract addendum or you won't leave this spot."

Avaya dug her nails into Siler's arm, and he cinched his arm tighter as a warning. He clasped his own hand for a reinforced hold on the choke from behind position. Avaya winced. "What kind of addendum?"

Semra stalked Siler in sidesteps, and he countered as they talked. *Keep him here, Zez.* The dragon split off from Semra and Siler eyed her and changed his footwork, dragging Avaya with him. "I've earned the next payout already by getting you out of Madensig alive under exigent circumstances."

Avaya pursed her lips. "I hired you *because* of exigent circumstances. I was led to believe they were your specialty."

Siler shrugged. "Even so. And considering you're about to enter a war zone, I'm going to need an advance if you want me to continue with next steps."

Zezura managed to get behind Siler, pinning him between the dragon and Semra, and he grimaced.

"I don't have anything," Avaya said. "If you hadn't noticed, I left with nothing but the clothes on my back."

"The clothes on your back, the rings on your fingers, the

pins in your hair...take your pick. Semra, tell Zez to back off. You know you're not going to kill me."

"You're right, I'm not," Semra said. "Just like you're not going to kill Avaya. Though nobody said anything about bodily harm, which I am absolutely still considering."

"Oh, me too. You've both caused me some headache in the past weeks."

"*I've* caused *you* headaches? Please." Semra stepped closer. "So if we aren't going to kill each other, what are we doing?"

"Catching up as old friends? You know, the type that drop you with a bow and no arrows in the middle of a forest?"

As if *she* were the traitor. Semra gritted her teeth. "You don't get to do that. You didn't say goodbye at Shamaran Castle. You vanished when I wasn't looking, then got me captured in Madensig and nearly killed, watched me be beaten, and rescued me to make yourself feel better afterward. You don't get to be angry. All I did was put you somewhere safe. And clearly not far enough away."

Siler set his jaw but said nothing.

Avaya swore. "Are you serious? Is *everyone* in love with this filthy tramp?"

Siler and Semra locked eyes and froze, but Semra hadn't a clue what he was thinking. Her stomach made an uncomfortable flop, but not from nausea. She had steadily been feeling better until now.

Everyone? Who is everyone? She knew Siler had some sort of feelings for her, or at least wanted to be around her, but she was also his ticket out of the mountain at the time they teamed up – and a convenient and understanding partner option afterward. No one had ever claimed to love her before, except the Framatar, who doled out his version of love and acceptance as a reward for duties well performed. And that had not exactly ended well.

"I don't know what you're talking about," she said, jerking her gaze from Siler and suddenly feeling quite awkward.

Avaya rolled her eyes. "Siler, I want your word you are committing to the full next phase as previously discussed, and then I will give you your advance."

Semra shook her head. "Siler. This is ridiculous. Stop this."

Siler ignored Semra and nodded in answer to Avaya's proposal. "Done. Give me something valuable now, and I'll let you go."

Siler loosened his grip and Avaya leaned back against him, then rotated into him so that his clasped hands were behind her neck and they stood nose to nose. Avaya slipped her arms around his waist, working a jeweled ring off her finger behind Siler's back. Red hot anger exploded in Semra at Avaya's attention-seeking display...or was it that Siler seemed all too willing to give it?

Semra's lip curled. "That's enough."

Avaya raised an eyebrow and cast a glance over her shoulder at Semra. "Oh? Does this bother you? If you're after Siler, why are you leading on my brother?"

Semra marched forward and seized Avaya's hand from behind Siler, wrenching the ring off her finger and flinging it at Siler. It hit him in the temple and fell to the ground.

"I'm not leading anyone on. No one is in love with me. Believe it or not, I do not use shameless flirtation to manipulate people the way that you do."

"Please. The long glances, the dancing in the stable loft... do you often let mere acquaintances wrap their arms around you?"

Semra's face flushed bright red as she yanked Avaya away from Siler. Siler let her go, his face set like flint. Avaya glanced between them and moaned. "Drag me anywhere you want, but a dance and a set of long lashes isn't going to be enough to make a queen out of a nobody, coming out of obscurity only to be known for her serial murderers."

Semra blanched and tightened her grip on Avaya's arm. "Why would I want to be queen? Why would I want to be anything close to royalty? The more time I spend with you, the less I would want to participate in the institution that made you how you are. But then again, the rest of your family seems much more reasonable. Is it your vanity that sets you apart?"

"Stay away from my brother."

"I haven't been chasing him." A woozy spell hit Semra and she stumbled, Avaya half-falling after her before catching herself.

"Watch it!" Avaya pulled at her wrist in Semra's grasp. Semra twisted Avaya's arm behind her and sent instructions to the dragon. *Keep Siler back.* Zezura huffed hot air in Siler's face and blocked off his approach.

Avaya went with Semra's motion, no longer fighting the restraint. "Why else would he be cutting meetings short to go find you, or waxing on to anyone who would listen about what a hero you are? Is that really how you see yourself?" She leaned around Zezura for another glance at Siler. "What's wrong with *him*? Are you allergic to spending time with people of your own status? Considering he actually seems to want your miserable company, I'd recommend jumping at the opportunity. And...well, he's certainly easy on the eyes." She flashed him a smile as Zezura mirrored every move he made to try to get to them.

Zephan had left meetings for her? He was talking about her around the castle? But Siler had said Firfell demanded he stay away. Zephan had admitted to keeping his distance. Had he really still sought her out in spite of them? Another wave of weakness came over her and Semra tripped again, this time causing both of them to tumble to the ground.

Avaya grunted. "I thought the poison was wearing off."

"It was. I'm not sure what's happening. We have to go."

"Semra! You're not responsible for the wars of this king or that king," Siler called to her from the other side of the dragon as he ducked, spun, and lunged, but was again thwarted by Zezura's nimble judgments. "Leave it alone. Leave *him* alone."

"You're in no position to be giving advice," Semra snapped. "You have your trinket. Go do the rich girl's bidding."

Semra gestured to Avaya, and she accepted Semra's hand to help her up onto the dragon. "Mountains and trees, Siler," Semra said, as she clambered up onto Zezura's back after Avaya. "You can be better than this."

She hoped it was true.

Zezura beat her wings against the air, and with a strained cry from the dragon, they were in the air again, leaving Siler down below once more. There was no guilt on leaving him this time. He'd chased down Avaya for more money, desperate to keep his employment. There were plenty of wealthy men with lists of people they'd pay to dispatch. Working for Avaya against the rest of the Shamaran family was slimy, and Siler knew it.

Anyone with half a brain knew it.

Semra and Avaya flew all that day, and made one more stop for Zezura to rest before rising into the air one final time for the ride to the battlefront. It was likely to have taken Zephan three and a half to four days to reach the battle, and he would likely only beat them by a day.

"They have explosives," Avaya had told Semra. "I don't want you depositing me in some hole like you did to Siler, so I won't tell you where they are until we get there. But they're going to turn the tide and force the Jannemar army into a trap."

It was afternoon before they left the Belvidore border behind, following the river as they crossed through Seddon and approached the Surion Strip. The city of Kinlock lay northeast and Belera to the west, and the Jannemar and Belvidore armies were engaged in battle. They fought across the river to the east, and on the south side of the river, but they were losing ground on the south and nearly retreated to the bridge. The sounds of war rose toward them in a cacophony of steel, horses, screams, and canons. Semra wondered where Zephan would be – to the east, out in the open, or backed up against the river, with little opportunity for escape.

A northeastern retreat toward Kinlock was inevitable. Semra scanned the scene and gasped as she looked west toward Belera and saw an additional force approaching from the side, only becoming visible to Jannemar's army on the ground. Avaya pointed down to the Kinlock side, and as they drew nearer Semra could make out wagons of explosives lining the east where she gestured. Between the fight with the main army, the explosives, and the advancing second force, Jannemar troops would have nowhere to go.

Semra leaned forward as Zezura picked up speed and swooped down low over the battlefield, and a cheer went up from the Jannemar soldiers at the sight of her. Zezura dipped and weaved as she made an arc over the front line, and Semra's heart skipped a beat. She was still suffering aftereffects of the poison. Had they flown her to hard?

Semra bit her lip and leaned into the dragon's kiss connection. *Not now, not now. You were feeling better, you can do this!*

Zezura opened her mouth to summon a deluge of fire, but even after several days' recovery, all she could manage were sputterings of green and purple fire. Zezura hacked and coughed, then spewed puffs of purple fire and smoke and tilted dangerously to one side as she made her turn in the air. She didn't have the impeccable control she was accustomed to.

Semra felt bile creep up her throat at the precipitous angle Zezura took in the turn, but she swallowed it down and steeled herself. She was fine. A few days should have been plenty of time to get whatever the substance was out of her system. Shouldn't it? Weakness rocked her, and Semra's grip on Zezura's back loosened. She slid a little to one side, and Avaya cried out and cinched her arms tight around Semra's waist.

"If you fall, I fall! Pull yourself together," she screamed in Semra's ear.

Semra wavered but nodded as the weakness passed. "Where is Zephan?"

There was a pause as Semra and Avaya searched the mass of bodies, then Avaya screamed and pointed. "There! There, on the Kinlock side near the river!"

Semra spied him then, in the thick of the fight before the waterfront shops, downing his man with a sword through the stomach and turning toward another. Her heart skipped a beat at the sight of him alive and well, but a moment later it stopped altogether. Some thirty paces away, stalking toward Zephan like a lion on the prowl, was Prince Axis in full battle armor. The afternoon sun glinted off his sword and shield, and his eyes zeroed in on his prey.

Zezura leveled off and angled toward Zephan and Axis, then screeched, whipping her head back and forth and retching, her putrid vomit raining down on the soldiers below. In the next instant the dragon rammed her head into the roof of one of the buildings, glancing off the building and plummeting to the earth. The force of the impact knocked Semra and Avaya from their places and sent them tumbling down Zezura's scaly hide and into the dirt of the battlefield.

Semra coughed as she was enveloped in a cloud of dust and green dragon smoke. Twenty paces off, Zephan jerked his head in her direction. His eyes widened and his mouth opened to scream something at her, but his words were swallowed up in the din. Axis closed the distance to ten paces, then five. Zephan hadn't seen him. A Belvidorian warrior on his right drove toward him with a sword stroke to his neck, but Zephan threw up a block without removing his eyes from Semra.

Her head spun. Her vision blurred. *Stop, Zephan! Turn around!* She opened her mouth, but no sound came. A heat-wave rolled through her and this time she leaned into it – she would stabilize after it came and went.

Semra recognized Axis's tall, broad-shouldered frame through the haze as it bore down on Zephan. The heat ebbed, and Semra found the strength to lift her finger. Zephan began to turn behind him, but it was too late. Axis struck him from behind with the butt of his sword and Zephan crashed to the ground.

46

———————

A guttural cry escaped Semra's lips as her voice unlocked and her strength returned. Fury gripped her, bubbling up through her stomach and rising into her chest. She flew at Axis with nothing but her bare hands and the rage of a thousand wyverns.

Somewhere in the back of her mind, the Framatar's voice nagged at her. *Emotion is weakness.*

Axis thrust his sword, and Semra turned into him, meeting his right shoulder with hers, trapping his arm, and tucking her head into his shoulder as he brought his shield down onto her back. She moved to sweep his leg, but he anticipated the move; Semra ducked under his arm and threw her whole weight into a torque on his arm, twisting it beyond its range of motion.

The Framatar's voice purred in her mind again: *Everything you are is because of me. You are nothing without me!*

Axis's body was rock-solid, and he ripped his arm from her grasp and slammed his elbow into her sternum, sending her flying backward. She gasped for air, but her lungs refused to fill. Zephan gathered his feet under him and flew into a low tackle. Axis sprawled backward but not quite far enough, and they fell together on the ground. Axis struck Zephan again and spun away, slashing a Jannemar soldier in the neck as he ran by and tossing his body on top of Semra as she lay on her back, the wind still knocked out of her from the fall.

Axis, the prince of Belvidore. The man who had her beaten against his father's command. The man whose greed for power would cause greater rifts between their two kingdoms than any king before him. She would not die at his hand.

Semra struggled to free herself from beneath the dead man's weight as she finally dragged a breath into starving lungs. Axis lined up three more Jannemar soldiers between himself and Zephan, killing each one in quick succession and heaping their bodies in a pile. Semra chanced a glance back at Zezura, but she lay unmoving on the ground.

Get up, Zez. Get up! Her heart sank. There was no flicker of response from the beast in response to her plea. Avaya stood awkwardly in front of the motionless dragon, unarmed, vulnerable, and completely out of her element.

Axis and Zephan locked eyes on Semra in the same moment, lunging toward her and crossing swords before reaching her. She shrank back with a yell, but the weight of the mountain of corpses locked her in place. Steel on steel rang in her ears, and the dust of their boots sprayed her in the face. Zephan knocked Axis backward, gaining the upper hand once again and positioning himself between the enemy and his sister.

Axis smashed his sword and shield together twice before giving a barely perceptible nod at two of his soldiers as they came running up from behind Zephan. Semra tried to cry out, to warn him, but her tongue stuck to the roof of her mouth. Zephan turned in time to see each soldier grip one of Avaya's arms and lift her off her feet. Zephan roared his dismay as his sister was dragged away on one side, and seeing his momentary indecision, Axis rushed him on the other.

The two men struck each other again and again, Axis pressing in with full armor, sword, and shield and Zephan pushing back with only a sword of his own. Axis had more brute strength, but Zephan was faster and had impeccable footwork. Semra was suffocated by corpses from her shins to her chest, and as the two princes battled, she worked to worm her way out from under the crushing weight. She flinched as Axis's heel struck her forehead as he made a hasty retreat nearly on top of her, then twisted to one side as she dry heaved from an empty stomach through another bout of nausea.

Sweat beaded her brow, and she padded down the torso of the easiest-to-reach dead body heaped on top of her burning lungs. Her fingers ran over chain mail and leather, but her hands picked up only blood in the pursuit. No tools. No weapons. Semra grunted and pushed and writhed against the bodies, but they would not budge, and her position gave her no leverage.

She glanced up, and the world seemed to slow as she took in the scene. Avaya screamed and kicked at the air, jerking this way and that in the iron grip of the Belvidore soldiers, to no avail. Zephan pushed Axis back and turned to reach for Semra, but Axis flew back at him and sent him crashing to the ground. He landed hard in the dirt, blood trickling down his face, and their eyes met.

Helplessness invaded her chest, and the weight bearing down on her soul was greater than the weight of the corpses crushing her to the ground. For the first time in a battle, all Semra felt was fear. Axis grabbed him by the ankle and dragged him away from her, her heart constricting in a fireball of pain as his eyes were ripped from hers. Semra's view was obscured by the bodies, but she saw Axis raise his broadsword, blade downward, over Zephan.

Is this what her life had come to? Kidnapped to be an assassin. Trained to be some conscienceless weapon, a machine to dispatch someone else's enemies. Betrayed by the dragonlord who raised her, nearly murdered by her mentor, and abandoned by a friend for money. In return, she exposed the dragonlord and threw him into the Shamaran dungeon, killing her mentor who had left her for dead, and dumped her foolish, untrustworthy "friend" and colleague in the woods. She had traveled, planned, fought, risked, escaped, and returned – and for what?

To watch her dearest friend in the world die?

Semra's mind reeled, and her chest tightened. Is that what he was? A friend? Her *dearest* friend? *You don't have friends. Whenever you do, they die like Brens or betray you like Siler.* A tear slipped down her face. *Zephan has never betrayed you.*

But was he just a friend? For a moment, she considered that he was her next-in-line monarch, but immediately she dismissed the thought. She had never cared much for giving her loyalty to royalty. They had no power over her, and she'd seen enough men in power to know that authority did not a good man make. But in Zephan's case, he was already a good man. Like his father.

A good man. The man who saved her when she had dangled from the balcony in the Shamaran castle with guards on the chase, who had believed her when she said she was an assassin but wanted to protect his family; the man who fought by her side in the throne room against evil itself, never judged her for nearly killing him when he had surprised her back at the castle, the man who held her close when she woke screaming from untold nightmares.

You're a murderer, Semra. The Framatar's voice echoed in her brain. *It's who you are.*

Ramas' rough growl joined in. *The only thing you were ever good at was killing, and now you can't even do that right.*

Perhaps your job, as you call it, is death ... but your inclination is life. It was a fresh new voice, warm and soft and smiling – the voice of the man who danced with her. Who wanted to protect her, even when her job was to protect him. The man who genuinely cared what happened to her, the man who had flirted with her, angered her, and made her stomach flip. The man who had once called her beautiful.

It didn't matter; whoever he was, he was about to be dead.

Axis's sword plunged down.

Semra screamed, the sound catching in her throat. Tears sprang to her eyes and rolled down her face, and she writhed uselessly under the weight of the corpses. *Is that all Zephan is now? A corpse?* Semra reached up and patted down the body of one of the men on top of her like she'd done before, but this time one of them shifted, and an axe toppled down the pile toward her face. She caught it an inch from her nose and twisted to see a horse-drawn wagon rumbling past her.

Semra swung and hooked the axe onto the back bar of the wagon when it rolled by. She gripped the axe with both hands, the top half of her body lifting off the ground, her muscles straining to keep a hold as the wagon pulled away from her. The horse plodded on. Semra's body jerked forward a few inches and then dropped, the axe ripped from her hands and falling from the wagon several paces away.

Tears ran a river down her dirt-stained face, and she swallowed a lump in her throat. *Focus. Focus, or you'll be dead too.* Was he dead? Semra looked up as a horse and fallen rider trotted by, the rider dangling from the stirrup. His foot bent at an unnatural angle in the stirrup, his hands dragged the ground over his head, and his eyes were glazed over, unseeing.

All Semra saw was an opportunity. She reached out and seized the dead rider's hands in a sudden burst of furious energy. No sooner had she taken hold of him did an explosion burst nearby. The horse spooked and took off, bucking at the resistance of Semra connected to it and then driving forward with power and speed. Semra's body yanked free from the pile of dead soldiers and met with freedom at last.

She released the dead man's hands and rolled in the dirt as the horse sped off. Two names raced through her mind as she scooped up an abandoned mace from the ground and the battle axe that had fallen from the wagon. *Zephan.* Was he alive? *Axis.* If Zephan was dead, Axis would be next.

Semra's lip curled as anger replaced the chasm of fear in her chest, and she whirled the axe and the mace, one in each hand, gaining momentum and running forward around the pile of bodies that had pinned her to the ground moments before. She took in the scene: Zephan, alive and strong, pushing Axis backward with a vicious series of attacks with the sword; Avaya, held kicking and screaming by one soldier who struggled to keep hold of his royal charge; the second soldier who had held Avaya, dead, spilling his blood into the ground between Zephan and Axis.

Zephan stepped over the Belvidorian soldier and – *thrust, parry, jab, slash* – pressed relentlessly into Axis, then spun away long enough to block Avaya's captor from escape and keep him engaged in the fight with a slice across the ribs as the man exposed his side to wrangle the princess. The soldier fell back, and Axis fell upon Zephan with lightning speed, locking him in combat. Axis disarmed Zephan with a guttural cry, sending his sword flying to the side. Zephan ducked the next blow and leaped back.

Semra flew the final few paces as if running on air, screaming his name as she tossed the battle axe through the air.

"Zephan!"

Just in time he turned, snatched the axe from the air, and brought it down on Axis'sshield arm with a thundering crash. In the same moment, Semra whirled and arced the mace around into the back of the soldier holding Avaya. Axis raised his shield to defend against Zephan's mighty blow, but not fast enough to have strong form, and he cried out in pain as the full force of Zephan's body weight snapped the bone in his arm. The soldier jerked his head back and opened his mouth, but no sound came, and Semra swung the mace again and bludgeoned him in the head with it. Blood poured from the crater in his skull, and Semra ripped Avaya from his hands as he crumpled to the ground.

Zephan and Semra exchanged a glance, and in a fraction of a second, they moved as one, each bringing their weapon to bear on Axis. Axis retreated in a backward run, wincing as he slipped the shield off his arm. He dropped the shield and held his crooked arm close to his body, raising his sword with the other. His face was drawn, his eyes dark with hate as he looked from his intended wife to her protectors.

"You think you can stop me with a few scrapes?" Axis growled.

"No, but that shield doesn't seem particularly effective at the moment." Zephan raised his sword, poised to engage.

Semra rocked on her feet, her head light, her knees weak. She'd nearly lost Zephan, and the taste of terror that had run through her at the possibility was all she needed to prevent his loss at any cost.

Axis lunged at Zephan and Semra whirled her mace, meeting the sword and yanking downward; Axis twisted and withdrew. He whirled the sword with his good arm and lashed out at Semra with a brazen downward icepick. Semra jumped back and the light prick of the blade bit her skin, drawing a trickly of blood as it grazed her arm. A *woosh* of air hit her face as Zephan's axe whipped over her head with gorgeous precision and knocked Axis's sword from his grip. Axis caught it before it hit the ground and followed up with a slice toward Zephan's abdomen, and the two danced apart.

"Semra, check on my sister!"

Her heart squeezed at leaving him, but she didn't stop to question the request. Semra spun to fend off attack from a Belvidorian soldier as he ran toward Avaya, but her knees buckled, and she stumbled halfway through her next stroke. Another woozy spell slugged her and she threw out an arm to catch her fall. Zephan darted in toward Axis and landed a blow to his injured arm. Axis reeled back and spat into the dust.

Zephan nodded toward Axis's arm. "You should get that looked at."

Axis jerked his head toward Semra. "You should get *her* looked at."

Semra's head spun and she swayed on her knees, her vision blurred. The figure of the soldier moved toward Avaya, but as he did, he split into three men. Semra blinked and shook her head. *Which one do I kill? Which one is real?* Exasperation bubbled up from inside and she swung blindly at the soldier trio.

Hardly aware of speaking, Semra heard her voice shouting as if far away. "Avaya, you *useless* clot! Stop standing there like a stuck pig and *do something!*"

Semra take another wild swing at the soldier, and from the corner of her eye she saw Zephan strike a final blow toward Axis, turn, and sprint toward the soldier overtaking Avaya.

Avaya dropped her body like a stone and rolled to one side. "Well, I'm sorry I haven't spent my life killing people! I'm a bit less practiced than you are!"

Semra opened her mouth to answer, then closed it as a second wave of weakness and nausea rolled through her. A deafening *boom* sounded and the earth shook, sending Semra crashing to her hands and knees. She dry-heaved.

Zephan skewered the soldier and yanked Avaya down with him to Semra. "Get up! They've got explosives, close! We need to get you and Avaya out of here *now*. And there's some sort of commotion on the Belera side."

Semra slapped her own face to orient herself. It didn't help. "There's a second force on the west. We're fending off attack on three sides."

Boom.

A high-ranking officer appeared twenty paces off and called to Zephan from across the way. "Your Highness! I thought you were lost! We're taking a beating south of the river!"

"Fall back! Retreat to the northeast!"

The officer nodded and sounded a horn, and Zephan surveyed the battlefield and turned back to Semra with a grim expression. "We called for reinforcements, but we've heard nothing back. What about you? You don't look good. Are you hurt?"

Semra's weakness was ebbing, but she had no time to respond. Zephan parried a blow from overhead as he knelt by Semra, sweeping the adversary's leg, and piercing him through as he fell. Zephan released Avaya and half-lifted Semra with his free hand, holding his sword out toward Axis with the other.

"Your people have nowhere to go." Axis spun his sword in a low arc and stalked toward them. "Your assassin rat is right.

My men are far more numerous than you accounted for. We have the river. Anyone across it now will be trapped there and die. It's time to pull back and give me what's mine – both the land, and my promised wife."

Zephan released Semra and stepped in front of Semra and Avaya. "You'll have neither!"

Axis and Zephan ran toward each other, Axis's broken arm tucked close to his body, and their swords met with a mighty *clang* of steel. Semra's stomach dropped. She lingered a moment longer as the weakness passed, and rose to her feet, mace in hand. This time she would not leave his side. Zephan and Axis fought tooth and nail, blow after blow, and Semra ran forward as Axis thrust his sword toward Zephan's abdomen. Zephan redirected Axis's blade with his own and stepped into him, reaching his second hand over and stripping the sword from Axis's hands.

Zephan adjusted his grip, a sword in each hand, and raised his arms for the final blow. Semra's heart lurched into her throat as a blur crashed into Zephan from the side, knocking him to the ground. Avaya.

A guttural cry flew from Semra's throat, but she choked on the sound with a half-sob as Zephan hit the dust. His sister had betrayed him. If Axis killed Zephan now, his blood would be on Avaya's head.

Semra changed direction at the last moment and grabbed Zephan's hand to pull him to his feet. Avaya snatched Axis's sword from where it had fallen and ran with Axis across the waterfront and toward the bridge. How willingly she fled from the love of her family to the belly of betrayal! If they crossed the bridge, they would be lost.

The mark on Semra's chest burned, and she glanced back again at Zezura. The dragon stirred, her wings fluttering slightly, but she did not get up. Semra swallowed the lump in her throat. *Not you too. Not now.*

Semra ran forward, still holding Zephan's hand, but a bottleneck of bodies closed in around them so tightly that they could not get through. Semra and Zephan broke apart to engage more Belvidorian soldiers as they fought between the shops closest to the river, and the sea of humanity converging on the bridge. Semra swung her mace, her opponent ducked, and she blocked his rebuttal, then chanced a glance toward the bridge. Axis and Avaya's heads were disappearing into the chaos on the other side. And there, moving steadily toward both bridges over the river, were wagons of explosives about to blow all chance of Jannemar's retreat from the south – and all hope of regaining Avaya.

47

———————

The nearest wagon rumbled toward the bridge. Belvidore troops surrounded the area in excess. There was no hope of reaching it in time. The Jannemar men south of the river would be cut off from escape, and Avaya would be lost. Semra looked frantically around her, but there was nothing but battling men, horses, and evacuated shops. She had been made into a weapon, exposing the Framatar for who he really was. She dismantled his assassin syndicate – but in the process, the queen had been murdered, and the court distrusted Zephan's association with Semra and the king's gracious hand toward her. She had repaid their kindness with the smallest of promises: protect their family and save Princess Avaya. She hadn't come this far from the mountain to fail them now, no matter how idiotic the princess had become. Semra turned to Zephan.

"Give me a boost!"

"What?!" Zephan and Semra each felled their opponents at the same time, and Semra pulled him around the corner into the shadows of one of the buildings. She stopped abruptly, and Zephan bumped into her. She gestured at the wall.

"Give me a boost and then get out of here!"

Zephan hesitated. Sweat, blood, and dust mingled in her nostrils, and her lungs dragged in long jagged breaths. Resolve hardened in her heart. She wasn't faithless like Avaya and Siler had been. She would carry out every promise. Semra dropped the mace and put her hands on his neck. "Trust me."

His eyes melted into hers, and as he looked at her, a fleeting thought intruded. The dragonlord would have called it weak, but an odd strength filled her. *Amber is the most beautiful color I've ever seen.*

Zephan sighed, then turned and squatted with his back against the house. Semra stepped on his knee, climbing up to stand on his shoulders. He grunted, gripped her ankles, and launched to his feet, tossing her upward. Semra pushed off his shoulders and clutched at the roof, tugging herself up and sprinting across the tops of two buildings. The explosives wagon was almost to the river now, swarmed by Belvidorian men.

Semra judged the distance from the roof. It would be a close call, but she couldn't wait.

She threw herself onto the wagon, tossing the man in the back into the mass of people before clambering to the horse driver's seat. She seized the top of his head with one hand and his chin with the other, snapping his neck with a sickening *crack* of bone and kicking him into the fray. Semra yanked the reins from the dead man's hands and pulled hard on the pair of horses. They veered off course from the bridge, but Semra felt the wagon tip. and twisted to see a young Belvidorian soldier hauling himself up behind her.

She knew in that moment she would never leave the

wagon. She couldn't chance the explosives getting to the bridge, and there would be nowhere to go after doing what needed done. There was no use wasting time thinking about it. Semra let go of the horses and dove into the back of the wagon as the soldier tumbled over the side. She snatched pieces of flint sitting next to barrels and several unlit lanterns, striking it against itself, and lit one of the lanterns.

The soldier swung at her, and she ducked, a wave of dizziness slamming into her as she did, and she smashed the lantern with its oil and flame into one of the wooden barrels of explosives. The flame would only take a moment to eat through the wood and reach the combustible mixture inside. Semra's hair whipped in her face, and the metallic smell of blood, smoke, and horses mingled in her nostrils. The world stood still. Soon it would go black.

"SEMRA!"

She snapped her head toward the sound, and her stomach dropped. Zephan stood alone and unarmed to one side, the wagon tearing straight past him. It was far too close. *No, no, no!* At least Semra would die with him, unavailable to tell Turian his daughter was lost and his son dead.

Zephan's face was dusty, his tunic stained with other people's blood. His arms were outstretched. Amber eyes beckoned her.

"Jump! Trust me!"

Trust me!

The Belvidorian lunged for her a split second too late. Semra launched herself off the wagon toward Zephan's waiting arms, and he caught her hips over his head, her body stretched out above him only a moment before the barrels blew. A shadow fell over them, and blue wings encircled them as Zezura descended out of empty skies to shield them from the flying debris of the blast.

Semra lingered before Zephan slowly lowered her in front of him, his arms tightly wrapping around her. His golden-brown eyes locked onto hers with an intense fire of their own, their bodies close, their arms wound around each other. Semra's breath caught as she looked back at him, and she felt a bizarre new thing.

Seen.

Wanted.

Not as an escape. Not for what she could do. She simply felt understood, wanted, despite everything. The strength of the feeling surprised her, and a strange warmth twisted her stomach into a knot before escaping into a trail of butterflies.

Zezura opened her wings, and Semra's heart soared. The dragon threw her head back and let out a stream of healthy white, yellow, and red fire. Jannemar soldiers flooded the area, and shouts went up from every side.

"The dragon! It's the dragon girl!"

"Reinforcements are arriving in the north! They're here from Kinlock!"

"We need them on the west! The bridge is secure!"

"Prince Zephan! His Highness is here!"

"To the prince! Get him out of there!"

Heat suddenly flashed through Semra's body, and the weakness took her; she dropped like a stone, and Zephan caught her up in his arms. His face lined with concern, and he let his men surround him and take over the fighting. Semra's vision blurred and numbness tingled her fingers and toes.

I'm so glad you're all right. Semra sent to Zezura's mind. *Go help. Target the wagons.*

Zezura bent over her and touched her nose to Semra's forehead, then unfurled her great wings and lifted off the ground. She tore along the east side, igniting remaining wagons of explosives behind Belvidore lines before they had the chance to move them forward, and flying low over the enemy pouring out streams of fire, relishing having her flame back again. Cheers went up as Zezura swept over the weary Jannemar warriors and the fresh reinforcements turning the tide on the west.

Semra felt herself lift onto a horse, and Zephan settled behind her, slipping his arms around her waist and pulling her close. He took the reins and set off at a canter, taking her away from the thick of the fight, flanked by Jannemar riders on all sides. She closed her eyes and leaned her head back against Zephan's shoulder, her body rolling with the motion of the horse, the weakness sapping at her tired muscles and pulling her toward sleep.

Two hours passed before Zephan's pace slowed, and Semra heard the quick hoofbeats of a new horse approaching, matching pace right beside them. The new rider spoke, and from her half-conscious state, Semra's heart lifted to hear it. Monac.

"Belvidore maintains control south of the river but has pulled back from the north, and their western force is retreating. The dragon unleashed all their unused explosives on them, and they are absolutely terrified. Our reinforcements pushed them back well, and this side of the Strip is ours."

Zephan's voice was soft but commanding in reply. "Good. I want an update on General Tallem's condition and will meet with him as soon as he can manage, and I want the commander's recommendations for next steps by nightfall. Send word to my father, and tell him we are stopping in Kinlock to get Semra assessed by a doctor."

"What happened?"

"I don't know. She and Avaya rode in on Zezura. Zezura was unconscious for most of the fight, and Semra went back and forth between risky and tenacious warrior and so nauseous and off balance that she couldn't keep her feet under her."

Monac grunted. "Perhaps some sickness going around in Belvidore?"

"Doubtful. Axis and Avaya are the picture of health. Well, except Axis, now. We managed to break his arm, but that's as good as it got."

There was a pause, then Monac spoke again. "Where is the princess now?"

Semra listened, but there was no answer. She struggled to open her heavy eyelids and saw Monac nod and look down at the ground.

"We'll need Coanor's skill when we get back," Zephan said. "We'll see if the Kinlock doctors can help ease things for the journey, but I want our finest healer evaluating Semra as soon as we're back at Shamaran Castle."

Semra's body ached, and she felt hot all over. She reached down to thumb Ramas' green serpentine amulet, but it was gone from its place on her belt. The corner of her mouth tipped up into a small smile – it seemed fitting, somehow. His voice, and the Framatar's voice, need not haunt her anymore. They need not follow her everywhere, plague her every thought, or be granted the time of day in her mind.

The dragonlord's voice tried again, once more:

My dear, my dear ... you know I am the only one who has never left you.

Semra waved it off in her mind's eye. Its power was lost as she recognized the lie. No, the Framatar was not the "only one who had never left her." Not anymore. And the arms around her now served as proof. Semra sank back against Zephan and allowed herself to drift off into the first dreamless, restful sleep she'd had in weeks. The future was uncertain, and her ailment was unsolved – but in this moment with Zephan, she was home.

ABOUT THE AUTHOR

Author of *The Forgotten Stone* and the *Blood and Flame Saga*, E.A. Winters loves pouring herself a cup of hot chocolate with a mountain of marshmallows and delving into creating epic fantasy worlds for you to enjoy.

Erin lives in Virginia with her husband and two boys. When she's not writing, Erin is spending her time with her family. She loves playing board games and reading, whenever the elusive "free time" opportunity arises.

ALSO BY E.A. WINTERS

Blood & Flame Saga

Book 1: Dragon's Kiss

Book 2: Broken Bonds

Book 3: Noble Claims

Book 4: Crimson Queen

Stand Alones

The Forgotten Stone